ROYAL
SPY

Praise for HEATHER FROST

"Royal Spy is a breathtaking page turner that leaves you wanting more! Frost has outdone herself with her irresistible characters and fascinating backdrop of Eyrinthia. This is a must-read for any fantasy lover!"
- Author Ashley I. Hansen on *Royal Spy*

"Royal Spy is a gripping story with strong, powerful characters. Excitement, betrayal, love with every turn of the page in this heart pounding adventure. I couldn't put it down!"
- Min Reads and Reviews (Mindy) on *Royal Spy*

"Reuniting readers with favorite characters and introducing them to new friends who jump off the page, Royal Spy is an immersion in exotic lands with richly detailed cultures. Frost effortlessly weaves a tale of adventure wrapped in romance, intrigue, and humor that leaves you anxious for more. An exhilarating read!"
- Author Rebecca McKinnon on *Royal Spy*

"Heather Frost is a force to be reckoned with! This is quite honestly my favorite Indie author series. Hands down, the best. Frost does such a phenomenal job of bringing the characters to life and giving them souls that you are instantly attached to...So many twists, turns and puzzle pieces, it truly makes Frost one of my favorite authors!"
- Author Sarah Hill on *Royal Spy*

"Action-packed, emotionally involving, and simply
astonishing... Colour me intrigued, this book
left me at the edge of my seat and I need to
know what happens next really bad!"
- Darkest Sins (Silvia) on *Royal Spy*

"From her very first book, Heather Frost has delivered solid
and vibrant characters and complex stories full of mystery
and romance, and Royal Spy is no exception. Every page
pulls you in and keeps you trapped until suddenly
the book is over and you're begging for more.
This book is excellent for anyone looking for an
adventure that will stick with you for years to come."
- Author Dana LeCheminant on *Royal Spy*

"...Everything was perfect about this book.
The story was beautifully written with an amazing world,
characters, and plot twists. This is one of my favorite
books of the year and if you haven't started reading
the books then I have no idea what you are doing.
Perfect for those who love royals and Sarah J. Mass."
- Thindbooks on *Royal Spy*

"This is a story that completely captured my attention from
the very beginning and didn't let go the whole way through
... I've been craving a book like this."
- Getting Your Read On (Aimee) on *Royal Decoy*

"This book has just about everything! ... The intrigue is
fantastic. This is a series that is worth reading. I will anxiously
await the next installment to see what happens next."
- Bookworm Lisa on *Royal Decoy*

"You know what I love? Fantasy. You know what really thrills me? When a story like this one works its magic on me in a way I still feel its power after finishing it. ... Full of action, conspiracies, exciting twists and turns, charismatic characters, and heart-warming moments—I demand my own Grayson! —this first installment is a fantastic opening."
- Darkest Sins (Silvia) on *Royal Decoy*

"This book was superb. ...Well thought out story that was action packed ... It was amazing ... a fantastic read that made me read it in one sitting. Heather Frost will be an author that I keep on my radar from now on. Can't wait for book two!"
- A Court of Coffee and Books (Stacy) on *Royal Decoy*

"If you are looking for a good read with royalty, mystery, intrigue, spies, war, and romance, this book has it all. Heather Frost certainly delivers a great read with Royal Decoy."
- Why Not? Because I Said So (Sheila) on *Royal Decoy*

"Frost has written a magnificent young adult fantasy romance that readers will absolutely love. The turn of every page is jam packed with fast paced, thrilling and adventurous twists and turns that will keep readers guessing and wanting more."
- Singing Librarian Books (Sydney) on *Royal Decoy*

"An amazing first book in a series! The premise of this novel was so interesting! It's something that I'm fairly certain I haven't read before in other books."
- Chapters and Pages (Caitlin) on *Royal Decoy*

"Super unique ... The story flowed and [...] was well-paced and
didn't end off in a cliffhanger. I totally recommend this book
to everyone especially those who want a fresh royalty read."
- Thindbooks on *Royal Decoy*

"*Seers* is a really good paranormal read mixed with a
great romance, and a some really fun characters."
- Mundie Moms Blog on *Seers*

"Heather does an amazing job of keeping the story rolling,
fast paced and full of intrigue and suspense."
- Author Cindy C. Bennett on *Demons*

"As soon as I finished the final pages of *Demons* I was on
a countdown until I had *Guardians* in my hands.
And it did not disappoint!"
- FicTalk Review on *Guardians*

Also by Heather Frost:

Fate of Eyrinthia Series
Royal Decoy

The Seers Trilogy
Seers

Demons

Guardians

Asides: A Short Story Collection

Royal Spy

FATE OF EYRINTHIA · BOOK 2

Heather Frost

Summary: Clare continues her adventures as the princess's decoy, facing growing threats on her journey to the kingdom of Mortise.

Hardcover: 978-1-7348919-2-8
Softcover: 978-1-7348919-3-5

For Anna and Laurie,
You were there at the inception of this story
and you've been with me at every stage since.
(Remember when it was going to be one book?)
Thank you for your forever friendship!

CHAPTER I

CLARE

CLARE SIPPED RED WINE FROM A LONG-stemmed glass, fighting to keep an easy smile on her face despite the lateness of the hour and the ache in her feet. The night was half-gone and the Harrington party did not look to be waning any time soon.

Torches flared in the night, bringing a glow of light to the gardens overrun by chatting nobles, rushing servants, and a perimeter watched by guards. The stars glittered above them, streaks of clouds lined in silver moonlight stretching across the sky.

Clare enjoyed the fresh air of the garden, heavily laden with the scent of blooming flowers. It was a nice change from the endless drawing room teas, lavish dinners, and the carriage that carried her to the next stop on their journey to Mortise.

Before leaving Iden, Serene and Clare had gone through a seemingly endless list of every noble Clare might meet on the tour. Serene had shared her personal background with the different nobles she knew, so Clare would know how to interact with them. In all her lessons, the princess had failed to mention how utterly draining these parties could be. Three days into the king's tour, and she was already exhausted. Her face hurt from smiling, and she missed sleep. Did nobles even *need* sleep?

She was beginning to think the answer was *no*.

She was trapped in a conversation with three ladies who were desperate to discuss every detail of Serene's wedding, including table arrangements—as if that was the most important aspect of the coming alliance between Mortise and Devendra.

"Of course, deciding what flowers to allow on the tables must not be put off," Lady Harrington said, her tone serious. "Choosing the wrong combination invites ill fortune."

Lady Firth nodded, which made the blue feather sticking out of her hair shudder. "My sister mixed peonies and roses for her wedding feast, and do you know what happened? Her husband's mother died a week later."

"No!" Lady Bent gasped, eyes wide as she clutched her wineglass.

Lady Firth nodded more vigorously, flapping the feather so much it looked like it was trying to take flight. "And that's not the end of it! They inherited all of the horrible woman's furniture and my sister's new husband was so deeply in mourning that, to this day, he won't let Elizabeth throw any of it out!"

Lady Harrington pursed her lips. "That's just the ill fortune we must avoid." She turned to Clare. "What flowers have you decided on, Princess?"

She gave the answer she thought Serene might—if she were in a diplomatic mood, of course. "I haven't decided, but I'd welcome your ideas."

The cluster of ladies tittered and started calling out possible arrangements and their alleged omens. Clare shifted her weight, trying to ease the ache in her feet. She envied Serene. The nineteen-year-old princess was a year older than Clare, and she was probably at an inn somewhere, blissfully asleep. Of course, that was the whole point of a decoy; Clare would take the risks of the highly-publicized tour, attending the social engagements, royal appearances, and dozens of appointments Serene had booked, all while the real princess traveled a safer, anonymous route. There were a few times their paths would cross, as King Newlan wanted Serene to handle some stops on the tour, most notably the dedication of a new road. But for most of the trip to Mortise, Clare would play the part of Serene.

She wasn't sure how she would survive six weeks of this.

"Wrong flowers aren't the only thing that can bring bad luck," Lady Bent cut over the discussion. She glanced at Clare. "Did, ah, Serjah Desfan offer to escort you to Mortise?"

Serjah, the Mortisian term for a prince, seemed to get a little stuck on the woman's tongue. Clare had been that way, before her tutoring. Now the Mortisian titles came easily; *serjan* for king, *ser* for lord, *serai* for lady. She wondered if Serene, after her marriage, would take on the Mortisian title for queen—*seraijan*.

Her lessons had taught her many things about Mortise, but she really didn't know much about Serene's future husband.

Serjah Desfan Cassian was the heir to the Mortisian throne. He was twenty years old, and he'd spent the last few years at sea rather than in court—an eccentricity many in Devendra's court speculated about. He was currently ruling as regent, since his father had fallen ill.

That was really all Clare knew. She hoped, for Serene's sake, he was at least kind.

Lady Bent was still eyeing her, awaiting a reply to her question. Clare shook herself from her thoughts. "No," she answered.

"He did not offer to escort me."

Lady Firth clucked her tongue. "Bad luck."

Lady Bent nodded in solemn agreement. "A man should always come to his lady. Not the other way around."

"I think," Clare said, "that if women always waited for men, nothing would ever happen."

Lady Harrington chuckled, but Lady Bent's brow furrowed. "I remember the last royal wedding Devendra saw." Her eyes pinned Clare. "King Newlan should have gone to Zennor to bring your mother to Iden, but he did not. He sent his cousin instead, and we all know how fate repaid everyone involved."

Clare barely held back a wince. Yes, she knew how that had played out. Newlan's cousin, Ivar Carrigan, had fallen in love with the queen he could not have and he'd started a civil war that had stolen many lives—including Clare's father's. Ivar had escaped the failed attempt to end Newlan's reign, and the lesser-known truth was that Queen Aren had aided his escape—and, according to proof Princess Serene had found—she had been quietly killed by her husband for her betrayal.

"I don't know how much stock I put into all that superstition," Lady Harrington said. "After all, Desfan's father traveled to Dorma to escort his bride, and yet that family has known nothing but tragedy."

Clare had only been a child at the time, but she remembered the shock on every face when the news reached Devendra. Half of the Mortisian royal family, dead in a shipwreck. Desfan hadn't been on the ship, or else he might have met the same fate as his mother and two younger sisters. Instead, he'd been left with his father to mourn their loss. Everyone had discussed the political ramifications and had even speculated if the terrible accident had been an attack by pirates, rather than the result of a violent storm. Clare, who had recently lost both of her parents, had whispered a prayer for the father and son who had lost their family.

"I've often wondered why Desfan spent so many years at sea," Lady Harrington said thoughtfully. "One would think, after what happened to his family, he would prefer staying on land."

"I've heard that he seeks revenge," Lady Bent replied. "That he longs to inspire fear and be known as the true terror of the sea."

Lady Firth rolled her eyes. "You should write novels, Lady Bent." She turned to Clare, and her serious expression was marred by the ridiculous feather pluming above her head. "Is it true the Mortisian emissary was thrown out of the castle?"

A knot formed in Clare's gut, but she forced a reassuring smile. "No, the emissary left of his own volition. He was grieved by his father's death and wished to return to Mortise with all haste."

Amil Havim had been more than grieved. He had been *furious*. His father had been killed at the castle during the farewell banquet King Newlan had held for Princess Serene. Clare had been acting in Serene's stead, and she would never forget the horror of that night. Including the moment Amil had killed the guard responsible for his father's death. Clare had liked and trusted Gavril, even though he had been trying to kill the princess—and, inadvertently, *her*—for weeks.

Lady Firth grunted—a very unladylike sound that Clare's etiquette teacher would have flushed at. "I suppose that makes sense."

"I heard Ser Havim refused a burial plot in Iden, even though King Newlan offered him a spot in the royal cemetery," Lady Harrington scoffed. "He demanded a pyre instead."

"Burning the dead is the tradition in Mortise," Clare said automatically, as if she were answering one of Master Ramus's many questions. The royal librarian had spent countless hours teaching her the languages and cultures of Eyrinthia. "A burial is considered an insult. Mortisians believe it traps the spirit, rather than frees it."

Lady Harrington blinked at her, while the other women stared.

Embarrassment heated her cheeks and she took a quick swallow of wine to keep from uttering any apology. Fates knew Serene wouldn't have apologized, even if her comments had made the ladies uncomfortable.

Lady Firth shook her feathered head. "I think it's barbaric. I can't imagine ever wanting to attend a funeral if that's the way they do it."

"I don't know that anyone ever *wants* to attend a funeral," Clare retorted smoothly.

"You're right, of course," Lady Harrington said, shooting her friend a sharp look.

Lady Firth shifted her feet, her lips pursed tightly. "Well, even if Ser Havim wasn't thrown from the castle, he certainly rode out the gates like a man pursued. I heard he didn't even wait until the pyre was cold before he and his guards galloped away."

Amil's fast pace would ensure he reached Mortise weeks before their ambling tour did. It would give him ample time to follow through on his threats. He had told Newlan he would convince Desfan to end the betrothal, and though Newlan had sent a letter to Desfan, Amil might arrive before the message did.

Clare hoped Desfan was a man not easily swayed. Losing the alliance was a terrifying prospect, with war looming on the horizon. All that was left to be determined was if the war would come from Ryden or Mortise.

"This topic has become far too serious," Lady Harrington said. "I think we should focus on the choice of flowers for the wedding . . ."

A prickle of awareness danced on the back of Clare's neck and she turned, searching the many faces in the crowd. Nobles were gathered in clusters, drinking, talking, and laughing. But beyond them, standing on the edge of the courtyard, was Bennick.

He stood near a torch, the flickering light catching every plane and angle of his face. His dark blue uniform fit him perfectly, from his broad shoulders to his tapered waist. His black boots matched his leather belt, which was adorned with a variety of sheathed weapons, including a longsword at his hip. He gripped the hilt with one hand, his crystal blue eyes trained on her. His dark blond hair fell over his brow and light stubble covered his angular jaw, lending a slightly rough edge to his soldier's appearance. Just seeing him brought warmth to her chest, but noticing the way he stared at her? The intensity in his expression? It was enough to steal her breath. The corner of his mouth twitched up in a slow smile and Clare's heart tripped in response.

She looked back to the women surrounding her, gently excusing herself. They curtsied, their conversation unbroken as they debated the merits of sea daisies.

Clare used the gliding step she had been taught, the courtyard stone unyielding beneath her sore feet. She nodded to several people who called out greetings, but she didn't join them.

Bennick's alert eyes followed her easily as she moved through the crowd. Her long skirt brushed the ground as she walked, and she knew the vivid red dress accentuated the dark brown curls that flowed down her back. Her skin tingled, knowing he watched her so closely.

She stopped before him, still holding her wineglass. "Captain."

Bennick's mouth twitched. "Princess."

"I'd like to explore the garden," she said.

His eyes warmed, but his tone stayed neutrally polite. "Of course."

Bennick took her wineglass, his fingers glancing over hers. He handed the glass to a passing servant and offered Clare his arm. The moment her hand touched his strong forearm, a flutter started low in her stomach.

Bennick guided her away from the courtyard and down one of the many paths that branched through the garden. Well-trimmed hedges formed a basic maze pattern, the walls of foliage tall enough that Clare couldn't see over them. There were still torches to light the way and they passed couples sitting on stone benches set in strategic places just off the path. They rose and bowed as she passed, giving congratulations on her betrothal and well-wishes for the alliance. But each corner they rounded took them deeper into the maze, and soon they were alone.

She breathed in deeply, enjoying the earthy smell of the moonlit garden. "It's a beautiful place, but I'm exhausted."

"Some of these parties go through the night, you know."

She groaned. "It's torture."

"Tonight *has* been torture," he agreed, his voice deeper than before.

She glanced over and was instantly caught in his stare. A stare that raised every hair on her body in the most delicious way.

They stepped around another corner and Bennick scanned the shadows around them. There were no torches lit this far from the courtyard, but the moon was nearly full. She could see Bennick clearly as he tugged her to a stop. His voice was pitched low. "What do you think of the garden?"

Her heart pounded. "I like it."

Bennick's hand drifted down her arm, making her pulse race. "It's peaceful," he said slowly, his eyes fixed on hers.

"It is," she agreed.

"And beautiful," he added.

"Yes."

Her heart tripped as he leaned in, his bristled jaw angled down so he could keep her gaze. "And private."

It was the way his mouth lifted at the corner that undid her. That half-grin melted her every time. She stretched up on her toes, her palms braced against his chest as she pressed her mouth to his.

Bennick's lips were the most intriguing mix of soft and hard as he kissed her, his hands going to her waist, though she wasn't sure if he was trying to steady her, or himself. Then his hands were moving, sliding up her back to bring her closer. Her body fit perfectly against his, his warmth chasing away the slight chill in the night air.

He stole her breath, her thoughts, her awareness of anything else but how it felt to be held by him. Her fingers curled into his dark blue jacket, pulling him impossibly closer.

He changed the angle of the kiss, his nose skimming her flushed cheek as long fingers tangled in her hair.

Oh, fates.

She groaned and pulled back, her breathing ragged. "My hair."

Bennick was also breathing deeply, his eyes cutting over her hair. "Oh." His gaze narrowed, and the hard expression on his face made her chuckle.

She ducked her head, letting her forehead fall against his chest. She could hear the thump of his heart, and it matched the rapid pace of her own. "We need to be careful."

He grunted, his fingers dragging gently through some of the

tangles in her hair. "Do you realize how hard it is to watch you and not touch you?"

His words caused a pleasant flip in her stomach, but she rolled her eyes. "You're being ridiculous."

"You're ridiculously beautiful."

She smiled. This thing between them was still new, and wholly exciting. But there were complications. Because it didn't matter what part she played—princess, decoy, or maid—a relationship with Captain Bennick Markam was forbidden.

Determined to be the responsible one, she eased back and combed her fingers through her hair. Thankfully, Ivonne had left it mostly unbound and there were only a few pins near her temples that needed adjustments. She looked toward the thick stone wall that loomed nearby, encircling the edge of the estate; she hadn't realized how far they'd wandered.

"You're doing well," Bennick said suddenly. "I don't know how you manage to keep smiling through so many hours of conversation."

"Most everyone has been kind."

He snorted. "They're self-important, grasping people who just want a chance to curry favor with the royal family."

The corner of her mouth twitched. "They probably wouldn't appreciate your assessment."

"Maybe not. But they couldn't argue, because it's true."

Unfortunately, she knew he was right. The king had been strategic in the stops he'd planned; Clare would be staying with noble families who were just notable enough to influence their communities. They would be flattered by the king's request to host the princess, and they'd be put in the awkward position of having to support the peace, no matter how they felt—and they would drag all their friends with them, or risk looking contrary.

And all the while, it would look like Devendra was uniting

to celebrate the princess's marriage to Desfan. It was why this journey would take so much longer than if they simply rushed their way to Duvan—they were making a statement.

Clare shook her head. "Sometimes I don't know how Serene lives like this. Everyone starts to look duplicitous."

"Politics are messy." His mouth dipped into a frown. "I've overheard some of the nobles talking. Many are planning to attend the prisoner exchange."

Serjah Desfan had initiated discussions for a prisoner exchange weeks ago, and the details had been negotiated in time for the exchange to be part of the princess's tour. This demonstration of good faith between their kingdoms would happen at the border town of Stills, and Clare would be overseeing it. Twenty prisoners from both kingdoms would be released; most had been captured during skirmishes along the border over the span of a dozen years. Devendra had only imprisoned Mortisian soldiers, but the Mortisians had arrested men and women who had fought to protect their homes. The thought that they might soon be free, after years of separation from their homes and families, warmed Clare's heart.

She eyed Bennick. "You don't sound happy about having spectators."

"I'm not. I understand the king wants people excited about the alliance, but I wish he hadn't encouraged them to go to the exchange. It will be a tense situation, and I don't like the idea of having a large crowd. It makes it too easy for the rebels to hide." His blue eyes met hers and promise lived in his voice. "I *will* keep you safe, Clare."

"I know." And she did. He would do everything in his power to make sure she survived. Not only because he cared for her, or because it was his duty as her bodyguard, but because she remembered the solemn way he had knelt before her ten-year-old brother and sworn to bring her home.

He seemed to shake off the heaviness of the last moment. "I have something for you." He reached into his uniform's jacket pocket and pulled out a stiff silver bracelet. The band was maybe as wide as her finger, though not as thick, and delicately engraved with twisting vines.

"Bennick, it's beautiful."

"I can't take credit for the design." He took her left hand and slid the bracelet onto her wrist. "Cardon gave one just like this to Serene, for one of her birthdays, I think. And it's more than simple jewelry." He ducked his head and ran a finger over the etching until the tip of his nail caught on a small notch. With a simple pinch, he drew out a long, thin wire from inside the bracelet. He looked at her from beneath his lashes. "It's a garrote."

She shot him a look as he fed the wire back into the wristband, as if on some kind of reel. "That is . . . unique."

The corner of his mouth lifted. "Serene loves hers and wears it often, so I thought it would be a nice detail if you had one. Besides, I like the versatility of it—decorative and defensive." He released her hand, and the bracelet suddenly seemed heavier. "The silversmith I hired didn't have it quite finished before we left Iden. It just arrived tonight."

She turned her wrist over, eyeing the silver band with some hesitancy. "I don't know if I can use this against someone."

"We'll practice," he assured her. "Try pulling it out."

She found the catch that hid the end of the wire and carefully dragged it out.

Bennick chuckled. "We'll work on your speed," he teased. "But it's fairly simple to use. The trick is to get behind your opponent quickly and wrap the wire around their neck. Preferably before they realize what you're doing and stick their hand against their throat. We'll practice until it becomes reflexive for you, and

I'll show you some tricks for how to use it effectively against someone taller than you."

She fingered the intricate design of twisting vines, the precious metal slowly warming against her skin. "Thank you. It really is beautiful."

"You're welcome." He stepped closer. "I think I can kiss you without touching your hair."

A smile teased her lips. "You're trying to distract me."

He leaned in, his lips brushing the curve of her ear and making her shiver. "You're the one constantly distracting *me*."

There was a muffled curse and then a growl. "Bennick?" Wilf snapped from around the corner. "Fates blast it, where are you?"

Bennick ripped away from Clare and she swayed at the sudden loss of his nearness. He grabbed her arm to steady her, then snapped back to a proper distance just as Wilf stepped into view.

The scowl on the huge man's face was both typical and impressive. But then, everything about Wilford Lines was impressive. He stood head and shoulders above most men and he was nearly three times as wide. His face was riddled with pox scars, and for a long time, Clare had been convinced the man might be trying to kill her. Now, his gruffness just made her mouth twitch.

He glared at them. "What are you two doing back here?"

"The princess needed to step away from the crowd," Bennick said.

Wilf's eyes narrowed on Clare. "Are you unwell?"

She smiled at his protective focus. "No, just tired."

There was an annoyed rumble in the giant's chest. "If you're tired, you go to your room. You don't—"

A scream rent the night, cutting off Wilf's words and chilling Clare's blood.

CHAPTER 2
CLARE

CLARE STIFFENED AND BENNICK DREW HIS sword. Everything about him had transformed in an instant—the second that horrible shriek sounded.

The silence the sharp cry had left behind was perhaps even more chilling.

"Guard her," he commanded Wilf.

Clare's heart pounded. "But—"

"Stay with Wilf," he told her, his jaw set.

Another scream rose, this one clearly coming from the courtyard. Bennick darted in that direction. Other shouts were taken up, a low roar of voices, a few rallying shouts; nothing distinct enough for Clare to understand what might have triggered the alarm.

Wilf stepped closer and gently gripped Clare's elbow. "We

need to get inside," he said tersely. "We'll stay on the edge of the garden and avoid the courtyard."

She swallowed back her instinctive protest. One of the first lessons Bennick had taught her was the importance of working with the guards, not against them. She forced herself to move with Wilf, even though desperate curiosity clawed at her.

They were halfway back to the mansion when Wilf tensed, turning to look down one of the maze's many paths. A young guard bearing a torch darted toward them, sweat dotting his forehead. He wasn't a royal bodyguard, or even one of the palace guards that had accompanied them. Clare assumed he was one of the men the Harringtons employed.

He paled at the sight of Wilf, then his eyes cut to Clare and he jerked out a bow. "Princess, forgive me—have you seen Lady Firth?"

"I—no, not for a while." Concern rippled through her. "Is she missing?"

The young man swallowed hard. "We heard that scream, and Lady Bent went into hysterics. She claims Lady Firth vanished, and now she's convinced that scream came from her. She's quite upset."

"We haven't seen anything," Wilf said, stepping slightly in front of Clare. "You should continue your search elsewhere."

Clare's eyes drifted to a small alcove carved into the hedge. It was one of the spots where a bench sat just off the path. She wouldn't have noticed it at all from this angle if they hadn't stopped. But there was something in the shadows behind the bench and she stepped closer, dread curling in her gut.

Her eyes caught the moonlit details slowly, painting a picture that made her hands shake.

A woman lay on the ground behind the bench. She might have been asleep, with the way her arm stretched out toward the path, her relaxed fingers slightly bent. Her blue dress was familiar, and then Clare saw the long feather sticking out of her hair.

A final step brought her close enough to see the woman's face, and a cry caught in Clare's throat.

Lady Firth's open gaze was aimed at the stars, but her eyes were glazed and unseeing. A crimson rose in full bloom was in her mouth, the petals spread over her lips, and a dagger was sticking out of her unmoving chest.

Clare stumbled back, pressing a hand over her mouth.

Wilf was suddenly there, pushing past Clare to kneel at the woman's side. He swore. "Bring that light over here."

Clare wanted to look away as the torch moved closer and illuminated the dead woman's body, but she was trapped by the macabre scene—which grew even more horrifying as orange light spilled on Lady Firth.

The rose stretching open the woman's mouth looked even more grotesque, but there was something Clare hadn't noticed in the darkness. The dagger that had killed Lady Firth was also serving to pin a bloodstained note to the woman's chest.

"Holy fates," the guard gasped beside her.

Clare's entire body shook as she watched Wilf lean in to study the note. "What does it say?"

He continued to read, his spine stiff. Then he pushed to his feet and snatched the torch from the guard. "Find Captain Markam and bring him here. Tell no one else what you saw. Go."

The guard stumbled away, still cursing under his breath.

Wilf scowled after him. "He'll tell blasted everyone."

Clare hugged herself, her stomach churning. "Wilf, what's going on?"

His hard gaze landed on her and she could see the tension in his eyes. "As soon as Bennick arrives to secure the scene, I'll take you to your room."

She stared back at him, but it was clear he had no intention of telling her what the note said. And so, just like Serene would have done, she stepped around him. He did not stop her, but she felt his eyes on her as she crouched beside the dead woman and read the small, precisely written words.

Princess Serene,

That feather looked ridiculous, didn't it? Shaking every time she talked. She wouldn't stop talking. I wanted to hear your voice, so I stopped hers.

I am delighted to see the tales of your beauty are not exaggerated. I look forward to watching you — nearly as much as I look forward to the moment you finally see me.

With Sincere Anticipation,

The Rose

Clare's throat was dry as she looked up at Wilf. "Who is the Rose?"

The guard's hard expression didn't alter. "A problem."

Clare stood in her suite, adrenaline still pumping through her body. She barely resisted the urge to pace the spacious sitting room; the sounds of Wilf searching every corner of the suite—again—put her on edge. Not that she didn't appreciate his thoroughness, but she hated the fact that he was so determined to find something when there was clearly nothing to be found.

Her fingers twitched with the need to do something. Or perhaps they just trembled because there was nothing to do. She folded her arms to stop the shaking, fingers digging into her elbows as she watched Venn scan the terrifying note Bennick had just given him.

At nineteen years old, Venn was the princess's youngest guard, and he sat on the edge of the room's settee, leaning over the low table. The blood on the note was slowly drying, causing the paper to bubble slightly. Venn's attention was fixed on the words, his mouth carved into a deep frown. Dark brows pulled together, furrowing his dark skin. His long hair was pulled back into its usual ponytail and one arm was in a sling; he was still healing from an injury he'd sustained at the princess's farewell banquet.

Vera and Ivonne—two of the princess's maids—stood near Clare. The sisters were pale after sneaking a look at the note. All thoughts of helping Clare from her gown had been abandoned the moment they'd seen the hard focus on Wilf's face when he'd escorted her into the sitting room.

It had taken Bennick nearly half an hour to join them, and

he'd brought the note. He confirmed that no sign of the killer had been found and he had increased the guard in the hallway as a precaution.

Finally, Venn looked up from the letter. "Well. That's the fates-blasted creepiest thing I've ever read."

"I don't understand." Clare looked to Bennick. "Who is the Rose?"

He exhaled slowly, not quite meeting her gaze. "He's an assassin. Perhaps the most well-known assassin in all Eyrinthia."

Clare frowned. "I've never heard of him."

"Well," Venn said, "you are pretty new to this world."

He had a point. She turned back to Bennick. "So, this assassin—he targets royals?"

"No." Bennick's expression was guarded, and that alone made Clare tense. Because if he was trying to hide his alarm, she probably wasn't as scared as she should be. "I don't think the Rose has ever targeted a royal."

"He killed a distant cousin in the Buhari royal family," Wilf offered, shutting a closet door on the other side of the room. "That was a few years ago. King Zaire nearly tore Zennor apart looking for the Rose, but he was never found."

"Royal targets aside," Venn said, "the Rose is known for killing influential figures, like wealthy merchants, prominent nobles, or even ambassadors. But sometimes it's just someone who crossed someone important." His eyes narrowed. "He killed a captain of the city guard a couple years ago. A Captain Olsen. The Rose left notes for him, too."

"They are part of the Rose's signature." Wilf double-checked the lock on a window before turning to face them. "He's not a typical assassin. He isn't hired just to kill, he's hired to taunt, spread fear and panic, and *then* kill. You hire the Rose when you want to send a message—and he never fails. Anyone stalked by the Rose ends up dead. And he always leaves a rose."

A chill rippled down Clare's spine, and her fingers dug more tightly into her crossed arms. Bennick's eyes flashed, noting the movement. His jaw tightened.

"No one knows which kingdom he hails from." Venn rubbed the back of his neck with his free hand. "He seems to kill indiscriminately."

"I heard a rumor that he was from Ryden," Vera said quietly.

Ivonne huffed. "He's probably one of those demon Kaelin princes."

Venn looked to Bennick. "What are the chances this is an imposter, just trying to scare us?"

"I'm not sure, but we're going to treat the threat as real." Bennick nodded to the note on the table. "I'll send that to Iden. My father investigated Captain Olsen's murder two years ago; he should still have the messages the Rose left, and he can compare the handwriting."

"Hiring the Rose to kill the princess while on her royal tour would have cost a great deal," Wilf mused. "She's a high-profile target on a highly publicized tour, well-guarded, with locations changing frequently. Not many could afford him. Especially if a request came to kill multiple people."

Venn snorted a short laugh. "Maybe the rebels took up a collection and pinched their coins."

"No," Bennick said, shaking his head. "They would want to make the kill themselves, not let an assassin claim the victory. If they used the Rose, they'd lose the power of their message."

"Agreed." Wilf stepped closer, finally abandoning his search of the room and joining them. "The fact he sent the note at the beginning of the tour is no coincidence. He's making it clear this is about the betrothal."

Bennick turned to Venn. "Check in with the house guards,

see if they managed to find anything new. And send someone to Camden's city guard headquarters for their fastest messenger. I want that note in the commander's hands as soon as possible." Venn dipped his head and left, and Bennick turned to Wilf. "How long has he been active? Do you know?"

"Not exactly, but several years. Maybe a decade. Long enough to establish a pattern and earn a reputation." He lifted his gaze and met Bennick's. "I don't think anyone in the business of professional killing would have the nerve to pretend to be him."

Bennick nodded, then gestured to the suite's door. "Let the guards know what happened and see if they know anything about the Rose. I'll take rumors and hearsay at this point."

Wilf nodded and moved for the door, obeying without question. Sometimes, Clare almost forgot that Bennick was the captain of the princess's guard. Not because he didn't take charge, but he was so much younger than the others; Dirk was in his fifties, Wilf in his forties, and even Cardon was thirty. But even though he was only twenty years old, Bennick had earned their respect.

Bennick turned to Ivonne and Vera. "May I have a private word with Clare?"

The sisters nodded, quickly moving for the bedroom and closing the door.

The moment they were alone in the sitting room, Bennick moved to stand in front of Clare, blocking her view of the bloody note. "Are you all right?" he asked, his voice low and intent.

She choked on a weak laugh. "Can I be honest?"

A muscle in his cheek tightened. "I'm sorry you had to see that."

She blinked slowly, knowing she would never get the images out of her mind. Lady Firth's sightless eyes. The dagger in her heart. The rose in her mouth.

She didn't realize she was shaking until Bennick set his hands on her shoulders, steadying her with his grounding touch. His words were quietly fierce as he said, "Lady Firth's death is not your fault."

Tears pricked her eyes. She supposed she should be surprised that he had read her so clearly, and yet, she wasn't. Her throat swelled with emotion she'd been trying to force down. "I feel like it's my fault. If I hadn't talked with her, then maybe . . ."

Bennick's fingers curled into her shoulders with gentle pressure. "You did nothing wrong, Clare. He's the one who murdered an innocent woman."

"He was watching me." She peeked up at Bennick. "He was watching me, and I didn't even notice."

The skin around his eyes tightened. "We'll catch him. He won't touch you."

Her stomach rolled. "He's never failed."

"Everyone fails. The Rose is only human."

"He sounds more like a nightmare," she whispered.

Bennick's lips pressed together and he tugged her to his chest. She leaned into his embrace, wrapping her arms around his waist. He rested his cheek against the top of her head, his arms completely enfolding her.

His embrace was exactly what she needed. As the moment lengthened, some of the tension in her body eased. Dread still iced her veins, but abandoning hope and trust for fear and panic would only give the Rose another victory. Her heartbeat gradually steadied, and she squeezed Bennick in silent thanks. "Will you promise me something?"

"Anything," he vowed.

She closed her eyes. "If something does happen to me, please look after my brothers." It was a promise she'd secured before they left the castle, but after tonight she needed the reassurance.

Bennick's arms flexed around her, tightening his hold. "Of course." His lips brushed the hair at her temple. "But nothing is going to happen to you. I will get you to Duvan safely and when the time comes, I'll get you home. I swear it."

She did not doubt him.

It was the rest of the world she doubted.

Clare lifted her arms so the seamstress could take her measurements. The poor woman kept shaking her gray head, mortification stark on her face. "I'm so sorry for this inconvenience, Princess. My apprentice must have made a mistake when she read your letter. Everything is slightly off."

"It's no trouble," Clare said, sending a reassuring smile toward the younger girl blushing in the corner. "It was an innocent mistake."

It had not been a mistake. The measurements the seamstress had received weeks ago were indeed the princess's—but while Clare and Serene were extremely similar in size, there were differences.

The seamstress—a matronly woman named Sylvie—continued to apologize, but the set of her shoulders relaxed as the fitting went on. The woman was known throughout Devendra for her spectacular designs and talent, and Serene had ordered several dresses from her. She'd been extremely angry when King Newlan had forbidden her to break from her alternate path to keep the appointment.

Sometimes the battles Serene picked with Newlan didn't make sense, but Clare was grateful this stop hadn't been canceled. The long afternoon was turning into a much needed break from the nobles who had been crowding her all morning and the terrifying memories that had kept her up most of the night. Even now when she closed her eyes, all she saw was Lady Firth's body and that terrifying note. The reality that she was being stalked by a professional killer who wrote chilling notes and shoved roses into his victims' mouths left a pit in her stomach.

Spending hours at a dress shop in relative solitude was exactly what Clare needed.

Ivonne had remained at the Harringtons manor with a headache, but Vera was in the dressing room with Clare, occasionally giving her opinion. The quiet girl had been even more so today; she seemed preoccupied, which Clare could understand after last night's events.

Sylvie continued her work, at times asking for Clare's opinion on a certain aspect of the design or a particular bit of embroidery. The seamstress also wanted the princess's opinion on several bolts of fabric imported from Zennor, so while the apprentice rushed to gather the final dresses to try on, Sylvie led Clare into the main part of the shop.

Of course, Clare knew nothing of how the silks compared to those found in Zennorian markets, but she sifted the smooth material between her fingers and praised the quality. Sylvie beamed. "Perhaps I could surprise you with a design in one of these silks? You have only to pick the color."

Her eagerness and enthusiasm made Clare smile. "You're very kind." And since Newlan could afford it, she picked a deep purple she liked and Sylvie lifted the entire bolt.

"I'll just put this in the back." She started to turn, but instantly twisted back. "I know many do not recognize the sacrifice you're making for us. For peace. But I want you to know that some of us do. Thank you, Princess." She dropped into a quick curtsy and—as if worried she'd said too much—hurried off with the fabric in her arms.

The woman's words were unexpected and touching. Clare promised herself she'd pass them on to Serene, next time she saw her. It was nice to hear something positive, when all around them were threats, anger, and rebellion.

Clare's eye was drawn to the corner of the room, where Venn stood admiring a length of maroon ribbon. He clutched the end with his good hand, the other still wrapped in the sling. He turned, the ribbon dangling in front of him. "Wilf, this is exactly your color!"

Wilf's arms were crossed over his chest and his pox-scarred face was set like granite as he eyed the ribbon. "Put that anywhere on me and I will break your arm."

"Rude." Venn caught Clare looking at them. His grin widened and he held the ribbon in front of Wilf's face. "It *is* his color, don't you think?"

Wilf snatched the swaying ribbon and threw it aside. But one could only throw a ribbon so harshly, so it fluttered almost gently to the floor.

Clare's mouth twitched. "We need to get you out of this shop."

Wilf grunted agreement.

"It's no crime to want to look your best," Venn said. "I bet I could convince Bennick to make it a new rule." He promptly raised his voice. "Bennick! Make it a rule that we each need to wear a ribbon with our uniform."

Bennick, who was peering out the storefront window, didn't even bother to throw a glance over his shoulder. "No."

"Couldn't we at least put one on our swords?" Venn asked.

"No," Bennick repeated.

"Thank the fates," Wilf muttered.

Venn pouted, but then his eyes darted to Vera, who was returning from the back of the shop with the seamstress's apprentice, their arms filled with the next round of dresses. The way Venn's gaze both brightened and softened spread a slow grin over Clare's face.

Vera flashed a smile at Venn before she disappeared back into the dressing room. Clare followed her, and Sylvie—who had returned from storing the purple silk—trailed behind.

Six more gowns were waiting to be tried, and Sylvie apologized once more that the dresses would not be ready to be taken today, though she assured Clare that she would send them to the next tour stop in Tarvin.

Clare was still wearing the final dress—a dinner gown in a light shade of blue that was almost an exact match for Bennick's eyes, with beautiful silver embroidery—when the apprentice ran out of pins and had to excuse herself to gather more.

Sylvie held the dressing room door for the girl, asking her to carry a few things to the back, since she was going anyway. She then turned to Clare. "We've kept you overlong, I fear. Allow me to fetch some refreshments while we finish up."

"I'm all right, but I'm sure my guards would appreciate something." If nothing else, Wilf probably needed a break from Venn's teasing, which she doubted had stopped. He loved riling the giant.

Sylvie bobbed a curtsey and exited the room, leaving Clare alone with Vera.

The seventeen-year-old maid was gathering up swatches of fabric and other items left behind in the chaos of the fittings. Clare picked up a pair of scissors before Vera could, and that was when Vera seemed to realize she wasn't alone.

"Oh, you don't need to do that," she said.

"Neither do you." Clare's brow furrowed as she studied the girl's face. "Is something wrong?"

Vera blew out a breath, and a tendril of blond hair that had come loose from her braid shivered from the long exhale. "Ivonne and I had an argument."

Clare's eyes widened. "Really?" The sisters always seemed so close; always in agreement.

Vera scrubbed a hand over her brow before dropping to pick up a discarded spool of thread. "It happened the night before we left the castle."

"I'm so sorry. I didn't realize . . ."

The maid shook her head, the spool of thread twisting in her fidgeting hands. "We agreed not to let it impact our work." She snorted. "But then she refused to come here today, so I suppose she broke that promise."

"She doesn't have a headache?"

"Oh, I'm sure her head aches," Vera muttered. "That happens when you're hard-headed."

Clare plucked the spinning thread from Vera's fast-moving fingers and met the girl's eyes. "What happened?"

Her mouth pursed as she weighed her words. Finally, she whispered, "I have feelings for Venn."

Clare's lips twitched. "I've noticed."

Color touched the girl's cheeks. "Yes, well, Ivonne doesn't approve."

"Why not? Venn is a good man and kind to everyone. Especially you."

"Venn himself isn't the issue. Ivonne doesn't approve of any man in a uniform." Vera curled the loose strands of hair behind her ear, her chest rising on a breath. "About a year ago, Ivonne fell in love with a member of the castle guard. He was handsome. Charming. And then she learned he charmed many of the maids, all at the same time." She shook her head. "She was devastated. She had given him everything and he . . . well, he took it and never gave her anything real in return."

"Venn isn't like that."

"Of course he isn't. But Ivonne won't see that. The night Venn was injured, I refused to leave his bedside. That must have been the moment she realized I had actual feelings for him. She had noticed his flirtations before, but I'd never acted on them, so she thought I felt nothing." Vera met Clare's gaze. "She thinks he'll hurt me. Maybe not like she was hurt, but she fears he could be killed, or reassigned . . . that something will force him to leave me."

"You can't live your life in fear."

"I know. And I told her that." She bit her lip. "For a long time, I was afraid of what I felt for Venn. I thought he did just flirt with everyone, but . . . not anymore. I think he truly cares for me, and I care for him. Ivonne will have to learn to accept my decision."

"I'm happy for you," Clare said with a smile. "And Venn."

"Thank you." Her cheeks pinkened. "Don't say anything to anyone—especially not Venn. I may not be afraid, but . . . I'm not ready to declare anything to him."

"Don't worry. I won't say a word."

Vera still seemed a little embarrassed to have shared so much, so when she offered to quickly take the box of scraps she'd gathered to the apprentice, Clare let her go.

She returned to tidying the room. The simple act reminded her of home, and she felt a sudden pang in her chest. She had been taking care of her brothers since Mark was an infant. Mothering them had been the sole focus of her life for so long, it was still difficult to be away from them. Knowing they had a wonderful caretaker helped, but she hated to think of all she was missing. Fates, she even missed mediating their fights.

And then there was Eliot. She had not left Iden on the best terms with her older brother, and she regretted that. She'd sent a letter, but it wasn't the same. If only she could have told him about being the princess's decoy . . . But in truth, Eliot had been more upset by Clare's proximity to Bennick than he had been about her leaving home to work at the castle.

Clare crouched to pick up an errant piece of lace. It had fallen by the dressing screen, which had been pushed to the back of the room during the fittings.

As she stood, a hand shot from behind the screen and snagged her wrist.

Clare jerked back, a scream trapped in her throat. Before any sound could escape, the man holding her arm darted from behind the screen and clapped a hand over her mouth, pushing her back until her shoulders thumped the wall. Her throat burned and panic clawed her insides, making her body freeze. The only thought that flashed through her head was that this was him— the Rose.

He wore plain clothes, mostly clean but heavily worn. He was taller than she was, maybe a couple of years older. His eyes widened as he scanned her face. His callused hand stretched over the lower half of her face, silencing her, and his thumb pressed into the tender skin under her chin.

"Easy," he said in an anxious whisper. "I'm not going to hurt you. Fates, Serene told me I wouldn't be able to tell the difference, but I was so sure it was her. Your likeness is incredible. Even the way you speak."

Shock and confusion mixed with the fear flooding her veins, making her heart hammer in her chest.

His features pinched. "Please don't call for the guards. I know you have no reason to trust me, but I swear I mean you no harm.

Serene told me you might help me, Clare."

She jerked, her breath quickening. He knew her name. Serene had told him—told him about the decoy.

Why?

Her wide eyes took in every detail of his face. He was tanned, as if he spent most of his days in the sun. A farmer, perhaps? That would explain the roughness of his hand. But why would Serene be in close contact with a commoner? And why would he use the princess's given name with such quiet confidence? How would he dare to touch her?

"We don't have much time." He shot a glance at the closed door, his throat working. "I'm sorry if I startled you. Just, please —*please* don't call the guards. Nod, and I'll release you."

Clare's first urge was to bite his hand, kick him between the legs, and yell until Bennick shoved into the room. But curiosity beat back her fear, at least for the moment.

She nodded, and the man eased his hand away.

Her heart still beat too fast as she quietly demanded, "Who are you?"

"My name is James." He winced. "I'm sorry for any alarm I caused. I was just so confident you were her."

She folded her arms over her chest, her cheeks suddenly burning. "How long have you been in here?"

The flush that washed over his face rivaled her own. He threw up his hands. "Fates, I didn't—I turned my back!"

Her eyes narrowed. "How do you know Serene?"

"That's not important right now."

"I disagree."

He shifted on his feet, clearly nervous. "Serene said we could trust you."

"Trust me with what?"

He tugged a small square of paper from his pocket. It was

folded and sealed with a small circle of red wax. "Will you give this to her when you see her next? Please. It's important."

"Who *are* you?"

His grip on the note tightened, his brown eyes pleading. "We'll both be indebted to you; that's all I can say. *Please.*"

Suddenly, Clare held the small missive. Had he shoved it into her hand? Surely she hadn't taken it. She was too frazzled to have made such a decision.

"Don't open it," James begged, anxiety edging the words. "And don't share it with anyone, or tell them I was here."

Before she could open her mouth, he was at the small window set high in the wall. She never would have thought he could fit through it, but he grasped the sill and slid out in seconds.

For some reason, she didn't stop him or call out.

The small letter seemed heavy in her hands. She eyed the simple seal, thoughts slowly piercing the confusion that still gripped her.

Serene had told James about the decoy. She'd even shared Clare's name. And the princess had been very upset when Newlan had refused her wish to make this particular appointment. In fact, she'd been upset when Newlan had canceled many dress fittings along the way . . . Those rare moments she could arrange to be alone, without even her guards.

Clare's jaw loosened.

James was undeniably handsome, in a rough-hewn way, with a strong build, dark hair, and high cheekbones.

Oh, fates.

The door opened behind her, Sylvie and Vera chatting as they returned.

Keeping her back turned, Clare stepped closer to the dress she'd worn to the shop, which lay draped over a chair. She slipped the small letter into the pocket, hiding it from view.

But even if she could no longer see the letter, it burned through her thoughts.

Serene—who was set to marry the future ruler of Mortise in perhaps the most desperate and highly fragile bid for peace in Devendra's history—was possibly in love with a Devendran commoner.

And Clare was hiding a piece of paper that had the potential to ruin them all.

CHAPTER 3

GRAYSON

A SHOUT RIPPED THROUGH GRAYSON'S throat, tearing him from sleep. He clawed at the blankets that tangled his legs and pinned him to the mattress, his shirt plastered to his back with sweat. His entire body shook and his heart exploded in his chest as his lungs heaved.

The darkness of his bedroom pressed in but he still drove the heels of his hands into his eyes, though it didn't stop the images from his nightmare. He still saw the old man he'd killed. A defenseless prisoner.

A test of Grayson's obedience.

He had slit the man's throat five days ago, and he had relived the horrifying moment every night since. But tonight, the nightmare had twisted. As Grayson had dealt the killing blow, it hadn't been the old man who had choked on blood.

It had been Mia.

He ducked his head, his fingers curling into his scalp, digging in with painful pressure as his pulse thundered in his ears.

He would never hurt Mia. He would cut his own throat first. But he still saw that nightmarish memory of the light leaving her eyes, the terror carved on her face; the wet slide of her blood on his hands as he'd held the wound and tried to save her.

His stomach rolled. He was going to be sick.

Not real. Just a dream.

Fear still knifed his gut.

It was the middle of the night. He should try to go back to sleep; fates knew his brother Liam would have another full day of training for him. But adrenaline pumped through his veins, leaving him tense and raw. He needed to see Mia. He wouldn't settle until he confirmed she was all right.

He shoved off the bed, bare feet hitting the cold rug. He padded over to the washstand in the corner, yanking off his shirt as he moved. He washed the sweat from his face and neck, then snagged a clean shirt from a drawer and tugged it on before turning to his weapons. He took three daggers of various sizes before stepping out of his room.

The hallway was deserted, with only a third of the torches lit. Shadows stretched long and deep in the corridors, and the castle was glaringly silent. Grayson moved quickly and soundlessly, almost wraithlike. The walk to the dungeon was one he knew well. Occasionally he spotted guards or servants, but they all bowed their heads and shrank back, eager for him to pass.

His hands twitched at his sides and he realized he'd forgotten his black gloves. He preferred to keep his scarred hands covered, though he hadn't felt the need to hide from Mia. Not anymore.

He'd found Mia when he was nine years old. She'd been a year younger, and a prisoner in the castle dungeon. Eight years had passed since then, and she meant more to him than the air in his lungs. He was still staggered by the fact she loved him.

And in three days, he would have to leave her.

His father had ordered him and Liam to travel to Mortise. They were expected to play the part of peacemakers until Grayson could assassinate Princess Serene Aren Demoi and spark a war between Mortise and Devendra.

Mia didn't know that part, though she clearly knew King Henri would never send Grayson on a mission of peace.

When he reached her cell, Grayson was surprised to see Fletcher, the quiet day guard, standing outside her door, rather than the usual night guard.

"What are you doing here?" Grayson asked, his low voice sounding loud in the shadowy hall.

Surprise flared in the old man's eyes, but he offered an abbreviated bow. "The night guard is ill, so I took his shift." Fletcher's eyes narrowed. "What are *you* doing here?"

Grayson wasn't one to normally explain himself, but he appreciated the man's fiercely protective tone. "I wanted to check on her."

The old guard grunted. "She hasn't been sleeping well. Not since Prince Tyrell came."

Grayson's hands rolled to fists. Five days ago, Tyrell had been sent by King Henri to punish Mia as a way to teach Grayson a lesson. When he'd burst into the cell and seen his brother wielding a belt against Mia, Grayson had nearly killed his brother in retribution.

Would have, if Mia hadn't begged him not to.

"Has she said anything to you?" Grayson asked.

"No. I just pay attention." Fletcher's gray hair caught in the torchlight as he sifted through his keys, a muscle thrumming in his clenched jaw. "I'm sorry I couldn't step in," he finally whispered. "When the prince came, I had no choice but to let him in."

The words were unexpected. He knew Fletcher wasn't heartless, that he had demonstrated kindness to Mia in the past, but his regret that he hadn't been able to stand up to Tyrell revealed the depth of his care for Mia. It gave Grayson the smallest bit of comfort, knowing she would have at least one ally while he was gone.

"There was nothing you could have done," Grayson said, his voice quiet. "Standing against him would have cost you your position. Probably your life."

The man's jaw tightened. "Still. She didn't deserve that."

Mia didn't deserve any of this. She had been taken by King Henri as a child and used to manipulate Grayson into obedience. Henri didn't spare a single thought for her well-being. The only value she had for him came from what she meant to Grayson—which was everything.

Fletcher unlocked the door and Grayson slipped into the dark room, pulling the door gently closed behind him.

He could hear snores from the back room. It was probably Mama, Mia's caretaker; she often drank herself into a deep sleep that nothing could pull her out of. King Henri had appointed the woman and her husband—who had no doubt already left for his shift in the lower dungeons—to care for Mia. They never showed her any true care, though. Just thinking of how cruel they'd been to her as a child made Grayson's vision haze red.

In the darkened stillness of the room, he eased his way to Mia's bed, near the stove. It glowed dimly, subtle heat wafting from it. Mia was curled on her side facing him, her hands tucked under her chin. Her face was smooth in sleep, her breaths slow and even. Her cheeks curved softly and a dark brown curl rested on her jaw, near a fading bruise from her fight with Tyrell.

She was safe. He should go. There was no reason to disturb her.

He turned for the door, but Mia's breath caught.

Grayson froze, hating that he'd woken her. But when he turned to apologize he saw her eyes were clenched shut, her expression twisted in pained sleep. A whimper escaped her parted lips and her forehead creased.

The pangs of his own nightmare lingered, and though he didn't know what terrors haunted her, he couldn't watch her suffer.

Grayson moved forward and set a gentle hand on her squirming shoulder. "Mia, wake up. You're—"

She thrashed awake.

He jumped back to avoid her swinging arms as she jolted up in the bed. She gasped raggedly, hands knotted in the blankets. She whipped her head around in the darkness, a cry pinching off before it could fully emerge as she shoved back against the stone wall. "Who's there?" she rasped, her breath too sharp and rapid.

His heart pounded as he lifted his hands, palms out. "Mia, it's me. You were just dreaming."

By the yellowed glow of the stove, he could see sweat beading her forehead. Her brown eyes were wild and her entire body shook, her hands pressed tight against her heart. When her eyes latched onto him, the tension didn't ease. It increased. Each breath rattled harshly out of her, wracking her entire body, and the pained sound clawed his insides.

He'd never seen her like this. "Mia? What's wrong?"

She didn't answer. She wasn't dragging in enough air; she wasn't truly breathing.

Fear locked every muscle for a horrible, frozen second. Then he was on the bed, grasping her shoulders. "Mia? Mia!"

The cell door banged open. Fletcher must have heard his

shout. The guard rushed in, drawing up short before he reached the bed. "Fates," he swore before Grayson could even ask for help. "Not again." He bolted for the trunk in the corner of the room and threw open the lid. He shoved things aside.

Mia fisted Grayson's loose shirt, her chest straining against her pale nightgown as her lungs fought for air. He clamped down on her arms, as if holding her more tightly would give her the breath she needed. He looked to Fletcher and demanded, "What's going on?"

A lesser man would have trembled from that tone, but Fletcher didn't even look at Grayson. "It's one of her panics."

"What?"

Fletcher cursed and twisted toward the bed, eyes shooting to Mia. "Where are they, girl?"

Mia couldn't speak. Her breathing was uneven, shallow, and tight. Fear was etched into every line of her face, her fingers desperately knotted in Grayson's shirt.

Fletcher was beside them in an instant. He snatched hold of Mia's arm and dragged her to the edge of the bed. Grayson kept a hold on her, his gray eyes slashing to the guard. "Fates blast it, tell me what's going on!"

Fletcher grabbed the back of Mia's head and shoved it down between her knees. Bent double, Mia's breathing still spiked and cut jaggedly.

The guard's eyes narrowed on Grayson. "Keep her head down. Rub her back. Make her feel safe. I'll be back as soon as I can."

"What—?"

Fletcher bolted from the room.

Grayson grit his teeth, his bare hand curved around the back of Mia's head. His free hand stroked up and down her bent spine, his throat burning and his lungs compressed. Confusion, terror, helplessness—they all washed over him, drowning him.

Make her feel safe.

He ducked his head to press a kiss to her temple. "I love you, Mia. I'm here."

Minutes dragged by. Mia's breaths grated out of her, wheezing and sharp. Each one cut him. Her body was strained and tight beside him—stiff as stone. Grayson's wasn't much better.

She was still hyperventilating when Fletcher finally dashed back into the room.

Grayson's jaw was so stiff he was surprised it hadn't cracked. "Where have you—?" He cut himself off when another man came into the room. "Who are you?" he demanded.

The stranger ignored him, lowering to his haunches in front of Mia. His long hands settled over her shaking knees, steadying them. His voice was smooth and calm. "Mia, you're all right. I need you to relax." He reached into the satchel slung over his chest and drew out a glass jar of smelling salts. He uncapped it and held it under her nose, encouraging her to breathe deeply. The smell was strong—so strong, it itched Grayson's nose. Lavender and something else—something sharper.

Fletcher lit a lamp, the additional light dispelling some of the icy panic in the room.

Grayson continued to rub Mia's back, his thoughts chaotic and his tension high as he studied the man before him. A physician. He had to be a physician. And he knew Mia's name. He knew what was happening—how to help her.

Not again. That's what Fletcher had said. The words made Grayson's blood run cold.

"That's it," the physician whispered to Mia, one hand still balanced on her knee. Her breaths were evening out as she breathed in the salts and, for the first time, the man glanced at Grayson. "Can you hold the jar, Your Highness?"

Grayson's fingers wrapped around the smooth glass while

the physician dug in his satchel and pulled out a thick candle. It was a pale purple color, and when he lit it, the scent of lavender grew stronger.

Grayson continued to grip the jar, holding it beneath Mia's nose. Watching her struggle to breathe was one of the most terrifying things he had ever experienced. Every nerve was drawn tight. And though he was relieved she was finally breathing again, tension continued to sing through him. Because it was clear this was not the first time something like this had happened.

The physician shot a glare at the closed bedroom door, his calm manner dropped in an instant. "They probably sold the salts I left for her."

Fletcher grunted in agreement.

Grayson finally found his voice. "This has happened before?"

Eyes flickered to him and he felt like a fates-blasted idiot. Mia's shoulder stiffened under his palm, making the silence even harder to bear.

The physician cleared his throat, his mouth offering a somewhat strained smile. "Nothing to worry over, Your Highness. Her panics are not as frequent as they used to be."

Grayson's fingers curled painfully tight around the jar. "I was not aware of them."

"It's nothing too serious," the physician replied. "Not if the salts are on hand."

Mia tugged the bottle from her nose. Grayson allowed it, because her breathing was less frayed. She peeked up at him, her cheeks still flushed. "I'm fine," she whispered, her voice hoarse.

Grayson's body remained taut. "How long has this been happening?"

She swallowed, shooting a look toward the physician, who answered, "About nine years, Your Highness."

The words struck him like a fist in his gut. This had been

happening ever since her imprisonment, then.

And he had never known.

"It's not often," she said with a low cough. "Not anymore."

Grayson's left hand tensed against her back, his right strangling the jar of salts still balanced on his knee.

"Really, I'm all right," Mia insisted. "Devon says it's not so uncommon."

"Indeed not," the physician—Devon—actually smiled, the expression soft in the dim lamplight. "I treat this all the time. Most noblewomen have several fits a day. It's the height of fashion from here to Zennor." He patted her knee and pushed to his feet. "Keep the salts and the candle, Mia. Tell Fletcher if they go missing again."

Mia nodded and Devon offered a quick bow to Grayson before he left, Fletcher trailing after him.

The door closed, leaving Grayson and Mia alone.

She twisted toward him, not quite meeting his gaze. Her voice was a bare whisper. "Are you angry?"

"No." He was furious, actually, but not with her.

There was a brief pause, then she said, "I'm sorry if I scared you."

He'd been fates-blasted terrified. He set the jar of salts near the flickering purple candle. "Why didn't you tell me?" he asked quietly.

Her eyes lowered to watch her fingers twitch in her lap. "There was no reason to tell you."

"No reason?" He stared at her, hand dropping from her back to fist against the bed. "You couldn't breathe."

She gazed toward the closed cell door, her eyes distant. "They happened all the time, in the beginning. The panics were triggered constantly because I was always so afraid. Then you came. Whenever you were near, they stopped." She ducked her head, long dark curls slipping over her shoulder, hiding her face. "I never wanted you to know. You're so strong, and I—" Her voice cracked.

Grayson gripped her upper arms, turning her so she faced him. "Mia, you are the strongest person I know. The bravest. Nothing will ever make me think otherwise."

She grimaced. "I'm not brave."

"You are." He hesitated, then asked quietly, "Did they start again after Tyrell?"

Her gaze cut away, color in her cheeks. "Yes, but what happened . . . that's not the only reason."

She didn't have to specify what she meant. That horrible night, Tyrell had beaten her—and Grayson had told her he was leaving for Mortise.

Silence stretched. He still held her arms, and he found himself thumbing the sleeves of her nightgown. "Is there anything I can do?" he asked. "Anything I can say that will ease your mind while I'm gone?"

She leaned into him, resting her head against his shoulder as she wrapped an arm around his back. "Just promise me you'll come back," she breathed.

He pressed a kiss to the top of her head. "I will." No matter what it cost him, it was a promise he would keep.

When he left her cell, it was an hour before dawn. He moved at a rapid clip to his room where he shoved on his black gloves, belted on a few more daggers, and palmed a small leather kit Liam had given him on their first day of training.

When he turned to face the door, he felt a moment of hesitation. A whisper that pleaded caution.

He pushed both aside, because he could not afford them.

It was the Black Hand who strode from his room, melting easily into the shadows of the corridor. He was the most feared prince of Ryden, the youngest son of a tyrant king and the queen of poisons.

No one saw him until it was too late.

There were two guards outside his father's room.

Grayson used the Zennorian blow darts from Liam and watched as the two men slumped to the floor, hands swiping uselessly against the small needles in their necks. The poison wouldn't kill them, but it paralyzed them, rendering them incapable of shouting a warning. Their rolling eyes, slowly glazing, could barely focus on him as he stepped over their bodies, pocketing the leather kit that held more darts and the bamboo cylinder that shot them.

He crouched before the door and drew out a set of lockpicks. In a breathless moment, the door clicked open and Grayson melted inside.

Grayson hadn't set foot in the king's apartment since he was a child, but the dim, pre-dawn light spilling through a crack in the mostly drawn curtains guided him around a table and pair of armchairs. There were no other guards in the room.

He heard the low snores of his father, but that was the only sound. Good. His mother was a lighter sleeper, so he was grateful she was in her separate suite. It would make this easier.

Grayson found the door to his father's inner sleeping chamber also locked, but he made short work of that and eased inside.

He let his eyes adjust as much as possible to the darkness, straining every sense to assure himself there was nothing else in the space—no traps, no last guard.

He sensed no one other than the man sleeping in the large bed.

His father, it seemed, had grown complacent.

Grayson ignored the tautness of his nerves as he withdrew a dagger and crept up to the bed, using the silent tread his father had beaten into him.

King Henri was sprawled on his back, one arm curved under his pillow, the other draped over his belly. His chest rose and fell in rhythmic breaths, his mouth partly open and surrounded by his beard. His brown hair, just beginning to gray at the temples, was an untidy mess that fell over his forehead. The sheets were shoved down his bare chest, as if even the coolness of Ryden's night air didn't dare touch him.

In sleep, he looked nothing like the monster he was.

Grayson lowered his dagger until the sharp edge lay against Henri's throat.

At the light touch, Henri's snores ceased. His eyes snapped open, his body tensing.

Grayson's voice was an even whisper. "I trust I have your attention?"

Confusion, fear, fury—they all swirled in Henri's eyes before his own indifferent mask slid over his features, banishing all emotion from his gaze. "You do."

"Good." Grayson increased the pressure of the knife against his father's throat and Henri's breaths thinned in response. He kept his voice pitched low. "I had hoped to make an impression."

Beneath the blade, Henri's throat flexed. There, finally, Grayson saw the spark of something he had counted on—the one thing that would keep Henri from outright killing him or punishing Mia: intrigue.

He had captured his father's curiosity.

Grayson's fingers twitched against the handle of the blade. For a brief moment, he thought about pushing deeper, drawing blood—maybe even ending his sire's life. But that would only end in his own death, and probably Mia's as well.

He eased back, spinning the blade in his hand. His mask was still firmly in place as he looked down on his father. He had never pinned Henri with this dark, soulless look. He had never worn the Black Hand's mask so fully in his father's presence.

And he had never seen such excitement on the king's face. Such pleasure.

Grayson's stomach churned, but he kept his gaze cold and his voice remote. "In one hour, you will meet me in your office."

The edge of Henri's mouth curled in a slow smile. "I look forward to it."

Grayson turned on his heel and strode from the room.

He had won the first round.

He hoped it would be enough to help him survive the second.

CHAPTER 4

GRAYSON

"YOU DIDN'T KILL THE GUARDS," HENRI SAID from behind his desk.

Grayson used the heel of his boot to kick the door shut behind him, sealing them in the king's office. "They weren't my targets."

Henri's smile thinned a little at the vague threat. The king sat in a cushioned chair behind his wide desk, his hair combed and a golden crown on his head. The low ceiling and crowded book-shelves made the room feel tight and stifling. There were no windows this deep in the castle, and even though lamps on the walls flared with light, it wasn't enough to drive out the oppressive feel of the place. Grayson had always hated his father's study, but the dark stain on the rug made him hate it even more. His lungs tightened at the sight of it, the memory of the life he had taken in this very space, but he had to shove away all emotion.

He was the Black Hand. To lose that mask now would be a deadly mistake.

Henri studied him, curiosity strong in his gaze. "Still, it would have sent a stronger message if you'd killed them. But no matter. For their incompetence, I slit their throats."

Grayson didn't flinch. He knew the king was testing him. "Do you really wish to discuss your dead guards?" he asked levelly.

"No."

He was not surprised his father was alone. To bring in even one guard would show fear, and Henri Kaelin was not that kind of man. The king would be armed, though, and the two guards outside could easily be summoned. Grayson needed to tread carefully. This path he walked was a knife's edge—if he didn't push far enough, this would all be for nothing; if he pushed too far, the king would kill him.

Henri leaned back in his chair, his expression speculative. "I sometimes forget you're a Kaelin. Then you do something like this. Something none of your brothers would dare."

"As I said, I wanted your attention."

"You have it." The king's head tilted to the side, as if studying Grayson from a new angle would shed new light on him. "What do you wish to discuss?"

"I have three demands."

"Indeed?" The king laced his fingers. "I'm most curious to hear them."

"I never want Tyrell near Mia again. Ever."

Henri's thick eyebrows lifted. "Interesting. What is your second demand?"

"I want Mia's caretakers removed."

"You don't approve of the couple I chose to look after her?"

He ground his teeth. "They abused her."

The corner of Henri's mouth twitched, and a new wave of

hatred swelled for his father. "And your third demand?" the king asked.

Grayson's lungs tightened. This was the one that mattered most. "When I get back from Mortise, I want you to release Mia, and give your word that no Kaelin will ever harm her, or cause harm to come to her."

Henri stared at him, unblinking. The silence lifted the hairs on the back of Grayson's neck, but he would not retract his request. He would not speak first.

Finally, the king shifted in his chair, his long fingers steepled in front of his mouth. "Are you sure you want that?"

The question was so unexpected, Grayson was frozen for a moment. "Of course."

Henri's firm gaze was unwavering. "What exactly do you think will happen if I set her free? Do you think she'll stay here, in the castle? That she'll choose to live with you?"

"She will be free to do whatever she wants," Grayson said, his voice too tight.

"Yes, she would be free. Free to leave *you.*"

A creeping chill invaded his veins, but Grayson refused to give in to the dread that clutched him. He stiffened his spine, ignored the tension gathering in his shoulders. "What Mia chooses shouldn't concern you."

Henri snorted. "You can be as grave-faced as you want, but I know the truth. You think you're in love with the girl, that she loves you. But have you forgotten? *You're* the reason she's here. If she knew the truth, she would hate you."

Irritation and something Grayson didn't want to name burned the back of his neck. "She already knows, and it doesn't matter to her."

"Oh, is that what she told you?" Henri shook his head, the crown glinting in the lamplight. "I'm doing you a favor by keeping her here."

"How?" Grayson demanded. "She deserves her freedom."

"Perhaps. But if she's free, she'll leave you. Surely you've considered that?"

Grayson said nothing. He didn't trust himself to speak.

He hadn't considered that. He hadn't thought past her immediate freedom. Getting Mia out of that cell, away from his family—that was all he could think about. But what did that actually look like? There was no way she could remain here, surrounded by the vile evil that was his family. No one would choose that. He wouldn't *let* her choose that. She deserved so much more.

The truth hit him hard.

If his father said yes . . . if Mia got her freedom . . . Grayson would lose her forever.

A smile played at Henri's lips. He knew what Grayson was coming to understand. Knew how much it was hurting him.

He relished Grayson's pain. And when he spoke, his voice was horribly soft. "I can see the fantasy you spun. You thought you would open that cell door and she would embrace you as her hero. That she would refuse to leave you because she loves you as deeply as you love her. You might have even thought to marry her. Have children with her. Create a life together. But why would she stay? A life with you is just another prison for her. She knows you're the enemy. I can guarantee she's never forgotten that." He snorted. "You are so easily manipulated," Henri said. "Especially by her."

"Mia has never manipulated me," he snapped, his cool mask cracking.

Henri chuckled. "She's manipulated you into this moment perfectly. Why else would you have risked your life by threatening me, when you're asking for something you don't even want?"

"I want her freedom."

"Do you, though? The panic in your eyes says something different."

Grayson's jaw locked. Fates, his father twisted everything. "Mia didn't ask me to come. She has nothing to do with this. We're here because I predicted your actions and you didn't disappoint."

"Ah, your own exercise in manipulating me." Henri nodded once. "Very good, Grayson. I'm impressed. And I must say, I like this version of you. This is what I bred you to be."

He hated everything about his father's words, including the possessive tone. The hairs on Grayson's body lifted, but he shoved back his discomfort and lifted his chin. "Then I'm sure you'll appreciate this. I reached you once—I can do it again. I can also reach your heir, and your wife."

The taunting smile vanished and Henri stiffened, his eyes shuttering. His voice took on a dark edge. "While I appreciate your ruthlessness, I do not appreciate threats."

"Then let us bargain instead." Grayson stepped closer, planting his hands on the desk as he leaned in. He kept his eyes trained on his father, his voice flat. "Give me what I want, and you will never have to fear my blades. I will be all you want me to be; do all you want me to do. I will no longer hold back or hesitate. I will be as ruthless as you trained me to be. I will use my blades to preserve your life even as I annihilate your enemies. I will be the Black Hand. The Scourge of Ryden. I will assassinate Serene and anyone else you ask me to. I will topple kingdoms for you." His eyes narrowed. "You know I've held back. That you've had to push me for each step. But I am ready to commit everything to you. All you need to do is give me what I ask."

The king's jaw tightened, but not in outright refusal. His thoughts were clearly spinning. "You promise complete devotion to me as opposed to killing me, my heir, and my wife?"

"It seems a good bargain."

Henri's eyes narrowed. "You have shown me a glimpse of what it would be like to be your enemy, Grayson. I thank you for that, because it makes me all the more eager to send you to Mortise. You truly are my masterpiece."

His father's words twisted inside him, tensing the muscles in his jaw. Grayson's gloved fingers tightened against the desk he was still braced over, his elbows locked. "Will you give me what I want, or not?" he demanded softly.

Henri watched him for a long moment, then dipped his head. "Serve me well in Mortise . . . and I will release the girl."

He hardly dared believe it. He swallowed, his tongue feeling thick. "You will?"

The king shrugged. "It's no concern of mine if she breaks your heart. In fact, it might teach you a valuable lesson." He leaned forward, and it took all of Grayson's willpower not to flinch back. "You are incapable of love, Grayson. You are incapable of *being* loved. You are soulless and unredeemable. It's who you are—carved into your very being, like the scars on your body. Nothing can change that."

His pulse pounded in his temples, his emotions rioting. Euphoria, because his dangerous plan had actually worked. Despair, because even if he succeeded in Mortise, it meant losing Mia.

The thought nearly destroyed him, but he would not let it shake his resolve. He owed Mia everything. He would gain her freedom, no matter how much it hurt him. It was the very least he could give her.

He pushed back from his father's desk, the sweat gathered on his palms sticking to his leather gloves. He curled his hands to fists, his spine straightening. "And my other demands?" he asked. "Will they be met?"

The king considered this. "I will not replace her caretakers. They have done their job of keeping her alive, and that is all I require of them. As for Tyrell . . . I will keep him away from the girl. Consider it a sign of good faith. But I would like a sign from you."

"I didn't kill you this morning," Grayson said tightly. "Isn't that proof enough?"

Henri's smile was cool. "Indulge me." He nodded to Grayson's right hand. "Remove your glove."

Balking would undermine everything he'd done so far, so he did not hesitate to strip the glove from his hand, leaving behind pale, scarred skin.

Henri's chin dipped. "Place your hand on the desk."

Grayson did, pressing his palm flat. His heart hammered. He knew what was coming.

He had counted on Henri's curiosity, his desire for Grayson's full, dark potential—his greed to own him completely. He had also assumed that—if he was still breathing at this point of his fool-plan—there would be some kind of retribution for what he'd dared to do.

The king of Ryden could not leave any exchange feeling lesser.

If this was the price required for securing a better life for Mia, he would pay it.

Henri's voice was smooth. "Take out the knife you put against my neck."

Grayson's left hand tugged the blade from its leather sheath.

"Put the blade through your hand. Slowly."

Grayson did, gritting his teeth at the pain. But he didn't make a sound apart from his altered breathing. His nostrils flared by the time the tip of the blade emerged through his palm and touched the desk. He gripped the hilt to stop his hand from shaking, his knuckles white, his eyes slowly lifting to meet his father's gaze.

Revulsion ripped through him at the pure glee in Henri's eyes. "Well done, Grayson. I believe you. There will be no more hesitation. No more forcing you to embrace your true nature. You are glorious." He glanced at Grayson's bleeding hand, noting the crimson sliding between his spread fingers. Then his attention turned to a stack of letters beside him. He flipped open the first one, not looking up as he said, "It's fortunate the trip to Mortise is long. You'll have plenty of time to heal."

The dismissal was clear.

Grayson's jaw flexed and his breathing thinned as he carefully pulled the knife out of his hand, trying not to make the damage worse. He had no bandage, so he simply put his glove back on. His hands trembled and sweat beaded at his hairline by the time he was done.

A smear of blood remained on his father's desk, and he had a feeling the king would leave it there, letting it stain the wood.

Grayson wiped the bloody blade on his thigh and returned the dagger to his belt. His hand throbbed, but he refused to show even a flicker of pain as he bowed to his father.

Henri did not look up from his letter, and Grayson would have believed he was completely absorbed by the missive—except for the smile teasing his mouth.

Grayson left his father's study, his jaw tight and his hand on fire. He had succeeded in gaining more than he'd ever thought possible, and he knew he should only be grateful his father had conceded so much, yet there was a metallic taste on his tongue. Not because of the agony in his bleeding hand, or even the vicious taunts his father had so cruelly thrown.

No, it was because after years of fighting, his father had finally won. Grayson had willingly become what Henri had always wanted—a ruthless monster. The Black Hand. And because of the bargain he had made, that is what he would always be.

It made his insides clench and his blood pound in his ears. He felt raw as he rounded a corner and caught movement at the end of the shadowed corridor.

Tyrell.

Every emotion that had been pounding through Grayson narrowed on his brother, heating his veins until he felt only a thirst for revenge.

His brother was one year older than him and wholly sadistic. He had dark features; dark hair, dark eyes, and a completely black heart. He had inflicted countless pains on Grayson, but when he spied Tyrell now, he wasn't thinking of the scars he bore. All he could think about was the last time he'd seen his brother.

He could still hear Mia's screams.

Tyrell's gaze was aimed down, a furrow between his tightly drawn eyebrows as he walked, but when he glanced up and caught sight of Grayson at the end of the hall, his steps faltered. It was a brief hitch, but even though his expression locked down quickly, Grayson had seen the flicker of fear.

Good.

Grayson's boots whispered against the stone and his hands hung at his sides. His right one sparked with pain, but that only fueled his anger.

Tyrell now stalked toward him with a confidence Grayson didn't fully believe—not after that hesitation he'd shown.

The hall was deserted except for them, and the muted gutter of the torches was the only other sound besides their soft footsteps and thin breaths.

With only a few paces left between them, Tyrell's mouth curled and he veered to the right.

Grayson blocked his path.

His brother's eyes narrowed and he drew to a stop.

Grayson stopped as well, leaving a small space between them.

"Get out of my way," Tyrell said, his voice dangerously low.

"No."

Tyrell's fingers twitched, clearly wanting to draw one of the knives at his belt. But his eyes darted to Grayson's hands, which also hung near his weapons.

Do it, he nearly begged.

His brother set his jaw and Grayson could make out the edge of a bruise. The area around his nose was also mottled blue and purple, spreading under his eyes. Satisfaction flared in Grayson's chest, but the darker part of him craved more. He wanted Tyrell to bleed. *Needed* him to bleed, after what he'd done to Mia.

His older brother lowered his chin, menace in his voice. "Step aside."

"Make me."

As the two youngest Kaelin princes, they had been pitted against each other since birth. Grayson didn't always win a fight with Tyrell, but he would win this one. He knew it.

He thought Tyrell knew it, too, because his brother did not immediately strike. He was rarely cautious, but of course the one time Grayson wanted his brother to attack, he didn't.

The fates hated him.

Tyrell grit his teeth. "Father has summoned me."

"He hates to be kept waiting."

His brother made a scoffing sound in his throat and stepped

to the right.

Grayson stepped with him, blocking him again.

Tyrell's teeth flashed as he growled. "I will kill you if you don't get out of my way."

"Doubtful. You're the one who almost died during our last fight."

A flush crept up Tyrell's neck, spreading over his cheeks. "I was following orders. Fates, you're losing your mind over some pathetic girl—"

His left hand was around Tyrell's throat in a split second. He shoved his brother until his back crashed into the stone wall.

Tyrell's hand shot to his belt, but before he could draw a weapon, Grayson had the tip of a blade against his stomach.

His heart thudded in his chest, echoing in his ears until they pounded. His bleeding hand screamed in pain as he clenched the hilt, keeping the blade steady. "You will not speak of her," he hissed. "Ever. Don't even *think* of her." His fingers dug more tightly around Tyrell's throat and he leaned in, letting his rage seep into his eyes so Tyrell would see it. "I will kill you for what you did. Not now. I want you to dread it. I want you to look twice at every shadow. I want you to feel my blade hovering between your shoulder blades every time the hairs on the back of your neck lift. I want you to know I'm coming."

A vein throbbed near Tyrell's temple and tendons flexed beneath Grayson's hand as he glared, unable to speak past the stranglehold at his throat.

Grayson leaned in, applying the pressure of the blade at Tyrell's navel until his brother hissed and Grayson could see a drop of blood seep through his shirt. "You will regret ever stepping foot in that cell," he told Tyrell. "Every pain you caused her will be returned to you a thousandfold."

Tyrell's glare sharpened. He snatched Grayson's wrist, attempting to snap the bones and draw the knife away from his body, but Grayson broke free, swiping the blade across Tyrell's face.

His body jerked, blood seeping from the cut that sliced over his cheek. A scar that he would always see and remember. A scar like the one he'd given Grayson not too long ago, though Grayson's blade hadn't been dipped in Syalla.

Pity.

"Well, this looks fun."

Grayson released Tyrell and stepped back, his eyes flashing toward the voice while Tyrell doubled over, coughing and clutching his throat.

Liam stood at the end of the hall, a single eyebrow raised. "Do you need some help, Tyrell?"

Tyrell shot Liam a glare, blood dripping down his angular jaw. The cut on his cheek would definitely scar, and that filled Grayson with a sick sort of satisfaction.

Tyrell straightened, his breathing a little ragged as his hand dropped from his throat. The skin was red. It would probably bruise.

Good.

His brother stalked away without a word, his shoulder smashing into Grayson's as he passed.

Grayson's mouth twitched, though admittedly the rush of emotion he felt wasn't exactly happiness. He'd scared Tyrell, but it wasn't enough.

It hadn't changed what Mia had gone through.

Farther down the hall, a door thumped closed as Tyrell disappeared into the king's office.

"What was that about?" Liam asked.

Grayson shoved his knife back in his belt. His right hand pulsed with pain, and he grit his teeth. "I had a message for him."

Liam's brows lifted. "Quite the message."

Liam was the middle Kaelin brother, and at twenty years old, he was easily the most well-traveled. He was Henri's spymaster, the Shadow of Ryden. Rumor said he could bring down a kingdom with a well-placed whisper. He had a closely trimmed brown beard and sun-bronzed skin from his extensive travels. Grayson had been spending more time with him since Henri had ordered them to go to Mortise together; his brother had been training him on everything from Mortisian politics to the foreign language.

Liam fiddled with the leather bracelet on his wrist as he eyed Grayson. "Are you all right?"

"Are any of us all right?" he asked.

The thin smile his brother cracked was not exactly mirthful. "We're Kaelins. I doubt we'll ever be all right."

Grayson snorted. That was certainly the truth.

CHAPTER 5

DESFAN

SERJAH DESFAN SAERNON CASSIAN, HEIR to the throne and current regent of Mortise, let his head thud against the desk. The scattered papers and endless piles of reports cushioned the blow, but his head still ached.

It had been aching for months.

Alone in his father's office, lamps burning through the night, he knew he needed to give up and retire. His best friend and bodyguard, Karim, had finally left an hour ago; he needed sleep so he could function during daylight hours and keep Desfan from doing anything stupid—like run and board the nearest ship leaving the harbor.

Ruling a country was exactly the nightmare Desfan had thought it would be. Give him his swords and pit him against pirates any day. A sea dragon, even.

Politics and paperwork would be the death of him.

The endless meetings. The blatant disapproval of the council. Waiting for a bride he had not met but was obligated to marry. Overshadowing everything was the agony of waiting for his father to recover, or finally succumb to the illness that had sent him into a nearly catatonic state and dragged Desfan back here, to the place he swore to leave behind forever.

When he lifted his head, a single paper stuck to his brow. He swatted it away, his focus moving to the painting on the far wall.

It had been commissioned soon after his mother and sisters had died, and the weight of that grief was clear in the slump of his father's shoulders. The serjan of Mortise had turned gray overnight. The fates had left him with only Desfan—a poor trade, certainly.

In the portrait, the serjan sat with eyes turned forward, his jaw stern. An eleven-year-old Desfan stood beside him, a hand placed gently on his father's shoulder, as if he were afraid to press too hard. His bronzed skin was the same as that boy's, though he had more scars now. The curling locks of hair were a bit longer now, too, but just as thick and dark.

Looking into that boy's wide brown eyes, Desfan could remember exactly what it had felt like to be him. The gnawing, incessant grief that plagued his every waking moment—and his nightmares, too. The ache that felt like it would swallow him whole. The tightness in his chest when he sobbed at night, wishing more than anything that his mother would come rushing through the door, gather him in her arms, and tell him it had all been a lie.

Nine years separated him from that boy, and despite the resemblance, he was a different person now. He'd had to become someone new to stop the pain from crushing him.

This was the last portrait Desfan had posed for. He'd refused all others. He didn't need another painter capturing his inner torment.

Fates, why hadn't he torn it from the wall yet? Maybe because he was usually too busy to look at it, or because he didn't want to change anything in this room because that might make it feel like he was settling in to stay.

Or maybe you left it up as punishment, a voice in his head whispered.

There was a knock on the door and Desfan turned eagerly toward the distraction. "Enter."

A middle-aged man strode in and it took Desfan a moment to place him. Manusch Arcas. He was a kiv in the city guard, and the soldiers under his leadership primarily monitored the docks and surrounding area. The man wore a red uniform, a gold-lined kurta that fell almost to his knees. He stopped in front of Desfan's desk and bowed deeply. "Your Highness."

"You're working late, Kiv Arcas."

"As are you." The soldier held out a piece of parchment, which Desfan took. "This is a matter of some urgency, so I would appreciate your immediate approval."

Desfan scanned the words, his pulse picking up. He straightened in his chair. "This is approval for a raid."

"Yes." Arcas gripped the hilt of his curved sword, which was sheathed at his side. "I have been monitoring this warehouse for some time, and I believe a shipment of stolen goods was just unloaded there. I have contacts at the harbor, and they swear to it."

Desfan glanced up. "You've already called up your men?"

Arcas nodded. "We leave as soon as you sign the notice, Serjah."

"Very well. But I do ask for one revision."

The man frowned. "And what is that?"

Desfan's grin stretched wide. "I'm leading this raid."

Desfan crouched lower to the ground as he picked his way to the back end of the alley. The smell of refuse, rotten food, and worse burned his nose, and he tried not to think about the puddles lapping the sides of his boots. That briny scent definitely wasn't seawater.

He was glad the weak light of the moon didn't reveal much; he didn't want a close look at what hid in the shadows of this forgotten alley.

He reached the corner and raised a closed fist. The silver light was dim, but the men behind him halted at once and followed his lead as he pressed his shoulders against the stone wall of the warehouse. A breeze swept up from the harbor, delivering a breath of fresh, salty air. He closed his eyes and could almost imagine he was back on his ship.

Adrenaline pumped through his veins, and his grin was unstoppable.

He only felt a little guilty that he hadn't woken Karim, but his bodyguard had become even more protective of Desfan since he'd been named regent. He was a year older than Desfan, and had been his bodyguard since Desfan was fifteen. There was no way Karim would have allowed him to join this middle-of-the-night excursion. But Desfan refused to miss it. Not when he was so desperate to *do* something.

He strained his ears and, after a moment, determined there were at least two guards on the warehouse door. They weren't speaking, but one shuffled his feet restlessly, and one a little further away kept clearing his throat.

Desfan lifted two fingers. From his periphery, he saw the nearest soldier nod.

His pulse thrummed with a fast tempo he loved. Danger, adventure, risk—he *needed* this.

With a flick of his brown fingers, Desfan sparked the attack. He was the first to round the corner, simultaneously drawing the two swords sheathed across his back. The twin blades cut through the air as he shifted his grip on the leather-wrapped hilts.

The two guards at the door were startled by the sudden appearance of the city guard and reacted too slowly. Desfan's swords tapped both their throats, stopping their shouts.

He smiled. "Keep quiet, and you can keep your heads."

The man on the left gulped.

"How many men are inside?" Desfan asked, his voice low.

The one on the right stammered. "I—I don't know."

"Hm. How disappointing." Desfan shifted his blade, increasing the pressure until a drop of blood appeared.

The man hissed. "Six. There are six men inside."

"Excellent." He eased back and one of the soldiers moved to take his place. "As long as they don't fight, they live," Desfan said.

Kiv Arcas arrived at his side. "Perhaps you should stay back during the initial sweep, Serjah."

He shot the man a grin, lightly swinging his dual blades. "Where's the fun in that?" He used his shoulder to shove open the door to the warehouse and the city guard poured in with him.

A warning shout went up and the cluster of men in the warehouse scrambled for weapons. The lamps hanging on hooks revealed that there were far more than six smugglers. Desfan's glance placed the count closer to twenty, which would make this a more even match.

Perfect.

"By order of the regent," Arcas boomed, "this warehouse is being seized for inspection on suspicion of illegal activity. Stay where you are and surrender your weapons!"

The smugglers didn't seem impressed. One lifted a crossbow and Desfan dodged left to avoid the fired dart. The clang of steel rang out as the guards crossed swords with the smugglers, the sound echoing high in the lofty warehouse.

One of the smugglers bolted for a side door and Desfan ran after him. He leaped over a row of crates, rather than skirt around them. As he came down, his booted heel caught the edge of one and he stumbled—but he didn't stop.

The smuggler had nearly reached the exit when he glanced back and saw Desfan. The middle-aged man glared, but there was an edge of fear. Even without a crown, it was clear the man knew who Desfan was. The distinctive double blades were a pretty easy marker.

Besides, after almost five years patrolling the sea, every smuggler from Zennor to Ryden knew of Desfan Cassian.

The man raised his sword just in time to meet Desfan's downward swing.

The blow vibrated up to his shoulder. "Going somewhere?" Desfan smiled.

The smuggler only growled. He was wider than Desfan, with thick arms that bulged with muscle. But Desfan was tall and lithe, and he used that to his advantage as he fought with both swords, slowly maneuvering until he blocked the man's path to the nearest door.

Fury sparked in his eyes and he battered Desfan's parrying blows with more power, striking fast and hard.

Desfan ducked and spun, making a shallow slice to the man's left side. The smuggler snarled, but before he could retaliate, Desfan delivered a kick in his back, sending the man crashing into a pile of crates. The wood buckled beneath his weight, snapping loudly as the pile collapsed. The smuggler's legs were visible in the wreckage, but he wasn't moving.

Desfan moved forward to check on the man, praying he was only unconscious—the kiv would want him for questioning—but movement from the corner of his eye drew his attention to a nearby table. A small shape huddled underneath. In the dim light of the lamps, it looked like a child.

He halted, aiming his swords at the ground as he moved carefully toward the table. "Easy," he said to the crouched figure. "You won't be harmed."

The shadow recoiled, scrambling out from under the table and shooting up on the other side.

The boy was maybe eleven years old. Dirt streaked his face and blood dripped from his nose. He wore a torn red vest and his bare arms were marred with the beginnings of several bruises. A dark tattoo was inked around his wrist and the whole area was rubbed raw—he'd been bound recently. Bound and beaten.

Desfan's stomach clenched. Anger rose, but he kept that out of his expression as he faced the boy. "You're safe now," he said. "I promise, they won't—"

The boy threw a knife at him. The blade was so small, Desfan hadn't even noticed it in his hand.

Desfan cursed as he dodged the knife. As he spun, the boy dove for a small crate on the floor. Before he could grab it, a dagger thunked into the wood, a breath from the boy's thin fingers.

He jerked back, darting a look at the man who'd thrown the blade.

It was the smuggler Desfan had kicked into the crates. He was back on his feet, blood wetting the side of his shirt and his temple. He snarled furiously, already reaching for another dagger. "You're dead, Ori!"

The boy's battered face paled. He scrambled back from the crate, his horrified eyes stuck on the man prepared to kill him.

The smuggler hurled the second knife at the boy's chest.

Desfan widened his stance and swung one of his swords, batting the dagger in midair so it thumped harmlessly against the dirt floor.

The smuggler cursed.

The boy—Ori—shot a look at Desfan before he spun and darted for the nearest exit.

Smart kid.

Desfan faced the smuggler, blocking his path after the boy. "Smuggling, kidnapping, resisting arrest, and the abuse and attempted murder of a child. That's quite the list you've built for yourself. Do you really want to add to it?"

The man lunged at Desfan. Despite his wound, the smuggler delivered punishing blows. Desfan was trying not to kill him—clearly a goal his opponent did *not* share—but avoiding a death-blow was forcing Desfan steadily back toward the wall. Soon, he would be pinned. He needed to change tactics.

The man surprised him with a flash of his fist, and knuckles smashed Desfan's nose. Cartilage cracked and blood spurted. Desfan gasped at the sharp pain, one sword falling as his hand instinctively flashed to his throbbing nose. Broken. His nose was broken.

Fates, not again.

The watering in his eyes distorted his vision, but he still saw the man's meaty fist fly for his jaw. He cursed and spun to the right, his shoulders bumping against the wall.

He tensed as the man raised his sword, and he knew he would need to go for the man's exposed gut. It was his life, or the criminal's.

Desfan's fingers flexed around the hilt of his remaining sword, but before he could strike a deathblow, his attacker suddenly jerked forward, his expression freezing, then slackening. Blood dribbled from the corner of his mouth as he rocked forward.

Desfan kicked him back so the large body wouldn't crush him and the smuggler hit the floor, dead.

Several paces away, Karim's arm slowly lowered, clearly having just thrown the knife that had saved Desfan's life.

Karim was tall, trim, and his dark hair was pulled into a knot at the back of his head. His belt was weighed down with a creative assortment of knives. His beard was short and framed his angular face, which was generally locked in a smooth expression that gave away nothing.

At this moment, he'd traded that stoicism for a fierce glare.

Desfan swiped the back of his wrist under his bleeding nose, blinking rapidly to keep his vision from clouding. "Hello, Karim. How are you?"

His bodyguard's thick eyebrows pulled tightly together. "I'm going to kill you."

Desfan snorted—and immediately grabbed his nose. Fates, that hurt.

Karim growled as he stalked forward. "Did you break your nose? *Again?*"

"I had help." Desfan lowered his hand, still cringing at the pain. He nudged the dead smuggler's boot with his own. "I was trying to keep him alive."

"That's what I keep saying about *you*, despite all your efforts to get yourself killed."

Desfan snatched up his fallen sword and sheathed them both, the twin blades hissing into place against his back. He wiped again at his nose and looked beyond Karim to see the fighting was over.

Soldiers secured prisoners as Kiv Arcas scanned the room. The older man's eyes flared wide when he spotted Desfan's bloody face. "Serjah!" He darted forward, and Desfan barely smothered a groan.

Karim spun on the kiv before he could get too close, and the older man withered a little under his glare. "You let him come on a fates-blasted raid? Are you insane? He's the future serjan!"

"It's not his fault," Desfan said, his tone a little nasal. "I made him."

Karim ignored that, his glare still on the kiv.

Arcas's throat bobbed almost violently as he swallowed. "I'm sorry. I didn't—I wasn't sure—He insisted, and I—"

Karim shoved a finger in the man's face. "Never. Again. *Understood?*"

Karim was a man of few words, but he usually made them count.

Desfan caught sight of the small crate the boy, Ori, had tried to take with him. It was on the floor, the smuggler's dagger still embedded in the wood. Desfan moved for it, wiping his sleeve under his bleeding nose, perfectly aware of Karim following him.

Desfan crouched by the crate. It was smaller than the others he'd seen in the room. He dropped it on the table, taking the iron bar the kiv handed to him so he could pry open the lid. Karim merely folded his arms and watched, irritation bristling the very air around him.

The lid yawned open and Desfan plucked out tufts of packing straw. After a few handfuls littered the table, several stacks of drawstring pouches were revealed.

Desfan's pulse spiked at the sight. He snatched one of the small bags and tugged it open, already knowing what he'd find.

The white powder was ridiculously fine—perfectly refined.

He shot a look at Karim, who hissed out a breath. "Olcain? This was an *olcain* raid?"

Desfan palmed the open bag, the white powder almost glowing in the dim light. "We didn't know what it was, actually. Just stolen goods. Arcas and I had a bet. My gold was on Zennorian wine."

Karim turned very slowly to face him. "You came on a raid and you didn't even know what you were trying to seize?"

Desfan ignored his friend's glare and turned to Arcas. "I want a full report of everything you find here. Exact quantities. And I want full notes on the interrogations of all survivors. I want to know how this olcain got into the city, who owns it, and who intended to buy it."

Even this small crate was worth a staggering fortune. Olcain was the most dangerous and expensive drug in Eyrinthia.

Someone in Duvan was bound to be very unhappy with the city guard for seizing it, and Desfan needed to know who.

Arcas hurried away, shouting orders to his men.

Karim shook his head at Desfan. "You need to take care of your face. You've got a meeting with the council in three hours."

Desfan cringed, but it wasn't fully from the pain of his broken nose.

No, it was because his short respite was over and he was the regent once more.

CHAPTER 6

DESFAN

". . . THIS IS A MATTER THAT WOULD NEVER have been dismissed in the past. Frankly, I'm astonished that . . ."

After two hours of hearing the same bland tones, Desfan was beyond irritated—and exhausted, since he hadn't managed to get any sleep last night, due to the olcain raid. The gold crown—which he only wore when absolutely necessary—was heavy on his head. His broken nose throbbed and his muscles twitched at the inactivity of sitting on his father's throne and listening to the endless bickering of the council, the belittling and snide comments directed to him—about him—and the ceaseless arguments against a betrothal that Desfan had already agreed to.

In short, he was out of patience, and there was still an hour to go.

". . . Not to mention the obscene lack of regard . . ." Ser Zephan didn't seem to need breath—he just kept talking. The man had black hair, lightly graying at the temples, and dark eyes. Desfan had wondered more than once if he was a relation to the notorious, dark-bearded pirate Syed Zadir—also known as Crush, because of what he did to his enemies.

Probably just fanciful thinking.

Desfan barely held back his sigh. Would any of them notice if he fell asleep?

A glance at the twelve members of the council assured him they would. Those men and women missed nothing. Serai Essa was frowning at him, perhaps seeing wrinkles in his white shirt. Or maybe she—like Ser Jamal—was still caught on the black and purple bruising developing around his eyes due to his broken nose.

The sunlight coming through the tall windows caught the black ring on his forefinger, and he stared at it.

Years ago, his younger sister Tahlyah had found three identical obsidian rings while playing in the royal treasury—something Desfan and his sisters did often, much to the chagrin of their mother and the amusement of their father.

"One for each of us!" Tahlyah had beamed, tossing one to Desfan and the other to Meerah.

Desfan had been ten at the time, and he'd twisted the simple band between his fingers. The royal children were known for finding mischief, but this seemed different, and he felt responsible for his sisters. "Mother won't like us taking these. It's stealing."

Tahlyah rolled her eyes. "They were lost in the bottom of a dusty trunk, Des. No one will care."

"It's too big," Meerah said, the ring swallowing her six-year-old thumb.

"We can string them on a necklace for now," Tahlyah said

with a shrug. "We'll grow into them."

They hadn't grown into them.

Tahlyah and Meerah had died a year later.

Desfan's fingers curled into a fist, the ring biting into his skin.

". . . And that is all I can say about it!" Ser Zephan finished, his mustache twitching along with his left eye.

Everyone looked at Desfan.

Fates, it was his turn to respond. And he hadn't heard much of anything Zephan had said. He straightened and cleared his throat, making sure his voice was strong enough to echo through the stone hall. "Thank you for bringing your opinion to my attention. I shall think on this and have a response for you soon."

Behind him, Karim may have snorted.

One of Zephan's dark eyebrows lifted. "Does this mean you will consider retracting the prisoner exchange with Devendra?"

"No," Desfan said at once. "Of course not." Was that really what he'd been droning on about?

Zephan's mouth tightened. "Then what, exactly, will you be thinking on? What response can I expect from you?"

He could feel every eye on him, and he silently cursed his distraction. He should have been paying more attention. "I misspoke," he said carefully. "I will not change my mind about the prisoner exchange. It has already been negotiated and Ser Ashear is overseeing the details. The intent behind my response to you, Ser Zephan, was merely to assure you that I have heard your opinion and I will bear it in mind moving forward. You are correct that I could have handled the negotiations with King Newlan better, by involving the council sooner. But it is done and my word is final."

Zephan's nostrils flared, but he jerked out a bow before he dropped back to his seat.

Desfan did not get a chance to celebrate the averted disaster, because Serai Yahri wavered to her feet.

The fragile-looking woman held the senior seat on the council and was old enough to be Desfan's grandmother, though there was nothing warm or grandmotherly about her. Her mouth was usually pulled into a frown and her eyes were generally narrowed. Before Desfan had been sent to sea by his father, he'd been a menace. He knew that. But years later, Yahri still looked at him as if he were that out-of-control boy. Disapproval was about the only thing he'd ever seen shine in her dark eyes.

Well, that and disappointment.

Her braided silver hair still had some dark strands mixed in, and her steely gaze was cutting. "It has come to my attention that you took part in an olcain raid last night, Serjah."

The council sucked in a collective breath.

Desfan cracked a tight smile. Fates, this was just what he needed. "Your information is not wrong, Serai Yahri."

Her thin mouth pressed into an even thinner line, though her posture remained oddly regal; her long and slender hands clasped before her, the wide cuffs of her green robe—which all members on the council wore—nearly swallowing her fingers. She was tall, thin, and her chin seemed to always be tilted up. "Did it not occur to you, Serjah, that you are the only heir to the Mortisian crown?"

Only every fates-blasted day since he was eleven years old. But even as he bristled at her words, he forced his tone to remain easy. "Indeed, it occurred. Which is why I led the raid. A leader does not stand back when there is a battle to be fought."

"A true leader uses more than his swords," Yahri countered.

Irritation prickled, tightening his skin and his voice. "I have an obligation to serve this city."

"Your obligation reaches further than that, Serjah. You should not take such risks with yourself." She raised a hand, stopping him the moment he opened his mouth. "We will not speak of this again," she said. "But I do hope you understand the feelings of this council."

Oh, he understood her perfectly. She wanted him to sit down, keep quiet, and agree with everything the council wanted. This was just another reminder that this wasn't his council—it was his father's. They did not see him as their ruler, only a temporary stand-in until the serjan recovered.

Desfan didn't need the reminder, but there it was.

Serai Yahri shifted her hold on her cane. "Now then, I believe it would be prudent for us to discuss your decision to invite a Ryden delegation into the palace. No Rydenic men—let alone two princes—have set foot in Duvan in decades. Our history is too bloody—we barely retain our uneasy trade. Most of their business is done in Zennorian ports."

Desfan lifted a finger. "First, I did not invite them. King Henri wrote to me with an offer of sending a peaceful delegation to witness the historic peace between us and Devendra, and I could not say no. If memory serves, you all agreed with me." *Reluctantly*, he almost added drily. "Which brings us to my second point. Our bloody history is exactly the reason why we had to accept them. The driving force behind our alliance with Devendra is to defend against Ryden. This was my father's fear when he first began discussing his plans of an alliance with Devendra. Our spies haven't gleaned much from the north, but we do know that King Henri's army is growing."

Serai Yahri's eyes narrowed. "It could have been stipulated by you that the delegation did not consist of two Kaelin princes. Might I add, it *would* have been stipulated, if you had consulted this council prior to sending your message."

The back of his neck heated. "Would you like to look over all my messages?" he said, his tone a little too stiff for the sarcastic bent he'd been aiming for. "I've been drafting a love letter to Princess Serene, if you'd like to help."

The woman lifted one eyebrow. "Only if you need my help in such matters, Serjah."

A few chuckles coughed out, rippling through the cavernous room.

Desfan smiled thinly, the action putting pressure on his broken nose. "I don't think that will be necessary."

Yahri tipped her head. "Very well. Then I suppose it is time we turn to the concerns of the people . . ."

Desfan grit his teeth.

It was going to be a long day.

CHAPTER 7

CLARE

CLARE STOOD ON THE WIDE BALCONY, basking in the warmth of the summer sun as she overlooked Lady Rendell's grassy yard. She felt lighter than she had in the six days since leaving the castle, probably because she was wearing the simple maid's uniform instead of the princess's attire.

They had reunited with Serene late last night at an inn just outside Tarvin. King Newlan had deemed it necessary for Serene to play herself during their stay with Lady Rendell, as the aging widow was a dear friend of the old queen of Zennor, Aimeth Buhari—Serene's grandmother. The noblewoman was practically a second grandmother to Serene and would probably see through Clare after spending any length of time with her. They were only staying with the widow for one day and night. Lady Rendell refused to throw large parties, and the point of Serene's tour was for her to mingle with as many people as possible. Newlan had chosen not to completely bypass Lady Rendell, however, because she was considered almost family, and the widow would have been quite vocal about the slight. Tomorrow morning, Serene would leave in disguise and Clare would move on to another manor in Tarvin to stay with Lord and Lady Wensil for a couple of days. But for nearly twenty-four hours, Clare could just be herself.

Princess Serene came to stand beside her, resting one elegant hand on the gray stone railing of the balcony. Her dark hair was unbound, her skin a slight shade darker than Clare's. They had the same blue eyes; deep, Devendran blue. Sometimes when Clare looked at Serene, with all her beauty and confidence, she had a hard time seeing how she managed to fool anyone into thinking she was the princess.

In the suite behind them, Clare could just make out the voices of Vera, Ivonne, and Bridget as the maids debated what dress Serene should wear to breakfast.

"I suppose you're grateful for the break," Serene said.

The corner of Clare's mouth lifted. "Do you blame me?"

The princess cracked a smile. "Not in the least."

In the gardens below, a servant called out to Lady Rendell's dog, who was bounding over the lawn. The rustling leaves and the errant birdsong made the moment quite peaceful.

Serene's eyes were on the horizon, her voice low. "We didn't get a chance to speak much last night, but I'm grateful for your discretion with James."

Clare had managed to slip Serene the letter when they met at the inn, with a very brief explanation of how she had received it in the dress shop.

The princess shifted her weight, one hand gripping the rail. "I hate to ask more of you, but I have a reply for him. I know he'll be in the city, awaiting word. Would you be willing to deliver my letter?"

A knot tightened in her stomach. "I can't just go into Tarvin."

"I'll make an excuse. I woke with a desperate need for new combs. I'll send you and Vera. James will find you in the market, and you can slip him the letter without the guards ever knowing."

"Should you be writing to him at all?" Clare asked softly.

The princess was silent for several long heartbeats, obviously thinking carefully about her answer. "I can see your concern," she finally said, her eyes on the oaks that lined the spacious yard below them. "But I assure you, this will not impact my betrothal to Desfan. I will fulfill my duty."

The firmly spoken words brought an ache to Clare's heart. "All right," she said quietly. "I'll take the letter."

Relief sparked in Serene's eyes. "Thank you." She drew out a small sealed letter from her pocket and passed it to Clare. "This will be the last time you have to see him."

Two reasons for that promise leapt to mind. Either Serene was telling him to not contact her again, or . . . "You're telling him your stops so he can come to you."

Serene's lips pressed into a line, but she didn't deny it.

Clare's brows pulled together. "Your location on this tour needs to remain a secret. It's for your safety." It was the entire reason Clare was here.

"James will not betray me."

Her firm reply effectively ended the conversation, so Clare sighed and slipped the letter into her pocket, her fingers brushing the tin soldier she always kept close, since it reminded her of home.

There was a brief silence, then Serene tightened her hold on the balcony railing. "So. The Rose. That's an unexpected development. Are you all right?"

Her skin still crawled at the thought of the assassin. There had been nothing new from him, which left Clare with a complicated mix of relief and anxiety. She knew it was only a matter of time before he struck again. "Honestly, I don't know."

"Bennick and I talked for over an hour last night about who might have hired him. He's become convinced it's someone from Mortise, but I fear this is more personal." She shifted her weight. "It feels too soon to have been Amil. He left Iden just before us, and I imagine it takes a little searching to find the Rose."

Clare stared. "Do you really think Amil would hire an assassin to kill you?"

"I think he hates Devendra for what happened to his father, and that includes me." A frown pinched Serene's features. "I suppose his father could have made arrangements before his death. He came to negotiate the peace because he was loyal to Mortise, but he didn't want it."

Clare shook her head. "I don't think Ser Havim hired the Rose. He spoke to me right before he was killed and he sounded confident that the serjan would recover from his illness, see the alliance Desfan had arranged, and put an end to it all."

"The serjan would not stop the alliance. It's a misconception people have. They think Desfan started talks of the alliance on his own, after his father's collapse, but Serjan Saernon had been writing to my father months before his illness. Desfan merely picked up where his father left off." Serene's fingers tapped against the railing at her hip, her thoughts clearly churning. "It's not my father. He wants this alliance too badly, and my death would cost him that. I'm not so confident about my brother."

Unfortunately, Clare could not dispute her words. Even though Prince Grandeur had been Clare's first friend among the royals, she had overheard a conversation between him and an unnamed man. They'd been in the castle garden, and though they hadn't seen Clare, she had grown cold as she'd listened to every word. If she wouldn't agree to spy on Serene for Grandeur, they would threaten her brothers. And the prince had even made it clear that he would sacrifice his sister's life if Serene turned against him.

Overhearing that conversation had brought Clare to the princess, who had finally confided why she did not trust her father or brother—Serene had proof that King Newlan had slowly poisoned Queen Aren to death after learning that she had helped Ivar Carrigan in the civil war. And Grandeur had known about the poisoning and done nothing.

That was how Clare found herself in the middle of these dangerous political games amid the royal family. Newlan had forced her to become the decoy, Serene had invited her to spy on Grandeur, and the prince thought she was a spy for him. He had even given her a ring with his personal seal so she could send him messages about Serene and warn him if she posed a threat to Devendra. He feared she was planning to sabotage the alliance, or even make a grab for the Devendran throne.

The irony was, Serene *did* plan to take the throne from her father and brother, as soon as she was in a position to do so. First, she needed this alliance with Mortise to succeed.

"I want you to send a letter to my brother," Serene said. "Tell him about the Rose, show him your fear. I want to see if he reassures you—if he knows the Rose won't harm you. If my brother hired him, he would have told the assassin about you being the decoy. The taunting messages might come your way, but he would wait to strike at me when I am myself."

Clare eyed her. "Like today?"

Serene flashed a grim smile. "Exactly. I'll be on my guard."

"I hate to think Grandeur could be capable of this."

"He has proven himself capable of many atrocities. Least of all is supporting my father." Her shoulders dropped with a sharp exhale. "They both suspect every citizen in Devendra to be part of a conspiracy against them. My father kills so many on suspicion alone. And he taxes the people so ruthlessly—not because he needs the extra coin, but because if people struggle to even survive, they have less time to rise against him. He's terrified of another civil war."

But the more ruthless he was, the more violent the rebels became. And, unfortunately, they had chosen to focus their efforts on Serene. They didn't want Newlan to have allies when they finally staged their open revolt, so even before the betrothal was officially announced, they had started targeting Serene.

Clare eyed the princess standing beside her. "The rebels are trying to kill you to stop the alliance, but what is their ultimate goal? Are they hoping to put someone else on the throne?"

Her mouth pursed. "I'm not sure what their end-goal is, as no one has stepped forward as their leader. They don't have a message, other than general outrage directed at my father. They're spreading chaos, fear, and making the king rule with an ever-tightening fist—which only incites the rebels more, and it all leads to innocents being hurt from both sides."

"Do you think Ivar Carrigan could be the leader?"

"An interesting thought. What makes you think of him?"

Clare shrugged. "He started the civil war ten years ago. And no one knows where he ended up. What if he didn't leave Devendra at all?"

Her brow creased. "I didn't know my father's cousin well, as I was quite young when he dissented. But I have a hard time believing Carrigan is behind the rebels now. I think he would have organized them better. And I imagine he would have declared his involvement by now, especially if he was leading the group. Many in Devendra stood with him before, and I imagine many would again."

"Princess!" Bridget snapped from inside the room. "If you don't want to look a wreck for this breakfast, you need to get in here! And Clare, you can make yourself useful!"

Serene arched a dark brow. "One would think *she's* the princess, with how she orders everyone about."

Clare chuckled as she followed the princess into the suite. Dresses were flung on the bed and Ivonne was sorting through them with Bridget. When the head maid saw Serene, she wordlessly pointed to a stool set before a mirror. Serene rolled her eyes, but sat.

Clare was exceedingly grateful Bridget traveled with the princess, and not with her.

While Vera set out several different options for Serene's jewelry, Clare lifted a comb and started working it through the princess's dark hair. There were a couple of knots, but nothing serious—until the teeth of the comb caught on a thin, tightly woven braid buried in the thickness of Serene's hair.

Clare fingered the unexpected, almost hidden braid.

Serene stiffened. "Leave it."

Clare dropped it at once. "Sorry."

Vera set down the necklaces she had been sorting and hurried to Clare's side. "I can do her hair," she said, with a somewhat tight smile. "Why don't you untangle those infernal chains? We'll need to pack them better next time."

Clare handed the comb to Vera, but even as she took over managing the jewelry, she kept glancing at Serene, her curiosity about the odd braid and the even odder exchange only building.

CHAPTER 8

CLARE

TARVIN'S STREETS WERE BUSTLING WITH morning activity. Shops lined the large square of the market and carts overflowing with wares filled the open area, leaving people to weave between the narrow spaces left between. The crowds were thick and the atmosphere jovial. Pipe music played somewhere, accompanied by drums. Delicious foods scented the air, children laughed and darted around in games of chase and catch. The mood was infectious, and despite the weight of Serene's letter in her pocket, Clare couldn't stop grinning.

Before Serene had joined Lady Rendell for breakfast, she had insisted that Clare and Vera go into the city and locate a new set of combs and several other personal items. Bennick had tried to offer alternatives, such as sending one of the guards, but the princess had propped a hand on her hip as she stared him down.

"Captain Markam, you know I care for you all deeply. But the day I let any of you pick my personal items is the day I have tea with the Poison Queen."

Bennick had relented. He hadn't loved the idea of the decoy going on the innocuous errand, but Serene was insistent on Clare going, and he soon gave up. As the captain of the princess's guard, he needed to remain at the Rendell estate with the princess, but he had sent Cardon and Venn with Clare and Vera.

Cardon walked beside Clare, dressed in his royal guard uniform. His stance was relaxed, though he was carefully scanning the crowd around them. Clare had missed him, as both he and Dirk traveled with the princess on her alternate route. Cardon was thirty years old and he had a distinctive scar that cut diagonally across his right cheek. He had a gentle smile and a warm gaze, and he had always been kind to Clare.

Venn and Vera wandered slightly ahead of them, the two of them chatting and laughing as they explored the market.

The sight widened Clare's smile.

"He's besotted," Cardon said, following her gaze.

Clare watched as Venn leaned in to catch Vera's words, his dark, half-Zennorian eyes seemingly trapped by her animated face. He barely looked away as they walked. Clare chuckled. "I'm not sure who is more besotted, really."

"Him," Cardon said. "Definitely him."

Clare glanced over at him, suddenly curious. "You're not married, are you, Cardon?"

"Oh, fates no. I'm never going to marry."

"You wouldn't be the first man to say such a thing."

He tipped his head. "True. But on this, I'm confident."

"Perhaps you just haven't met the right woman."

His smile tightened a little at the corners. "Perhaps. Royal bodyguards don't often marry, though. We give our lives to our careers. Sometimes literally."

"Wilf married."

"Yes, but Rachel was special. He could hardly resist her. Their love was enviable." Cardon's eyes softened. "Poor man."

Bennick had once told her about Wilf's wife. She had died from the pox—an illness she contracted while caring for Wilf, who had been deathly sick. Pox scars still covered his body; the scars from losing the woman he loved were not as visible, but just as real.

"It's good he has all of you," Clare said.

"We're family," Cardon said, his answer simple but strong. He glanced at her. "Bennick mentioned that he gave you the garrote bracelet."

"Oh. Yes." Warmth rose in her cheeks, even though she knew Cardon's words were only innocent conversation. He didn't know about her deepening relationship with Bennick—they were being careful to keep it private. She cleared her throat. "He said you gave an identical one to Serene."

"I did. Fates, that was a long time ago." He tapped a finger against the scar that sliced his cheek. "I'd gotten this only a few weeks before."

"How did you get it?" she dared to ask.

Cardon didn't seem to mind the personal question. "I let a would-be assassin get too close. He would have killed me, but he was shot first. The arrow in his back made his knife easy to swipe aside, though it still got me a little." He smiled a bit crookedly. "Venn says it makes me look ruggedly handsome."

She returned his smile. "It does."

He drew his thumb over the scar. "I haven't thought of that day for a long time. Serene was almost fourteen. I'd been her bodyguard for maybe a year."

"I didn't realize you'd been her guard for so long."

He nodded. "Dirk is the only one of us who has served her longer. He's been watching over her since she was born."

Clare's eyes widened. "Nineteen years?" She had seen Serene and Dirk interact, and she'd thought their bond was strong. She'd had no idea he'd been with her all her life, though.

"Technically, Wilf has been a royal bodyguard for just as long. He was one of the queen's guards until Grandeur was born. Then he was transferred to guard the prince." Cardon took a breath, returning to his story. "The royal family used to vacation at Lambern Lake every summer, and they would go on hunts in the forested foothills. Queen Aren was particularly fond of hunting, and, unfortunately, many knew this. During my first summer as Serene's guard, there was an ambush. The king and queen were the focus of the attack, and their guards were dropping rapidly. Dirk ran to assist, and I was covering the princess. I saw Wilf carrying Grandeur, and even though the prince was twelve at the time, he didn't slow Wilf down."

Clare didn't think *anyone* could slow Wilf down.

Cardon's eyes narrowed in memory. "I was fighting one of the assassins when I heard Serene cry out. An assassin had gripped her braid and was yanking her back. I threw my knife and hit his shoulder; it was enough to startle him back. It saved her life, but I had no weapon against the assassin trying to kill me, and with my distraction, he quickly gained the upper hand.

"While we grappled, I heard Serene run. But she didn't actually leave. She was only retrieving her bow, which was already strung for the hunt." He eyed Clare. "She shot my attacker. She saved my life when she should have run."

Clare could barely imagine the scene his words painted, but she knew enough about Serene to believe that even as a young girl, she had been fierce.

Cardon exhaled a short laugh. "All I could do was stare at

her. I remember her standing there, her hair a loose mess, the bow still in her hands, and she lifted an eyebrow and said, *You're welcome.*" He shook his head, a smile still tugging at his lips. "I had that garrote fashioned for her as a mark of my thanks."

"Bennick thought it was for her birthday."

"The occasions happily coincided."

They passed a pastry shop, the scents of baking flour and sweet sugar wafting out into the street. Clare breathed in deep, hearing snippets of the conversation that snaked around her. It seemed there was to be a party in the square tonight, to celebrate Princess Serene's arrival in Tarvin and the coming marriage.

"It's strange," Clare said. "That some celebrate the alliance while others will do anything to stop it."

"Some must think the reward is worth the risk. Many lost family members—and profits—during the border wars. Some let that loss turn them bitter, but others came away just wanting peace. Even if it means trusting someone who used to be an enemy."

Clare spotted an artist at her cart, trying to sell paintings of Serene. Some were of the princess in Tarvin's square, others showed her on a beach in Mortise, standing next to a handsome dark-haired man with a golden crown who could only be Desfan.

"Sometimes I feel sorry for her," Clare said quietly. "That for the alliance to work, she has to marry a stranger." She glanced at him. "Do you think Serene will be happy with Desfan?"

Cardon's gaze swept the collection of paintings. "I think the princess is capable of anything." He slowed, nodding to a cart in front of them. "Some of that looks promising."

Clare stepped up to the cart, and Cardon stood nearby while she sifted through the decorative combs, colorful ribbons, painted fans, and assorted cosmetics. She also stole glances at the constantly shifting crowd around her, hoping for a glimpse of James.

"Anything yet?" Cardon asked.

She lowered a pearl-studded comb, still searching the crowd from the corner of her eye. "Not yet."

The young man overseeing the cart sidled closer. "If you're looking for more variety, this is only a small taste of our wares. My father's shop is just over there. We have all sorts of magnificent pieces—crafted by the best artisans in Devendra, and even some from Zennor."

Something brushed Clare's hand. She looked down just in time to see a young boy dart back into the crowd, but he'd left a small slip of paper in her palm.

While Cardon quietly listened to the over-eager shopkeeper, Clare stole a quick look at the hastily scrawled words.

Meet me at Harrow's End. - J

Clare glanced around and almost immediately spotted the tavern, which was on the other side of the square. The name *Harrow's End* was carved onto a wooden sign hung over the door, which was propped open. Even from here, she could see the room was full of people.

"Clare?"

Her attention snapped to Cardon. "Yes?"

"Would you like to explore the shop?" he asked, the patience in his voice making it clear he was repeating himself.

The young man at the cart watched her closely, eagerly waiting for her answer.

Since the shop took them closer to Harrow's End, she nodded. But nerves danced in her stomach as Cardon guided her forward, calling out to Venn so he and Vera would know where they'd disappeared to. They entered the shop, which was just as crowded as the square had been. The patrons were mostly women, and in the summer heat of the day, the decorative fan display seemed to draw everyone closer, which clogged the entrance. The overpowering mix of perfumes being sold nearly made Clare sneeze as she tried to wriggle her way through the elbows and hips of the milling women.

Cardon slipped in front of her, using a charming smile and gentle nudges to help them make faster progress. With his back turned to her, Clare knew this would be an ideal moment to slip away.

Her heart pounded as she melted into the crowd, moving back to the entrance. She knew it wouldn't take long for Cardon to notice her missing, and she hated to make him panic. But she had promised Serene she would try to deliver her message to James, and she didn't want to risk being seen. That meant leaving Cardon behind. She hoped to be quick enough to pretend she'd only been caught up in the crowd and pulled away briefly.

Outside the shop, Clare lowered her head and cut through the crowded square. She skirted the cart where Venn and Vera had paused to admire a silversmith's trinkets and kept her gaze on Harrow's End. The skin on the back of her neck prickled, the sensation of being watched nearly making her shiver. She dismissed it as her guilty conscience and finally reached the tavern.

Wide front windows revealed the crowd, and Clare quickly climbed the stone steps and stepped through the open door. Savory meats and steamed vegetables salted the air, with sweet-smelling pastries scenting the edges of the wafting smells. The scent of ale was also strong, and the booming laughter and celebratory atmosphere made the tavern feel even more overwhelming. Card games were in progress at several tables and the rest were filled with groups of both men and women as they ate and toasted the princess's health.

Pausing beside one of the large front windows, Clare scanned the room for James, her palms sweating. Movement to her right drew her eye, and she finally spotted him. He was sliding around a crowded table, headed for her.

She met him halfway, drawing out Serene's letter and passing it to him.

He slid it into his jacket, his handsome eyes intent. "Thank you."

"You're welcome." She bit her lower lip, nerves still dancing in her stomach. "I can't linger. The guards will be looking for me."

She started to turn, but he snagged her wrist. "Wait. Please." The skin around his eyes tightened. "Can you tell me how she is?"

She glanced around them, but no one seemed to be paying them any attention. Still, she lowered her voice. "She's well." It didn't feel like enough, so she added, "She was pleased to hear from you."

James released her, his hands rolling to fists at his side. "Good. That's . . . good."

There were many things she wanted to ask him, if only she were brave enough. How he had met Serene. What exactly he thought was going to happen, once she married Desfan.

James's voice interrupted her thoughts. "I heard a rumor that the Rose has targeted her."

A chill ghosted down her spine. "Unfortunately, it's not a rumor."

"Fates." He shoved a hand through his brown hair and his thick eyebrows drew together as he viewed her. "Be careful, Clare."

Surprised by the sincerity in his tone, she only managed to nod before he turned and walked away, vanishing into the crowd. Almost as if he hadn't been there at all.

Feeling a bit unnerved by her foray into spywork, Clare turned toward the door—and swore when she saw Cardon through the window. He was frantically searching the crowded street outside the tavern. His eyes fell on the open door of Harrow's End, and he started for the steps.

If he found her in here, there was no way she could claim she'd simply lost him in the crowd. Even now, he probably wouldn't believe it, but as it would be her best defense, she needed to avoid being seen in here.

She hurried deeper into the tavern, and after some pushing she found a side door. It was also propped open—presumably to let the slight breeze inside—and it let out into a narrow side street. A couple of people passed her as they left the square, but no one looked at her as she hurried down the stairs.

The square was close, but she hesitated to rush into it. Finding Cardon a little further from Harrow's End felt like the better option, so she followed the side street away from the square, searching for a cross street she could use to double back and re-enter the square in the thick of the crowd.

Her cheeks were warm, and she willed herself to feel nothing but calm. Her ability to lie had grown greatly since becoming the decoy, but she didn't know how convincing she would be when she came face to face with Cardon. And she didn't even want to think about Cardon telling Bennick about the incident. Perhaps she could convince him to keep the whole thing between them.

So attuned to her own thoughts, Clare didn't sense the man behind her until it was too late.

Hard fingers dug into her arm and jerked her into an alley. Her hours of training kicked in without thought. She dug in her heels and dropped her weight. The attacker grunted and staggered, nearly losing his grip.

Her heart pounded and she yanked harder, but the man grabbed her forearm with both hands and swung her into the alley wall. Her shoulder hit the unforgiving stone a second before her head cracked against it. Agony burst across her cheek, dazing her.

In the space of a blink, her chest was forced against the wall and her arms were wrenched back, wrists held in a bruising grasp. Her shoulders screamed in pain and her entire body shook, dizziness still swirling in her head.

Hot breath fanned over her ear. "Be quiet and listen closely. We have your brother, Eliot Slaton. We will not hesitate to kill him. You will do everything we ask, and you will not tell the princess's guards about us." His grip changed so he could hold both wrists with only one hand. He gripped so tightly, the bones in her wrists grated together.

She gasped, tears stinging her eyes.

"You see how easily we got to you. We can reach you again. And if you resist in any way, or if you tell the guards, we will kill your brother." A hand slammed against the wall in front of her face, making her jerk in his grip.

A piece of paper crinkled, pinned under his palm. "This is from him, so you know we aren't lying." He leaned closer, pressing her body more painfully against the wall. Clare shuddered when his bearded jaw brushed her cheek. "Eliot resisted quite a while, but he screamed when we broke every finger on his left hand. Then we moved on to other things. Had to leave the right hand alone, so he could write to you."

Revulsion, hatred, pain, frustration, fear—it all rushed through her, tightening her throat. "What do you want?"

"Your cooperation. We will be in touch." With a shove, he released her. Clare's aching arms dropped, but she forced them to press against the wall, to steady her.

The man stepped back, the paper he'd slammed to the wall

fluttering to the ground. "We're watching you, Clare. And we'll know if you betray us."

She whirled, but it was only to see him stalk down the alleyway. She tried to take in the details of his appearance, but there wasn't much to see with his back to her. He was dressed plainly, tangled brown hair brushing the tops of his wide shoulders. Her heart thundered in her chest, pulse racing, eyes blurring with unshed tears. She wanted to chase after him—demand answers. She wanted a chance to actually fight him. The dagger Eliot had given her was strapped to her thigh, and it had been utterly useless once he'd pinned her.

We have your brother.

She forced her aching body into a crouch, her trembling fingers struggling to lift the discarded paper.

It was crinkled from its rough treatment and folded once. She remained on the ground as she flipped it open.

The familiar handwriting was a punch to her gut, once again driving out all her breath.

> Clare,
> I am being forced to write this as proof that their threats are real. I was taken by the rebels during one of my patrols. They instruct me to tell you that I will be kept alive if you follow the instructions they send you. Do not tell anyone. Especially the princess's guards.
> Forgive me,
> Eliot

The rebels had her brother.

She folded the letter and stood, looking around the now-empty alleyway as she slipped the paper into her pocket. Her heart pounded and the hairs on the back of her neck lifted. She could feel eyes on her, knew she was being watched. Maybe from one of the windows overlooking the alley?

"Clare!" It was a distant shout, but she knew it was Cardon.

Her throat constricted. She was unable to answer his shout. She pinched her eyes closed, allowing herself one moment to breathe, to think.

For Eliot's sake, she needed to tread carefully.

When she opened her eyes, she knew what she needed to do. "Clare!"

She moved for the mouth of the alley, spreading her hands over her skirt to make sure nothing looked amiss. She entered the side street and there, near the entrance to the square, was Cardon. His slicing gaze cut to her and the scar on his cheek jumped, his shoulders falling a little in evident relief. He hurried over to her. "Where have you been? I've been looking everywhere. I was about to call on the city guard."

"I'm fine." She forced a smile, ignoring the pain radiating from her cheek. "I lost sight of you in the shop, and those perfumes were making my eyes water."

Cardon frowned. "So you just left?"

"Yes. I'm sorry."

"Clare, you can't just wander off like that."

"I know. The crowd pulled me, and I . . . I enjoyed having a moment to myself. I'm sorry."

His voice lowered, his gaze sharp. "Anything could have happened to you. You can't take risks like that."

Her throat cinched and her eyes misted. "I know," she repeated. "I'm sorry for any panic I caused."

He blew out his breath, one hand scrubbing the back of his neck. "I have to report this to Bennick."

She was too preoccupied with what had happened that she didn't argue as Cardon took her elbow and guided her back to the square—even though a part of her was screaming for help.

CHAPTER 9

GRAYSON

TOMORROW, GRAYSON WOULD LEAVE for Mortise. As if
that did not make his morning bleak enough, he had received
a summons from his mother. As he dragged himself up the tall
flights of stairs to her private tower, he dreaded whatever en-
counter he was about to have with her.

The Poison Queen was everything her title promised. She
was cold. Conniving. Brilliant. When it came to poisons, she was
the most knowledgeable person in Ryden, perhaps in all Eyrinthia. She pitted her sons against each other, playing favorites
when it suited her. She didn't know about Mia, which was a rare
blessing from the fates, but she knew other things about Grayson
that Henri didn't. Treasonous things. It made him even more
wary of her.

Grayson rapped his knuckles against the thick wooden door

at the top of the tower. There was a slight pause, then his mother's voice rang out, inviting him inside.

He entered cautiously, his eyes sweeping the space. Tables and shelves laden with bottles of potions and potted plants, dried herbs and stained books dominated the circular room. Standing at the window, overlooking the dawn, was Iris.

The queen wore a long white dress, as she usually did, with a simple pale blue sash tied around her waist. Her dark hair was gathered into a long braid that trailed down her back, and when she twisted to face him, cool gray eyes met his. She smiled without warmth. "Grayson, thank you for coming so quickly."

He bowed to his mother, his spine stiff.

When he straightened, her smile only grew. "Are you excited for your mission to Mortise?"

He assumed she knew every detail of the mission, including his orders to assassinate Princess Serene. Clearly, it didn't bother her at all.

He gripped his hands behind his back, forcing himself not to show any weakness. "I will serve Father well."

"I'm sure you will." Iris moved to a long case sitting on a narrow table on the other side of the tower room. "It's a little tradition of mine to give a gift to each of my sons before they leave Ryden for the first time." She peeked over her shoulder at him. "You know I have always loved you most, Grayson."

He barely held in his snort. If she had a favorite, it would be Carter. He was her protégé, studying poisons almost as religiously as she did.

"You're stronger than your brothers," she continued, lifting the case and carrying it toward him. "You always have been. You endured their tortures, until the day you finally rose above them. They fear you, now. After what you do in Mortise, no one can deny your destiny." She held out the flat, rectangular case and

Grayson hesitated the slightest second before taking it. At her silent urging, he flicked open the clasps and lifted the lid.

Two daggers with blue hilts rested in the velvet case. They were decorative, expensive, and he recognized them at once.

They were the same poisoned daggers Tyrell had used against him weeks ago. The scar on his cheek suddenly burned in memory, as did the mark on his arm.

"Beautiful, aren't they?" she murmured. She'd shifted closer, and it took all of his self-control not to ease away from her. She peered down at the daggers in the case. "They're coated with Syalla, though you already know that." She darted a look to the fresh scar on his face.

She knew exactly what those daggers had done to him.

Grayson's jaw stiffened and the corner of her mouth lifted in a thin smile. "There is also a bottle of Syalla in the case. Apply it to the blades after they've been well used, to keep a fresh covering. Are you pleased with them?"

"Yes," he managed to speak past the dryness of his throat. "Thank you."

She beamed, a spark of true joy in her eyes. It was unsettling. "I'm glad you like them. Because I also have a favor to ask of you."

Tension coiled inside him as his mother closed the case and set it aside. She drew out a small vial from her pocket. A pale, cloudy liquid was corked inside. "Ieannax," she told him, something like reverence in her voice. "An extremely rare poison. It comes from a snake found only in the heart of Zennor's eastern jungles. It's difficult to harvest and refine, thus very expensive. It is practically undetectable. No scent. No taste. There's not even any pain. And there is no antidote. Once ingested, death is the only outcome." She rolled the bottle between her long fingers. "Of course, some people add other poisons to it. Danura, Tarvu,

Porallis—any poison that will add pain to the experience. But this is pure Ieannax. Painless death."

Grayson nearly pulled back as she took his gloved hand and laid the vial in his palm, rolling his gloved fingers over it. She kept her hand curled over his as she met his gaze. "Once you have settled into the Mortisian court, you will use this to kill Liam."

He jerked back. "What?"

Iris frowned, letting her hand fall. "Is something unclear?"

"I can't kill Liam."

"He has become a liability to your father. To Ryden. His time in the other kingdoms has altered his perspective. He has shown signs of weakness." Her dark brows pulled together. "Your father doesn't see what I see. He thinks Liam can still be controlled, but he must be destroyed before he can do harm to Ryden. I offer you the Ieannax to spare him unnecessary suffering, but you may kill him however you wish."

Grayson shook his head, still gripping the small vial. His stomach clenched. "I can't . . . How can you ask me to kill my own brother? Your son?"

Her eyes narrowed, the gray color turning icy. "You refuse me?"

"Father ordered me to keep him safe. I can't kill him."

Iris twisted away, her long braid swinging as she moved back to the window. Her breathing was strained with anger, almost reedy. When she spoke, her voice was thin. Clipped. "You will kill Liam in Mortise. Your father will forgive you for failing to bring him back—after all, you will be in a dangerous kingdom and accidents happen." She peered over her shoulder at him. "If you do not do as I say, I will tell your father about your treason in Gevell. That you helped fugitives escape the king's tax and turned your sword against Ryden."

Grayson's heart turned over in his chest. "You have no proof," he whispered. But he knew she could convince Henri of anything—especially this, since it was the truth. And while Captain Reeve may not have reported Grayson for what he suspected, he did not imagine the man would continue to protect him. Not if the queen asked him to speak against him.

If Henri learned the truth of his betrayal, he would lose everything he'd bartered for. He had to believe Henri wouldn't kill Mia; that threat had been reserved for if he failed to kill Princess Serene. But he would punish her—hurt her. And he would never grant Mia's freedom.

His right hand, still barely healing from when he had been forced to stab it two days ago, ached at the thought of how it had all been for nothing.

But how could he murder Liam? His brothers had all hurt him, but Liam had been almost kind at times. He wasn't like the others.

Iris turned fully to face him, her arms folded over her chest. Her chin tilted up. "You know Henri will punish you for what happened in Gevell."

"He'll also punish me if I return without Liam."

"Yes, and you'll survive his wrath as you always do." Her head tilted to the side, her gaze piercing him. "But there are three people who won't survive if you fail to kill your brother."

A churning started in his gut, though he tried not to reveal his growing horror.

Iris's voice was horribly soft. "I sent a few of my men to Kevid. They found a physician who was paid handsomely for tending a widow and her two children. The physician was only too eager to share that the woman and children journeyed south, to Valn, to make a new home. The younger boy still struggles with a cough. Perhaps his lungs will never fully heal from his illness.

But he's happy. And so is the older boy. Apparently, he plays with the other children in the village and tells stories of how a heroic stranger saved them one terrible night." Her lips curved upward, a horrible facsimile of a smile. "What a charming boy, that Brant."

Grayson wasn't breathing. Fates, he'd never told anyone the boy's name. That alone convinced him that she was telling the truth. He hadn't known where the family had ended up—helping them escape Gevell had been the end of it.

Saving their lives had been one of the only decent things he'd ever done, and all he'd really succeeded in doing was making them targets.

He felt sick.

Iris continued smoothly. "The widow recently found work at a tavern in town. She works every day, leaving the boys alone for hours. Anything could happen to them. But I wouldn't worry too much—they're all being very closely watched." Her chin dipped, her smile dropping. "I think you misunderstand, Grayson. If you don't kill Liam, I will find someone else to do it. He *will* die. That is a fact. But Brant doesn't have to. Neither does Garyn, with his poor lungs. And they don't have to watch their mother die." Iris stepped forward, and Grayson's instincts roared for him to run. Fight. Something.

He did nothing as she came to a stop in front of him.

Her hand lifted, her fingers tracing the line of the newest scar that cut across his cheek. Her voice was a whisper. "You are so striking. Your harsh beauty is stunning. My scarred prince. And yet, you don't want anyone to know how soft you are underneath the cruelty they all see." She suddenly gripped his chin, her fingernails digging into his skin.

Grayson stiffened in pain but made no sound. He held her gaze, his skin crawling as he stared into her cold gray eyes.

"Do not make the mistake of failing me, Grayson. More than

your life is at stake." She released him with a shove and he was a little surprised there wasn't blood on her fingernails. His jaw ached and his skin stung from her punishing grip.

Iris moved back to the window, the hem of her white skirt dragging over the stone floor. "Safe travels," she said over her shoulder. "I look forward to your successful return."

Grayson ground his teeth, heart pounding against his ribs as he strode from the room, the bottle of Ieannax in his fist.

"You're forgetting one," Liam said from across the small table.

Grayson tightened his grip on the back of his neck, eyeing the maps and papers spread before him. "I named them all."

"No. There are twelve seats on the Mortisian council. You named only eleven."

"I don't remember, then."

Liam sighed. "Ser Omar Jamal. He's the youngest on the council, and the newest."

"I won't forget," Grayson said, his tone a little too stiff.

His brother leaned back in his wooden chair, which creaked. They were in the castle library, a somber place that smelled of dust and mold. Sporadic windows let in the vibrant light of a dying afternoon. Grayson had always enjoyed the large room because most everyone in his family avoided it. That made it an ideal place for their current studies because they didn't have to worry about being disturbed.

"Would you like to talk about what's troubling you?" Liam asked.

Iris's face flashed through his mind, tightening his jaw. "No."

It had only been a few hours since she had ordered him to kill Liam, but it had already felt like an eternity. The two paths that stretched out before him both held death.

If he didn't kill Liam, his mother would betray him. The Hogans would lose their lives. Mia would lose her chance at freedom.

If he killed Liam, the Hogans lived and Grayson might somehow be able to convince his father to set Mia free, despite his failure to bring Liam back to Ryden. But he would have to live with killing his own brother.

It wasn't much of a choice.

Liam studied him in silence, twisting the leather bracelet that encircled his right wrist. His brother was tanned from all the time he spent abroad, and his carefully maintained beard—short, by Ryden standards—added a foreign flair to his features. He was only three years older than Grayson, and yet he always looked confident and in control. "You haven't paid attention to this lesson at all."

They'd started with memorization drills and then moved to solving riddles and puzzles. "You need a sharp mind," Liam had said, and that was the only explanation Grayson got before he was given another thing to solve. As their lesson moved toward an end, Liam had switched to quizzing Grayson about the Mortisian council.

Grayson hadn't done well at any of it.

Liam eyed him from across the table. "You're often quiet, but today is worse. What's on your mind?"

"Nothing."

Liam snorted. "I can tell." He looked to the towering bookcase beside them and shook his head, then fingered the nearest shelf, watching as the dust built against his finger. When he spoke, his voice was quiet. "Sometimes I think the cruelest thing our parents ever did to us was kill our ability to trust. Least of all each other."

The words were low, but there was a vehemence to them that made Grayson wonder if Iris was right about Liam.

His brother withdrew his hand from the shelf and brushed the dust against his leg. "I think that's all we're going to manage today. I'll continue to train you during our travels." He pushed to his feet and stepped around the table. He paused there, then twisted back to face Grayson. His mouth opened, closed, and then he shoved his hands into his pockets. "Enjoy your last night in the castle. I'll meet you in the courtyard at dawn." He strode from the room without a further goodbye, leaving Grayson alone.

The silence pressed around him. His skin felt too tight. Anger, grief, and hopelessness rushed through him.

In another life, he and Liam might have been friends.

In this one, he would probably have to kill his brother.

Grayson didn't know how long he sat at the table, smelling dust, moldy leather, and aging parchment. But the maps and papers spread out before him held no answers, and neither did any of the thousands of volumes surrounding him.

When he finally pushed up from the table, the scuff of the chair against the stone floor grated loudly in the cavernous room. He left the maps spread on the table. He wondered if anyone would even come in here to put them away, or if they'd still be here when he returned from Mortise.

Because he would return. Despite all the uncertainty and confusion he felt, that was something he knew. Nothing could keep him from coming back to Mia. Even if it was only to see her freed.

He would have to learn how to be strong enough to let her go.

His boots clipped against the floor, the setting sun that

streamed through the dirty glass of the tall windows cast the rows of books in a reddish glow. The harsh light was broken intermittently by the shelves, so each step Grayson took was in shadow, then light.

He was nearly to the exit when the hairs on the back of his neck lifted, instinct screaming that he was no longer alone.

His steps slowed and he looked to his left.

At the end of the row of towering shelves, Carter stood, watching him.

Carter was the second oldest Kaelin. His long dark hair brushed his shoulders and he always reeked of herbs and potions.

Grayson drew to a stop, his pulse kicking. Not in fear—he could easily beat Carter in a fight. But dread wormed inside him, because nothing good ever came from one of his brothers seeking him out.

Carter started down the aisle, drawing toward Grayson on nearly silent feet. As he got closer, he reached out with his left hand and ran his fingers over the leather spines. His forefinger was mostly gone; Peter had cut it off years ago.

"I thought you might still be here," Carter said.

Grayson's jaw tightened. "What do you want?"

The corner of Carter's mouth twitched up, but he didn't answer.

Grayson stiffened as a light scuff of a boot sounded behind him. Twisting a look over his shoulder, he saw Peter at the end of the other aisle, slowly walking toward him.

They were hemming him in.

Chapter 10

Grayson

GRAYSON COULD HAVE RUN. **C**ARTER and Peter were drawing closer, but he wasn't surrounded, and the library's exit was near. But he had stopped running from them years ago.

Tension climbed his back, but he didn't let anything show in his expression.

"So glad we managed to catch you," Peter said. The signet ring on his right hand glowed in the red light of sunset, the emerald eyes of the snakes flashing. The crown prince was the shortest brother, but his ruthlessness was something they had all felt over the years. He had brown hair and an angular face, and intelligence shone in his light-brown eyes.

He would make a terrifying king one day.

Carter and Peter both drew to a stop. Grayson eased back a step so he could view them both.

Peter crossed his arms over his chest. "We want a quick word before you leave us."

"Peter has a request," Carter added.

Fates, not another request. Grayson was already drowning in them. He gritted his teeth and eyed his older brothers. "What?"

Carter's gaze narrowed. "Be careful of your tone. He is your future king."

Perhaps it was being pushed into a corner that made him reckless, but Grayson lifted his chin, one hand dropping to rest on the hilt of one of his belted knives.

A spark of fear lit Carter's eyes, but he managed not to shift back a step. Impressive, because Grayson could feel the mask of the Black Hand drawn over his face. Most would run from him. He forced himself to edge out a thin, dangerous smile. "I'm well aware of what you both are."

Carter's mouth pressed into a thin line, but his eyes flared.

Peter clucked his tongue. "Easy, Carter. The Black Hand merely wishes to stretch his dark wings."

A muscle popped in Carter's jaw and annoyance flashed in his eyes, but the fear was still there.

Grayson's sharp smile spread a little wider.

Peter propped a shoulder against the overstuffed wooden shelf. "This request is to remain private. Do you understand?" Grayson didn't bother giving an answer, and Peter didn't wait for one as he said, "I have no wish to marry Yemma."

That wasn't exactly a secret. Peter had grown bored with his betrothed by the time he was fourteen.

Carter seemed unable to help himself, so he jumped in. "He wants to end the engagement, but Father will only allow it if Peter can find a better match. I've been helping him."

"What a lovely matchmaker you must be."

Carter scowled.

"Yemma's father will not take ending the betrothal lightly," Peter said. "So Father must be in total agreement that my new bride would be of greater advantage."

"You'll not find better in Ryden," Grayson said. "Her name is nearly as old as ours."

Peter smiled thinly. "True."

Grayson's skin itched. This was not where he wanted to be right now, and it certainly wasn't a conversation he wanted to have a part in. His breath came out sharply. "You want a foreign bride, then?"

"Yes. And you'll meet her in Mortise."

Grayson's dark brows drew together. "Princess Serene?"

Carter snorted. "Peter is intrigued by the tales of her beauty, but no."

Peter shot Carter a silencing look and he snapped his mouth shut. Peter then shifted his focus to Grayson. "I want Princess Imara."

Grayson's knowledge in foreign politics was limited—that was more Peter and Liam's territory—but he knew Princess Imara was one of the Zennorian royals. Since King Zaire Buhari had half a dozen daughters, that didn't really narrow things down.

"I know Father isn't concerned with Zennor right now," Peter continued. "But I've been there and they're ready for the taking. All we have to do is snatch the opportunity."

Carter leaped in, eagerness edging his words. "The oldest two princesses are married, but the third—Imara—is not. She's betrothed to a man named Skyer, a leader of one of the Zennorian clans, but that is of little consequence."

"You intend to marry her, then?" At Peter's nod, Grayson barely held back a snort. Or perhaps he didn't succeed, because his brother's eyes narrowed. "And you think she—and King Zaire —would negate the betrothal so she could marry you?"

Carter's fists tightened at his sides. "They'd be fools not to accept the match. As the third daughter, she could have never dreamed of such an honor. To be the future queen of Ryden?"

"A position you covet, no doubt."

His face flushed darkly, but Peter's voice was cool. "Negotiations will not be an issue and Father would not be able to find fault with the match. After we take over Devendra and Mortise, we will be close neighbors with Zennor. Forging a marriage alliance is in our best interests."

Grayson folded his arms over his chest, more than done with this conversation. Mia was waiting, and he would much rather spend his last evening in Ryden with her. "Congratulations on your perfect match."

Peter smiled thinly. "Thank you. But you'll have a part to play in this."

"How?"

"Jahzara came by some interesting information," Peter said.

Grayson was not social by nature, but he'd met Jahzara several times. Peter's mistress was a calculating woman who watched everyone around her with sharp eyes and a cruel smile. She and his brother were perfectly suited, which was probably why Peter hadn't dismissed her, even after two years—certainly longer than any other mistress had lasted. They'd met when Henri had sent Peter to Zennor to meet with King Zaire. From what Grayson had gathered, Peter had found Jahzara to be a perfect ally; the noblewoman came from a strong Zennorian line, but her family had fallen out of favor with King Zaire and she thirsted for revenge and power. Peter had probably promised her both.

Peter's eyes brightened as he continued. "Some of her contacts in Zennor sent word that Imara is not in Zennor at all."

"Wait." Grayson stared at his brother. "Your mistress helped you choose your future bride?"

"Yes." Peter's expression didn't change.

Grayson could only shake his head. "I'm sure you, Jahzara, and Princess Imara will all be very happy together."

Peter ignored that. "Imara has left Zennor and gone to support Princess Serene's betrothal in Mortise, which means your paths will cross in Duvan."

Grayson's eyebrows drew together. "You want me to share your proposal with her?"

Peter laughed, the burst of sound echoing loudly off the library's tall ceiling. "Fates, Grayson. She'd probably take one look at your scarred face and run away screaming. No." He set his hands on his hips, chin tilted up; it was strange how he could be the shortest one in the room, but still look down on them all. "If I wanted a message delivered smoothly, I'd send Liam. I could have ordered him to seduce her, even, but that's not how I want to play this hand. I've met Imara. We didn't speak much while I was in Zennor, but she knows me, and she does not . . . Well, she doesn't exactly like me."

Grayson felt a prickle of unease. "Then how do you intend to—"

"When it's time for you to leave Mortise," Peter overrode him calmly, "I want you to bring her back with you."

Grayson blinked. "You . . . wish me to abduct Princess Imara?"

"Yes." Peter didn't even have the decency to look the least bit ashamed.

His fingers dug into his crossed arms, a hundred protests on his tongue. He settled for the one Peter might understand. "There's no way I'll be able to do that. Father's orders—"

"I know Father's orders," Peter cut in. "You and Liam are to play the part of peace-seekers until the moment is right. Then you will assassinate Princess Serene and start a war between Mortise and Devendra. It is during that chaos that you will take

Princess Imara and bring her to me."

"This would start a war with Zennor—a war Father doesn't want yet."

"Peter and Imara will be married before Zaire Buhari even learns she's gone," Carter said. "It will be too late. He'll have no choice but to accept it."

"Jahzara and my other sources in Zennor all indicate that King Zaire would not be able to muster an army in time to save his daughter," Peter added. "Besides, Zennor will already be pulled into the conflict between Mortise and Devendra, or risk losing their alliance with Devendra. Zaire's hands will be tied. He won't be able to do anything."

Carter nodded, his long black hair brushing the sides of his angular face. "By the time a threat could even reach us, Imara will probably be carrying Peter's child. What could the king do then?"

Make Princess Imara a widow, Grayson thought. But that was not the argument he used. "Even after Liam and I complete our mission, we're supposed to keep our covers—Ryden isn't supposed to be implicated in Serene's death. Abducting a foreign princess would be impossible."

Peter lifted one shoulder. "I'm sure you can make it work."

The muscles in Grayson's neck tensed. "I'm not so confident."

The crown prince's eyes narrowed. "Let me rephrase: you *will* make it work. I don't think I need to describe the ways I'll punish you if you don't do as I order. I will be king, Grayson. I am your future, and I can make that future a nightmare."

He knew Peter was telling the absolute truth. He would make Grayson's life miserable.

But the thought of stealing a young woman and dragging her to Lenzen, throwing her at Peter's feet and beneath his non-existent mercy . . . It made him ill.

He would not be a part of this. He may not have many choices right now, but this was one he could make.

"All right," he lied, his quiet voice echoing in the silence. "I'll bring her back."

Carter smiled, and so did Peter.

Fates-blasted fools.

And the joke was truly on them because when Grayson made it back from Mortise, he was doomed to incur the wrath of either his mother or his father, and neither of them would leave much of him for Peter to torture.

The sun was just peeking over the pine-covered mountains when Grayson left his bedroom. He had one bag slung over his shoulder and his weapons were sheathed in all the usual places across his body. He hadn't slept well. Between nightmares about the man he'd killed in his father's office and all the things weighing on his mind, it really was no wonder.

He didn't look back as he left his room and locked it, then moved for the dungeon. When he arrived at Mia's cell, Fletcher was already standing guard. The older man reached for his keys, but Grayson halted him with a raised hand. He set his bag aside and then pulled out a small drawstring bag.

Fletcher frowned as Grayson placed the weighty pouch in his palm. "What's this?" he asked.

"I'll bring you more when I return, if you watch out for her."

The old man actually scowled. "I don't need your coin." He tried to hand the bag back, but Grayson refused it.

He tugged out a key. "This is to my chambers. Twelve stones in and seven to your left, the square is loose. There's a map inside. It will lead you to a cave not far from here, and there are instructions on how to find a chest I buried. Half the coins inside are for you, and half are for Mia." He took a breath, knowing he was asking too much. But he had no choice. "If something happens to me, I need you to get her out."

"Are you mad? We'd never make it out of the castle."

"There are instructions on the map that will help you navigate the guards."

"No."

Grayson's voice tightened. "My father brought her here to control me. If I'm gone, she no longer means anything to him. He will kill her."

Fletcher's eyes widened and he muttered a curse.

Grayson grasped the man's free wrist and folded the key into his palm. "Please. I'm not above begging."

The guard grimaced. "Please don't do that." He gripped the key in his fist and blew out his breath. "I'll do all I can to keep her safe, but I can't make any promises. Not with the king."

Grayson nodded, knowing it was the best he could expect.

When he reached into his pocket again, the man groaned. "Fates, what else?"

Grayson lifted a sealed letter. "If something happens to me, I want you to give this to her. Please don't read it."

The man sighed. "I won't." He took the letter, then eyed Grayson. "You're a legend, Your Highness. If you want to come back, you'll make it happen. So make it happen."

Grayson swallowed, his throat feeling suddenly tight. "I'll do everything in my power to return."

He also knew he wasn't invincible. He could fail. Which was why he'd needed to take these precautions for Mia. It was also why he wouldn't tell her about the possibility of gaining her freedom until he returned. He didn't want her to have that dream ripped away, in case something happened to him.

Fletcher unlocked Mia's cell and tugged the door open. Before Grayson could step inside, the old guard did something he never had before—he bowed.

Unnerved by the show of respect, Grayson hurried into the room.

Mia waited for him. She stood in a soft pink dress, her dark curls falling around her shoulders and framing her round face. In her hands was a folded sheet of paper, and she was fingering the edges. She fidgeted where she stood, chewing her bottom lip as she eyed him. She took a bracing breath as the door clicked shut, and then she held out the folded paper. "I don't want you to open it now. Wait until you're . . . away."

He took it, thumbing one of the stiff corners. He swallowed, suddenly losing all words.

She wrapped her arms around his waist, drawing him close. He embraced her in return, breathing in her jasmine and lavender scent, pressing his body closer to hers. She was so small in his arms, but she was everything to him. His entire world.

He let her go slowly and Mia eased back to cup his cheek, guiding his gaze to meet hers. "Promise me you'll be careful." There was vulnerability in her voice, and fates knew his own fears were rising.

"I will be back," he promised. "This isn't goodbye."

Yet.

He forced that away. He couldn't afford to be conflicted. Gaining Mia's freedom, letting her go . . . that was his only goal, now. He owed her everything. He swore to the fates he would give her this, no matter what it cost him.

He reached into his pocket. "I have something for you, too."

Color invaded his cheeks, but he tried to ignore that as he tugged the necklace out. It sat on his gloved palm between them, looking suddenly pathetic to him. He'd made it last night. A gray pebble was the only ornament, bound to the leather string with crisscrossed strands of twine. He should have gotten her a book, or paints, or—

"Grayson, is that . . .?" Mia clapped a hand over her mouth. "That's the pebble. The pebble we first played with." Her gaze lifted to his, and moisture brightened her rich brown eyes. "You kept it?"

He was fully flushing now, but he jerked out a nod.

"That's . . . amazing. You're amazing. Will you put it on me?" Mia asked, already putting her back to him as she grasped her hair in one fist, exposing the back of her neck.

Grayson slipped the paper she'd given him into his pocket and tugged off his gloves. His heart kicked against his ribs as he grasped the necklace in both hands. He brought it around her neck and secured it, his fingertips brushing her bared skin. When he was done, he let his thumbs slide down the column of her neck, coasting over the smooth ball at the base. She shivered under his touch and he dropped his hands. Before she could see the newest wound on his palm, he hurried to fit his gloves back on. He refused to tell her how he got it.

Mia slowly turned, releasing her curls to fall down her back once more. She was looking down at the pebble that rested under the hollow of her throat. Her fingers wrapped around the small stone and when she looked up, a tear rolled down the curve of her cheek.

Grayson brushed the tear away with the gloved pads of his fingers, his gut twisting.

Mia sucked in a breath, her body vibrating with emotion. "I promised myself I wouldn't beg you to stay. But I want to."

That killed him, in every way.

Left without words, he ducked his head and set his lips against hers, holding her face with both hands. He thumbed the delicate curves of her cheeks and angled the kiss so he could taste her more fully. He needed this, and he knew she did, too.

She gripped his wrists, holding him close. And as the kiss deepened, she slid a hand up his arm, shoulder, and neck, until her fingers got lost in his hair. Her other hand moved to his chest, resting over his racing heart. Her fingers curled into his shirt, dragging him closer, and her other hand shifted in his hair, shooting tingles across his scalp. He shivered, wanting this moment to last forever. To be lost in her kiss, her touch, until everything else in the world disappeared.

When they needed air, he tugged his lips away, but he placed a last kiss against the corner of her mouth before he tipped his forehead against hers, keeping them close. They were both breathing roughly, their sharp breaths mingling. He closed his eyes, his lungs tight. "I love you."

Mia's hand flexed against the back of his neck and her brow pressed tightly against his. "I love you, too, Grayson. Never forget that."

He kissed her again, refusing to acknowledge the burn in his throat or the pressure building behind his eyes. His heart tripped, and he kissed her longer than he should have—it still wasn't enough. But they were out of time. Because even down here, away from the sun, he knew it was rising.

It was time to leave.

He eased away, but Mia grasped his hand. He flinched as pain shot out from his wounded palm.

Her grip eased, concern in her eyes. "Are you all right?"

"Fine." He forced a smile. "I hurt my hand. It's nothing."

Her hold loosened further, and then she gently brought his

gloved hand to her mouth, placing a gentle kiss on the center of his palm—right over the painful throbbing. His heart rolled in his chest.

When her gaze lifted, he was surprised by the almost desperate edge that had crept into her eyes. His shoulders tensed. "Mia?"

She stared at him, still gently holding his hand. Her breathing thinned. "Grayson, there's something I . . . I need to . . ." Her lips pursed and she closed her eyes, exhaling deeply. "Please be careful."

He frowned, certain that hadn't been what she wanted to say. "Of course." He hesitated. "Is there something you want to tell me?"

There was a moment of stillness. A weighted silence as they both held their breath. He never pressed her. Not for anything. But this felt different.

Mia's mouth opened, and he could feel her hand tremble against his as their fingers slowly twined.

"You can trust me, Mia," he said softly.

"I know," she breathed, not looking at him.

Grayson gently squeezed her hand, ignoring the pain that flashed through his wounded palm. "You're from Mortise, aren't you?"

Her shoulders stiffened.

"I can try to find your family," he said, his voice quiet. "I can give them a message. Or just learn about them—see how they are. If you tell me what city you called home, or give me your full name, I—"

"No."

"But—"

"I am dead to all who knew me," Mia said, her voice low but sharp. "And I . . . they died . . . I . . . I can't—I can't do this." She ducked her head, but not quickly enough to hide her grimace.

He heard the tears in her voice, and they were knives against his skin. He cupped her cheek and gently forced her tortured gaze to meet his. "You don't have to tell me a fates-blasted thing," he whispered. "You don't have to explain anything. Nothing you say, or don't say, will change how completely I love you."

She blinked through her tears, her mouth opening once, but no words came out. Finally, she lifted onto her toes and pressed a kiss to his jaw.

When she rocked back, he brushed a thumb over her knuckles. It killed him to move for the door, but Mia stepped with him, still holding his hand. Her fingers clenched his as Fletcher unlocked the door, and when it swung open and Grayson hefted his bag over his shoulder, Mia still held on to him, his fingers trapped in hers.

Her hand shook as she flexed her hold one more time, and then—their eyes locked on each other—she slowly pulled away. Their fingertips brushed a final time, then Grayson's hand was empty.

He tightened his hold on his bag and stepped out of the cell, a knot in his throat.

Mia watched him go, her hands clasped in front of her, knuckles resting against her closed mouth. Her shoulders were tense and her deep brown eyes burned with a thousand emotions he couldn't even begin to decipher.

Aware that Fletcher was watching, knowing their time was gone, Grayson turned away.

He'd barely taken a step when Mia called his name.

She gripped the edge of the open door and her toes brushed the invisible line of the corridor, but Fletcher wasn't even watching—he'd turned to give them privacy.

"Can you do something for me?" Mia asked. "When you're in Mortise?"

Of all the requests being made of him lately, this was one he was eager to hear. "Anything."

Her grip on the wooden frame tightened, her knuckles going white. "When you're there, I . . . I want you to visit the beach."

"The beach?" It was the last thing he had expected.

"Yes. Find a place where you can be alone. Take off your boots and sink your toes into the sand."

This request was getting stranger by the moment. "Why?"

Her mouth twitched, but she didn't answer him. "I want you to stand just inside the ocean and let the waves roll over your feet. Let it be sunset, and close your eyes and feel the warm sun on your face and the cool water on your feet. Feel the shifting sand beneath you, and whisper my name. Let me be there. With you."

Grayson stepped back to her slowly, his heart thumping too hard and fast. He rested a hand on her cheek and stared into her eyes. His voice came out low and rough. "You are always with me. You're the best part of me."

She rolled up on her toes and kissed him, the gentle press of her lips searing all the way to his heart.

CHAPTER 11
DESFAN

AFTER A DRAINING DINNER WITH THE council and their families, Desfan knew he needed a reprieve before he could face another evening in his father's office, trapped with reports and half-written letters—including one to Princess Serene that he'd been struggling to finish since the betrothal had been accepted.

He'd wanted to write a letter to her—not her father, not about the alliance—but to *her*. He wanted to introduce himself, ask questions about her. The only issue was, of course, he didn't know what to say. Every question felt arbitrary, since they had already agreed to be married, and when it came to describing himself, well . . . He knew he wasn't the polished diplomat Serene was known to be, or the stately ruler one would expect from his title. And then, of course, he'd delayed in reaching out for so long, it felt awkward to send it now.

Desfan wanted to escape the castle, just for a few hours, but he knew he couldn't. So he went to visit his father instead.

The serjan was in the same place he'd been for six months —his bed.

Saernon Cassian breathed. Sometimes he blinked. Sometimes he swallowed water and broth. But he didn't otherwise move. When he was awake, it was really no different than when he slept. He never spoke. His eyes, when open, registered nothing. Sometimes his body twitched, or he would moan. But otherwise, it was as if his body was the only thing left of him. And even that was wasting away.

In many ways, it was like he was already gone. His soul was no longer here.

And yet Desfan still visited him.

He sat beside his father, the physicians and attendants having slipped respectfully from the room when he arrived. He'd left Karim outside, and he knew his friend would keep anyone from disturbing him.

Karim couldn't save him from his thoughts, though.

Desfan balanced his arms on his knees, hands dangling, shoulders slumped as he viewed his father. "Fates, I wish you were here," he whispered.

When Desfan was a child, his father had been so large and powerful. He'd had a booming laugh, a gleam of mischief in his warm brown eyes, and his hugs had been rib-crushing.

Then he and Desfan had received the news—a sudden storm just off the coast of Dorma had caught the royal ship and dashed it to pieces. Just like that, at eleven years old, Desfan's life had irrevocably changed. His mother and sisters would never return from their summer trip. He would never see them again.

Mortise had lost their beloved Seraijan Farah and two cherished seraijahs that day.

Desfan had lost everything.

His mother's tender smile, the way her long fingers sifted through his hair as she sang him to sleep.

Tahlyah's hitching laugh when she made him grin, her shrieking scream when he'd toss her in the water—and her retaliating pinches.

Meerah's ever-ready smile, the way she'd crawl into his bed at night and beg him to tell her a story, or how she'd hang on his arm until he would help her build a castle in the sand.

He'd lost his childhood. His security.

And he'd lost his father.

When the news came, the serjan had collapsed and wept. And though the tears had eventually dried, the sadness had never left his gaze. He was no longer the vibrant man he had been before. He was a shadow of himself.

Desfan remembered standing by his side in the royal mausoleum and looking upon the markers that belonged to their family, no ashes in the vault because the sea had claimed their bodies. That was the last time his father had embraced him, his hold almost strangling—as if he feared Desfan, too, would be lost.

And he *had* become lost.

Those first few months had been a daze; he hadn't wanted to do anything. And then, as if something inside him flipped, he suddenly had to do *everything*. He couldn't sit still. He had to be in motion.

He avoided his tutors, skipped his lessons—except for fighting. He'd relished that.

He refused to pray to the fates or attend religious ceremonies; the fates had abandoned him, so it seemed only fair.

He stole things for the thrill of it. He gambled. He learned how to cheat. He ran away, only to be hauled back a day or three later by the guards. He snuck out of the castle most nights and by the time he was thirteen, the guards would find him in dirty alleys, his body swollen and bruised from street fighting.

The more frustrated his father became, the more Desfan acted out. Because anything was better than seeing his father's eyes so cold. So empty.

Anything was better than feeling that way himself.

As the years passed, Desfan kept pushing himself and his father. Drinking, drugs—he'd done it all by the time he was fifteen.

The night of his birthday had changed everything. He'd avoided the party at the palace and snuck into the city instead, roving the betting tables for any diversion from the oppressive reminder that he was still alive, still aging, while his sisters and mother never would.

The guards had found him eventually, as they always did, and they'd dragged him back to the palace for what had to be the thousandth time.

But this time was different.

The drugs and drink might have clouded his mind, but he knew something was wrong when he was hauled not to his room, but to his father's. And when he saw the man's face flushed red in anger . . . He knew he had pushed the serjan too far.

For the first time in years, the serjan had touched his son. He'd struck Desfan so hard he'd fallen to the floor, blood bursting across his tongue.

His father had stared down at him, heavy breaths sawing out of him, his eyes finally flashing with something. Anger. Frustration. Hopelessness. The serjan had looked . . . *raw*.

"No more," he gasped. "This ends tonight. There's a ship at the harbor. I've given you to the captain for a year."

Desfan had trembled, still curled against the floor, his jaw throbbing, ears ringing, lips smeared with blood. His father didn't want him. He'd given him away. To the sea, of all places—the monster that had swallowed his mother and sisters.

It felt like his chest was collapsing around his heart and lungs. He couldn't breathe.

"Maybe someone else can do something with you," his father had snapped. "The fates know I can't." He'd stalked to the door, stopping only to throw one last look at Desfan. "Your mother would be disgusted with you."

The words were a knife in Desfan's stomach; they gutted him.

Filled with his own pain, he barely heard the note of it echoing in his father's hollow voice as he muttered, "She would be disgusted with us both."

He'd walked away, leaving Desfan on the floor. He hadn't even said goodbye.

Guards had escorted him to the ship, and he'd felt like a criminal being led to prison. And there, at the docks, he had met Karim.

His father had assigned him a young bodyguard, probably in hopes they would become friends. Karim had been unbearably good, even then. And though their relationship had been rough at first, they *had* become friends. Eventually.

What had started as a horrible nightmare became Desfan's saving grace. A year at sea turned into another, and another. He didn't want to go home. He didn't want to be the serjah. With the deaths of his mother and sisters, the palace had become a mausoleum, his father slowly rotting inside those stone walls. And Desfan had been rotting, too.

But at sea, life was simple. He worked alongside the crew. Bled with them. Fought shoulder-to-shoulder with them, kept the islands and trade routes safe. And perhaps he wasn't saving his mother and sisters, but he had saved others. He'd made a difference, served his people.

Then, six months ago, he had received the message from Serai Yahri.

His father had collapsed. He couldn't speak. Couldn't communicate in any way. They expected him to die within days.

Desfan had returned, his gut a bottomless pit of dread. He had hated and loved his father, and he didn't want to lose him. He didn't want the crown. He didn't want this life.

He didn't want to be truly alone—the last Cassian in Eyrinthia.

But his father hadn't died. Desfan had not become Serjan, but regent—and even that was enough to smother him. He'd spent the last nine years of his life running away from the palace and his responsibilities, and now he was stuck here. And though his father was still alive, he wasn't actually here.

"I'm sorry," Desfan said, his voice a dull whisper. "I'm making a mess of everything. Like always."

His father, of course, said nothing. He was staring vacantly at the ceiling. A bit of drool gathered at the corner of his mouth, and Desfan's hands clenched into fists.

The fates could be so cruel.

The physicians weren't sure what ailed him. He'd simply collapsed one night. He'd been in his office. Working too late, too hard.

No one outside this room knew how dire his condition was, except for the council. But no one could assume by now that the chances of the serjan returning to the throne were good. He had been ill for months.

But Desfan knew they still had hope. They clung to it, chanting prayers and holding late-night vigils in the streets. Even most members of the council seemed to refuse the dire truth because the alternative was to have Desfan crowned. He knew they assured themselves repeatedly that the serjan would get well soon. Because to have Desfan on the throne permanently was an unthinkable option.

Desfan eyed his father's lax profile, spinning the obsidian ring on his finger. What if he hadn't forced the man's hand all those years ago? What if he had been here? Been the royal figure he should have been? He could have taken some of the burdens from his father's shoulders. Perhaps his father's health wouldn't have deteriorated so quickly.

Not that speculating did any good.

Sitting here didn't do any good, either.

So Desfan pushed up from his chair, bent over his father, and used a cloth to blot away the drool at his mouth before it could spill. "I'll visit again soon," he said quietly. "I promise."

His father gave no indication of hearing him. But then, he never did.

Desfan strode from the room. The problems with the council weren't magically solved, but he could visit Kiv Arcas. It had been three days since the olcain raid, and the kiv should have a full report with detailed interviews from every smuggler they'd arrested.

Running a country was overwhelming.

Hunting smugglers and drug masters? That, he could do.

CHAPTER 12

DESFAN

"Serjah Desfan, do you have a moment?"

Desfan looked up from the papers spilled over the desk and blinked to bring Serai Yahri into focus. It had been another late night of sifting through reports, and he'd returned to his father's desk first thing this morning so he could again go over Kiv Arcas's report of the olcain raid.

Not to mention he hadn't slept well after visiting his father last night. Too many memories had been stirred.

A visit from Serai Yahri wasn't what his morning needed.

The older councilwoman was wearing her ceremonial green robe, even though the council session would not start for hours yet.

Perhaps she liked flaunting the power of her position.

Desfan straightened behind his desk. "Of course." There was

no other polite answer.

The woman moved with surprising grace, her cane tapping the stones as she advanced. Karim started to move forward, but Desfan waved him back. It didn't send a great message if he was always seen with his bodyguard, especially in a private meeting with the leader of the council. Karim tipped his head and remained in the hall as he closed the door.

Desfan shuffled some of the papers on the desk to hide the olcain report. Yahri had already reprimanded him for his involvement in the raid, and he wasn't in the mood for another lecture. "What can I do for you, Serai Yahri?" he asked, settling back into his chair as she sat across from him.

Serai Yahri settled her hands atop her cane, her thin shoulders up despite the slight curve of her back. "I'm grateful I caught you. I know your schedule is full. I've been sending you cards for the last two weeks, trying to find a time for us to meet."

"I'm sorry I wasn't able to fit in an appointment sooner." The messages were probably still on his desk. He'd read them and set them aside with intentions to get back to her soon—another failing, but, fates blast it, he was exhausted every day and the last thing he wanted was to endure her disapproving words in the council chambers, and then again here.

A corner of the serai's wrinkled mouth twitched. "Well, lucky for me to have caught you at a good time."

"Is there something in particular you'd like to discuss?" Frankly, he couldn't think of any lecture that she hadn't already delivered to him in front of the council.

"A couple of things, actually." She lifted a silver eyebrow. "I have consulted with the royal physician and he informed me there has been no change in your father's health, except for the continued weight loss. There is no telling how long this will continue."

Desfan's hands fisted under the desk. "I don't think it is your place to discuss my father's health with his healer. You could have asked me."

"I planned to, but you never returned my messages." She shook her head. "Times are uneasy, as you well know. I believe there are those who would take advantage of our weakened state."

"You mean my ineffective rule?" he asked drily.

"Yes." Her simple response shouldn't have surprised him, but it still felt like a slap. She sighed. "Desfan, you are young, inexperienced, and impulsive—often reckless. One look at your face confirms this."

His broken nose flared with pain. He wanted to point out that the swelling had gone down dramatically, but instead he tried to keep his voice level as he said, "Your feelings about me are no secret, Serai Yahri. I've known of your low regard for me since I was a boy."

Her head tipped a little to the side. "Do you know what I see when I look at you, Desfan? And no, it's not what you're thinking."

It grated that she'd dropped his title. Normally, he wouldn't care—he'd spent years running from it—but from her, it felt like a calculated insult. "How do you know what I'm thinking?"

"I know exactly what you assume," she said. "That I am an old fool who still regards you as a child. And in some ways, you're right. But when I look at you, I don't see the drug-addicted hellion who wreaked havoc wherever he threw himself. Nor the boy who skipped his lessons and refused to learn how to lead this country. No, instead I see the pain, despair, and disappointment of your father."

Desfan's jaw tightened even as his gut sank.

Yahri didn't even blink as she continued. "When I look at

you, I see how your childish tantrums and complete disregard for your life, your safety, your future—your *identity*—impacted the serjan. You broke his heart. Repeatedly. You forced him to send you away, and then you never came back. You abandoned him after he had already lost so much."

Heat crawled up Desfan's throat. "You have absolutely no right to say these things to me."

"You leave me no—"

"My father abandoned *me*," Desfan bit out. "He shut me out first. And after ignoring me for years, he paid a man to take me away so he didn't have to deal with me anymore."

The woman's forehead wrinkled. "I did not say he was perfect. But neither were you."

"I was a *child.*"

"And what are you now?"

Trapped. Alone. Judged.

He couldn't give voice to any of that.

Her whisper was almost loud in the sudden quiet. "You do not want the crown."

Desfan didn't answer. He wasn't even looking at her anymore, but at that fates-blasted painting across the room. The one of him and his father, their faces so bleak.

Yahri's voice was quiet. "I think it may be time to discuss some options. For the best interests of Mortise."

His spine was as stiff as his tone. "Such as?"

There was a pause, long enough that he forced himself to meet Yahri's eyes. The woman's expression was relaxed. Almost poised. He had the thought that she must have been quite beautiful in her youth. "You could refuse the crown."

The words hung between them, heavier and more terrible than a weapon.

"No," Desfan said, his voice low and hard.

The serai shifted, tightening her grip on the cane. "It has happened before in our history."

"I know the story," he nearly snapped. "The heir was feared to be insane."

"And he denied his birthright so his brother could rule—your ancestor."

He huffed a dry laugh. "If memory serves, the serjah in question was locked in the dungeon for a month and tortured, and it was with a knife to his throat that he disavowed the crown."

"An unpleasant part of the story, to be sure. But he was not in his right mind and he would have made a dangerous—no, *disastrous*—ruler."

"And you judge me to be insane as well? A dangerous choice?"

"Not insane, obviously. But you do not want the crown."

The words cut deeply, because they were true. He didn't want the crown.

He also refused to give it up. It was his birthright. And for all the ways he had disappointed his father and the memory of his mother, this was a line he would not cross.

Strange, though, how much more willing he was to fight for it the moment someone told him he should give it up.

His voice was edged as he asked quietly, "Is this you holding a dagger to my throat, Serai?"

The woman straightened her spine. "Of course not. I merely bring the story up as an example. There is a precedent for a royal to refuse the throne the fates granted him."

"Yes, well, the fates took all the other Cassians away. I'm all that remains of the royal line."

"Then perhaps it is time to discuss the difficult subject of ending the Cassian line," Yahri said gently.

Desfan rose in one fluid motion. "You speak treason."

The woman also stood, swaying a little as she gripped her

cane. "No. I speak of an opportunity. You do not want the crown. We could find a graceful way for you to walk another path. You could assign an heir. And when your father passes—"

"Get out." Desfan's chest tightened, his lungs burning as he tried to hold onto his anger. "If I could remove you from the council, I would. But I can order you from this room so *get out*."

She paled, but her fragile jaw firmed. "Desfan—"

"I am the serjah," he said, hands braced on the desk before him. "You will address me as such. This conversation is over. And I don't want you to visit my father anymore, or speak to the physician about him. You can be assured I will deliver my wishes to the physician myself, and he will report to me if you so much as walk by my father's room. Do you understand me?"

The councilwoman lifted her chin, her eyes sharp. "As you will it, Serjah." Without another word, she left. But even after the door closed behind her, Desfan knew that Yahri was not done with him.

Desfan wanted to go to the docks, find the worst sort of pub, and drink until he found a good brawl to join. Since that would only prove Yahri right, at least on some level, he asked Karim to join him in his apartment. He'd needed to escape his father's office, be in a new space before he was due in the council meeting chambers.

Karim closed the door behind them and watched with one brow raised as Desfan paced the blue and gold carpet.

"Are you going to tell me how that old woman got you so

worked up?" he finally asked.

When Desfan told him, Karim's eyes lost their humorous edge. "She *what*?"

"Abdication would be her preference, but I'll admit, she might not be above hiring an assassin." He was only partially joking.

"Did she mention anyone else?" Karim asked. "Was she alone in the request, or do others on the council feel this way?"

"She didn't say, but I wouldn't be surprised if she has allies. None of them are loyal to me." Well, Jamal seemed agreeable. He was also the youngest on the council, though, and he didn't hold much—if any—sway over the others.

"What she said to you is serious," Karim said.

"I know." Desfan shoved a hand through his dark curls, pushing them off his heated brow. A light breeze drifted through the open windows, carrying the scent of the sea into his room. It calmed him a little. "She didn't actually threaten me. I can't label her a criminal for expressing her opinion."

"It was seditious. That's enough to see her thrown off the council."

Desfan didn't disagree, but his hands were tied. "As long as my father breathes, he is the serjan. Since he instated Yahri, I can't remove her. Not unless she is guilty of committing an actual crime."

Karim growled low in his throat. "I still think this should count as a crime. She's dangerous, Des."

"Yes. But if I imprison her, how does that make me look? Paranoid. Weak. And as you said, if more people agree with her, it won't do any good—it could silence them to the point where they *do* hire an assassin, rather than approach me as she did, and I need to know my enemies."

"Even if you know which ones oppose you, what then? As you said, you didn't instate them, so you can't remove them."

Desfan considered this, and a wonderful, reckless idea occurred to him. "Yes, but if they *did* commit a crime, then they would lose their office."

Karim's eyes narrowed. "I don't like that look you have."

The corner of Desfan's mouth curved. "I just have to make them angry enough that they reveal themselves—either as Yahri did tonight, or better yet, through action."

"Like hiring an assassin to kill you in your sleep?"

"That would be perfect, actually, if I can get proof of the hire."

Karim shook his head. "You're insane."

"Not insane enough to give up the throne. Besides, I've always liked a challenge."

"Do you hear what you're saying? You want to incite the council until they either demand you step down, or they try to kill you."

"At least I'll know who is loyal to me."

Karim folded his arms over his chest, his dark brows lowering over his sharp gaze. "What exactly are you planning to do?"

"Oh, I've got a few ideas . . ."

Karim grit his teeth. Desfan could see his friend warring with something, some internal battle. Finally, his mouth opened. "Did you read Kiv Arcas's report?"

Desfan blinked, surprised by the unexpected question. "Yes. Why?"

"He inventoried the olcain that was recovered at the warehouse. I went and recounted this morning."

Ah. Desfan's expression relaxed into a neutral state. "Did you?"

Karim stared Desfan down. When the silence stretched, he stalked around him and started opening drawers in his small desk.

Desfan crossed his arms and leaned a shoulder against the

nearest sandstone pillar. "Can I help you find something?" he asked mildly.

Karim ignored him, just continued pulling out drawers. He even checked the hidden compartment in the middle drawer. When the thorough search of the desk yielded nothing, he moved for the bedroom. Desfan thrust his hands into his pockets and followed at a leisurely pace. By the time he entered the room, Karim had already jerked open the top drawer of his dresser and was rummaging inside.

"You could ask me, you know."

Nothing from Karim. After another moment of searching, he grunted, slammed the top drawer closed, and jerked open the next.

Desfan sighed. "You're working yourself up for nothing."

Karim punched the drawer closed and rounded on him, his eyes narrowed. "Tell me there is no olcain in this room."

Desfan's silence was answer enough.

His hands fisted. "You promised."

"I'm not taking olcain anymore."

Karim's eyes flashed angrily. "Then why did you steal two pouches of it from the kiv's storage room?"

Desfan strode to his nightstand and slid open the top drawer. When he straightened, he had two pouches of white powder in his palm. He tossed them to Karim, who snatched them from the air.

"Both are full," Desfan said. "I haven't taken any drugs since that night."

The night he'd nearly died from taking too much. Karim had saved his life and he'd secured a promise that Desfan had not broken. Would never break.

Karim's throat bobbed and he looked up to meet Desfan's eye. "Then why steal these?"

"Someone in Duvan is expecting that olcain. We only caught some of the smugglers, and they didn't know who sold the olcain, or who bought it. But with a few well-placed questions in the city, we could find the answers to both."

There was a beat of silence. "You planned to disguise yourself, walk the streets, and sell stolen olcain?"

"If it helps, I was going to invite you."

Karim closed his eyes, his nostrils flaring as he pushed out a breath. "Do you want *everyone* in Duvan to take a stab at you? The council isn't enough, you want to incite drug masters as well?"

"I have a bad feeling about this olcain." Desfan shook his head. "It's dangerous, and the last thing I need is this flooding the streets. And I can't help but think the timing is significant."

Karim frowned. "You think this could be one of the other kingdoms trying to weaken us?"

"With my father ill and my attempts to forge peace with Devendra, Mortise is more vulnerable than ever. There is unrest in the city and protests tearing across the country. My gut tells me the olcain is a weapon wielded by an enemy who wants to see how far I can be pushed. It will drain Mortise of gold, hurt our trade with the increased security searches, and the worst part? It could be anyone in Ryden, Zennor, Devendra . . . or even Mortise."

Karim sighed. "Where do we start?" As ever, his loyalty was undisputed.

"I've asked Arcas to search for Ori, the boy who was at the warehouse during the raid. He is connected somehow—an enemy to those who ran the warehouse, clearly, so he might be willing to work with me for protection."

"You expect the kiv to find that waif? Duvan is full of orphan boys."

"True, but Ori has a tattoo. Hopefully that will help lead us to him, since he's probably affiliated with a gang."

"Wonderful," he muttered.

"Then of course there's the part of the plan where I come in."

"I hate it already."

Desfan grinned. "I have some old contacts in the drug trade . . ."

Karim grunted. "Isn't that just fates-blasted perfect."

CHAPTER 13

CLARE

CLARE SPUN AND DELIVERED A KICK TO Bennick's knee. He grunted with the impact, his leg nearly buckling, but she didn't have a moment to celebrate the good hit. His wooden knife sliced toward her and she ducked, breathing hard.

Lord and Lady Winsel's garden made a perfect training ground. The grassy area past the flower gardens was flat, with surrounding trees and bushes offering privacy. If anyone thought it odd that the princess would practice defensive training with her bodyguard, they didn't say anything.

Wilf and Venn were out of view, watching the entrance to the area. They were prepared to ward off the talkative Lady Winsel, who had rarely left Clare's side.

They had been here for two days, and Clare struggled to focus on anything other than the fact that the rebels had her brother. The frustration of not being able to do anything, and the fear that he might already be dead, made it hard to be patient or kind when Lady Winsel refused to give her a moment of privacy. She thought that might have been why Bennick had carved out time for their training. He knew what weighed on her mind, because she had told him everything.

She had decided to tell Bennick about Eliot's capture even while she'd stood in that alley in Tarvin. The rebels had ordered her to silence, but holding that note in her hands, staring at her brother's words . . . she knew it was too much to handle on her own. She didn't *need* to handle it on her own, because for the first time in years, she had people she could rely on. And working with Bennick, rather than against him, would give her an advantage when it came to saving her brother's life.

She hadn't said anything to Cardon while in Tarvin, for fear of alerting the rebels, in case they were watching her. But as soon as they returned to Lady Rendell's, Clare had searched out Bennick.

Something in her eyes must have shown him how urgent the matter was, because he had immediately asked Venn to take his place outside the tea room, where Serene and Lady Rendell were visiting. Clare wasn't really surprised when Cardon followed her. The man had been eyeing her the whole ride back to Lady Rendell's estate, his instincts clearly calling that something was wrong. Wilf, who had been standing guard with Dirk, also followed them into Lady Rendell's library. And there, Clare had pulled out Eliot's note and handed it to Bennick.

His blue eyes scanned the words, his jaw tightening. When he looked up at her, his gaze burned. "Tell me exactly what happened."

She did—without any mention of James or Serene's letter, of course. When she explained how the rebel had dragged her into the alley, Bennick's eyes flared.

"Are you all right?" he demanded.

Her chest felt tight and her eyes stung, the fear of that moment rushing back. "He didn't hurt me," she said. But she touched her aching cheek and Bennick's gaze narrowed.

He stepped closer and brushed strands of hair away, his fingertips running over the tender area. His shoulders stiffened. "He struck you?"

"Not exactly." She told him that she hadn't managed to get a good look at his face because he had held her against the wall.

Bennick's expression hardened. "What did he say?"

Clare swallowed hard, her words coming out in a rush. Bennick listened, silently passing Eliot's letter to Cardon and Wilf to look over.

When she finished, Wilf asked, "Can you confirm this is your brother's handwriting?"

She nodded.

Cardon glanced up from the page, the skin around his eyes tight. "You didn't tell me what happened because they may have been watching."

"Yes. I'm sorry."

"Fates, I'm the one who's sorry." His brow creased. "I wasn't paying enough attention."

Guilt threaded through her, but she bit her tongue. She couldn't admit that she'd intentionally slipped away.

Bennick looked to Cardon. "Where was Venn?"

"With Vera." Cardon winced. "I let him be distracted. We're both to blame."

Clare's cheeks flushed. "No, it was my fault for wandering."

"Assigning blame is useless," Wilf said, waving the letter. "This is also useless. The rebels probably killed your brother the moment he signed it."

Pain knifed through her. "I have to believe he's alive." She turned to Bennick. "Please, you have to help me find him—without raising any suspicions. The rebels can't guess that I've told you anything."

Bennick's brows lowered, his blue eyes flashing with too many emotions to name.

"Where would we even start?" Cardon asked. "They have no headquarters, at least that we know of."

"And we can't send Tarvin's city guard in search of this rebel, because we have no description," Wilf added.

"I'll write to my father," Bennick finally said. "He can start an investigation into Eliot's disappearance. It won't alert the rebels, because it would not be uncommon for the commander to be involved if a city guard member is missing."

"Eliot has a friend in the guard." Clare spread a hand over her forehead, wracking her brain. "Fates, I can't remember his name . . . But perhaps he knows something."

"I'm sure my father will question all of Eliot's acquaintances." Bennick blew out his breath. "The bit of good news is that our ploy is working. The rebels don't know Serene has been taking a different route."

"True." Wilf frowned. "Do you think any of the other maids will be targeted?"

Bennick shook his head. "No. They picked Clare because she's new." His lips pressed together. "I'll ask my father to increase the guard on Thomas and Mark."

Ice shot through her veins. "Do you think they're in danger?"

"I don't know. But I would rather be overly cautious." His eyes grew more serious. "The rebels will attempt to contact you again. You need to promise that if they manage to slip past us, you will come immediately to me—even if you feel it will put

Eliot in danger."

Her stomach twisted, but she nodded. "I promise."

Two days later, and her insides were still in knots. But as she dodged Bennick's attempt to grab her arm, she was grateful for the distraction of training, as well as the physical exertion. The chance to be alone with Bennick was an additional reward, though the longer they trained in Lady Winsel's private garden, the more she wished they could simply talk. An idea had been churning in her mind, and she had not yet had an opportunity to share it. Though, in all honesty, she didn't think Bennick would like it.

She kicked at his shin and he took the hit as he stalked toward her, the training knife held low and tight to his body, ready to stab her.

Her ribs hurt where he'd managed to land strikes throughout the training session. Thank the fates she'd managed to stab him a couple times, too. But she was clearly missing the more regular training she'd had at the castle—it had taken most of this training session for her to relax and fall back on her training.

Bennick slowly circled her, his wooden knife held at the ready. She kept her knees slightly bent as she slowly pivoted to keep him in her center vision. "I've been thinking," she said.

"About what?"

"Eliot."

The skin around Bennick's eyes tightened, though he continued to circle her. "Anything in particular?"

"I think there's a way to help him, rather than simply rely on the commander's investigation." She leaped back, evading his strike, and managed to catch his arm with the tip of her mock blade.

He eyed her. "Go on."

She swallowed, her throat suddenly dry. "Well, I've been

thinking about what you said the other day. That it's good the rebels don't know about Serene taking another path. It gave me an idea. We could set a trap for them. When they reach out, they'll clearly want me to betray the princess—and I can, without ever risking her. I can—"

"No." His voice made the word wholly final.

Her grip on the wooden knife clenched. "Serene would never be in danger. I can be the bait."

"No," he repeated.

"But—"

"Risking your life is unacceptable." Tension bracketed his mouth. "You're the decoy, Clare. Deliberately putting yourself in danger would be the same as betraying Serene—it would be treason in the king's eyes."

"It wouldn't be the same thing. Not exactly. And if we could set a trap for them, then we would have a much better chance at saving Eliot."

Bennick shifted back a step, their gazes level. "I don't know how else to say this, but no. I'm not risking your life."

Frustration rolled up her throat, making her words come out tight. "I can't just do nothing. This is my brother's *life*."

"I understand that, but I'm trying to keep you alive. *That* is my job."

"And Eliot means nothing?"

True bafflement sparked in Bennick's eyes. "I didn't say that."

"Your history is messy," she pointed out, her tone sharp.

Before Bennick had become the captain of the princess's guard, he'd been a captain in the city guard. In a horrible, drunken accident, Eliot had killed his partner, and Bennick had been responsible for deciding his punishment. He had personally flogged him, rather than sentence him to death.

Bennick drew back from Clare. "I won't deny that Eliot and I have a complicated past, but that has *nothing* to do with this."

"Are you sure?" she shot back.

"Yes," he said firmly. "Your brother might hate me for what happened—he certainly blames me—but I have no malice toward him. The only reason I refuse to use you as bait is because I'm trying to keep you alive. *That* is my priority. You will *always* be my priority. And Eliot would agree with me on this."

She didn't drop her stare, but her eyes suddenly stung. Shame for lashing out at him, fear for her brother—they swam inside her, sapping the fight out of her. "I'm sorry," she whispered, shoulders slumping.

Bennick said nothing for a short moment. Then he spoke, his voice quiet. "You're worried about your brother. I understand."

She shook her head. "It's not just that. I *have* to help him. This is my fault."

His forehead creased. "Nothing about this is your fault."

"The rebels targeted him because of me. Because of my proximity to the princess. How is that not my fault?"

He stepped forward, one hand settling on her shoulder. "Don't take this on yourself. You're not to blame."

She wanted to believe him. And maybe there was a part of her that did. But the knot remained in her stomach and she blinked back tears. "We argued. Eliot and I . . . Our last conversation was an argument. He told me it was too dangerous. He begged me to leave the castle. I couldn't, but he didn't know that. He believes I ignored him, and now . . . they *tortured* him."

Bennick squeezed her shoulder. "No matter what, Eliot loves you. He wouldn't want you to feel this guilt. And he wouldn't want you to put yourself in danger, either."

"But if we could safely lay a trap for them . . . would you consider it?"

His shoulders fell as he expelled a slow breath. "Capturing them won't necessarily save your brother."

"I know. I know he could already be dead, but . . . I can't just do nothing. Please understand."

"I do. And I promise, if there's a way to lay a trap for the rebels without endangering you, I'll consider it." His eyes sharpened. "But you have to promise not to do anything without me. We will do this together, or not at all."

She wrapped her arms around his neck, drawing him in for a tight embrace. "Thank you," she breathed against his strong chest.

His arms locked around her, his head ducked by her ear. "I have your word, then?"

"Yes."

When they finally pulled apart, she felt steadier than she had in days. "Thank you," she said again. "Not just for this, but for writing to your father. I know how hard it is to ask him for help."

The corner of Bennick's mouth lifted. "Well, when it comes to you, I think I'm capable of anything." He nodded to the wooden blade in her hand. "Let's test your offensive skills, then we'll go back to the garrote."

Clare's sore body wanted to refuse, but she ignored that and lunged. Bennick dodged the training blade, but kept striking. He did not make things easy for her, and she appreciated that. She had been in enough dangerous situations to know that an attacker would not make things easy for her. Besides, it gave her deeper satisfaction when she did manage to hit him.

They spun and twisted around each other on the grass, and Clare saw a perfect opening. She kicked out, aiming for his unguarded middle, but Bennick snatched hold of her ankle and jerked her off-balance. Her arms swung out, strangling her wooden knife as she fought the pull to topple.

Bennick still held her ankle and he smiled as she hopped on one foot to keep her balance. "You should definitely approach all attackers like this. You are utterly disarming."

She exhaled sharply, wisps of loose hair fluttering around her flushed face. "And you're utterly annoying."

His features softened as he continued to view her. "On second thought, I want to keep this image for myself."

Pleasure spread warmth through her chest. "Clearly, you're also ridiculous."

He grinned. His hold was firm, but still managed to be gentle.

She arched a brow, very much like Serene. "Are you going to let go?"

His head tipped to one side, blue eyes calculating as he studied her. "Maybe. For a price."

His flirtation sparked tingles all over her body, tightening her flushed skin. "What price?"

His fingers flexed around her ankle as he leaned in, his voice dropping. "A kiss."

She fought a shiver, even though she was flushed from training. She dropped her own voice, though it came out a little too thready—she had yet to catch her breath from their sparring, and the way he looked at her wasn't helping. "You do realize if you want a kiss, you'll *have* to release me."

"Hmm. But I don't think I should just let you go. You're looking rather unsteady on your, well, *foot*."

Before she could toss a retort, he shifted his hold on her ankle and slowly, measuredly, sank to his haunches before her.

Her breath caught. Her pulse pounded fast as she locked eyes with him. His neck was craned back, his intense gaze never leaving her face as he gently shifted her captive foot to the ground. "I wouldn't want you to fall," he said, his voice deeper than before.

A shiver danced up her spine when he eased back to his feet, his hands trailing up her body as he rose. Her skirt rippled from his gliding touch and she could feel the heat of his fingers through the layers of cloth.

Her chest rose sharply as his hands rounded her hips and hesitated at her waist, his thumbs pressing low against her stomach. "I will *never* let you fall," he promised softly, before leaning in to press his mouth against hers.

She kissed him, her skin flushed and her heart racing. Her palms were against his chest, her fingers curling into his loose white shirt, dragging him impossibly closer.

One of his hands lifted, callused fingertips brushing her cheek. Her hair was done in a braided crown, though loose tendrils of dark hair had escaped and now curled against her jaw. He thumbed her smooth skin, cradling her head as he changed the angle of their kiss. His touch was a careful exploration, a caressing gentleness that threatened to melt her.

When they finally pulled back for air, their breaths were coming quickly, their gazes holding. With his full lips slightly swollen and color high in his sun-bronzed cheeks, he was beautiful. Her heart squeezed, her smile unstoppable.

"Fates, you're beautiful," he whispered, his voice uncharacteristically hoarse.

"I was thinking the same of you."

He huffed, affection and amusement locked in the sound. "I'm *beautiful*? Not fiercely handsome?" One hand curled around the back of her neck and his forehead pressed against hers. The ball of his thumb slid up and down the side of her neck, his other hand still warming her waist. "Clare—"

"Princess!" Lady Winsel called out, her voice winding from around the trees. "Princess, I have news!"

Clare froze, but only for an instant. She jerked back the same moment Bennick did. She stooped to grab the wooden dagger that had fallen into the grass. She couldn't hear much of anything beyond the pounding of her heart as she squared off before Bennick, both of them flushed as Lady Winsel, Venn, and Wilf came around the screen of trees.

"Oh, there you are!" Lady Winsel called out. While she was beaming, Wilf and Venn looked decidedly tense.

Clare straightened alongside Bennick, her instincts screaming. "Is something wrong?" she asked, striving for Serene's controlled tone.

Lady Winsel shook her head. "Not at all! I just wanted you to know that a delivery has come for you."

Clare shot a look at Bennick, whose expression had hardened. "Delivery?"

"Yes, my parlor is overrun with it all. Jewelry, dresses, flowers, and—"

"Flowers?" Bennick cut in sharply, his body tensing. "What kind of flowers?"

Lady Winsel blinked. "Well, all sorts. Daisies, lilies, roses— wait, where are you going?"

Bennick stalked past the woman and Clare scrambled to follow. Bennick spoke rapidly. "Wilf, take the princess to her room. Venn, you're with me."

Clare's stomach knotted. Flowers. Could it be a message from the Rose? She hurried to follow Bennick, Wilf striding along beside her. Lady Winsel blustered behind them, asking what was wrong.

Bennick and Venn moved quickly through the gardens so by the time she, Wilf, and Lady Winsel reached the manor, Bennick and Venn were already at the end of the long main hall, Bennick's hand wrapping around the handle for the parlor door.

Clare ignored the staircase on her left and marched after them. Wilf grumbled, but didn't attempt to stop her as he shadowed her steps.

They entered the sitting room together, where boxes of gifts littered the space along with endless collections of bright flowers. But the most surprising sight was a young woman, probably Clare's same age, standing in the midst of it all. She was beautiful, with dark brown skin and even darker eyes. Her hair was black and piled atop her head in an elaborate bun, elongating her round face. She was rather short with high cheekbones and a pert nose. Her traveling dress was a deep emerald and covered in dust, but that didn't detract from her easy elegance. Her slightly pointed chin was lifted and a grin split her face when her eyes latched onto Clare. She threw out her arms and cried, "Surprise!"

Clare could only stare. While fondness resided in the girl's eyes, she was a stranger to Clare. Obviously, the woman thought she was Serene.

Bennick stood near Clare's side, still gripping the door handle, but slowly the tension in his shoulders released. "Princess Imara. What an unexpected honor."

Princess Imara Buhari winked. "Sorry if I caused you any distress, Captain Markam. I know bodyguards don't appreciate surprises."

"Not generally," Bennick agreed. He glanced back at Clare, though his eyes immediately bounced behind her. He lifted his chin. "Lady Winsel, perhaps you could order some tea and refreshments for the princesses."

Clare was still staring at Serene's cousin, trying to calm her racing heart. There was no threat. At least not at the moment. Now she needed to remember everything she had been taught about Imara. The princess was the third daughter of King Zaire, and it was known she was one of Serene's closest friends.

Fates, Serene probably would have embraced her by now.

But then, maybe Serene would be just as shocked to find her cousin standing here without any warning whatsoever.

Imara rolled her eyes. "You're cross with me, aren't you?" She did not wait for an answer, merely set her hands on her hips. "I know you didn't want me to come, but how could I stay away when you needed me?"

Bennick spoke before Clare had to stumble out some kind of reply. "Princess Imara, where are your guards?"

"Oh, they're getting the rest of the gifts." She gestured to the flowers and riches surrounding her. "These are from the Zennorian court, signs of congratulations on your impending matrimony."

Wilf took up a position in the hallway and Bennick closed the door.

Imara frowned. "Is something wrong?"

Bennick sighed. "Your guards cannot know."

"Cannot know what?" Imara looked to Clare. "What is he talking about?"

Clare shot Bennick a look and he sighed. "She'll figure it out," he said. "Better to tell her now."

"Tell me what?" Imara demanded. She was small, but her tone was uncompromising.

Clare exhaled slowly. "I'm not Serene."

Imara blinked. Then her eyes narrowed and she studied Clare thoroughly. "Who are you?"

"Clare Ellington."

"I see. A pleasure, I'm sure." She turned to Bennick. "Markam, what by all the blasted fates have you done with my cousin?"

"It's a long story," Bennick said.

Imara eyed Clare. "Clearly, you're a decoy. A very remarkable one, I might add. The resemblance is uncanny. Have things truly become so dangerous?"

"Yes, unfortunately." Bennick's arms folded over his chest. "Imara, what are you doing here?"

Her delicate face smoothed, the picture of innocence. "My father sent me. He wished me to be with my dearest cousin and to express Zennor's enthusiasm with the coming peace between Devendra and Mortise."

"Somehow, I don't quite believe your presence here is official," Bennick drawled.

Clare gaped at him. Could he really challenge a foreign princess like that?

But Imara merely chuckled. "Oh Markam, I've missed you. You're such fun." She angled toward Venn. "And how are you, Grannard?"

He dipped into a smooth bow. "Quite well, Your Highness."

"Good. I—"

"Imara," Bennick cut in. "You can't be here."

She glanced around the space. "Actually, I find that I can." At Bennick's pointed look, she rolled her eyes and moved for a small beaded bag sitting on the settee. She opened the flap and dug around inside. "I do have an official letter from my father, as well as an invitation signed and sealed by my uncle."

"You don't need to bother fetching them," Bennick said. "I'm aware you somehow managed to get your hands on Newlan's seal years ago."

Imara glanced up from her bag and winked at Clare's gaping expression. "We all need our diversions," the princess said.

Bennick snorted and glanced at Clare. "Princess Imara is perhaps the most talented forger in all Eyrinthia."

The princess's eyes twinkled. "Markam, you do know how to flatter a woman." She tugged free two letters and fanned them out with a flick of her dark fingers. "Are you sure you don't want to look? They took hours."

Bennick ignored the proffered letters. "I assume Newlan has no idea you're here. Does your father know?"

"He knows it was my greatest desire," Imara answered promptly.

Venn coughed rather suspiciously, the crinkles around his eyes betraying his amusement.

"That's not the same as knowing you're here," Bennick said. "Let alone granting his permission."

"I have his signature right here," Imara said, waving the sealed letters. "It's not my fault you won't take a look."

"Princess, it truly is more dangerous than you know."

"Clearly." Imara tucked the letters back in her bag. "Who in this house knows about Clare?"

Bennick sighed. "Only the royal bodyguards and maids."

She nodded approvingly. "And where is my cousin?"

"She is taking an alternate route with Cardon, Dirk, and a few other guards. Our paths will intersect rarely."

"Then I *must* stay a while. I haven't come all this way to leave without seeing her." Imara turned to Clare. "I'm sure the tea will be here soon, and I'd love to learn all about you. I have a feeling we'll be friends."

"Imara." Bennick's tone grew harder. "You cannot accompany us."

She waved a hand at him. "I have my own guards. You won't be put to additional trouble."

"There is a great deal of unrest in Devendra, and Serene has been targeted. You will be in danger. I don't think Serene would want you to take this risk."

"Well," she quipped with a smile. "I'll just have to stay until she can tell me otherwise."

Venn leaned toward Clare, his voice low. "I don't even know what to say right now. There's already enough humor in this."

Clare swallowed a chuckle.

"Does anyone in Zennor even know you're here?" Bennick asked Imara, exasperation coloring his tone.

She picked at a thread near her narrow waist. "Well, I'm assuming by now my father found my note. So, yes."

Bennick's eyes narrowed. "And what about your betrothed? Does he know you're here?"

Imara shrugged one shoulder. "I would assume my father has informed Skyer."

He scrubbed a hand over his eyes. "Princess . . ."

"You won't get in trouble for this," Imara assured him. "That's why I have the letters. They will cover you from all blame. But you cannot make me go back. I will support Serene by going to Duvan. That fact is unchangeable."

Bennick seemed to reach the same conclusion. His shoulders lowered and the room filled with silence.

Clare was the first to finally move. She stepped forward and dropped into a short curtsy. "It is a pleasure to meet you, Princess Imara."

The young woman grinned. "Please, just Imara. And no need for courtly niceties. We are *cousins* after all." She reached out a hand, which Clare took with an answering smile.

Venn elbowed Bennick's ribs. "Just wait until Imara teaches her forgery."

Bennick muttered a curse.

CHAPTER 14

CLARE

THE CONCERT HALL ECHOED WITH THE final swell of music
from the stage, the strings and flutes twined together and supported by a rolling drum in the last crescendo of the evening.
Applause rang out, Clare clapping along with the rest of the audience. She shared a private box with Princess Imara and Lord
and Lady Winsel.

The evening had been exciting for Clare, as she had never attended a concert before. The performance had been beautiful
and exhilarating, and during the intermission she had enjoyed
the fact that the gathered nobles were eager to speak with Imara.
The Zennorian princess was an excellent conversationalist and
had a natural ability to make those around her feel important.
After only one day around the princess, Clare was already beginning to see her as a friend.

On the floor below, the audience filtered their way to the exit, talking and laughing as they went, with many stealing glances at the box the visiting royals occupied.

Bennick and Venn stood guard at the back of the box, along with two of Imara's bodyguards. Wilf had gone to help bring the carriage to the front of the concert hall. Until it was in place, Bennick had asked them to remain in their seats.

"Did you enjoy the performance?" Lady Winsel asked, perched on the edge of her cushioned chair.

"Oh, yes," Clare said. "The musicians were very talented."

"Agreed." Imara glanced to the stage, where the large velvet curtain had just swished closed. "I love comparing the differences between Devendra and Zennor, especially when it comes to the arts."

"What differences might those be?" Lady Winsel asked, her tone politely curious.

"Usually in a performance like this, there would be an accompanying narration between the pieces. It helps bring the songs together with a story."

Lord Winsel—who Clare had only heard speak a handful of times—glanced up from his book. "That sounds like the better way to do it. It's easy to grow bored when it's just the music."

His wife shot him a look. "I'm sure you jest, my dear." Her fan fluttered, teasing her hair. "The music tells its own story, if you'll only listen."

Clare looked at Imara. "Do you have a favorite symphony?"

"I have several favorites. But if I had to choose . . ." She nodded once. "The Widow's Braid."

Lady Winsel's fan stuttered in her hand. "If I might be so bold, that sounds quite depressing."

"Oh, it is," Imara said. "*Tragically* depressing. And yet, beautifully romantic."

Lord Winsel lowered his book. "Forgive my ignorance, but is the widow's braid still practiced in Zennor?"

"Yes, it is. I'm surprised you know the custom, my lord."

"When I was a child, I spent a couple years in Kedaah, as the son of an ambassador."

"Oh, how wonderful!" Imara smiled.

"It was," he said. "I've always thought it beneficial for people to live in other kingdoms. One can learn a great deal about themselves and others by simply walking roads they would have never otherwise traveled."

"A lovely sentiment," the Zennorian princess said.

Lady Winsel frowned, clearly not appreciating the fact that she'd been left out of the conversation. "What is a widow's braid?"

Clare had been wondering that as well. She had studied about Zennor, and even had Zennorian ancestry through her maternal grandparents, but she was unfamiliar with the term.

"It's a tradition," Imara said. "And like all traditions, it began with a story."

"Perhaps you could tell it," Lord Winsel said, actually closing his book. "It has been many years since I've heard it, and we have the time."

"Well, I'm not exactly a performer, but I suppose I can try." Imara cleared her throat, her voice taking on a richer tone, clearly enjoying her attentive audience. "Long before the Zennorian monarchy was organized, Zennor's borders belonged to a nomadic people. The clans were ruled by the strongest warriors. One warrior was well-known among all the clans. His name was Jaymet. He had a beloved wife, Helenera, and when news came that she was with child, Jaymet returned from his latest war campaign to be with her. The unborn child's time was half-fulfilled when a rival clan made a surprise attack on their main encampment.

"Jaymet and his warriors fought as fiercely as panthers, but they knew the rival clan would soon overpower them because most of Jaymet's men were still away on their campaign. When he realized defeat was imminent, Jaymet ordered men to guard the retreat of the women and children. They used their bodies as shields to allow their precious ones to escape into the jungle. Jaymet learned Helenera lingered, urging other women to precede her to safety. He left the front lines to personally guard her retreat, but when he took her arm, an enemy warrior jumped out of the foliage. Helenera could do nothing but watch as her brave husband was struck from behind—felled in one surprise blow. Helenera fell to the ground with her husband and held him as he died. Her heart broke in that moment."

Clare's heart clenched, feeling pain for Helenera—even if it was just a story.

"Fates," Lady Winsel breathed.

"She would have been killed as well," Imara said, "but the enemy warrior was slain by one of Jaymet's most loyal men, and he continued to guard Helenera as she mourned her lost husband. Helenera and Jaymet were so respected, there is no doubt the valiant warrior would have guarded her and the clan chief's body until every drop of blood was wrung from him, but Helenera was not unaware of the danger. To save her unborn child and the selfless warrior, she rose from Jaymet's body. She continued to weep as she braided her hair, binding it so she could run with ease. She left her beloved where he lay and fled with the warrior into the trees.

"The brave warrior and Helenera found refuge with a neighboring clan, and that is where—months later—the child was born. He was given his father's name: Jaymet. Helenera treasured her son. And even though her husband's death weighed on her, their child was not raised on revenge and despair, but honor and hope.

Helenera braided her hair every day in memory of her lost husband, until one day—when her son was nearly two years old—the warrior who had saved her life asked if she would become his wife.

"Helenera was troubled at first, for how could she forget Jaymet and marry another? She went into the woods to ponder the warrior's offer, and it is said she spoke with the spirit of her husband. Regardless of whatever spirits did or did not appear, her peace became complete. She unbraided her hair before making one small, tight braid behind her right ear. She cut it off and held the small braid in her hands. Three gathered strands made up the braid—one for love, one for honor, one for memory. Helenera dried her face, buried the braid, and returned to the valiant warrior who had claimed her heart."

Clare's lips pressed into a smile, her throat constricting with emotion. Serene would have no doubt heard this before, so she said nothing, but the story was undeniably moving.

"That's a beautiful ending to the story," Lady Winsel said, her eyes shining.

"It is," Imara agreed. "But there's never a definite end to a story, only a pause before the next development. You see, the brave warrior became their clan leader, and he had a unique vision—that the violence between the clans might be stopped. He set out to unite the clans into one strong kingdom. His name was Zennor."

Lady Winsel blinked. "He was Zennor's first king?"

"No. Unfortunately, Zennor didn't live long enough to see the completion of his dream. But his son, Jaymet, did. When he managed to unite the clans in peace, he called the kingdom *Zennor*, to honor the man who had loved him and his mother.

"To this day, widows in Zennor follow Helenera's example. When a husband is lost, all the widow's hair is braided. After the funeral, the large braid is traded for a thin braid that trails from behind the right ear. Some choose different positions, and some even dye it so it stands out more, but when a woman has decided to open her heart again, she cuts the braid and returns it —if possible—to the grave of her husband. Some women wear the widow's braid until the end of their days, while others may cut it sooner. The tradition leaves the healing period up to the woman."

Clare stared at Imara, but she was no longer seeing the princess. The memory of combing Serene's hair mere days ago rushed through her. She had found a thin, tight braid hidden in her long dark hair, and Serene had stiffened at the discovery. Vera had quickly given Clare another task, and the moment— while odd—had faded from Clare's thoughts.

Until now.

But it couldn't be a widow's braid. Serene had never been married.

And yet, the more Clare thought on it, the more certain she became, even if it didn't fully make sense.

Serene had a widow's braid.

Her mind reeled. Why would the princess wear one? Had a man she loved actually died? Of course, there were many types of loss.

She thought of James, the mysterious man Serene had written to. She had wondered if their connection went deeper than friendship, and now, considering the widow's braid . . .

What if Serene wore the braid not for a man who had died, but for one she could not have—because she was betrothed to another?

Lord Winsel's deep voice pulled Clare from her thoughts. "How is the unrest in Zennor? I've heard that tensions with the dissenting clans run high these days."

"Unrest is a strong word." Imara's tone was carefully diplomatic. "There have always been disagreements between the clans and the monarchy, but my father continues to honor their independence."

"And of course your marriage to one of the clan leaders will help settle things," Lord Winsel said.

Imara smiled, though the corners were tight. "Indeed."

Lady Winsel beamed, the glow of the candles highlighting her sharp cheekbones. "Two royal weddings in such proximity. What an exciting time for Eyrinthia!"

Wilf returned, letting them know the carriage was ready. They all filed out, Imara's arm linked through Clare's. The Zennorian princess leaned in as they walked the corridor, her voice low. "You do a remarkable job, you know."

The compliment caught her by surprise. "Thank you."

"No, thank *you*." Imara's brow furrowed, her voice still a low whisper. "I'm grateful for the risks you take for my cousin. You're very brave."

"Most of the time I don't feel brave."

"And yet you continue to protect her. That is true bravery."

They descended a carpeted staircase and entered the lobby, which still housed clusters of nobles huddled together after the performance. Clare was grateful Bennick and the other guards were there to keep them moving across the marble floor and through the tall double doors.

The silver moon hung low in the sky, and several torches spaced along the front of the concert hall spilled light onto the waiting carriage. At their approach, the footman opened the door and bowed low.

Clare was lifting her slippered foot to the carriage step when Bennick's arm snaked around her waist and jerked her back from the open door.

Her heart pounded. "What is it?"

Tension radiated from Bennick as he continued to hold her. "Wilf," he snapped.

The large man slipped past them and ducked his head into the shadowed carriage.

Bennick lowered Clare to the ground, but he didn't let go of her.

Venn darted forward with a lantern, holding it high so the light could spill over Wilf's tall shoulders.

Venn's curse sent a chill down Clare's spine.

Finally, the large guard straightened, his face grim as he met Bennick's gaze. "We'll want another carriage."

Clare twisted in Bennick's grasp and managed to see past Wilf. With the light in Venn's hand shredding the shadows, Clare could finally see the interior of the carriage.

Her stomach dropped and her knees went weak.

Crimson rose petals were strewn on the floor and bench seats, and there—in the center of the floor—was a man's severed head, a rose stuck in his gaping mouth.

Lady Winsel screamed.

"He was one of the ushers," Venn said quietly. "He showed us to the box."

Clare's gut churned. Sitting on the settee in her room, she tried to keep her expression calm. Bennick had already asked her if she would like to go to bed, and she knew if he saw her terror, he would end this discussion immediately.

But she needed to know everything.

Lord and Lady Winsel had retired. Imara had also disappeared into her room, leaving Clare in the sitting room of her suite with Bennick, Venn, and Wilf.

The Rose had left another note, but this one was different than the last. This time, it was a poem.

Settle the petals around your bed,

Let dreams of me dance through your head.

Your soldiers can't save you, try as they might;

I'll steal your breath as I steal your life.

I'll touch you and taste you and smell

your perfume—

I've already picked out a rose for you.

The horrible rhyme raised every hair on her body. But it was the second note that truly terrified her.

It had been wrapped around a small stoppered vial, no bigger than her smallest finger, and filled with a red-tinted liquid. The message on the tightly curled note was short.

For you, Markam.

In case the fear becomes too much.

Wilf held the vial now, and he was frowning at the liquid. "I don't know what this is, but I doubt it's good."

Bennick glanced up from the poem, which he had been reading yet again. "It's Raebris, I think."

Clare eyed Bennick, her insides knotting. "Why would the Rose send you poison?"

Bennick didn't look up this time. "I don't know."

"I think he's insane," Venn muttered.

"Possibly," Bennick said, his tone mild.

Clare stared at him. "How can you be so calm? An assassin sent you a vial of poison."

"I'm really not worried about the poison."

"But he threatened you."

"No," Bennick's eyes found hers. "He taunted me. There's a difference."

"Clare has a point." Venn crossed his arms, his dark brow furrowed. "It's strange that he singled you out. It breaks his pattern. Or you're a target now, too."

One of Bennick's eyebrows lifted. "You think whoever hired the Rose to kill Serene also paid for my death?"

Venn shrugged. "The Rose isn't known for taunting anyone but his victims. And you said it yourself, that gift of poison was a taunt."

Bennick's brow furrowed. "Why in all of Eyrinthia would anyone pay to have me killed?"

"It doesn't have to be personal," Venn said. "It's no secret you're the captain of the princess's guard. Your name would be easy enough to learn, and threatening you adds tension to all of us."

"Or it *could* be personal," Wilf countered. "Either for the Rose, or the one who hired him."

"I don't have any enemies," Bennick said. "Not like this."

Wilf grunted. "That you know of."

Bennick shook his head. "This is all just speculation. I'm more concerned with how the Rose managed to behead a man and arrange everything in the carriage without the driver, footmen, or guards noticing."

"They stepped away," Venn said. "Just for a few moments."

"Which only proves how closely the Rose was watching them," Wilf said. "The fact he also killed the usher who assisted us also proves he was inside the concert hall."

Bennick's eyes narrowed. "I don't like how he keeps blending in."

"He could be dressed as a servant," Clare said, drawing their attention. "It would be an easy enough disguise, and none of the nobles would look twice at him. The other servants would be too busy to question the extra hand." Servants were practically invisible. She knew this from experience, even though as a maid she'd rarely left the castle kitchen.

"Good point," Venn said.

"He could also be dressed as a guard," Wilf pointed out. "Or a noble. Frankly, he could be one of the shadows on the wall, for all we've been able to detect him."

Bennick gathered up the Rose's messages. "I'll send these to the commander for review, and I want to question the driver and footmen again. They never should have left the carriage unattended." He turned to Clare. "Get some sleep. We have a long day of travel ahead of us."

But even though she was exhausted, she did not sleep. Because long after she was in bed, she imagined she could smell roses in the dark.

CHAPTER 15
MIA

MIA SAT AT THE TABLE, ONE HAND PLUNGED into her thick hair, the other lying flat on the book spread open before her. She was trying to practice her Devendran because it was her worst language and she needed any distraction she could get.

Grayson had been gone three days, and even breathing hurt. She'd been without him before, but not like this. Traveling to Mortise would take a month at least, and the length of his stay in Duvan was undetermined. It would be months—very possibly an entire year—before she saw him again.

There were things she should have told him. Things she had tried to say, but couldn't. She'd physically locked up, her throat constricting as sweat broke out over her body. Her heart had hammered, fear and shame keeping her silent until it was too late.

Her breathing hitched and she forced herself to focus on her breaths. To draw them out. To relax her body so her heart stopped racing and her lungs didn't ache.

Devon, the physician who had tended her for years, had told her she needed to keep calm. That breathing slowly and deeply would help keep the panics at bay. That, and she needed to avoid stressful thoughts.

Which was why she was trying to focus on the Devendran poetry.

Grayson had given her many books over the years. Pilfered them from the library, mostly, though some he had purchased during his travels throughout Ryden. He knew she loved to learn, so many of the books were about life in the other kingdoms. This particular volume had been thrown into a pile by Queen Iris when she'd visited the library once. She'd called the poetry wasteful, and the servants had thrown it into a box with other books the queen had deemed useless. The queen had become bored with her tirade and the box had been carried out with the other castle waste.

Grayson, at thirteen years old, had saved every book he could carry and Mia had them—and others—stacked under her bed. Books also lined the shelves on the walls and more were stacked in the corners of the room. Books and art—these were her escapes.

And Grayson, of course.

She wondered, not for the first time, what Grayson was *really* doing in Mortise, because he certainly wasn't on a mission of peace. Henri never would have sent him for such a reason, which left her with all sorts of horrible ideas. She worried about what he would do to others—and what those actions would do to him.

Sometimes all Mia felt was fear, which she hated.

Fearful little thing.

That was the first thing King Henri had ever said to her, when she was seven years old and hauled into the throne room. It had been late at night, but he'd seemed fully awake. And when he'd grinned at her, she had never felt so frightened in her entire life.

Which was saying something, because she had tasted horrible fear before coming to Ryden. Fear, pain, anger, denial, and grief.

That little girl in that ragged dress had wanted nothing more than to scream at the king, *I'm not afraid!*

But she had not screamed. She hadn't said anything, because she *was* afraid.

She was still afraid.

She was a coward.

Some days, she convinced herself she wasn't. That living through such horrors somehow excused her from being measured the same way others were.

But there was no denying her cowardice. If she was brave, she would have told Grayson the truth a long time ago.

She slapped the book closed, set her forehead against the leather cover, and groaned.

Grayson had once told her that he envied the way she sang. With confidence, uncaring if others heard. But what he didn't know was that she only sang so bravely when Mama and Papa were gone.

Fearful little thing.

Fates, she missed Grayson. She missed how strong she felt when he was here. She missed the security that came from knowing he was close, even if he wasn't with her. And she missed the training sessions they'd shared. After Tyrell had attacked her, she craved Grayson's lessons more than ever.

She had nightmares of that night. The belt. Tyrell's dark eyes. Being bound to the foot of the bed . . .

But those weren't her only nightmares, and they were not

the worst.

She saw the faces of her family, sightless eyes staring at her with accusation and horror. She saw the faces of the men who had taken her away from everything she had ever known.

She had started to see Grayson's death.

She pushed back from the table and rose, snatching up the slim volume of poetry as she crossed the room to her bed. She knelt on the hard stone floor and flipped up the quilt that hung nearly to the floor, revealing the stacks of books underneath.

Before she could replace the book, a sound froze her.

Voices in the corridor, just outside her door.

Mia's stomach twisted and she shot a look over her shoulder.

The voices on the other side of the door were muffled. One belonged to Fletcher, but the other . . . It wasn't Mama; the voice was too deep, and she had gone into the city for the day. And it was too early for Papa to be back from his duties in the lower dungeon.

Her breaths ran shallow as she strained to hear through the door. There was a pause in the conversation. Or perhaps it was the end of it. Just a brief visit from another guard come to see Fletcher, perhaps?

That theory was shattered by the metallic slide of a key going into the lock.

Mia lurched to her feet, still clutching the book of poetry in one hand. She barely resisted the urge to reach for the pebble that rested just under the collar of her blue dress. But when the door swung open and she saw who stood in the frame, she was glad she hadn't grabbed for the comfort of the necklace.

She needed her hand free to fight.

Tyrell stood in the corridor, taller than she remembered. And wider. His shoulders were so broad they nearly took up the whole doorway. His hair was the same dark shade as Grayson's, but similarities between them ended there. Tyrell's expression was cool and his features were sharp—cruel. A red cut sliced over his cheek, standing out starkly against his pale skin.

That had not been there the last time she'd seen him.

When his brown eyes focused on her, she locked her knees so she wouldn't tremble.

Over his shoulder, Mia saw Fletcher. He was pale as he darted a look to her that said, *I'm sorry.*

Mia tried to give him a thin smile, something to assure him, but her lips were pressed into a tight line that could not relax.

Her heart pounded painfully against her ribs.

This was like last time. So horribly like last time.

Except Grayson wasn't in the castle. He wouldn't be coming to save her.

Tyrell stepped into the cell, his eyes coasting over the space. He kicked the door shut with the heel of his dark boot and the slam echoed through Mia's bones, making her flinch.

Relax, Grayson's voice rang in her mind. *You need to keep loose so you can move quickly. Don't let yourself get pinned. Go for the eyes.*

She hadn't managed to gouge Tyrell's eyes last time, but her nails had caught his skin. She doubted the small cuts were still there, though. He'd hurt her far more than she'd hurt him.

Her arms and back throbbed in memory.

"Hello," he said.

His voice was deep and the book in her hand shook. But she managed to keep her expression hard, and she was proud of herself for that.

He wandered over to the table, rapping his knuckles lightly against the wooden top as he eyed the shelf in the corner. He scanned the carefully labeled jars of food stores, not paying her any attention.

Mia's body tightened and she shifted slowly, keeping him in

her sights as she eased back a step.

His eyes cut to her, and she froze. He lifted his chin. "You're probably wondering why I'm here."

Her throat was too dry to speak. She merely watched him, her pulse roaring in her ears. Every instinct screamed at her to run, but there was nowhere to go.

Tyrell leaned against the side of the table as he faced her. "My father has ordered me to visit you."

Considering King Henri's last ordered visit had ended with Tyrell beating Mia with a belt, this revelation didn't bring any level of comfort. Terror flooded her body.

Tyrell must have seen something in her eyes, because his eyebrows lowered. "I'm not here to hurt you. Those aren't my orders."

If Mia felt any relief from his words, it barely registered. She gripped the book in front of her like a shield—or a weapon, if he came toward her.

The prince gripped the table's edge with both hands, his posture still managing to look lazy as he reclined against it. "Trust me when I say I would rather be anywhere else. But with Grayson gone, my father worried about your lack of company. So, for as long as Grayson is in Mortise, I have been ordered to visit you."

"No." The word popped out of her, a quiet denial.

Tyrell cocked his head, and the action felt predatory. "*No?*"

She swallowed, her teeth aching as she ground them.

The corner of his mouth curled up. "Lost your tongue?"

Mia's grip on the book of poetry was vice-like. She could feel her knuckles creak as they protested the pressure. "I don't want you here."

"That doesn't matter." He eyed her. "If you want to blame someone for this, blame Grayson."

Shock roared through her. "Wh-what do you mean?"

"He tried to make a fool of our father. Threatened him. Demanded your safety from me and all others." Tyrell crossed his arms over his chest, shaking his dark head. "The king doesn't respond well to threats. So, he's ordered me to visit you twice a week for an hour each time. That's Grayson's punishment, not that he'll learn of it until he returns. There is no negotiation on your part. The king will be watching, and I will not disappoint him."

Mia stared at Tyrell, her thoughts spinning so quickly she felt dizzy. Grayson had *threatened* the *king*? What had he been thinking?

But she knew the answer already. Like always, he would have been thinking of her.

She was relieved he didn't know the consequence of his actions. The knowledge that Tyrell was going to visit her would have tortured him.

It was torturing her.

Had she truly been dreading the emptiness of the weeks ahead? Now she had something to dread even more.

Her lungs tightened, but she forced herself to breathe deeply. She would not have a panic attack. Not now. Not in front of Tyrell.

He was once again studying the cell. "Fates. It's horrible in here. No window. It feels like the walls are closing in. You'd think you'd be grateful for my company."

It took every bit of strength she had to keep her voice from shaking. "I would rather be alone in here for an eternity than spend a moment with you."

A thin smile ghosted around his mouth. "That's a considerable amount of loathing."

"Did you expect anything less? After what you've done to

me—to Grayson?"

His eyes flicked to the mostly faded bruise on her face, and she could not stop herself from taking a step back.

The skin around his eyes tightened. "The last time I was here I was following orders. As I will do now. So." He edged out a smile. "How should we pass the time, Mia?"

CHAPTER 16

DESFAN

"You did *what?*"

Seeing Serai Yahri's shock, Desfan's grin was effortless. "Well, I mentioned a week ago that I was working on a love letter to Serene. I decided a gift was in order, and I thought reforming our system for the care of orphaned children would appeal to Serene. She has, as I'm sure you all know, paid particular attention to such charities in Devendra."

And Desfan couldn't stop thinking about that boy, Ori. If Mortise cared better for the waifs in their cities, perhaps Ori would not have been beaten or mixed up in street gangs dealing in olcain.

Besides, if he was going to rile up the council, he might as well do some good at the same time.

The sunlight filtering through the tall council room windows caught in Yahri's silver hair and highlighted the wrinkles on her face, making her look even older as she stared at him. She could not seem to find her voice.

Ser Zephan did not have that problem. "Withdrawing such a large sum from the royal treasury demands discussion." His dark beard did nothing to hide the color rising in his face. "Beyond that, this level of reform should have been voted upon."

"I do apologize if I've caused offense," Desfan said, setting a hand over his heart. "Causing distress was never my intention. But I was under the impression that I am the regent, and that I alone act in the stead of my father."

"The serjan would not have disregarded our protocols. You have blatantly offended everything this council stands for!" Zephan moved to rise, but Yahri snapped at him and he remained seated. He closed his mouth and glared at Desfan.

He wasn't the only one glaring, either. And Serai Essa just looked . . . appalled.

It seemed his plan to upset the council was working. He could almost feel Karim's stiffness as his friend stood behind the throne.

Clearly, Serai Yahri was taking the lead on the council's response, as was her right as the senior member. Her thin jaw was hard as she addressed him. "Serjah, while I'm sure I'm not alone in admiring your noble sentiment to help the orphans, Ser Zephan is right that such a major endeavor should have been carefully debated within this space. It should not have been decided without discussion on the details of the reform and the sustainability of such a new course. And it certainly should not have been all thrown into a letter and sent to another kingdom without this council's knowledge. Your promise to Serene to reform the orphanages in Mortise will now be seen not as a gift, but as part of the negotiations, and we must now be responsible for seeing that everything goes according to the plan you outlined.

Surely you can see the less than ideal situation you have placed us in."

Ser Jamal, the youngest and newest on the council, cleared his throat. "I think this makes a good betrothal gift. It shows that we have looked to Devendra and found something they do well, and now we want to emulate their system. It shows good faith."

Zephan turned his glare on the youngest council member.

Desfan tipped his head. "Thank you, Ser Jamal."

Ashear, who was generally more mild-mannered, frowned. "While I think Jamal may have a point, Yahri and Zephan are both correct that this should have been discussed with us. Could you not send a rider to reclaim the message, Serjah?"

"I'm afraid not. I sent it days ago. I forgot to mention it until now."

Essa sighed and shook her dark head. "Then it is done. We must discuss the best way to salvage this."

"Let us go over your plan for continued funding," Yahri said, her sharp eyes on Desfan. "I'm sure you have a plan, Serjah."

The words were a challenge, and Desfan had to smile. "Always."

"Your stupid plan with the council just might work," Karim muttered as they strode down the crowded streets of the lower city. Walking this close to the harbor with the darkness of night growing around them, shadowy figures crept out to roam the streets. Law-abiding citizens would be hard to find at this hour.

"Thank you."

Karim rolled his eyes. "It wasn't exactly a compliment, Des. You might just get a knife in your back."

Desfan and Karim were both dressed in the plainclothes they'd used for years while at sea. Desfan was more comfortable in them than any of the fine kurtas or tunics he wore these days. It was just the two of them, as it had been the last few nights they'd ventured out. Karim didn't like it, but he kept his complaints mostly to himself. Probably because he worried Desfan would go without him if he kept insisting on more guards. Desfan had opted to leave his dual blades at home, as they tended to draw more attention. He had a dagger and a curved sword buckled to his sides.

Karim shook his head as they went around a cart of silks that had stopped in the middle of the street. "Zephan has always been against you, but Essa and Ashear have seemed generally supportive—until today. You offended everyone, except for maybe Jamal, and that could have also been a weak attempt of his to get on your good side, thinking it might advance his political career." He shook his head. "If you're not careful, you're going to *make* enemies in your attempt to flush them out."

"It will be worth it if I can learn who I can trust."

Karim grunted, accepting this.

Desfan stole a look at his friend. "Any luck with finding the boy, Ori?"

"No, not yet."

Too bad. Desfan had a feeling the boy from the warehouse would be able to shed light on the seller—or the buyer. He'd clearly been viewed as an enemy by the people at the warehouse, which made Desfan wonder if some kind of double-cross had happened at some time.

Karim changed the subject. "Who are we trying tonight?"

"A man who goes by the name Fang. He used to sell all manner of drugs from his cousin's tavern, The Red Cobra."

Karim leveled a look at him. "Just how many drug masters do you know?"

Desfan smiled a bit grimly. "Enough. When I was younger, I had to change dealers often. Not all of them were willing to sell to me, once the royal guard managed to track me down. I'd have to find someone new each time that happened. Same for tattoos, in case you were curious."

"I wasn't," Karim replied easily, even as he scratched his bicep. Because his shirt was sleeveless, Desfan could see the small, knotted tattoo on his brown skin. It was an exact copy of one Desfan had, an ancient symbol of Eyrinthia that every sailor knew—*My life, tied to yours.* It used to be a superstitious symbol, a way for sailors to bind themselves to the sea—as if marrying her would somehow tame such a fierce and dangerous mistress. But time had changed the meaning until it became more widely known as a show of fealty, or the sign of a life-debt. They had gotten them when Desfan was fifteen and Karim sixteen, because even though they had been forced together, they had forged an unbreakable friendship.

As far as Desfan knew, it was the only tattoo Karim had. Well . . .

"Did you ever tattoo Razan's name over your heart?"

Karim stumbled, his head whipping toward Desfan. "What kind of fates-blasted question is that?"

He shrugged. "You really liked her."

Karim's jaw worked. "She lied and nearly got us killed."

"So, things were complicated. But you liked her."

"I did. Then I hated her, and now I'm indifferent."

Desfan eyed Karim's curled fists. "You don't look indifferent."

"Well, I am." He scowled. "What is the point of this conversation?"

He slipped his hands into his pockets. "I guess I'm curious. I haven't seen you pay attention to anyone since Razan, and that was years ago."

"I need a woman like I need a knife in my back."

"That's a rather intense response."

Karim rolled his eyes. "This conversation is over."

"Is it really?"

"Yes."

"You're grumpy tonight."

"I'm always grumpy."

"Thus your need for a woman."

Karim punched his shoulder and Desfan laughed as he stumbled.

Karim's mouth twitched, and they walked in a short silence until he asked, "What about you?"

Desfan glanced over at him. "What about me?"

"Is there anyone you have an interest in?"

He snorted lightly. "It wouldn't matter if there was. Princess Serene will be my wife. That's the end of it."

"Really?"

"Yes." Desfan's hands fisted in his pockets. "I keep thinking about the night Yahri brought up abdication. How I felt. There was no doubt—no temptation. Fates know I'm not ready to rule anything, and even though I sometimes want to run away from all of this . . . I refuse to leave." He looked through the shadows at his friend, who watched him closely. "My father began arrangements for my betrothal to Serene, and I will see it through. I will be the serjah Mortise needs."

He had done a lot of things over the years. Things his father detested, things his mother would have hated. Maybe, in part, that's why he had done them. But of all the things he had done, he knew he could not turn his back on his parents, and that is what he would be doing if he gave up the crown.

They reached The Red Cobra and ducked inside. Desfan tugged the lightweight hood of his vest lower over his brow, further shadowing his face. Karim fell into step behind him as they weaved their way through the crowd. Laughter, pipe music, and the thump of tankards hitting the stained tables filled the tavern's large room.

Fang wasn't there. At least not yet. So Desfan steered Karim to the bar and they ordered drinks. Then they joined a game of dice. Finally, after about an hour, Fang appeared in the doorway. He had two bodyguards, and they cut through the crowd and went straight for a table in the back corner of the room.

Desfan dumped the yellowed dice from his cup and they clattered over the table. Spectators hooted at the roll, but he didn't look—he was focused on Fang, who sat at his corner table with a mug gripped between his hands.

Karim scooped up the winnings and shoved the coins into Desfan's hands. From the corner of his mouth, he said, "He doesn't look happy."

No, Fang did not. The man's eyes were narrowed, his lips curved into a snarl as he nursed his ale.

"Perhaps we should reconsider approaching him," Karim murmured, taking the cup of dice passed to him.

"No," Desfan whispered. "He could be upset from the loss of the olcain. He could be exactly who we need."

Karim threw his dice. "Fine. We finish this round."

Desfan nodded and the game of dice continued. He kept sneaking glances at Fang. The man was probably in his fifties, his dark skin leathery from too much sun. His guards sat with him, one of them talking rapidly into Fang's heavily pierced ear.

Of all the drug masters they'd approached thus far, Fang

was the first Desfan worried would see through his disguise. His voice lower than before, he said, "You take the lead."

Karim's chin dipped in silent agreement.

They both lost coins this round, and no one thought twice of them leaving the game; there were always others eager to join in the game of chance.

Karim led the way to Fang's table, cool confidence in every step. They were nearly there when one of Fang's guards rose and put a hand on Karim's chest. Desfan took the role of guard and put his hand on his belted knife.

"Easy," Karim said, his voice softer than usual. "I only want a moment with Fang."

"Not tonight," the guard barked. "Get out."

Karim lowered his voice. "I'm not a buyer. I've got something he'll want. Trust me."

Desfan didn't see the knife the guard pressed warningly against Karim's stomach, but he saw Karim tense. "Get. Out."

Desfan stepped closer, but before he could do anything, Karim lifted a hand, palm up. "Rev? The package, please."

It was Desfan's cover name, and he forced himself to listen. But even as he drew the packet of olcain from his pocket, he was eyeing the exit. He shouldn't have dragged Karim into this.

Karim took the offered pouch and held it between two long fingers. "Fang will want to see this."

The second guard had risen, and he plucked the pouch from Karim's grip.

Activity in the tavern continued, no one seeing—or more likely not caring about—the tense group in the back. The guard checked inside the draw-string pouch and his eyes widened. He handed the bag to Fang, who took it carefully, eyeing the powder inside. Without looking up, he flicked his ringed fingers, the red and green gems twinkling in the lamplight.

Karim was shoved into the seat across from Fang and Desfan took up a position behind him. No one bothered taking their weapons—clearly, Fang wasn't worried about his advantage.

He probably had the fealty of half the men in the tavern—or at least held their debts, which bought a certain level of loyalty.

Fang tugged the strings of the bag, closing it. "Who are you?" he asked. His voice was low, nearly lost in the commotion of the room.

Karim fell easily into the role Desfan had been playing the last few nights. "Vek. I'm a man with a dream, and I think with my olcain and your connections, we could make it happen."

"Do you have more of this?"

"Yes."

"How much?"

"Enough to make a worthy profit. You won't find purer powder in all of Mortise."

Fang lowered the pouch to the table. "I'll need to see it all."

"In good time."

Fang's gaze turned lethal. "Where did you get it?"

"That doesn't matter. I've got it. Lots of it."

Fang leaned in. "You will tell me where you got it, or you'll wake up gutted on the street."

Karim's throat bobbed. "One could argue I wouldn't wake up from that."

Fang's eyes narrowed. "I've already got another throat to slit tonight. Yours will be no issue for me. Now, tell me where you got this."

Karim shifted in his chair. It looked like uneasiness, but Desfan assumed it was a way to work free one of his hidden knives. Desfan forced his body to relax, to be prepared for the inevitable fight.

"I may have lifted it," Karim said.

Fang glanced at one of his guards. "Why don't you tell them what we heard?"

The guard eyed them. "There was a raid on a warehouse, maybe ten days ago. Many things were taken. Including olcain, packaged just like this."

"Oh." Karim blinked. "I see."

"Good." Fang smiled a little, and it was the most unpleasant thing Desfan had probably ever seen. "Tell me where the rest of it is."

"Well, that's the trick of it. I have another partner, and he hid it—"

A knife slammed into the table, a breath away from Karim's fingers. It was a testament to Karim's control that he did not even twitch. "Enough lies," Fang snarled. "That olcain was seized by the serjah himself. So, you are not the quick-finger you'd have me believe. You're a soldier. City guard, I assume. You're trying to sniff out who it belongs to." Fang bared that horrible smile once more. "Too bad you'll never live to tell your kiv about this conversation."

Fang lifted a single finger and half the tavern rose, weapons drawn.

The pipe music stopped. Several men and women darted for the door, fleeing to the streets.

Desfan eased closer to the table and lifted the edge of his hood so Fang could see his face.

It took a moment for the drug master to see the truth, but it was clear the moment he did. His eyes widened.

"Call them off," Desfan murmured.

For a horrible moment, nothing happened. Then Fang lifted his hand and the room settled back to normal; the games re-started, the music began again.

"Serjah," Fang muttered, an edge to his low tone. "What a

displeasure to see you again. It's been a few years."

"Indeed."

Karim stood and Desfan took the seat. He flashed a smile at the drug master. "How is your daughter?"

Fang growled low in his throat. "If not for her pleas, I would have killed you that night."

"The arrival of the royal guard may have also played a part in you backing off."

Fang bared his teeth in a grim smile. "Oh, perhaps they helped save you in that moment. But I'm lithe as a serpent. I could have reached you easily enough in the palace."

Desfan tipped his head. "So we understand one another."

Fang eyed the door. "I assume your men are outside."

"Yes."

"And you know that I can kill you later if I like."

"Yes."

"Then, yes, we understand each other."

"Perfect." Desfan leaned in. "You have all but admitted that the olcain belongs to you."

"Those words did not leave my mouth. And it was my guard who shared the rumor about a warehouse. Rumors cannot always be believed."

"You're right, of course. But I heard a rumor that the olcain belongs to you. Who were you selling it to?"

"You must think me a fool."

"No, I just think you like your head where it's at."

Fang chuckled, the sound cold. "You have grown, but you haven't changed."

"Who was the buyer?"

"I wouldn't know; I'm not involved in this."

Desfan settled against the back of his chair. "Give me something and I'll keep your name out of this. For your daughter's sake."

"Mention her again, and I'll filet you."

"Noted. A name, Fang."

He pondered this a moment, glancing again at the doorway. "I don't know anything but rumors, you understand? But word is, someone in the palace promised protection for the safe delivery of the olcain."

"Who?"

"Don't know any names. But it must be someone with some kind of power or influence. They said they would make sure nothing went wrong. It may have been one of the nobles in residence, a kiv in the guard, or even someone from the council."

"And this someone paid you for the olcain?"

"That's not how the rumor went. My understanding is that someone in the palace would get a cut of profits as long as things went smoothly with the delivery. Which it didn't. Now, I don't own the powder, and I don't know who does. But rumor has it, whoever the palace contact is, he's a dead man."

Desfan considered this. "So even though you won't admit it, you own the olcain and you're telling me that someone at the palace promised safe delivery. Who is the buyer? Or were you going to distribute it yourself?"

His eyes narrowed. "For the last time, it's not mine. Now, there are rumors that I may have agreed for a cut of some powder in exchange for lending the use of a distant relation's warehouse for temporary storage, but that's clearly false. My bet? The seller is from Zennor. It's the buyer I would focus on."

"Do you know anything about the ship it came in on?" From Arcas's report, it wasn't a registered ship. Probably stolen, and a dead end.

"Rumor has it the ship belongs to Rahim Nassar," Fang said, clearly feeling no loyalty.

Desfan frowned. "That name is familiar."

"Should be," Fang snorted. "The Nassars have been merchants in Duvan for generations, and smugglers for even longer. They're good, though. Nothing is ever proven. Their profits are never *too* good. But word is, Nassar has run drugs out of Zennor before."

"Olcain?"

He shrugged. "Don't know. Could be."

"I'll be sure to pay him a visit. What do you know of the buyer?"

"Nothing. But rumor has it Zadir is involved."

Syed Zadir was more legend than man at this point, and though Desfan had spent time at sea chasing the infamous pirate, he'd never gotten close to catching him. He was almost a ghost.

Zadir's involvement in this olcain mess could be real, but it was also possible Fang was just using his name to send Desfan on a worthless chase. Frankly, Fang himself might be the buyer—unless he *was* just taking a small cut for the use of his relation's warehouse.

Regardless, Desfan was out of time. Much longer, and the men Fang had no doubt silently signaled to search the perimeter of the tavern would report back that there were no royal guards stationed outside.

At which point Desfan and Karim would both be slaughtered.

Desfan pushed up from his chair, nodding to the pouch. "Keep it. As a thank you."

"You are a very interesting serjah."

"Thank you."

"I'm not sure that was a compliment," Karim muttered.

Fang chuckled, a hard edge in the sound. "Indeed."

Desfan stepped away from the table and Karim was right beside him.

They were nearly to the door when two men stepped in front of it, blocking the way.

"A question for you," Fang called out, still seated at his table, admiring the rings on his left hand. "How many men do you have outside?"

Desfan twisted to face the drug master, trusting Karim to guard his back. "Enough."

The corner of Fang's mouth twitched up. "A serjah's ransom is surely enough to see me into a comfortable retirement."

Who would pay it? Desfan nearly shot back. Serai Yahri would probably receive the notice, and since she wanted him off the throne anyway, it wouldn't be insane to think she'd ignore it.

Once again, everything in the tavern stopped as men rose from the tables and drew weapons.

Karim sighed. "Des? Someday I'll kill you."

Desfan eyed the men closing in on all sides and snorted. "I think you'll have to get in line."

CHAPTER 17

DESFAN

THE AIR AROUND DESFAN'S FACE WAS HOT in the burlap sack that had been thrown over his head. He was sitting on a dirt floor, his arms secured around a wooden post at his back. His shoulders strained after being in the painful position for what had to have been close to an hour, and the rope around his wrists chafed his skin as he carefully sawed the rope against the sharp corner of the wooden beam.

"You know," he said conversationally. "We could view tonight as a success. At least we know Fang is involved."

"You're lucky Fang decided to ransom you, rather than slit your throat," Karim snapped somewhere across from him, his voice muffled by the bag over his own head.

"Quiet," their guard ordered. It sounded like the criminal was several paces away, angled toward them. Desfan had heard him alternately drink and sharpen a blade—and bark at them to keep quiet or stop moving.

Desfan pushed back against the post, trying to ease the ache in his arms and back. His breathing was loud in his ears, every exhale trapped in the bag around his head. "Do you think Fang has already sent the ransom note?" he asked.

No response—from Karim, or the guard.

"He's probably waiting," Desfan mused. "He'll want to make sure everything is carefully arranged." Ransoms were risky to carry out, especially with royalty involved. Of course, that was assuming anyone at the palace valued him enough to pay for his release.

He could only imagine how that council meeting would go. If Yahri even bothered to put it to a vote.

Silence reigned in the warehouse, and Desfan sighed. "Karim, are you asleep?"

"If you must know," Karim said, his deep voice flat, "I'm counting all the times you've nearly gotten us killed."

He snorted softly. "That will be a large number."

"It is. And I'm not nearly done."

"Stop talking," the guard said, sounding almost bored.

Desfan flexed his hands, grimacing as the rope cut into his skin. "When we get out of this, we can look into Nassar and Zadir, and obviously we can arrest Fang."

"*If* we get out of this," Karim clipped, "Fang is going to flee the country with his gold and you'll never see him again."

Desfan opened his mouth, but before he could speak, a low groan rose from somewhere nearby.

Desfan tensed. Fang had mentioned he had a throat to slit tonight. Was this other prisoner the one he'd meant? "Hello?" he called out.

"I said be quiet," their guard rumbled.

Footsteps approached, and one of Fang's men spoke to their guard, speaking too low for Desfan to make out any of the words.

Wood creaked as their guard presumably stood from a chair or crate. "I'm not going far," the man told them, warning in his tone. "You'll still be in my sights, so don't try anything."

Two sets of footsteps drifted away, and Desfan turned his head in the opposite direction, the sounds of groaning and strained breathing reaching him. "Hello?" he tried again. A prisoner of Fang's might know something about the olcain.

The shallow breathing hitched. "H-hello?"

The voice was pained and young. Desfan frowned. "Ori?"

A pause, then, "How do you know my name? Are you from the crew?"

The last part was spoken with a hint of hope.

He hated to dash it, but he told the truth. "No. I'm Serjah Desfan. I saved your life during a raid. Do you remember?"

A longer pause. "I threw a knife at you." He sounded a little terrified.

"You aren't the first to do that," Desfan quickly assured him.

Karim grunted. "Won't be the last, either."

Desfan ignored that. "Ori, are you tied up?"

"Yes. To a post."

"Are you hurt?"

". . . A little."

Disgust for Fang doubled in an instant. He grit his teeth. "Ori, I need to know everything you know about the olcain and Fang. All of it."

Silence.

Desfan eased his head back against the post behind him, the burlap sack itching his face. "Ori, I want to help you. We're both prisoners right now, but I swear I can help you once we get out of this. Just tell me what you know."

The silence stretched.

Desfan sighed. "I know you're part of a gang. That tattoo on your wrist? It's a mark of your membership. Can you tell me about them?"

Nothing.

"Are you—"

Glass shattered on the far side of the warehouse. Men roared, and blades rasped from their sheaths and then clashed, ringing sharply in the cavernous room.

Desfan swore and shoved to his feet, his back and arms scraping up the wooden post. He dropped his head, shaking until the bag fell—thank the fates it hadn't been tied around his neck. He blinked as light from a nearby lamp pierced his eyes, and he struggled to focus on Karim.

His bodyguard had also pushed to his feet and dislodged the burlap sack, but he had made it a step further—he was slamming a booted heel against a nearby crate, attempting to break a piece off.

Desfan did the same, cursing the fact that his hands were tied behind him; it made everything more awkward. Finally, a piece of the crate snapped off. Desfan toed it closer, then twisted his body around the post so his back was to Karim. He dropped to a crouch, ignoring the burn as the wooden post scraped his spine. His bound hands snatched the broken piece of the crate, his fingers blindly finding the small nail buried in the wood. He concentrated his efforts with the nail on the weakened part of the rope, which was frayed due to the last hour of careful sawing. The nail was small but sharp, the metal tearing into the worn rope.

His thighs began to burn from his squatted position, and sweat slicked his fingers and forehead. The sounds of fighting continued unbroken, but a wall of crates blocked his view. It wouldn't be a rescue; guards would have announced themselves by now, called out for him or at least ordered Fang's men to surrender. No, the attackers were probably enemies of Fang's, and Desfan didn't want to stick around long enough to become their prisoner.

The rope snapped. His arms were nothing more than dead weights as they swung forward, the sudden lack of tension pitching Desfan forward. He managed to keep from landing flat on his face and pivoted in time to see Karim climb to his feet, his arms swinging uselessly at his sides, his eyes darkly focused. "Go. I'll get Ori."

"No." Desfan darted in the direction Ori's voice had come from, quickly rounding a mountain of crates. He winced as sensation rushed back through his deadened arms, but he tried to ignore that as he wiggled his fingers, willing all feeling to come back.

Ori was tied to a post, just as they had been. Unlike them, no sack covered his face, and it was clear he had been beaten. The young boy's face was a swollen, bloody, and bruised mess. Fury ripped through Desfan. No one should hurt a child. *Ever.*

He dropped behind Ori, tearing at the knots that bound him. He hadn't bothered to bring the small nail—his fingers had learned a wide variety of knots during his time at sea.

While Desfan freed Ori, Karim searched for a weapon. Throwing crates aside, he finally found an iron bar. It was used for prying open crates, but it would work in a fight. He gave it an experimental swing, but it was clear from the sagging arc and the grimace on his face that his arms were still recovering from being bound.

The rope loosened and Ori's arms fell uselessly to the ground. He hissed in pain, one eye swollen shut as he eyed Desfan. "Are you arresting me because I tried to kill you?"

"No, I'm saving you." Desfan hauled the boy to his feet, but Ori's legs buckled.

Fates, how long had he been bound?

Desfan grit his teeth and threw the boy over his shoulder; he didn't trust his still-tingling arms to carry the waif.

Karim led the way as they bolted away from the fight. There was always a back door, they just had to find it. Then maybe they could find a city guard patrol, and get reinforcements back here before the fight was over. Desfan would love to arrest all of them.

Regardless, getting to safety was the priority. And questioning Ori, once the boy was seen by a physician. Whether or not the boy helped him, Desfan was determined to get Ori into a safer life. He was only nine or ten years old. He deserved so much better than this.

They rounded a tower of crates, and there was the back door.

Karim rushed for it, Desfan right behind him with Ori still slumped over his shoulder. Karim yanked open the door and drew up short.

Several armed men stood outside, blocking the way with their curved swords.

Desfan froze. Karim's shoulders tensed.

One of the men grinned, a menacing edge to it. "Drop the boy."

Desfan eased Ori to the ground, keeping a protective and supporting arm around him. "Let him go. He has nothing to do with this."

"That's where you're wrong," the man said, his gaze drifting to Ori. "He's the reason we're here."

Karim's grip on the iron bar shifted. "You touch him, I kill you."

"Oh, I don't think the dramatics are necessary," a new voice said. The wall of men parted to reveal a man in his forties. He was large without being overweight, and he had a black beard and black eyes. A sword hung at his side and his hands were braced on his hips. Desfan had never seen him before, but he knew him at once—even if the drawings had failed to capture the full height and breadth of him.

Pirate captain Syed Zadir smiled. "Serjah Desfan Cassian. What an unexpected pleasure."

Ori glanced up at Desfan, the corner of his swollen mouth lifting a bit smugly. "I don't belong to a gang, Serjah. I'm part of a crew."

Desfan and Karim were tied up again, though this time their hands were bound in front of them. His shoulders appreciated the change. They were also in a different warehouse, locked in one of the small offices, sitting across from Syed Zadir. A wall of men stood behind him, arms crossed and eyes narrowed.

"Well," Zadir said, eyes sparking with amusement as he studied Desfan. "This night has taken an interesting turn."

"Is Ori all right?" Desfan asked.

"He's being cared for now, and he will be fully avenged." Zadir's head tipped to the side, a man evaluating a puzzle. "Your concern for him is touching."

"I didn't realize the infamous Syed Zadir recruited such young boys to fight his battles."

"I don't." Zadir leaned back in his chair. "I have boys in every port. They keep an ear out, let me know what's going on. I reward them with gold and protection, and the possibility of one day joining my crew. Ori was a little too ambitious and involved himself in things he shouldn't have. He thought he was doing me favors." His dark brows lowered. "He wasn't."

"What will you do with him?"

Zadir chuckled. "I'm not a murderer. A killer, yes, but only when the occasion calls for it. There is never an occasion to kill a child, so Ori is safe."

"And what about us?" Karim asked, his voice low and dangerous.

The pirate waved a hand. "I don't kill important people, either. Too many repercussions. So I'll be letting you go. First, I wanted to explain something so you don't get the wrong impression. I was only at that warehouse tonight to rescue Ori. I heard he'd stuck his neck out for me, chasing some ridiculous rumors that I'm involved in the drug trade. I'm not. It's a nasty business full of double-crossers, and it hurts more people than it helps."

That actually tracked with what Desfan knew of the pirate, but he kept that to himself. "I will get to the bottom of this," he said. "If you are involved, I'll figure it out."

Zadir snorted. "Not if you continue like you are. From what I can see, you're making a clumsy mess of your so-called investigation. Fang is still alive, angrier than ever now that he's lost all his prisoners—not to mention the olcain. Word will spread that talking to you is a bad idea. You won't learn anything else from your contacts."

Unfortunately, that was probably true.

Zadir flicked his fingers and one of his men stepped forward, drawing a dagger.

Karim snapped to his feet, ready to protect Desfan even with his hands bound.

"Relax," Zadir drawled. "He's only cutting you free."

Karim did not relax, but he held out his tied wrists. The pirate swiped the blade and the ropes fell. Karim flipped over a hand, his jaw set. "Knife."

The pirate frowned, glancing back at his captain.

Zadir's voice was amused. "I already said I don't kill important people. The serjah is safe from us."

Karim's stance didn't falter. "That dagger doesn't get any closer to him unless I'm holding it."

There was a short pause, then Zadir lifted his chin. "Give him the knife, Whistler."

The pirate passed the blade to Karim, who cut Desfan free while keeping a wary eye on the pirates.

"Will I get the knife back?" Whistler asked.

"Probably not," Zadir said, studying Karim's hard profile. "I'll replace it."

Whistler nodded his thanks.

Desfan could feel Karim's silent command for him to stand, but he remained seated, gently rubbing his wrists as he eyed Zadir. "You say you're not involved in the olcain deal, but Fang mentioned your name."

"A lie," the man said smoothly. "Ori was chasing the same rumor. He wanted to find out who was using my name, and he put his nose where it shouldn't have been and got caught." A furrow appeared between his black eyebrows. "He mentioned you saved his life during that raid, and you were clearly trying to help him tonight. Thank you."

Desfan tipped his head, acknowledging the words. "I would like to talk to Ori."

"No. The boy has no further information for you. All he learned was that Fang was storing the shipment."

It was nice to know, but that wasn't his primary reason for asking. "I want to offer the boy a job."

Zadir cocked an eyebrow. "Excuse me?"

Desfan gestured around them. "Clearly this isn't a safe place for him. I can give him a position at the palace."

"Kind of you to be concerned, but I must decline the offer on his behalf. He enjoys working for me." Zadir slapped his hands on his thighs and pushed to his feet. "Now, I think it's time for us to go our separate ways."

Desfan didn't move to stand. "I'm not ready to leave yet."

Zadir smiled wryly. "Thinking of joining my crew, Serjah?"

The pirates laughed.

Desfan smiled a little. "What do you plan to do about the lies being spread about you?"

Zadir frowned. "I don't see how that's any concern of yours."

"It doesn't concern me. But I think it should concern you."

The pirate folded his arms over his chest. "That sounds mildly threatening, Serjah."

Karim shot Desfan a hard look, which he ignored. "I think we could be allies, Zadir. I want to find out who is involved in the olcain deal, and you want to find whoever is throwing around your name. Our goals align."

"They really don't," Zadir said. "You want to make arrests. I just want to kill whoever is spreading lies about me." He nodded to the door. "Please go."

Desfan settled back in his chair. "You said it yourself, Zadir. What happened with Fang tonight will spread, and none of my contacts will talk to me. The city guard can conduct raids, inspections, and interrogations, but this requires a subtler approach. That's why I involved myself in the first place." Well, that and life at the palace had been strangling him. But Zadir didn't need to know that.

Zadir's forehead creased. "Your city guard must feel left out, with you doing their jobs."

Desfan ignored that. "I want to hire you."

The pirate shook his head. "I work better on a ship."

The corner of Desfan's mouth lifted. "So do I."

Zadir's lips twitched. He hadn't given an outright no.

Beside him, Karim was rigid. Oh, Desfan would be lectured for this later.

There was a beat of silence, then Zadir leaned forward. "I like you, Serjah. You gained quite a reputation on the sea, and I'm pleased to know the rumors are true. You're tenacious. Fair. Reckless. All things I admire." He threw a glance at his men, then focused back on Desfan. "As you said, I've got a personal interest in this mess, so I planned to look into things. I don't like people using my name for their personal gain, and I could share what I learn. For a price."

"Name it."

"Oh, I will." Zadir flashed a grin. "Give me five days, and I might have something to share. I might be at Four Winds for a drink after dinner, as long as you come alone. Do you know the place?"

"Yes." Desfan rose and clapped a hand on Karim's tense shoulder. "He'll be with me, though."

"Well, then I might see you both." Zadir pointed to the door. "Now, please go before I have to call the city guard and complain about your trespassing."

CHAPTER 18

CLARE

CLARE STOOD BEFORE THE TALL MIRROR inside her bedroom, taking in her appearance for the Paltrow's ball. She looked nothing like herself in the lilac-colored gown, the voluminous skirt so long that it brushed the floor. The sleeves were tight against her arms and silver gloves hid her hands. The neckline was square-cut and revealed her sharp collarbones. Vera had applied makeup over her freckles and her hair had been left down in large curls, falling just beneath her shoulders. A silver band—the delicate crown of a princess—encircled her head, resting high on her forehead, and matched the intricate silver needlework on the fitted bodice of the dress.

"You look beautiful."

She spun to face Bennick, who stood in the doorway. "How long have you been there?"

The corner of his mouth twitched. "Just since Vera left."

Her eyes narrowed. "That's been minutes."

"Has it really?" He stepped into the bedroom and her stomach flipped as he stopped in front of her, only a thin space between them. His voice lowered. "As beautiful as you are like this, I have to admit I prefer how you look when we spar."

Her chest swelled at the compliment, but she noted the serious edge in his eyes. "Has something happened?"

He sighed. "I received word from my father."

Her lungs tightened. "Any news of Eliot?"

"Not really." His jacket strained over his shoulder as he shoved a hand through his hair. "My father questioned everyone in Eliot's barracks. Michael Byers was said to be Eliot's best friend and was with him on patrol the night they disappeared—two days after we left Iden. There was no sign of a struggle—no sign of them at all."

"Fates," she breathed, dread slithering through her. There had been a small hope that somehow it had all been an awful trick. That Eliot would be safe at his barracks. Now, that hope was dashed. He really was a prisoner of the rebels. And as for Michael . . . He was either a prisoner as well, or dead. She had only met her brother's friend once, but she felt horrible about his fate.

"My father didn't have a lot of information on the Rose, either. Basically everything we already know—which isn't much." His shoulders stiffened. "He also let me know that my mother's health has worsened."

"Oh, Bennick, I'm so sorry." She didn't hesitate to wrap her arms around him. She knew all too well the pain of losing a parent.

He returned her embrace, tugging her body close against his chest. "I wish I could be with her. I hate that she only has him."

She brushed a quick kiss against the rough stubble of his cheek. "I wish you could be with her, too. But she knows you love her."

"I know." He eased back, his hands skimming down to rest against her waist. His thumbs pressed gently against her stomach. His head was ducked, his voice low. "I'm not like him, Clare. I will *never* be like him."

His father had betrayed Bennick's mother in the most despicable way, with many different women. Bennick had learned the truth, and Clare knew he still carried guilt over telling his mother. Her health had plummeted, and his relationship with his father was practically non-existent.

Clare cupped his jaw, gently forcing his head to lift so their eyes could meet. "I know that, Bennick. You're nothing like him."

His throat flexed as he swallowed, but before he could respond, the main suite door opened loudly and Imara's voice reached them in the bedroom. "Are you ready yet? The guests are arriving!"

Bennick and Clare broke apart, her cheeks hot as Imara stepped into the room. The Zennorian princess brushed her hands over her long white skirt, which was accented with swirling turquoise beadwork. Her dark hair was piled into an elaborate knot atop her head, which she lifted, her eyes darting between Clare and Bennick, who stood at strict attention.

A small smile teased the corner of Imara's mouth. "I'm sorry, did I interrupt something?"

"No." Clare stepped forward, linking her arm through Imara's and steering her for the door.

A knowing look crept into Imara's eyes. "I can come back later."

Even Clare's ears were burning. "No, we don't want to be

late."

"If you insist," Imara said.

Fates, they needed to be more careful.

———◆———

Flutes and violins twisted melodies together to create music just loud enough to be heard over the murmuring voices of the crowd, the swishing skirts, the tittering laughter, and the foot-steps of the couples spinning over the polished wood floor. The ballroom was brightly lit by iron chandeliers loaded with flick-ering candles spaced along the high ceiling and sconces set along the walls between the tall windows. Glasses chinked together as the nobles drank to the coming alliance. The room was warmer than Clare had anticipated and her palms were sweating in her gloves as she danced with Lord Tripp.

The nobleman was an elegant dancer with near-flawless form. Unfortunately, that was the only compliment Clare could give the man. She had made his acquaintance yesterday at a gar-den party hosted by Lord and Lady Gates, another prominent family in Lindon. His clothes were bright, his smile too even, and his blond hair perfectly combed. His favorite topic was him-self, and he had a rare ability to always bring the conversation back to him.

"The ball is quite lovely, don't you think? Of course, dancing has always been a talent of mine. One of my dance instructors said I could have a career in it, though such a thing would not be seemly. The Tripps are a family of leisure, that's something my father taught me . . ."

Clare nodded occasionally, even made a few non-committal sounds, but Lord Tripp hardly needed the encouragement to keep talking. He told her how he had designed his clothes, and his tailor wanted to hire him to make more designs, but, of course, he couldn't . . .

Her attention wandered to the room at large. There were perhaps a hundred people present, and each one was anxious to have a moment of her attention. She had quickly learned there were two types of people, and she could determine them by their questions.

The first group wanted their curiosity satisfied. *What has been your favorite stop so far? Are you excited to marry Serjah Desfan? Is it true the Rose has targeted you? How terrifying!*

The second wanted to poise themselves to get more out of the coming alliance. *Do you know the king's plan for the Mortisian trade tax? My lands have the best orchards in Devendra; do you think there's a market for apples in Mortise? We'll be attending your wedding —do you know which Mortisian merchants will be invited?*

Her answers had become rote, her smile inflexible. She supposed she should thank Lord Tripp for changing things up.

She could feel Bennick's eyes on her from the edge of the dance floor, and she knew Wilf and Venn had both taken positions near her as well. With Bennick's heightened precautions, she was never far from them. Additionally, the other palace guards and the Paltrow's guards were fully alert, placed at nearly every window around the room.

Despite the concerns of growing unrest, the Rose, and the fact that the rebels had yet to strike, the ballroom was full of merriment. Everyone was smiling and laughing, clearly enjoying themselves. Or at least pretending to.

The song ended on a swell of strings, and the crowd applauded the musicians while the couples bowed and curtsied to their partners.

Clare added a polite nod to Lord Tripp, but her eyes widened when he bowed with such a large, sweeping gesture, that included both arms. The flung limbs forced a nearby lord to take a quick step back to avoid being struck.

Lord Tripp seemed unaware of the near miss. "Princess, I am so glad we had this chance to dance." He straightened with yet another flourish and clasped his hands behind his back. "I've not been able to get your radiance out of my head since yesterday."

She smothered a chuckle and instead forced a tame smile. "You flatter me."

"Excessively, I hope." He winked. The music started up again and his smile hiked wider. "Perhaps you would care for another dance? My waltz is particularly—"

"Princess, may I steal this dance?" a new voice asked.

Clare turned, taking in the man beside her. He was dressed well, though not as excessively as Lord Tripp. He was also older. While Tripp was probably only a couple years Clare's senior, this man was probably thirty. He had brown hair that curled a little over his brow and at the nape of his neck, just brushing the collar of his jacket. His stance was relaxed and a small smile curved his lips up at the corners.

Clare spoke before Lord Tripp could. "Of course."

Lord Tripp's face was frozen into a hard expression for a split second, but then he smiled tightly at the newcomer. "But of course." He bowed with another flourish to Clare. "Until we meet again, Princess."

As Lord Tripp walked away, the other man took Clare's gloved hand and pulled her easily into his arms. "My apologies if you wanted another dance with him. I thought I saw your eyes glazing, though."

"Oh dear, was it that obvious?"

"Not to worry," he assured her, his voice deep and rich. "Anyone who has spent more than five seconds with Lord Tripp understands."

She chuckled. "Perhaps I was in need of rescuing."

His smile bent wider. "Well, I'm happy to have saved you."

"And you are . . .?"

"Lord Finch."

"Thank you for your timely intervention, Lord Finch."

"I can't take all the credit." His chin lifted in a quick gesture toward two young ladies who stood at the edge of the dance floor, watching them. "My sisters noticed the situation and sent me to your rescue."

"My thanks to you all, then."

Lord Finch's dancing was much smoother than Lord Tripp's, his hand sure on her waist, the other warming her gloved fingers. "I suppose I should offer my congratulations on your betrothal," he said. "My sisters have informed me that your love affair with Serjah Desfan is excessively romantic."

"Really?"

He nodded. "Sarah deems herself an expert, actually. She and her friends have been informing us all about Desfan's attributes, from his roguishly good looks—her words, not mine—to his many known exploits as a pirate hunter on the high seas. Apparently, you were destined by the fates to love him, and the royal wedding will be perfect."

"Well, I'm relieved to hear my future happiness is assured."

He smiled. "You're as charming as your reputation suggested."

"I hate to disappoint."

"Never fear, Princess. You don't disappoint me."

He spun her suddenly, one hand ghosting across her back as he helped her come fully around. Clare clutched his hand, feeling off-balance even though he barely let her sway.

The spin had brought her closer to him and she took a slightly longer step back than the dance required in order to maintain a proper distance. A quick look proved that Bennick was still watching her closely from the edge of the dance floor. He was frowning, his hand resting on his sheathed sword.

"Ah." Lord Finch had followed her look. "I've made your bodyguard nervous. No more spins, I suppose."

"He is quite protective."

"As he should be." His gaze lingered on Bennick, and curiosity prickled at the back of her neck.

"Do you know him?" she asked.

Lord Finch looked back at her. "I've followed his career."

"Really?"

"I suppose that's a strange thing for me to admit, isn't it?" Color touched the tips of his ears. "I used to dream of being a soldier when I was a boy. My father wouldn't allow it, but he couldn't stop me from taking an interest. I had friends who attended the military academy, and they would tell me stories about the legendary Bennick Markam. I was fascinated by his achievements. His father was every bit as legendary, and yet every success Bennick enjoyed was his alone. I admire that. Not all of us can claim such independence from our fathers. Too often, they make us who we are." He cracked a somewhat wry smile. "I apologize, that was long-winded of me."

"No need to apologize." Clare stole a glance at Bennick, warmth building in her chest. "He is very talented."

"Indeed he is." Lord Finch spun her again without warning, and Clare tightened her hold on him. The man flashed her a grin, a dimple popping into view. "Sorry, I couldn't resist. Do you think the captain will come after me?"

Clare couldn't help but laugh. "Very possibly. You're quite

daring."

"I like to think so." His head canted to the side. "I'm sure you've heard this before, but your laugh is beautiful."

He wasn't the first lord to flirt with her, but she had to admit he was more charming than most. Her lips curved into a smile. "Thank you."

"I wanted to thank you, actually. For the prisoner exchange that has been arranged with Mortise."

"Oh?" No one had thanked her for that yet.

He nodded. "One of the prisoners to be released is actually the brother of a dear friend. His whole family wept for joy when they received the letter from King Newlan."

"I'm so happy for them. It will be a joyous day."

"Indeed. I would not miss it."

"You're coming to Stills?"

"Yes, and I'm not the only one. So you'll be seeing me again, Princess. And, I'm sure, Lord Tripp. If the man were not so besotted with himself, he would be entirely entranced by you."

The song concluded and couples across the floor parted.

Lord Finch lifted her hand to his lips for a brief kiss. "Thank you for the dance. It was most enjoyable."

"Thank you again for saving me." She tipped her head toward the opposite side of the dance floor where Lord Finch's sisters stood, offering the girls a smile and a wave, which they quickly returned. "Please convey my thanks to your sisters as well."

"I will." He offered a bow, his eyes lingering on her as he stepped away. "Until our paths cross again."

Another young man moved to take his place, but Clare gently excused herself with an apologetic smile and the excuse of needing a drink.

She spotted Bennick easily, as he was standing prominently

on the edge of the crowd. He had a slight frown on his face, and his focus was beyond her as she approached. Her lips twitched, knowing who he must be watching.

When she reached him, his voice was low, nearly buried by the music. "Who was that?"

She glanced back to just see Lord Finch disappear into the other side of the crowd. "Feeling jealous?" she asked teasingly.

Bennick glanced down at her. "Would it lower your opinion of me if I said yes?"

"No. It's rather amusing, actually."

He huffed a breath. "For you, maybe." His fingers glanced over the small of her back, and to anyone who saw, it probably looked like a purely guiding gesture as he led her into the crowd of loudly chattering people that ringed the dance floor. To Clare, the brush of his fingertips meant something far more. Tingles raced through her body and she breathlessly enjoyed each second of the simple contact as they wound their way to a back corner of the room, where a table with refreshments waited.

The corner was mostly deserted, as everyone had edged closer to the dance floor, and Bennick's hand lingered a little longer than necessary before he took a measured step back.

Clare took a glass of water and sat in one of the many empty chairs, feeling the ache in her feet. She patted the seat beside her. "No one will care if you join me." No one was even looking at them—they were too absorbed in the party.

Bennick remained standing in front of her, his arms crossed over his chest. "I'd better not." His brow furrowed. "What was his name? I didn't recognize him."

She twisted the tumbler in her hands, watching as the water rippled inside. "Lord Finch. You're not really jealous, are you?"

"Watching you dance with an idiot like that Lord Tripp is one thing, but seeing you in Lord Finch's arms is different."

"Why, because he's handsome?" She fluttered her lashes.

Bennick shot her a scowl.

She laughed and took another sip of water. "You really don't need to be jealous, you know. Lord Finch might be charming, but he's not you."

His eyes narrowed. "You think he's charming?"

She rolled her eyes. "I'm only teas—"

A window across the room shattered, and cries of shock exploded throughout the ballroom.

Bennick's hand landed on Clare's shoulder, keeping her seated. "Stay down," he said, his gaze focused on the broken window.

Her heart hammered as shouts rang out.

"Rocks!"

"They're on the lawn!"

"*Who?*"

The music had stopped and musicians scrambled to their feet as another window exploded. The crowd nearest the broken windows had scrambled back, but those on the edge of the ballroom crowded closer, trying to get a look outside.

Venn shouldered through the cluster of people and cut toward them, Wilf only a few steps behind.

Venn's expression was set with tension. "People are throwing rocks at the windows, chanting for the alliance to die."

"Rebels?" Bennick asked.

"I don't think so. Doesn't seem quite bloody enough for them."

Wilf growled. "We need to subdue them before it becomes bloody."

Bennick pulled Clare to her feet. "Venn will take you to your room. You'll be more secure there. Wilf, you're with me."

Clare grabbed his arm, her stomach dropping. "You're not

going out there?"

"Someone has to talk to them."

"Why does it have to be you?"

"I'm the highest ranking officer here. And I have a feeling the Paltrow's guards will only make things worse in their effort to keep this from escalating." His eyes softened. "I'll be fine. Just stay with Venn."

She watched him stride away, Wilf at his side. The chanting outside had grown louder, and she could hear them clearly.

No alliance! No alliance!

Venn took her elbow, his voice low. "They'll be all right. Come. We should hurry."

Many of the gathered nobles seemed to be of the same opinion, and were pushing to exit the ballroom and find refuge in one of the sitting rooms across the hall. Venn led her past one woman who had fallen into a faint in the arms of her husband, who seemed just as petrified.

Clare's heart beat faster, her steps quick to keep up with Venn's longer gait. "If this isn't the rebels, then who?"

"I got a quick glimpse of them through the window. They just look like men and women from the city. Farmers. Merchants." He shot her a look. "We knew the unrest would probably grow. I just didn't expect an actual attack. With rocks."

"Will they be arrested?"

"Too many to arrest. Bennick will need to calm them and hopefully convince them to leave peacefully. The city guard can investigate the instigators later."

"What happens if they don't leave?"

A muscle in Venn's dark jaw ticked. "Let's hope they do."

Dread pooled inside her. She didn't know how many people formed that mob, but she knew it would be a terrible fight if they decided to storm the mansion. People would die.

They climbed the wide staircase to the second floor, and Venn opened her suite door. He remained in the hall, updating the two guards stationed there, while Clare entered the sitting area of her room.

Vera and Ivonne were both standing at the window, their faces nearly pressed to the glass as they tried to glimpse what was happening in the front yard below. They spun when Clare closed the door.

"What's going on?" Ivonne demanded.

She quickly explained what she knew, and the two sisters immediately turned back to the window. "Fates," Vera whispered. "They're so angry."

Clare hurried to join them, but though the mob carried torches, this room was far to the left of the courtyard, so there was not much she could make out. But the crowd was much larger than she'd imagined, and that was enough to tighten her lungs.

"Perhaps I should try addressing them," Clare said.

Ivonne shot her a look. "They would be more likely to throw a rock at you than listen to you."

Though she was probably right, Clare still felt restless. She could barely hear the roar of the crowd, sealed safely in this room, but she knew what they were screaming. She hated to picture Bennick standing in front of them, trying to calm them.

Clare turned from the window and paced away, nerves tightening the knots in her gut. On her second loop around the room, she realized the chanting was louder by the maids' room. A glance inside showed why—the small window was open.

She stepped inside, not entirely sure if her intention was to close it, or lean out and try to hear Bennick. But the moonlight spilling through the window shone on a slice of the floor. Lying at the base of the window was a white card.

The hairs on her arms lifted with sudden apprehension, but she stepped closer. When she crouched beside it, she realized it was a small sealed letter. Written in a hand she knew as well as her own, were five letters that formed one word: Clare.

She cracked the seal with shaking hands and flipped the letter open. She angled it to catch the light of the moon, and her heart stopped as she read Eliot's message.

> There will be a distraction at midnight. Get the princess into the gardens. Do this, and I will be returned to you tonight. Fail, and you will find me in a pool of blood.
> Eliot

"You're alive," Clare breathed, blinking rapidly at the sudden sheen of tears. Though she had told herself repeatedly that Eliot still had to be alive, she'd had moments of doubt. Nightmares that her brother had been murdered the moment he finished writing that first letter. And now, here was proof that he lived. More than that, if this letter was to be believed, he was close. How else could he be with her again tonight?

Her breaths were coming too quickly. She forced herself to close her eyes. To breathe. To think. But it was difficult with the mob shouting.

Her eyes snapped open.

Fates, the mob. They were the distraction.

Clare shoved to her feet, her pulse racing. She needed to tell Venn—she needed to get Bennick. They could set a trap, but they had to hurry—

No. It was already midnight. That meant the rebels were already in the back garden, waiting to strike.

Eliot could be out there right now. And if Serene didn't appear, he would be killed.

There was no time to make a plan with Bennick. No time to

argue with him—for he would argue. Putting Eliot's life above hers was not something he would ever do. But she couldn't just let her brother die.

Thoughts spinning, Clare folded the note and strode out of the room. She went right for the suite door and jerked it open.

Venn cut off speaking to the guards and turned to her. "You need to stay inside."

"I need you to get Bennick," Clare said. "Now."

His eyebrows drew tightly together. "Why?"

"Please, just trust me, Venn. I need him. Right now."

He studied her, and clearly something in her expression assured him she was serious. "Are you all right?" he asked, peeking over her shoulder. "Has something happened?"

"I can't explain. Please, get Bennick."

Venn frowned, but he nodded. "Stay here." He shot the guards a look, which was a clear order despite there being no words. He hurried away, disappearing down the stairs.

Clare turned, coming face-to-face with Vera, who had crept closer. She handed the girl the note. "I need you to promise you won't open this. Give it to Bennick the moment he arrives."

Vera's eyes widened. "Why? What is this?"

Ivonne stepped closer, her eyes narrowed. "Where will you be?"

Clare swallowed thickly. "There's no time. I need to go." She eyed the two guards. "I need you to come with me."

"Apologies, Princess, but we have orders to stay here," the older one said.

She lifted her chin, trying to exhibit every bit of Serene's confidence even though she was vibrating with terror. "I believe your orders are to guard me. So, guard me."

CHAPTER 19

CLARE

CLARE STEPPED INTO THE PALTROW'S GARDEN, the hem of
her skirt whispering over the ground. She could hear the low
roar of the mob, but it was distant. Though there was only the
mansion between them, it may have been another world. The
gravel that formed the path bit through her thin slippers and
crunched as it shifted underfoot. Her skin tingled and her eyes
kept darting to the deepest shadows, wondering which one hid
her brother—and the men determined to kill her.

She knew this was reckless, knew Bennick would be upset
with her for leaving the manor. But Eliot was here. She was incapable of turning her back on him.

Her plan was simple. Probably too simple, but there hadn't
been time to think of anything more elaborate.

The garden, which she had explored earlier today, was full

of tall hedges, overflowing flowerbeds, and winding paths. The chances of the rebels having an archer placed to kill her were slim. They would probably resort to a knife, which meant they had to get close. It should give her the briefest moment to react, and more than that, it would draw them out.

Even if Vera and Ivonne did open Eliot's note, they would not be able to get it to Bennick much sooner than Venn was able to fetch him. She had minutes only until Bennick, Venn, Wilf —and probably several guards—stormed the garden.

One of the guards she had forced from her room was standing at the garden's entrance. He would be able to tell Bennick which way Clare had gone, which would get Bennick to her even faster. The other guard walked behind Clare, and she sincerely hoped his presence would not be enough to keep the rebels from attacking. She needed them to reveal themselves before Bennick arrived—but hopefully not too long before. Then, while the fighting reigned, she could find Eliot.

Her fingers twisted in her skirts, hiding the dagger she gripped in her hand. The manor stood behind her, lights glowing from the ballroom windows. The scents of roses and lilacs swirled in the cool summer air.

There was a rustle of leaves, and then the shadowy form of a man stepped into the path three paces in front of her.

Clare froze, and the guard behind her cursed.

He didn't like her plan.

"Hello, Princess," the rebel said, a few other shadows drifting from the foliage to stand behind him. She could hear others stepping onto the path behind her, surrounding them.

Her hold on the knife tightened. "Where is Eliot Slaton?"

"So she told you, did she?" The man grinned, his teeth flashing in the moonlight. "Well, it makes no difference. We just needed to confirm it was you."

More shadows stepped onto the path. Maybe five men? And from the sound of it, there were a few more taking up positions behind the guard.

Her heart pounded. "There's no need for this."

"Oh, there's plenty of need." Derision edged his words, and fury flashed in his eyes as he stepped closer.

"Don't hurt the guard. He's done nothing."

"He supports you."

Clare took a step back, her entire body tensed. "Wait—"

He lunged, and Clare sidestepped, bringing up her knife in the same motion. Training with Bennick had made these movements instinctual, but the moment her blade sank into his belly, everything about this moment felt like a nightmare.

His gasp of pain, shot with surprise, was hot near her ear. She jerked out the blade, feeling more resistance than she'd expected. The sound was wet. Sickening. Her stomach churned as she stared at him, her jaw loose and her eyes wide, panic swelling in her chest. He grabbed his belly and fell to his knees, his breathing ragged.

There was a moment of stillness, then the shadowy rebels lurched forward. Not to help their fallen friend, but to grab her.

Clare swiped her blade at the hands that reached for her, her chest rising and falling as she struggled to breathe past her fear. The knife knocked against something—an arm?—and there was a strangled curse as one of the shadows reared back. She flinched, her grip on the bloody knife spasming. But she didn't drop it.

The sounds of the guard fighting behind her were horrible. Fists striking flesh, grunts, and the snick of daggers slashing against each other. There was no room on the path for swords.

A man slid behind her and wrapped a thick arm around her chest, pinning her upper arms down. She moved reflexively, as Bennick had prepared her for just such an attack. She stomped on his foot with her heel and dropped her weight, then twisted and kicked the side of his knee.

There was a terrible crack and he howled as he staggered back.

Another man grabbed her, hauling her close, both arms crushing over her chest and arms. She shifted her grip on her knife and stomped on his foot, but he merely grunted, his hold flexing painfully around her. "Kill her!" he rasped, his chest rising against her back. "I'll hold her!"

Clare froze. That voice . . . It was twisted with rage, but wholly familiar. She knew it as well as her own. She just couldn't believe it. Couldn't understand it.

"Eliot?" she gasped. The raw emotion drove away her practiced tone, changing it from Serene's voice to her own.

The arms around her stiffened. "Clare?"

Her pulse thudded in every part of her, too hard and too fast. Confusion flooded her. Nothing about this moment made sense. *Eliot* was the one holding her. He wasn't a prisoner.

He was one of them.

Eliot spun her, his fingers digging into her upper arms with so much pressure she winced. His gaze raked her face in the moonlight, his eyes widening as he saw past the dress, the crown, the makeup.

Beside them, the guard had been subdued—but he was alive.

"Eliot?" one of the rebels snapped. "What's wrong?"

"It's not her," he breathed, shock behind each word. "She's not the princess. She's . . . my sister." His hold on her tightened, and she grimaced as he shook her. "What are you doing?" he demanded. "What—?"

"Release her!" Bennick's hard voice cut through the night, and chaos exploded.

The rebels tore past Clare and Eliot, rushing the path to engage the soldiers. Clare tried to twist free of Eliot's grip, but he held her too tightly.

He cursed as he dragged her away from the mansion, the fight—and Bennick.

She stumbled, struggling to pull free. "Eliot, stop!"

He only hauled her forward, plunging them deeper into the maze of the garden. "We have to get out," he snapped. "*Now*. What were you thinking? Coming out here, dressed like her?"

"I was trying to save you!"

He rounded on her, his eyes blazing. "You shouldn't have risked your life for hers."

She glared, her heart slamming against her ribs. "You were never in danger. You're one of them. A rebel." Tears stung her eyes, and she blinked quickly, wishing she could see his shadowed face more clearly. She wanted to truly see him—to know this was really him.

The fracturing in her heart told her it was. "Those messages," she rasped. "The man who grabbed me in Tarvin and told me you were being tortured—it was all a lie."

He grit his teeth. "You weren't supposed to be in any danger."

Emotion clawed her throat. "You used me."

"We have to keep moving." Eliot said, his voice hard.

Her lungs were so tight she could barely breathe. "Why would you do this? Why would you become one of them?"

"Newlan killed our father," Eliot growled. "And losing him killed our mother. The royals destroyed our lives, just like they've destroyed so many others. And now they want to make an alliance with the enemy? We can't let this continue. It has to end. *They* have to end."

They rounded another hedge, the sounds of the fight drifting further away.

Eliot glanced at her, and even in the filtered moonlight she could see his hard face as it twisted. "You look just like her. Fates, you even sounded like her. This wasn't your first time pretending to be her, was it?"

Clare said nothing, only glared.

He ground his jaw. "You're a decoy. Not a maid. You've been her double all this time." His fury rippled through the darkness between them, burning her skin. "Fates rot them all. They dress you up like her, parade you around in front of everyone—and that fates-blasted Markam. He kisses you, then dangles you in front of killers? That's sick, Clare. Once I get you out of here, I'll rip his throat out."

"I'm not going anywhere with you." Clare yanked against her brother's strangling hold, but when Eliot barely slowed, she changed tactics. She made a fist with her free hand and plunged it into his gut.

Her brother grunted from the blow, obviously not expecting it, but he recovered quickly and dodged her second hit, then jerked her forward. Fire sparked in her wrist, and in the span of a pained breath, her back was pressed to his front, his arm banded around her, once more pinning her arms to her sides.

His breath was hot against her ear. "I will knock you out and carry you over my shoulder if I have to, but you're coming with me."

Gravel crunched behind them and Eliot spun to watch a shadow run up to them. It was a young man, and he looked vaguely familiar. "What are you doing?" he hissed at Eliot. "You can't bring her with us. They'll come after her!"

Eliot tensed against her back. "I'm not leaving her."

The man shoved a hand through his hair, and Clare suddenly knew him: Eliot's best friend, Michael. "Fine," he exhaled sharply. "Bring her. But we have to move. *Now*."

Clare stiffened. "I'm not going—"

Eliot's sweaty palm clamped over Clare's mouth, his fingers clenched so tightly her jaw ached. She tried to scream, but his hand smothered all sound. "I'm doing this for you," he grunted, his arm flexing more securely around her.

Michael led the way and Eliot followed, dragging Clare to the back garden gate. The half-moon cast a dim light on the open gate, and the body of a guard stretched out on the ground before it. Blood pooled under his head and around his middle.

Nausea rose inside her and she trembled in her brother's arms. Eliot may not have been the one to kill that guard, but even if he hadn't delivered the killing blow, he had been involved in his death.

Her brother truly was capable of things she had never imagined.

"Stop!"

The shout came from behind them and relief punched through Clare at Bennick's voice. She would not have been able to face his death. Especially not when his blood would have been on her hands.

Eliot and Michael whirled, Michael's sword leaving its sheath with a dull ring.

Bennick stood several paces away. His sword was lifted, every inch of him rigid as his eyes sliced over her. His eyes narrowed on Eliot. "Release her."

Eliot's arms flexed around her, keeping her secure. "Stay back, Markam."

"You've lost," Bennick said, his voice menacingly level. "Release her. *Now.*"

"You might be willing to watch her die," he sneered, "but I'm not."

Bennick's eyes narrowed. "You're the one who nearly got her

killed tonight." He shifted a step forward. "Let her go. You're hurting her."

"Stay back!" Eliot snapped, his hold clenching.

Clare sucked in a pained breath and Bennick halted, his face shifting into a snarl. "Let her go or I'll kill you."

"I'm fine!" Clare gasped. "Bennick, please, don't hurt him!"

He wasn't even looking at her. He was focused solely on her brother.

"She's coming with me," Eliot said, edging back a step. "You're going to get her killed if she stays with you."

A growl lived in Bennick's throat. "She doesn't want to go with you."

"She's not thinking clearly."

"And you are?" His glacial eyes narrowed, and even Clare shivered. "Do you really think there's anywhere you can go that I won't find you?"

Michael looked to Bennick, his sword angled protectively in front of him. "If you let us walk away, we'll leave her."

"Done," Bennick vowed, no deliberation, his sword still held at the ready.

Her brother's hold only tightened. "No."

Michael shot him a look, his voice low. "We can't win this. We need to go, before more soldiers come."

There was a horrible, frozen moment. Then her brother's hold loosened until only one arm trembled around her. "I'm sorry," he breathed.

She twisted free and looked up at his shadowed face, feeling gutted and angry and hurt as she took a step back. "So am I."

Eliot's throat bobbed, his eyes pained.

"Clare." Bennick's voice was taut behind her.

She turned away from her brother, blinking quickly to push back the tears that stung her eyes.

Bennick stepped forward, lowering his sword as he extended a hand, relief finally surfacing in his stormy gaze.

Foliage snapped and a second later, white-hot pain pierced her right side, jerking her entire body. Her hands flashed to the source of the pain—

A dagger was sticking out of her.

She sucked in a shocked breath, the agony so intense her knees buckled.

Bennick roared.

CHAPTER 20

BENNICK

BENNICK DROPPED HIS SWORD SO HE could catch Clare with both hands. His body shook as she fell against him and he crashed to his knees. He was vaguely aware of Clare's brother springing for the shadowed figure who had pushed through the cover of bushes to fling the knife at Clare.

He bit back a curse as he lowered her to the ground, his insides clenching.

Clare cried out as he moved her, her stiff body arching. He froze, but he hadn't hurt her—the bloody knife was now in her hand.

She'd ripped it out.

"No." Bennick clutched the bleeding wound with both hands. The knife had hit just above her right hip, and though he wasn't sure if it had hit anything vital, she was losing blood far too quickly now that the knife was no longer plugging the wound. His fingers were already slick with it.

Clare hissed when he increased the pressure of his hold. She dropped the small knife and clutched his wrist, her nails digging into his skin as she gasped for breath. Panic flared in her tear-filled eyes and pain twisted her beautiful face.

"You're all right," he said through gritted teeth. "You're going to be fine."

He tensed when Eliot Slaton dropped to his knees on the other side of Clare. "How bad?" her brother gasped.

"I need something to stem the blood."

Slaton tore off his jacket and Bennick snatched it from him, balling it up and pushing it against her side.

She gasped, her entire body shuddering.

Bennick's jaw locked.

Slaton breathed hard beside him, blood on his hands. Bennick assumed the rebel who had hurt Clare was no longer breathing.

"Is it lethal?" Slaton asked.

"She won't die." It was a promise, because Bennick refused to lose her. He set bloody fingers against the side of her neck. Her skin was cool, her pulse erratic.

Of course it was. She was bleeding out.

"Eliot." The man with the sword—who Bennick guessed was Michael Byers—stepped closer, urgency in his voice. "We have to go."

Bennick's concentration was fully on Clare. He didn't care if the rebels left or died. He brushed dark strands of hair from her pale face with his free hand, his heart beating as fast as hers. Her eyes would not focus and her eyelashes kept fluttering, as if keeping her eyes open was a struggle. "Stay with me," he breathed, his insides compressing. "Clare, stay with me."

"She needs a physician," Slaton said. "I'll stay with her, and you—"

Bennick's head cranked up, his eyes locking on Slaton. "I'm not leaving her with you."

His eyes narrowed. "She needs help. They'll listen to you—"

"Clare!" Vera screamed.

Venn's hand stopped her from darting forward, his sword leveled at Slaton, his eyes on Michael. "Bennick?" he asked, his voice hard.

The order rose to his tongue. It would be so easy to order their deaths, or at least their arrest. They were rebels. They had attempted to kill the princess. They had used Clare—hurt her. But as much as Bennick wanted to kill Slaton for what he'd done to his sister . . . it would hurt her. And he had made a promise to let them go.

Tension sang through every nerve, but in the end, his focus needed to be on Clare and nothing else. "They're leaving," he said to Venn.

Slaton glared. "I'm not going anywhere."

Every muscle in Bennick's body throbbed with the need to hurt the man across from him. Clare's blood soaked his hands, her dress, the ground. His voice was dark and rough. "You are seconds away from a death sentence, Slaton. Get out of my sight. Now."

Clare's breathing hitched. Bennick had not even realized she was still aware of them. "Eliot," she whispered weakly. "Please go."

Her brother's face crumpled. "Clare, I . . ." In the end, no other words came out.

Michael grabbed his arm and hauled him to his feet. He pulled Slaton away and the two men vanished through the gate.

Venn still held his sword, his body tight. "Should you really have let them go?"

A voice of warning screamed in Bennick's head, but his words came out on a whisper. "I don't know."

Venn released Vera and she dropped beside Bennick, a cry strangling in her throat as she viewed Clare.

Bennick tightened his hold on Slaton's jacket, pressing it deeply against Clare's bleeding side. He pushed vengeance, regret, denial, panic, and fear from his mind as he looked to Venn. They'd wasted too much time already. "Find the nearest physician. One was probably invited to the ball. We'll be in the library." It was the nearest room he could think of, with glass doors leading right into the garden.

Venn bolted to obey.

Vera stared at Bennick, her hand on Clare's forehead. "Should we really move her?"

"She's losing blood too quickly. If the physician has to come all the way out here, it could be too late." He jerked his chin toward Clare's side. "Hold the wound. Apply as much pressure as you can."

Vera's hands shook, but she did as Bennick said. "Will she be all right?"

"Yes."

He would *make* her all right.

Bennick scooped Clare into his arms and rose. She gasped, her body going rigid against him. His breath locked in his chest and he tried to gentle his hold. "It's all right. I've got you. You're going to be fine."

Vera moved with him, keeping Slaton's jacket pressed against Clare's side.

Clare's soft moans of pain stabbed him, but he didn't slow his pace. His goal was the manor, his focus on keeping his gait steady, his steps quick. He monitored every pained breath Clare sucked in, each strained exhale.

When he had been working to calm the mob and Venn had come to him, saying Clare needed him, anxiety had sliced through him. He'd left Wilf in charge, and had immediately followed Venn back into the mansion, his heart beating too fast. Clare would not have asked for him if the matter wasn't urgent.

When they had reached the base of the stairs and he saw Vera and Ivonne bounding down them, pale as ghosts, his fear had spiked. His hand had shaken while he read Eliot's note.

He had never run so quickly.

And the moment he had seen her standing on the path, surrounded by rebels, his fear had been all-consuming.

None of that compared to the terror he felt now. Her blood coated his hands

She was dying in his arms.

"Bennick?" Clare's voice was hoarse.

"I'm here." Her head rested against his arm, near his shoulder. Impulse had him setting a kiss against her brow, not caring what Vera thought. "I'm right here," he breathed.

She shivered. "I—I'm sorry." She suddenly slumped against him and his pulse roared in his ears. But she was still breathing. She was only unconscious.

Not dead.

His breath rattled out of him.

They hurried past the guards who were dragging the bodies of rebels into a pile. A couple of men took up positions around them, asking no questions but darting anxious looks at the woman in Bennick's arms, whom they assumed was the princess.

They climbed the stone steps that led to the library's glass doors. Two guards ran up to them, one hurrying to open the doors, the other rushing to light the nearest lamps. Bennick ordered the first guard to keep anyone from entering through the library's main door, except for the physician. As the man darted away, Bennick eased Clare onto a low settee. Her head tipped back against the cushioned bench and his hands shook as he took over Vera's job of holding the jacket in place. "Find bandages, any supplies you can think of."

Vera nodded and was gone.

The guard lighting lamps carried them closer, then stationed himself outside the glass doors, keeping watch.

Alone in the room with Clare, Bennick bent and set his lips against her cool cheek. "Stay with me," he breathed. "Please, stay with me."

Boots clipped the carpeted floor and Bennick threw a look over his shoulder. Venn and a stranger hurried to the settee. He was middle-aged, his eyes a light green and his brown hair long enough that it brushed his shoulders.

"Knife or arrow?" he asked, his voice a surprising mix of authoritative and calm.

Bennick forced his voice to work. "Knife."

The physician crouched beside Bennick and peeled back the bloody jacket. "Thrown or stabbed?"

"Thrown."

"I need bandages."

"I sent someone for supplies."

The physician tossed a look at Venn. "Hurry up the servant we sent for my bag."

Venn ran out the door.

"I need to see the wound." The physician scanned the room, then snatched a pair of embroidery scissors that were sitting on the end table. He made some cuts in the lavender dress, baring Clare's side.

In the glow of lamplight, Bennick got his first clear look at the injury. It was smaller than he had feared, and yet he knew the danger was in the depth of it. Even though seeing the cut in her flesh turned his stomach, he was relieved by the placement. If the knife had hit closer to her gut, or been thrown with more force . . . She would already be dead.

With this wound, she had a chance.

The physician quickly cut a length from Clare's skirt, balled it up, and shoved it against the still bleeding wound. "Hold this. I need more light."

Bennick obeyed at once, his fingers brushing her soft skin. She trembled. Or maybe it was just his hands that shook.

The physician gathered every oil lamp in the room and crowded them close to the settee. By the time he was done, Venn and Vera had both returned.

The physician turned to Bennick. "I need you to hold her down in case she wakes."

The mere thought made his gut churn, but he nodded and set his hands on her shoulders.

The physician worked quickly and efficiently, cleaning and then stitching the wound. Bennick ordered himself to be objective. To remember all the times he had watched his men get stitched up by a surgeon.

But this was Clare. It was different. Entirely different.

Thank the fates she remained unconscious.

When the physician finished, he sat back on his heels. There was a bead of sweat at his temple, but that was the only sign of distress he had shown in all these tense minutes. "The bleeding was severe, but the damage was not. Infection is a danger. I need to clean the area again and when she wakes she'll need something for the pain. Recovery may take a couple of weeks and I'll need to monitor her closely for fever." He looked at Bennick. "You can breathe, Captain. You haven't lost your career.

She'll be all right."

Bennick still couldn't breathe. He would never forget the terror of these moments. He also realized he was still touching Clare's arm with one hand. He couldn't seem to pull away.

The door burst open and Wilf barreled in, his face whiter than Bennick had ever seen it. The man's expression was fierce as he eyed Clare. "Is she . . .?"

"She should be fine," the physician said. "The immediate danger has passed."

Wilf's huge shoulders slumped, relief flashing over his face. He wrenched his gaze to Bennick. "Tell me the one who did this is dead."

"He's dead." If only he had been the one to kill him, maybe he would feel better.

Venn eyed Wilf. "You were supposed to wait in the hall. Didn't the guards mention that?"

"One might have tried to stop me."

"Is he still alive?"

Wilf grunted.

Princess Imara peeked into the room, her knuckles whitening on the frame as she clutched it. "She's all right?"

"Yes." The physician rose. "There are a few wounded guards. I will tend them and return soon."

Imara pursed her lips. "I should tell Lord and Lady Paltrow that Serene's all right. They're beside themselves." The princess and the physician left, both promising to check in later.

After the door closed, Wilf turned and set his hands on his hips. "What by all the blasted fates happened?"

Venn took the lead, with Vera chiming in about the note she and Ivonne had been left with.

Wilf's brows tugged together. "Foolish girl. But smart, too. Delayed reinforcements. Clever."

Bennick grit his teeth. While he was thanking the fates Clare had sent Venn for him, he could not help but want to curse her, too. She should have waited for him. She never should have gone out there.

But she was selfless, and she'd thought her brother was in danger. She thought she could save him.

Instead, Eliot had used her. Manipulated her. He had put her in danger, and she had nearly died.

Bennick knew he would never be able to forgive Eliot Slaton for that.

Bennick slumped in a chair pulled up to Clare's bed. One hand was wrapped around hers while the other braced his ducked head.

Vera slept curled in a chair in the corner of the room. Ivonne and Imara had remained for quite a while after Clare had been settled into bed, but eventually they had each left. Dawn could only be a couple hours away now.

No one had said anything about Bennick staying at her bedside. He'd only left once, briefly, while Vera and Ivonne changed Clare out of her ruined dress and into a white nightgown. He'd scrubbed his bloodstained hands until they burned from the lye soap and then he'd returned to sit beside her.

He was so closely attuned to Clare's breathing, he knew the moment she woke.

He lifted his eyes and saw her blink at the ceiling. "Clare."

Her head turned toward his soft whisper and she cringed as

her injured body stretched.

He leaned in and squeezed her fingers. "Try not to move."

Grogginess swam in her eyes as she gazed at him, the dim light from the lamp making her rounded cheeks appear even softer than usual. She swallowed. "May I have some water?"

He reached for the glass and pitcher on the nightstand. He measured out a bit of the powdered medication the physician had left, and he watched it dissolve into the water, turning it a bit cloudy. "This is for the pain," he said softly.

"What time is it?"

"I don't know. Nearly morning." He cradled her head in his palm and tilted her up gently, pressing the cup to her lips. She drank only a little and then settled back against the pillows.

He set the glass aside and placed one hand against the top of her head, fingers smoothing her hair back from her forehead. "You terrified me," he admitted in a whisper.

Clare's pale lips pressed together. "I'm sorry."

Their fingers interlocked on the quilt and Bennick let out a slow breath. "We don't need to talk about that right now." He hated that she had put herself at risk tonight, but he didn't want to lecture her. He was too fates-blasted relieved she was alive. Besides, it was clear in her eyes that she was berating herself enough.

"Did Eliot leave?" she asked.

"Yes."

Her eyes drifted closed.

Silence stretched in the shadowed room. His thumb traced slow circles on her hand.

When she spoke, her voice was thin. Pained. "I can't believe he manipulated me like that."

Bennick squeezed her fingers. He knew the pain of a loved one's betrayal, though his father's sins had never put his life at risk. "I'm sorry."

She peeled open her eyes. "How many died?"

"Three guards. Five rebels. A few escaped."

Her throat clenched as she swallowed. "Eliot figured out I'm a decoy. The others probably guessed it as well."

"There's nothing we can do about that now."

"It will complicate things, though."

"Maybe. But right now, I need you to focus on healing."

She pursed her lips. "How badly am I hurt?"

"You'll be fine, in time. The physician said the damage could have been far worse." He'd repeated that to himself the whole time he'd scrubbed Clare's blood from his shaking hands.

She released a slow breath. "We won't be leaving for Halbrook tomorrow, then."

"No. We'll be delayed by a couple of weeks."

Clare winced. "Newlan won't be pleased."

"I don't care."

She pursed her lips. "Dangerous words, Captain."

He leaned in and pressed his mouth against hers so suddenly, he was as startled by the kiss as she was. The feel of her lips, the heat of her breath—they punched through him, reassuring him that she was alive. He pulled back and leaned his forehead against her temple, eyes pinched closed. "You truly terrified me," he admitted.

"I'm sorry." Her fingers sank into his hair, keeping his head against hers.

He held her, his breathing finally normalizing. She was alive.

But she wasn't safe. She wouldn't be, so long as she was Serene's decoy.

CHAPTER 21

ELIOT

"WE HAVE TO REPORT THAT SERENE HAS a decoy," Michael said. "It changes everything."

Eliot grimaced, rubbing a hand over his aching forehead. This wasn't the first time they'd had this conversation. It had been two days since that horrible night where everything had gone wrong. He could not forget the sharp betrayal in Clare's eyes. He could still see her bleeding on the ground, practically begging for him to leave her.

With Markam.

"I'm sorry," Michael said. And, again, it wasn't the first time he'd said that.

The sounds of the small-town common room seemed louder when neither of them were speaking.

Eliot had not touched his food. He hadn't been able to eat

since that night. He and Michael had fled, stolen horses, and they'd been hiding in the woods and at roadside inns ever since. Everything had devolved into a nightmare. Their perfectly laid plan had failed. Clare hated him. She had nearly died, and Eliot had killed the man who'd thrown the knife—a fellow rebel. He hadn't known the man, but his hands still shook when he thought about it.

And the worst part of all was that Serene would never be vulnerable again, because they'd just keep using Clare like a puppet.

"She's alive," Michael said gently. "You heard the news, clear as I did. The princess's tour was delayed, but she's healing."

"Clare never should have been hurt." Eliot raked a hand through his brown hair. "Bloody fates, she shouldn't be anywhere near this mess. She shouldn't be a target for Serene's enemies. It isn't right."

"No, it's not, but there's nothing we can do to stop them from using her. So we need to report that a decoy exists."

Eliot lifted his eyes. "We could take Clare from them."

"Even if we could get past their defenses, you heard it from her own mouth—she has no desire to leave."

"I could persuade her. If I'd had more time . . ."

Michael shook his head. "She doesn't trust you now."

He clenched his teeth and stared at his untouched food. "I won't let the rebels use her again. I was a fool to go along with things as I did." He shot his friend a glare. "And you didn't have to tell her I was being tortured."

"I wanted her to feel the gravity of the situation. Your note didn't sound desperate enough."

Eliot thrust a hand through his messy hair. Guilt had been creeping in long before the disaster at the Paltrow's ball. He'd had misgivings about using Clare from the start, especially when he had crouched near an open window in Tarvin and watched as Michael had grabbed Clare and forced her up against an alley wall. He had seen the terror in his sister's eyes.

He had helped put it there.

He scrubbed his face with both hands. "I shouldn't have agreed to this."

"You wanted to see if she would choose you."

That only increased his guilt. He had agreed to do all of this for such selfish reasons. The fact that he'd been drunk when he agreed only made him feel more disgusted with himself.

He'd wanted his sister to choose him.

And she had, in a way. She had risked her life for him. And then she had rejected him, choosing to stay with Markam to be used as a target.

That hurt on nearly every level.

Michael's lips compressed. "The rebels need to be told Serene has a decoy. It's the best way to keep Clare safe."

It was an argument they'd been having for two days, but Eliot nodded now. "Yes. We need to tell them. But I don't want them to know it's my sister. They would want to use her."

Like he had already used her.

Michael leaned in, his voice serious. "I know you're upset. I don't blame you for that. But there's no going back. We are known traitors now. We can never return to Iden."

That was like a punch to his gut. He thought of his brothers, Thomas and Mark. Fates, he'd never see them again. At least not up close. He couldn't be a part of their lives.

And Clare didn't want him anywhere near her.

"We've lost everything," Michael continued. "The only way to make this sacrifice worth it is to ensure the alliance fails."

"Our position is painfully clear," Eliot said tightly. "What's your point?"

Michael's shoulders slumped. "I'm sorry. You joined the rebels because of me."

Eliot's lungs emptied in a slow breath. "Not just for you. I joined for me—for my family. For everyone Newlan has hurt." He shook his head. "You're my brother, Michael. Mortisians killed your family at the border, and after you became a soldier for Newlan, he wants to betray you—betray their memories— by allying with the enemy? No. He doesn't get to do that. He doesn't get to play with our lives anymore."

Michael nodded slowly, and Eliot took his first bite of food in days.

Several minutes later, their contact arrived.

Eliot had met John several times. He had coordinated the attack at the Paltrow's ball, and he looked harried now that things had failed. He slid into the chair next to Eliot, dispensing with all niceties. "I'm grateful you two survived. We have a new plan we'd like you to take part in."

"We have some information that might change things." Michael looked to Eliot, waiting for him to explain.

His stomach cramped, but he spoke anyway. "The princess has a decoy. That's who was there during the attack."

A scar on John's forehead nearly disappeared when his brow furrowed. "A decoy?" He cursed. "That throws off everything. How are we supposed to know if our next attack is even worth it?"

"I would know the decoy again," Eliot said, hit with sudden inspiration. "If I was close enough, I would know her. Give me a position close to the strike, and I can tell you if the kill should happen or not."

If he was close to Clare, he could protect her. And if he got close and it wasn't Clare . . . Well, he would happily slit the princess's throat. She was a traitor to Devendra, and a selfish coward for hiding behind Clare.

John eyed him. "Are you sure? You would face the brunt of the danger."

"I'm sure."

The man tipped his head. "Thank you for your offer. Let me reach out to the others. I'll be in contact soon with your next orders." His eyes narrowed. "The princess will not make it to Mortise. We'll make sure of it."

CHAPTER 22

MIA

MIA WAS READING ON HER BED WHEN Tyrell entered her cell. It was his fourth visit, and he stalked in without a word—as had become his habit.

His first visit had been a shock and, truthfully, most of it was a blur. His second visit, he had wanted to talk, and she'd spent most of the hour refusing to answer, her back pressed to the far wall. Annoyance had sparked in his eyes, and he'd finally gone silent.

He'd spent his last visit sitting at the table, sharpening some daggers while she'd pretended to read. He'd barely spoken to her, not that she'd relaxed. Her body's reaction to him wasn't something she could control. The locking up of her muscles, the freezing of her lungs—it was just something that happened the moment he stepped into her cell.

And even though she didn't back away from him like she had that first day, she was always careful to keep space between them.

The door thumped closed behind him and Tyrell strode to the table—but this time, he didn't sit. He turned to face her, his arms crossed.

The break in pattern shot a chill down her spine, but she forced herself to look up from her book.

He stood with his hands on his narrow hips, his expression smooth. "We're training today."

Her insides hollowed. "What?"

He shrugged. "Clearly, Grayson gave you some training. You fought me quite admirably the first time we met."

Her bruises may have faded by now, but Mia would always remember how he'd hurt her. She refused to forget. And her heart thudded painfully at the thought of training with him. It would be too real. He would grab her. Touch her.

Panic swelled in her chest, and she fought to crush it. "I will not train with you."

"You don't want to lose your skills while he's gone." Tyrell took a step back, holding his hands out to the side. "Besides, don't you want a chance to hit me? I promise I'll let you get in at least one hit."

"No."

He rolled back on his heels, his jaw tightening. "I'm not doing this with you anymore. The silence. It's driving me mad. If I have to come down here, we will interact. But because I'm generous, I'll let you choose what we do today." He lifted a finger. "You can read aloud a book of my choosing." A second finger rose. "You can sit at the table and carry on a conversation with me." Three fingers were lifted now. "Or you can train with me." The corner of his mouth twisted up at the corner. "We'll do all of these things eventually, but you get to choose today."

Her skin felt too tight. "We will never train, because I refuse to touch you—or let you touch me."

There was a horrible silence, and Tyrell's expression didn't change as he stared at her. Fear flashed through her body, igniting every nerve. Her words were a challenge. She knew that. And she also knew how easily he could overpower her. Hurt her.

But, fates, she would hurt him back.

Tyrell's eyes measured her, and then he dipped his head. "Very well. No training today, then."

"Not ever."

He ignored that. "So what will you choose? Reading aloud a book of my choice, or conversation?"

Surprised he hadn't retaliated against her stubbornness, Mia swallowed back the flash of victory and tried to focus on his question. "What book would you make me read?"

Tyrell chuckled. "So suspicious." He reached behind him and plucked a thin book from a back pocket. He handed it to her, and Mia's face flushed at the highly inappropriate title. She threw it back at him and he laughed as he caught it. "Very well. Conversation it is." He swept a hand toward the table, a silent invitation.

Mia nearly refused, but what was the point? Eventually, his patience would snap. She was a little surprised it hadn't already, with how she'd been treating him. So she clutched her book to her chest, slid off the bed, and skirted around him on her way to the table and took a seat.

Tyrell clucked his tongue as he sank into his chair across from her. "You're quite moody. I suppose that's why you and Grayson get along."

The back of her neck prickled, but not with fear. No, it was annoyance.

Fearful little thing.

She heard King Henri's words in her mind, and she hated them more than ever.

Not anymore, she vowed. Even if terror flooded her body, she would not give Tyrell the satisfaction of knowing it.

She lifted her chin, meeting his stare even though her hands shook on her lap. "I don't see the point of these visits."

"My father ordered them. That's point enough."

"Don't you have anything better to do?"

He considered this. "I've got a soldier to flog. If you really want me to leave, I suppose I can go do that."

Mia grit her teeth. "What do you want to talk about?"

He leaned back in his chair, looking far too pleased with himself. "Perhaps you can tell me how you met Grayson."

"No."

"Why not?"

Because it was too personal. Too beautiful. She would never share that with Tyrell.

As she kept her silence, he rolled his eyes. "Fine, you can tell me why you even like him. Fates know no one else does."

Her back teeth ground together. "I don't want to talk about Grayson."

Tyrell's eyes dipped to the necklace she wore, the pebble resting against her skin. "Did he give you that?"

She snatched hold of the pebble, locking it in her fist to hide it from his view.

His twisted lips were mocking. "He gave you a worthless rock? I knew my brother was pathetic, I just didn't think he would insult you like that. Peter treats his mistresses like queens."

"I'm not Grayson's mistress."

Tyrell cocked a brow. "Then what are you? His friend?" He actually laughed. "I hate to be the one to tell you this, but my brother's feelings for you obviously go far beyond friendship. He's insanely in love with you, as evidenced by the fact that he attempted to threaten my father over you."

Mia released her hold on the necklace and let the book drop to her lap. She leaned forward, holding Tyrell's derisive gaze. "I love him."

If the declaration surprised him, he didn't show it. "Love. A truly idiotic emotion." He crossed his arms as he studied her, his smile mocking. "Do you miss him?"

She refused to dignify that with a response.

Tyrell lowered his voice. "If you refuse to have a conversation, we can always read that book I brought—"

"Have you always been cruel?" she snapped.

"Yes," he said without hesitation. "All Kaelins are."

"Grayson isn't."

"Of course he is. He's the Black Hand. My father's enforcer. He may have more blood on his hands than I do."

"But you enjoy what you do. That's the difference between you."

His head tilted to the side. "There are many differences between us. And yet, in the end, we're exactly the same."

"No, you're not."

Tyrell leaned back, drawing his finger over a fresh scar on his cheek. It was still healing. She had noticed it before, because it was a mark he hadn't had the night he'd come to hurt her. "Did you know Grayson gave this to me before he left? He cornered me in a hallway and cut my face open, just because he could."

She met his gaze, her jaw set tightly. "Grayson would never hurt anyone without provocation."

"I did nothing but try to step past him. He kept blocking me —and then he grabbed me by the throat and gave me this. You see, his temper can get the better of him." Tyrell spread his hands. "We both follow our father's orders, Mia. Every time."

She looked down at her lap and watched her knuckles grow whiter as she clutched her book. "He's nothing like you," she repeated.

"Perhaps he convinced you of that, but I could tell you stories about him that would turn your stomach. If you knew him as I do, even your blind faith would be destroyed."

"I know him," Mia said evenly, lifting her gaze to his. "But you don't know me. Not if you think you can convince me Grayson is evil like you."

There was a tense beat of silence, then Tyrell leaned forward. Her eyes tracked his every movement for any sign he was about to strike her, every nerve in her body taut and alert.

He set his hands on the table, his eyes on her. "Did he tell you about his mission in Mortise? What he's gone to do?"

She clenched her teeth. Her breaths were coming too quickly. She needed to keep calm—keep the panic from clawing out.

Tyrell studied her, triumph flashing in his eyes. "Clearly, he doesn't trust you as much as you trust him." He leaned back once more. "Perhaps we *should* talk about something other than my brother. What else do you do besides read?"

Mia's lungs ached as she fought against her rising panic. "I draw. Sometimes I paint."

"I want to see your work."

"No." Tyrell opened his mouth, but Mia overrode him. "I agreed to a conversation. That was all."

His dark brows slammed down, but surprisingly, he didn't argue the point. "What are your favorite books?"

The interrogation continued, pointless and irritating. Mia gave stilted answers and never asked a question of her own. She didn't want to know Tyrell. She already knew enough about him;

he had tortured and abused Grayson all his life and he found pleasure in cruelty.

Finally, the hour was over. Tyrell unfolded from the chair, looking totally at ease while irritation bit at Mia's skin. He smiled a little, as if he sensed her frustration and reveled in it. "I look forward to our next visit."

CHAPTER 23

DESFAN

DESFAN STOOD ON THE PALACE RAMPARTS, watching as Ser Ashear led the Devendran prisoners through the gates and into the city. There were twenty in total, men and women. Most were Devendrans who had been captured during the border skirmishes years ago. He knew not everyone on the council agreed with his decision to free so many prisoners, but as he looked at the prisoners being escorted toward freedom, there was a lightness in his chest.

They'd all been given new clothes, and Ashear had seen to it they were given a better diet weeks ago to prepare them for the trip to the border. Though their wrists remained tied with rope, their shoulders were not drooping.

They were going home.

Desfan set his folded arms on the stone ledge and glanced

toward the sea. The shrieking of gulls flying over the harbor overlaid the sound of the rolling waves that called to him, an endless pull he didn't think would ever ease. It was a fist in his gut, clenching tighter with every day. He missed the freedom. The thrill that came with riding out a storm, or facing a new island with no real expectations. The excitement that pumped through him when he boarded an enemy ship.

He could see a merchant ship leaving the port and he very nearly ordered the guard next to him to run and flag it down so Desfan could climb aboard. He didn't care where it was going—another Mortisian port, or south to Zennor—he'd take any destination.

Instead, he tapped his fingertips against the stone barrier and watched the ship as it drifted farther away.

"Serjah Desfan," a deep voice said. "The palace guard said you would be here."

He straightened and faced Ser Zephan. "I wanted to see Ser Ashear off."

Zephan stepped up to the wall, his dark eyes aimed toward the city below. "Ah, yes. The prisoner exchange."

Desfan could see Zephan's curled fist at his side, so he knew he wasn't as calm as his measured tone indicated. He couldn't help but needle the man a little. "I'm relieved to hear you've come to terms with the exchange."

"Well, we had little choice." The Mortisian lord eyed Desfan. "You know I think this is a mistake. As is the alliance. You are doing too much, too fast. All of this should have been discussed more with the serjan, once he has recovered."

Desfan turned to face him fully, hip propped against the ledge beside him. "Are you reprimanding me, Ser Zephan?"

"Merely stating my opinion. We are still allowed to do that, I hope?"

"Indeed."

Zephan glanced away, his eyes on the azure sea. "I sought you out because I need to be excused from court for a couple of weeks. Perhaps a bit longer."

"Oh?"

"I've had some personal matters arise. Nothing too serious, just some minor issues with my estate. Things will be solved quickly, I'm sure. I requested leave earlier this morning from Serai Yahri, and now I need only your approval."

It meant one less snake to deal with in court, but something about the man's leaving made Desfan's nerves tighten. "Have you named your temporary replacement?"

"Ser Anoush will take my seat while I'm gone."

Desfan knew the name, but little else about the man. But if Anoush was trusted by Zephan, then Desfan was instantly wary. "I wish you safe travels."

"Thank you, Your Highness. I hope the serjan's health improves over my absence."

"As do I."

The man dipped his head and retreated into the castle.

Desfan remained at the wall, now frowning out at the sea.

That was how Karim found him. "What did Zephan want?" he asked.

"Do the guards report everything to you?"

"Yes. But they weren't close enough to hear what he said."

"He asked for temporary leave. Something to do with his estate."

Karim grunted. He shifted his weight, turning to face Desfan. "It looks like Fang has vanished. I don't think he's foolish enough to actually try to kill you, but I've increased the guard on your room and you're not allowed to go into the city until things have calmed down."

Truthfully, things could have been a lot worse. At least Fang had never sent that ransom note to the palace, or he was sure Yahri would be calling for his immediate abdication for recklessly endangering himself.

Desfan slowly spun the ring his sister had given him, the obsidian band twisting around his finger. "I will try to take fewer risks," he said. "But I have to meet Zadir tonight."

"No," Karim said smoothly. "If you insist on hiring a pirate to do a kiv's job, then I will be the one to arrange it. You'll stay here and keep out of trouble."

"That's not exactly my strong point."

He snorted. "I'm well aware."

Desfan smiled, but it faded too soon. "I have to meet Zadir." He raised a hand to stop his friend's protest. "We both know he won't talk to you alone. We'll be cautious. We can even bring some guards most of the way with us."

Karim blew out his breath, his shoulders falling. "Fine. But can I at least say that I think this is a mistake?"

"You certainly can, I just heard you." Karim's punch to his shoulder had some strength behind it, and Desfan rocked back with a grin. He leaned against the stone wall that edged the sharp drop-off of the palace wall. The pounding of the waves against the cliffs echoed up from far below, punctuating the short silence. "Do you really think it's foolish to trust Zadir with this investigation?" he asked quietly.

Karim didn't answer right away. The wind ruffled his dark hair and his red uniform tightened across his shoulders as he pulled in a deep breath. "I think he has connections that could get the answers we need. But in the end, he's a pirate. Easily bought, and invested only in his self-interest. He is not loyal to you."

"Unfortunately, he's not alone in that." Desfan's list of friends in the palace was alarmingly short.

"Anything new on Rahim Nassar?" Karim asked.

"No." Desfan had gone to the Nassar warehouse the day after Fang had dropped the merchant's name, but Rahim's associates said he was away in Zennor. They assured Desfan the boat in question was not theirs, and that as soon as they could get a message to Rahim, he could attest to that as well.

Desfan had spent the last couple of days reviewing every report that had ever been submitted about the Nassars, and even though there was no sure evidence of them being smugglers, it did seem to be a part of the family business. Rahim had taken over a few years ago, after his father retired to one of the islands. There was no proof of illegal activity, only strong hints.

Karim frowned. "I know you want to solve the olcain issue, but you need to be focused on things at the palace as well. The council seems more aggravated with you than ever, and then there's the Rydenic princes coming for a visit. I have a bad feeling about all of it."

"You always manage to cheer me up, Karim."

He rolled his eyes. "You're a fates-blasted idiot, you know that?"

Desfan cracked a grin. "How could I forget, with you always reminding me?"

Syed Zadir sat at a back table of the crowded Four Winds, a mug held loosely in one hand. A couple of crew members sat beside him, their eyes searching the room for any hint of danger.

Desfan and Karim sat opposite the pirate captain, Desfan flashing a smile. "You came."

"So did you." Zadir thumped his tankard onto the table and glanced around the room. "I don't even see any soldiers."

"Karim and I really don't need them."

The pirate chuckled and scratched his dark, bearded chin. "I must say, I like your arrogance."

"That's not something I hear often."

"I can imagine." Zadir leaned in, elbows braced on the table. "You've probably noticed, but Fang fled the city. I suppose it has more to do with the buyer or seller, and less to do with the threat you might pose."

"Were you able to confirm that Fang was only storing the olcain for them?"

"I haven't found a pretty stack of evidence for you," the pirate captain drawled. "But I didn't think that was where I should be spending my time. I'm focused on the truth, and I have interviewed men who swear Fang was just holding the olcain."

Fair enough. "Have you learned anything about the buyer or seller?"

"The seller is Zennorian. Don't know a name yet. And from what I've gathered so far, the buyer is a nobleman living in Duvan." He cracked a smile. "Maybe being born rich doesn't pay as well as we all thought."

Zadir's men chuckled.

Desfan frowned, caught on the fact that a nobleman was involved. That confirmed his rising suspicion that the olcain was being used as a political maneuver—a way to destabilize the city.

Not good.

"Has anyone from your sphere fled the city recently?" Zadir asked.

"Zephan left this morning," Karim said slowly. "Maybe he wanted to leave before he was discovered—or to avoid the drug war that might break out."

"It's possible." But Desfan didn't want to lose sight of other suspects. There were plenty of nobles living in Duvan, and it could be any of them. He glanced up as a serving girl arrived at the table. He ordered a couple of drinks, which were brought quickly. After they were alone again, Desfan leaned closer to Zadir. "Fang mentioned that someone at the palace was offering protection. Any clues about who that might be?"

"No, but it seems likely someone in a position of power is helping to move the pieces. For all we know, the one offering protection is the buyer as well. I'll continue to ask around, especially at the harbor. Dockhands and port authorities have a tendency to know things."

There was a burst of shouting at a distant table of the crowded tavern, an explosive burst in an already loud environment.

Karim's voice was tense when he spoke. "We paid a visit to Nassar's warehouse, but we didn't learn much. Do you know him?"

"Never met him," Zadir said. "But I've heard we have some mutual acquaintances. Didn't know he smuggled drugs, but I can always ask some questions."

"Look into him," Desfan said at once. "I'll begin looking into the top suspects at the palace, and I want you to focus on the nobles who live in the city. We'll focus on the buyer for now, but if you happen to learn who the Zennorian seller is, I'd like to know."

Zadir settled back against his chair, his eyes sharp on Desfan's face. "In my digging, I came across a rumor. Apparently, there is a belief circulating that the serjan's illness was not an act of the fates."

Desfan stiffened. "What do you mean?"

"There are some who believe the serjan was poisoned."

"Impossible. It was illness that seized him." Karim glanced at Desfan, as if for assurance.

Desfan kept his eyes on Zadir, a pit opening in his gut. "Did the rumor claim anything else? Offer any details?"

"Not really. The story goes that the serjan was not alone in his office the night he collapsed, and that someone has been working hard to keep that fact hidden." Zadir's forehead creased. "Some have said the serjan was killed by your order, actually."

The words drove the air from Desfan's lungs.

"That's insane," Karim snapped.

Zadir shrugged his broad shoulders. "I didn't create the story, I only heard it. Thought it might interest you."

Desfan grit his teeth. "I didn't poison my father."

"It's possible he wasn't poisoned at all," Zadir pointed out. "But it might not hurt to ask yourself, Serjah . . . Who might have wanted your father off the throne?"

It was a chilling question, but he would learn the truth. He would question the physician and the guards who had been on duty that night, and servants who might have seen anything. He would pursue every lead.

Because if his father *had* been poisoned, the would-be killer would meet the most painful justice Desfan could deliver.

CHAPTER 24

DESFAN

"POISON?" THE ROYAL PHYSICIAN'S BROWS shot up. "I'm sorry, Serjah, but that is simply impossible. The serjan's collapse, though unfortunate, was completely natural. He had been working too hard for too many years. He did not care for himself as he should, and he hadn't been sleeping well for months. He carried a great deal of stress, and his body simply gave out. Recovery is unlikely, but his illness is not the result of a poisoning."

Desfan stood behind his desk, too agitated to sit. He'd summoned the physician at first light, anxious to question him. He'd barely slept after Zadir had shared the rumor last night.

Karim stood in the corner, a silent observer as Desfan asked, "Did you check for poisons, though?"

The man blinked. "Of course. But I found no evidence of anything amiss."

"Who summoned you to his office?"

He frowned. "A guard."

"Was my father alone?"

"In his study? Yes."

"You saw no one else in the room?"

"Just a couple of guards." His shoulders lifted, the motion stiff. "What is this about?"

Desfan ignored his question, but not the fact that the man was growing defensive.

"Were you aware of anyone with the serjan before his collapse? Was anyone in the room with him when it happened?"

"No. Not that I'm aware of."

"Didn't you question the guards about his collapse?"

The man's angular jaw flexed. "Of course I did. But they didn't see it happen. They were positioned in the hall. The serjan often worked late, odd hours."

"But no one was in there with him?"

"No. As I already said."

"How did the guards know he collapsed?"

The physician clasped his hands behind his back, his eyes narrowing. "They heard him fall, and then they found him on the floor, convulsing."

"Had he eaten anything recently?"

"Dinner, I presume."

"You presume? You didn't investigate his last food and drink?"

"No, I did not."

"Then how did you rule out poison?"

The man spread his hands, his exasperation clear in his tone. "There were no signs of poisoning. No discoloration of the tongue, no foul smells, no spots or rashes. He had a seizure of the mind and body, but this is an illness that can strike a man his age, especially one who has been over-worked for years. It is not unheard of. Unusual, yes, but not a sign of poisoning. Jumping to such a conclusion is radical."

Desfan grit his teeth. "So you didn't check his food and drink."

"There was no need." The physician's throat bobbed as he swallowed, his voice calmer than before. "Serjah, as difficult as it is to accept the will of the fates in this, I must insist that the serjan's condition is nothing other than illness." He straightened. "May I now go and tend your father?"

Desfan dismissed him, and the moment the door closed, he turned to Karim. "Thoughts?"

"He was defensive. Nervous, at the very least. Possibly lying about something."

That was Desfan's assessment as well. "I'll increase the guards on my father's room, though it's unlikely the physician is a danger to him, since he has been caring for him for months. I suspect he is protecting someone."

"Or himself. If he didn't investigate everything as he should have, he could be worried about the repercussions."

"I think someone else might have been there that night. And I think the physician knows who."

"Do you want me to bring him back here?"

"No. I'll ask Arcas to assign someone to trail him, see who he might seek out."

"I can also find another physician to check on the serjan and his health reports, see how someone outside the royal physician's sphere might interpret his condition."

Desfan nodded. "Good idea."

There was a knock on the door, and when Jamal entered, Desfan dismissed Karim. He knew his friend would arrange the tail for the royal physician, and everything else.

The youngest member of the council bowed deeply, sitting

only after Desfan lowered himself into his chair. "I'm sorry to intrude," Jamal said. "I hoped to catch you before the council meeting."

"Of course. What can I do for you?"

"I wanted to see how your investigation into the olcain problem was progressing."

"Quite well, though I've mostly turned it over to others." Not exactly a lie, though the man probably assumed "others" meant guards, not pirates.

Jamal nodded, his hands rubbing over his knees in a nervous gesture.

Desfan's eyes narrowed. "What did you really want to ask me, Jamal?"

Sweat beaded on Jamal's forehead. "I don't want to speak too hastily, but I overheard a conversation yesterday that I cannot remove from my mind. It could mean absolutely nothing. And as the youngest on the council, I know I should tread carefully, but . . ."

"You can speak freely here."

The man's throat bobbed. "I was passing the council chambers yesterday, and I heard voices. I was curious, since the council was not yet in session, and the room should have been empty. I found Ser Zephan and Serai Yahri within."

Desfan frowned. He didn't like the thought of those two having secret conversations.

Jamal shook his head. "I nearly joined them, but something held me back. I know I shouldn't have lingered, but their voices were low. Frantic. My curiosity got the better of me, I'm afraid."

"What did you hear?"

"Zephan told Yahri he would not stand by. Not like last time. Yahri demanded that he stay in Duvan, but he overrode her. He said she could orchestrate her plans and wait for things to fall into place, but he was a man of action." Jamal's face reddened. "They moved for the door then, and I left before I could be discovered. I know this isn't anything more than hearsay, and there is nothing overtly wrong about what they said, but I felt you should know about the exchange."

"I appreciate that, Jamal." Desfan's mind was reeling, trying to overlay what Jamal had shared over the mysteries he was trying to unravel. The olcain, the possible poisoning of his father . . . in any case, it spoke of a friendship—or at least a partnership—between Yahri and Zephan that Desfan had not been aware of.

Which did not bode well.

They were in the middle of a council meeting when the doors to the chamber pushed open without warning and a guard rushed in.

Even before he spoke, Desfan knew it wasn't going to be good.

"What is the meaning of this interruption?" Serai Yahri demanded. "This chamber is to remain closed during council meetings!"

"Apologies." The guard continued toward Desfan and he offered an awkward bow as he moved. His throat bobbed anxiously. "Serjah, Emissary Amil Havim has returned and demands to see you at once. I told him—"

Desfan rose along with the twelve council members as Ser Amil strode into the vaulted room. He was covered in dust and sweat and the hollowness in his cheeks bespoke missed meals. There were purple marks under his eyes, showing a lack of sleep, and the men trudging behind him looked just as haggard.

"Serjah, I must speak with you immediately." Amil's voice cracked through the hall.

Desfan tensed. "Amil. What are you doing here? You should be in Iden, with your father."

Amil stopped at the base of the raised throne. He did not bow as he gazed up at Desfan, fury in his eyes. "My father will never leave Iden. He was murdered."

Desfan stopped breathing. Shock rippled through the room, ripping gasps from some of the council.

"Explain," Desfan demanded.

Amil sneered. "What is there to explain? My father was murdered before my eyes. Devendra is to blame. We must attack!"

Desfan grit his teeth. He eyed the flustered guard who had first burst into the room. "Seal the room. No one else comes in."

Amil's hands opened and closed at his sides, his rage palpable. "You doubt my word?"

"No. But I will not have rumors spread until I know everything." Desfan crossed his arms over his chest, his dark brows pulling together. "Did King Newlan order your father's death?"

Amil ground his teeth. "No. But he is not guiltless."

"Tell me what happened and we will seek justice."

Amil worked his jaw, his dark beard unrulier than Desfan had ever seen it. He had never considered Amil a friend, even when they were children, but he felt pity for him in this moment. He knew what it felt like to lose those you loved. He knew the denial. The hopelessness. The rage.

He also knew that blame was an easy thing to throw on others, even when there was no one to really blame.

"My father was killed in an attack made at the farewell banquet held for Princess Serene three weeks ago," Amil finally bit out. "He had no chance to defend himself. It was an ambush. A coward's strike. The attack was organized by a Devendran soldier, a palace guardsman. He intended to kill the princess as well, but failed."

"Fates," one of the councilmen swore.

"I burned my father's body and rode straight home so I could deliver the truth of Devendra's weakness, cowardice, and pointlessness as an ally. There can surely be no peace now. There would be no point. They're tearing their own kingdom apart and if we try to ally with them, we will be slaughtered—as my father was slaughtered. We need to retaliate."

Murmuring broke out among the council.

Desfan lifted a hand, forcing the room back into quiet. He stepped down from the dais and set a hand on Amil's shoulder, his grip tight. "I'm sorry for your loss," he said, hating the words that had been spoken so uselessly to him once, but feeling the need to say them anyway. "Mortise mourns with you, and we will tell everyone of your father's brave sacrifice. But I will not attack Devendra, nor will I put an end to the alliance."

Amil's gaze sharpened, his nostrils flaring. "They are a pack of ravenous wolves. There is no honor for their king. Even now, the rebellion against Newlan rages strong. Their kingdom will be fractured by another civil war, and you would have us be pulled into that? For what?"

"Peace. Stability. Financial gains. Stronger ties with Zennor. And as a guard against an attack by Ryden." Desfan glanced at the council, knowing every eye was on him. "There are reasons for everything I've done. And though it's not something I've spoken of, I know some of you are aware that these plans for a marriage with Princess Serene were laid down first by my father. Even if you do not respect my command as regent, you should respect his as your serjan."

He focused back on Amil. "A room at the castle is yours. Eat, wash, and rest from your travels. I will visit you later and we can discuss the state of Devendra and all that happened." He tightened his hold on Amil's shoulder and lowered his voice. "I truly am sorry for the loss of your father. But if the alliance is made, then I promise his death will not have been in vain."

Amil stared at him for several long heartbeats, and Desfan had no idea what he was thinking.

After the uncomfortable pause, Amil shrugged off Desfan's hand and took a step back. His face betrayed nothing as he bowed stiffly. "As you decree, Serjah." He turned on his heel and strode from the room, his men falling into step behind him.

Desfan glanced at the council. "We will dismiss until tomorrow."

None of them spoke to him as they shuffled from their seats and moved for the door. But they whispered among themselves, and the back of Desfan's neck prickled in response.

Karim came to stand beside him, his voice low. "Amil was not appeased."

"No." And Desfan wasn't sure he could blame him. He scrubbed a hand over his brow. "Fates, why did I send them?"

"You thought they would be good emissaries," Karim said.

It was true. Amil had never shown hostility towards Devendra, and even though it was known Bahri Havim didn't want peace, he was loyal to Desfan's father. Unflinchingly so. Desfan knew he would not go against a royal order, even if he hated it.

It hit him, then. Desfan had sent a man to his death. It hadn't been by design, but the result was the same, and he felt the full weight of that. His shoulders dropped. "Sometimes I feel like

I can't win."

"Sometimes you can't," Karim said. "What will you do to calm things with Devendra?"

He blew out his breath. "I'll write some letters. I don't know what Amil's last words to Newlan or Serene were, but I need to assuage any fears. The smallest spark could turn into a flame that destroys us all."

Karim grunted. "That spark could very well come from Prince Liam and Prince Grayson's arrival."

"I suppose we'll find out soon enough."

Unfortunately.

CHAPTER 25

GRAYSON

SEVENTEEN DAYS SINCE GRAYSON HAD seen Mia.

It had taken fourteen days for him and Liam to reach the coastal city of Vyken, where they'd boarded a large boat in a vast shipyard. Grayson had stood on deck and watched as the coast disappeared.

That was three days ago. The captain of the ship estimated eleven more before they reached Duvan, if the weather cooperated.

Fates, he hoped it cooperated. The ship already pitched and rolled enough on calm waters. Grayson had never felt so sick in all his life. The first time Grayson had lunged for the side of the ship, Liam had chuckled. "You'll get used to it."

He'd spent the past three days swaying on his cot, his stomach rolling, or gripping the wooden rail on deck and heaving until his insides ached. The sailors had largely ignored him, though he heard snickering now and then—especially from the guards sent to protect the two princes.

At least he wasn't retching right now. In fact, his legs didn't tremble like they had the last few days, and even though his palms were sweating in his gloves, he didn't feel terribly sick. Only a little dizzy, his stomach a bit uneasy, but the cool breeze and fresh air helped with that. Standing at the rail, Grayson supposed Liam had been right. Maybe his body was adjusting. But fates, he hated sailing.

If a ship wasn't the fastest way back to Mia, he would never step on a deck again. He'd been utterly miserable, unable to even think, but since his stomach was calmer today, he pulled out the folded piece of parchment Mia had given him. He'd opened and refolded it so many times that the folds were deep creases. Holding it carefully in the teasing breeze, he viewed the drawing again.

On the page, two figures knelt across from each other on a sandy beach, looking down at the waves frothing up on shore. The picture only gave the profiles, with the sea in the distance. The view was trained at an angle, looking slightly down on the couple.

It was him and Mia. On the side of his face, there were light tracings of scars and his dark hair fell over his brow. Mia's profile was softened by the curls tumbling over her shoulders and her gaze was fixed on him. He could see the love in her stare. The emotion she had captured in this sketch . . . it gripped Grayson's heart, making it hard to breathe.

In the drawing, Grayson was not looking at her. Instead, he was looking down at their reflections in the rippling water of the sea, the corner of his mouth tugged up in a grin he rarely used in life.

But the reflections in the water . . . they were not an exact mirror.

It was Mia's young face—exactly how she had looked the first time he saw her—that beamed up from the water, as if she could see the older version of Grayson looking down at her. Beside her, a young Grayson's eyes were fixed on her. He was absolutely blinded to anything else, adoration carved across every line of his face.

At the bottom of the picture, Mia had written three words. *Forever with you.*

The drawing captured so many facets of their relationship —the depths of it. Their friendship, love, and dedication to each other. Letting his eyes trace over the page . . . it was akin to feeling Mia's arms wrapped around him. It was almost like she was holding his hand now, squeezing it.

She loved him. And he would do whatever was necessary to return to her, and give her the freedom she deserved. Even if that meant assassinating Princess Serene and starting a war.

And ensuring Liam never made it home.

"You're looking better."

Grayson glanced over his shoulder and saw Liam approaching. He quickly folded Mia's drawing and tucked it into his pocket.

His older brother did *not* struggle with life at sea. His legs didn't falter and he didn't get sick. In fact, he seemed happier with every hour that took them further from Ryden. And while Grayson's skin burned and peeled, Liam's tanned face almost glowed.

Liam reached the side of the ship and leaned back on the rail beside Grayson. "I'd say you might be back to your old self, but you've been quiet since leaving home." He flashed a grin. "Well, when you aren't retching."

Grayson tightened his hold on the rail when the ship crested a wave and then dropped. His gut churned and he clenched his teeth. The only consolation was that when he gripped the rail now, his hand had healed enough that it didn't flare with agony. The scars were already forming, slightly raised in the middle of his palm and on the back of his hand. There didn't seem to be any permanent damage, thank the fates. Just two more scars on his body. A physical reminder of what he had already sacrificed for Mia.

A reminder that he needed to stay focused, and not become distracted by a brother who might have, under any other circumstances, become a friend, rather than someone he would have to kill.

"Sorry." Liam folded his arms, still leaning easily against the rail. "You do seem to be doing better, though."

"A little," he admitted.

"Are you feeling well enough to resume our lessons? I still have much to teach you."

Liam had been imparting all sorts of knowledge, helping Grayson hone skills that would be useful in Mortise—including the spy language. The covert sign language was a minimalistic way to communicate; a flick or tap of the finger, the occasional twist of a wrist. It could all be done with one hand, and the movements were small, concise, and a trick to do with gloves. But Grayson could see the appeal of having such a language, so he had dutifully practiced until the motions came more smoothly. He had a hard time catching the meaning when Liam moved quickly, though.

"I also thought we could go over some poisons that Mortisian assassins seem particularly fond of," Liam added. "Just in case."

Another roll of the ship had Grayson searching for the horizon. Fates, he hated the sea. "Maybe tomorrow."

Liam chuckled. "Very well." He glanced across the deck. "Looks like we'll get some entertainment."

Grayson followed Liam's gaze to where a cluster of soldiers had gathered. The guards were drawing swords, preparing to mock fight. Sailors crept closer to watch, placing bets on the guards they thought would win.

"You could kill any of them, couldn't you?"

Grayson shot his brother a look. "Why do you ask?"

Liam shrugged a shoulder, still looking at the gathered men. "I suppose it wasn't really a question. More of an observation." He eyed Grayson. "You really are a legend, you know. And not just in Ryden."

Grayson's gut knotted. He told himself it was from the ship's rocking, and not the memories that assailed him. All the times he had made arrests, pulled families apart, overseen executions —killed.

Or when he had willingly become the Black Hand so he could threaten his father.

When he'd cut a blade into Tyrell's skin purely because he could.

Or when he'd made the decision to kill Liam, because the alternative was to see innocents suffer.

Grayson knew Liam was waiting for some response. He cleared his throat. "You sound like Father."

The corner of Liam's mouth twitched. "You mean prideful and possessive with a touch of insanity?"

He wasn't used to hearing King Henri insulted; not that he disagreed with his brother's assessment. "You seem happier since leaving Ryden," he commented.

"I'm not sure happiness is an emotion we're suited for." Liam fingered his bearded jaw. "But it's freeing to be away. For me, anyway. It seems to disagree with you. Thus my reason for wandering over here—you look pensive. Maybe even upset."

"I don't like sailing."

Liam almost smiled. "The whole ship has heard how violently you hate it—several times a day. You're wasting away, little brother."

"I'm fine."

"I'll try to fold my mothering instincts away, then." He reclined against the railing, obviously not worried about the ship pitching him over the side that dug into his lower back.

Grayson looked back out at the horizon. He didn't like turning his back on the deck, especially now that the fights were underway and he could hear the strike and scrape of swords. The space between his shoulder blades itched, but staring at the horizon helped ease the churning in his stomach.

Liam watched the fights for a moment before speaking. "I remember the first time I left Ryden. I was so nervous, I made myself sick." He shook his head a little, his eyes trained on the fight but clearly not seeing it. "You were young, so you probably don't remember that." His eyes darted to Grayson, a thin, humorless smile twisting his lips. "I'd been sent to train with father's best spies in Ryden before then. Forced through endless tests and shoved full of information that I could repeat in my sleep—or withhold when . . . questioned."

Shock flashed through Grayson, but he really shouldn't have been surprised at the way Henri would treat a young boy. Fates knew he had enough firsthand experience. But even though he'd seen each of his brothers tortured by their parents, he had never heard them talk about it.

Liam's voice was just loud enough to be heard over the rush of water as the ship cut through the sea. "I was twelve when they gave me my first mission and dropped me in Devendra.

I was alone with no support. It was winter. I was freezing and starving. I got lost, and I remember wandering around, knowing I was going to die. I felt like . . . like I was *drowning*."

Grayson's scalp prickled. That was exactly how he felt. He tightened his hold on the rail as he shifted toward his brother. For some reason, he needed to know. "How did you survive?"

"The only way anyone ever actually survives—I had help." His eyes grew hooded. "I managed to stumble upon an estate. A wealthy Devendran family took me in and nursed me back to health. They showed me kindness." His throat bobbed as he swallowed. "They thought I was Devendran—I'd mastered the language and accent. I told them I was an orphan and I was given a position in their house as a kitchen boy. By then, I realized who they were."

Dread curled in Grayson's veins. This was not going to be a good story.

"I served in their house for two weeks. The lady of the house checked me personally every day. She wanted to make sure I had enough to eat and that I fully recovered from my illness. Knowing her habits made it easy for me to sneak into her chamber. I stole the letters Father had wanted all along—documents that proved she was a traitor to King Newlan. I completed my mission when I placed them in the hands of one of Father's spies." Liam's jaw tightened. "I later learned that the lady worked for Father. Her son had been captured during a raid years ago. He was a Devendran soldier, and Father threatened his life as a way to control her. She turned spy against her own kingdom, without even her husband's knowledge, all to preserve the life of her imprisoned son. When she failed Father in one of her missions, he didn't only execute her son, he also betrayed her to Newlan with the letters I stole." Liam's eyes flashed with some unnamable emotion and his voice dropped low. "Newlan had her beheaded."

The sails overhead snapped with a stiffening gust of wind. Grayson's voice sounded hollow, even to his own ears. "I . . . don't know what to say."

Liam's stare was intense. "There's not really anything to say."

There wasn't.

His brother scrubbed a hand over his bristled jaw, and when he exhaled, the sound was rough. "I know what it's like to be a prince of Ryden, Grayson. I know what it's like to be controlled. Hated. Feared. I know what it's like to hate yourself, the very blood in your veins. But there is one thing I've learned out here —Father's reach is not as long as he thinks."

Grayson looked away, toward the rippling water that glittered in the sunlight. There were so many things he wanted to say—to ask. *Are you a traitor? Do you know Mother suspects? Do you know there's a bottle of Ieannax in my bag and I'm supposed to use it to kill you?*

And then the most dangerous question of all . . . *If you are a traitor, do you have a plan to defeat them?*

Grayson didn't voice any of his thoughts. He didn't dare. Because if there was even a chance that Liam was loyal to Henri, Grayson couldn't risk it.

Liam shoved his hands into his pockets and pushed off from the rail. "Meet me here tomorrow after breakfast and we'll continue your studies." His eyes flickered to a spot behind Grayson, and he grimaced a little. "That is, if you decide to eat breakfast."

Grayson turned to see an ominous roll of darkening clouds on the horizon.

His stomach twisted and he cursed.

Liam chuckled, though pity shone in his eyes. "Sorry, Brother. I don't think your outlook on sailing is going to improve any time soon."

CHAPTER 26

MIA

THE NEXT TIME TYRELL CAME, MIA WAS ready. When he stepped into the cell, she lifted two books. "Choose between these and I'll read aloud."

Tyrell lifted an eyebrow as he kicked the door closed. "Anxious to avoid another conversation with me?"

"Choose, or I will."

His mouth twitched and he strolled forward, leaning in to read the titles. His eyes narrowed. "Those sound like the two most boring—"

Mia tossed one of the books to her bed and moved to the table. She sat, flipped open the book, and started to read. "The study of moss can lead to great insights into our natural world—"

"Why is there a whole book about fates-blasted moss?"

"—which can in turn lead to a greater understanding of our

natural selves. My journal documents my—"

"Is he a gaffer, or a philosopher?"

"—thoughts on moss, and details my intense study of it."

She paused for breath, and Tyrell asked, "Where did you even find this?"

She ignored him. "Moss may be seen as insignificant, but it is more widespread and fascinating than anything else I have heretofore studied."

"Hmm," Tyrell said, his voice lower than before. Speculative. "Insignificant but fascinating . . . Reminds me of someone."

Mia swallowed, her mouth suddenly and uncomfortably dry. "Moss is soft, but fierce. It clings to the ground, stones, trees—whatever it can attach itself to—and is the most resilient form of flora, in my opinion. It is surprisingly vibrant in its shade, and . . ." Her voice faltered when she saw movement from the corner of her eye—Tyrell was strolling toward the bookcase near the table, putting him slightly behind her. "And the scent of moss is actually quite pleasant to me. While others may disagree, I find moss to be strangely compelling."

"Strangely compelling. Huh." From her periphery, she could see him leaning against the bookshelf. His hands sank into his pockets, and Mia could feel his eyes on her.

Her scalp prickled, and she tried to ignore his stare. "Moss is unassuming, but I think it controls more than a casual observer might expect. For instance, it may be overlooked in the shadow of a giant tree, but it surrounds the trunk and even the roots, more a part of the mighty tree than one might suspect. I first began my study by observing moss near water. Streams, rivers, and ponds are all fine places to discover the wonder of moss. There are—"

"Did you do these?"

Mia looked over and her stomach plunged.

Tyrell had twisted toward the shelf and plucked down one of her many sketchbooks. It lay open in his hands.

She dropped her book onto the table. "Put that down."

Tyrell ignored her and flipped to another page. His brows drew together as he studied the drawing. "You're quite good."

Mia shoved to her feet and snatched for the book, but he held it aloft in one hand.

He smiled down at her. "What about the moss? I was so intrigued."

"Give me my book."

"No."

She grit her teeth, her fingers curling to fists as her pulse thudded. "Those are mine. You have no right to look at them."

"I'm a prince of Ryden and you're my father's prisoner, so I have every right and you have none."

He flipped the book open again, still raised above her head. The page was tilted down, so Mia could see the simple sketch of a daisy. Grayson had given the flower to her long ago, his cheeks turning pink as he'd held it out. The white daisy was still pressed in one of her thickest books, along with other flowers he'd given her over the years.

"How old were you when you did this?" Tyrell asked. When she didn't answer, he shot her a look.

She glared. "Twelve or thirteen."

"Really?" Surprise colored his tone. "Can I see your current work?"

"No."

He clucked his tongue. "So stubborn." He flipped to the next page, which was a large, detailed spider. He blinked. "That's terrifyingly realistic."

"You're afraid of spiders?"

"I'm not afraid of anything." He studied the image. "Your

skill really is incredible."

Mia clutched the pebble hanging just below her throat, her heart pounding. "I don't want you to look at my drawings."

Tyrell ignored her and turned the page, revealing a drawing of a fluffy kitten who was missing half of his left ear.

Mia had been nine when she'd seen the poor creature. Grayson had found him in the castle yard, limping on a torn paw, his fur streaked with blood that spilled from his torn ear and multiple scratches along his ribs and legs. Grayson had been bleeding himself, Mia remembered. He'd just finished a training session, and his eye was bruised and swelling shut, shallow cuts on his arms and hands oozing blood. He'd plucked the kitten out of the weeds and smuggled him down to Mia's cell.

Her heart had broken for the little cat, who was clearly traumatized and hurting. "Hold him gently," Mia had ordered Grayson.

The ten-year-old boy's grip loosened a little, and he watched Mia as she rushed to pour water in a bowl and find a clean towel.

She had known Grayson for about two years. He was the youngest prince of Ryden, and his father was absolutely terrifying, but Grayson had never scared her. He was generally quiet, and he watched her intently, but she was never uncomfortable around him. Sometimes, she thought *she* made *him* uncomfortable. Even though he was older and bigger, there were times she would touch him and he would flinch. She'd never hurt him, though. He was her best friend.

She carried the bowl of water to the table, where Grayson sat. She pulled a chair in front of him and sat so close their knees touched.

Grayson tensed, but he didn't shift away. The kitten in his hands was muddy, fur matted with blood. He'd clearly fought for his life.

Tears stung Mia's eyes and her chest cracked. "Here, let me clean him."

Grayson passed over the kitten, and the moment Mia's fingers wrapped around the fragile thing, it hissed and raked its claws over her skin.

Pain flashed and Mia gasped, dropping the kitten on reflex. The small thing bolted under the bed.

Grayson cursed and grabbed her bleeding hand.

"I'm fine," Mia said in a rush. The scratches welled over with blood, and they stung fiercely. She swallowed back her tears, not wanting to make Grayson—or the cat—feel badly.

Grayson snatched the towel she'd carried over and pressed it to the cuts.

She sucked in a breath, but bravely pursed her lips. She felt her chin tremble, though.

Grayson had gone pale, which only made the bruising around his left eye more stark. "I'm sorry," he gritted out. "I don't know why he did that. He didn't hurt me when I picked him up."

"He didn't mean to," Mia said, her voice tight with swallowed pain. "He was just scared. It's all right."

Grayson's forehead creased. "I'll take him away."

"No!" Mia shook her head, brown curls dancing around her shoulders. "I want to help him."

Indecision sparked in his gray eyes, but he finally nodded. "Let's clean your hand first."

Mia wanted to argue that the kitten needed help more than she did, but she knew from the stubborn set of his jaw that Grayson would not budge on this. So she didn't protest as he tended her wound.

Once the bleeding stopped, he dabbed the residue away with a wet corner of the cloth, then gently wrapped a bandage around her hand. When he was finished, he leveled a serious look at her.

"He might have only hurt you because he was scared, but that doesn't make it all right. *No one* has the right to hurt you."

No one had the right to hurt Grayson, either. Or that kitten.

It didn't stop any of them from being hurt.

Heat rose in Mia's face as the memory vanished. She still gripped the necklace Grayson had given her as she watched Tyrell thumb through her sketches.

She didn't want him to see these things. They were glimpses of her past, windows to her thoughts. They were private. And no matter what he said, he had no right to rifle through them.

She released the pebble, her hands fisting at her sides. "Give me the book," she said firmly.

Tyrell glanced at her. "Or what?"

"I'll take it from you."

Something like intrigue sparked in his eyes, even as he cracked a cruel smile. "Didn't you already try that?"

Her fingers itched to grab the nearest chair and hit him with it. Grayson had taught her to see everything around her as a potential weapon.

She didn't think she would win the fight, but she would make him drop the book.

Tyrell glanced at the next page, which had fallen open. His eyes narrowed, and she followed his gaze.

It was a sketch of Grayson. He was probably fourteen in the picture, and he was staring into the distance, lost in a memory. Shadows were under his eyes, and her pencil had traced out the scars on his face. His shoulders were up, slightly hunched. He somehow looked both weary and alert. Vulnerable. Haunted.

Disgust curled Tyrell's lip. "Fates. Is this what you see when you look at him? He's pathetic. What a waste of paper."

Mia grabbed the chair and slammed it into Tyrell's side.

The prince stumbled at the unexpected blow, the sketchbook knocked from his hands. It slid across the floor and Tyrell whirled on Mia, a muscle ticking by his temple. "Strike me again," he said lowly, "and I will strike back."

Mia gripped the chair so hard, her knuckles protested. But she still held it in front of her—a shield and a weapon. "Get out," she ordered, her voice vibrating with fury. "*Now*."

"No."

Her breaths came too quickly, too sharply. "I don't want you here," she said.

"I don't really want to be here, either, but the king will be obeyed." Tyrell set his hands on his hips, his shoulders high and tight. "I think we're done with moss and drawings, and you clearly want a fight. So we'll train for the rest of the hour."

Her stomach lurched. "No."

He ignored her, turning to push the table to the wall to create more space in the room. "I'm assuming Grayson focused your skills on hand-to-hand combat. If you had a weapon, you would have drawn it on me by now."

She kept the chair between them, but her arms were beginning to tire from the weight of it. "I'm not training with you."

Tyrell finished moving the table and faced her, his eyes unreadable. "We're doing this, Mia. I have my orders to stay with you for an hour, and I refuse to spend it in silence while you glare at me. So we train."

"No."

He shot forward.

She swung the chair, but he batted it aside.

Her empty hands stung and her pulse snapped. Sweat broke out on her body and her lungs seized. She fell back a step, pure instinct, and then she attacked him.

She managed a punch to his gut, but he moved with the rapidness of a striking cobra. His hands snatched her wrists, halting her next hit, and he propelled her back until her spine hit the bookshelf. Items on the shelves rattled and her heart thudded painfully as he towered over her, his legs pressed against hers, his arms pushing hers up above her head, holding her immobile.

"Let go," she gasped, fear and adrenaline rushing through her body. She bucked against him, but he had caged her in completely with his body.

His fingers dug into her wrists. "Didn't Grayson teach you how to break holds?" he asked, his tone mocking. "Those are the basics."

Her chest rose and fell with jagged breaths, her lungs screaming, her heart crashing as panic clawed up her throat. "Let go," she repeated, a rasp edging the plea.

"This should be easy—you hate me, so hurt me."

"Stop it!" she cried, her vision hazing with tears, a heavy weight pressing against her chest. She couldn't breathe.

Tyrell shifted his grip on her wrists until he shackled them with one hand, his other now free. He grabbed the pebble necklace hanging by her throat. "Perhaps I'll take this. Give you an incentive to—"

She lost all sense of sanity. The panic attack was all-consuming. She only knew that her body had turned against her, and that Tyrell had threatened to take Grayson's gift.

She struck out, jerking her arms down—heedless of his punishing grip that nearly snapped her wrists, or his nails that scratched her skin as she yanked free. Her thumbs went for his eyes and he reared back, dropping the necklace—and her.

While he jerked back, she crashed to her knees, her aching hands barely supporting her as she gasped and wheezed for breath.

"Mia?"

Her fingers curved into the floor, her back arched as she struggled to drag in air. The pain in her chest was excruciating, the agony of a boulder crushing her lungs.

Hands grasped her shoulders, twisting her until she was lying on her back. Tears leaked from the corners of her eyes and she grasped her necklace protectively in one hand, the other raking at Tyrell's face.

He dodged the strike and snatched her hand from the air, the pressure of his grip carefully controlled. Nothing like his punishing hold only moments before.

He spoke through gritted teeth. "Easy, I'm not going to hurt you."

The words were strange, coming from him, but did nothing to impede the devastating wave of panic that assaulted her.

Tyrell leaned in, and Mia's hold on the pebble tightened until it bit into her palm.

He muttered a curse. "I'm not going to take that stupid rock, either. Can you just hold still? What's wrong with you?"

She couldn't answer. There was no air in her lungs.

Tyrell's head cranked toward the door. "Guard!" The bellow of his voice made Mia flinch.

His hand on her shoulder burned through her dress, and she tried to shrug him off, but she wasn't sure if her body had even really moved. There was a horrible roaring in her ears.

Devon had said a panic attack would not kill her.

She thought he might be wrong.

The door pushed open and Fletcher's eyes widened.

"I didn't do anything," Tyrell gritted out. "She just started gasping."

Fletcher ignored the prince and dashed out of Mia's view. When he returned, he knelt beside her, the familiar jar of salts in hand. He slid his palm under her head and gently lifted.

"You're all right, just breathe," he said, his quiet voice lined with steel. "Deep breaths, now."

Mia struggled to do as he said, her breaths ragged at first but gradually evening—deepening. The smell of lavender was familiar, and the more it filled her nose, the easier her breaths became. But her cheeks were flushed after the panic, and her eyes stung. She had gotten so much better over the years, her panics less frequent. Then she had panicked in front of Grayson, and she'd hated that he'd seen her like that. Now, Tyrell knew her weakness, too—and that was wholly humiliating.

Fletcher helped ease her into a sitting position, angling her so she was facing him. She was grateful, because that kept a kneeling Tyrell in her periphery.

Fletcher's large hand was warm on her shoulder. "There," he murmured. "You're all right now." He glanced at the prince. "I think you should go, Your Highness."

Tyrell's fist tightened against his bent knee, his eyes on her. "Mia, do you require a physician?"

"No," Fletcher answered for her. "Your Highness, I must insist that you leave her to rest."

Mia could feel Tyrell's eyes burning against the side of her face, but she refused to look at him as she spoke. "Go." Her voice was hoarse, and she didn't like how it turned her request into a plea.

There was a short silence, then clothing rustled as Tyrell pushed to his feet. He stood there a moment, hovering over them both. For a brief moment, she thought he might say something, or question her about her panic attack. But he simply turned on his heel and strode from the room.

Fletcher eyed Mia. "Are you all right?"

He was asking about so much more than this moment. He was asking about Tyrell's visits and Grayson's absence, and the cracking in her heart hurt so badly. Tears gathered in her eyes, watering her vision.

"No," she breathed. "I'm not all right."

CHAPTER 27

CLARE

CLARE CLOSED HER EYES, THE CORNER OF her mouth lifting as the morning sun warmed her skin. She pulled in a slow, deep breath, and there was only a slight pinch in her side.

"Maybe you should sit down," Bennick said, his voice laced with worry. "I'll send for a chair."

"No, I'm fine." She squeezed his arm, which she was proud to say she barely leaned on. "The physician said it would be good for me to be on my feet."

She was thoroughly grateful for the older man's change of orders. It had been sixteen days since the disastrous Paltrow's ball. She had been stuck in bed for almost two weeks after her injury, and though her side still ached if she over-exerted herself, the physician had allowed her to take short walks over the last couple of days. Today, he had encouraged her to join the party in the yard.

The Paltrows were hosting an annual fair to help raise funds for the orphanage in Lindon, and the grassy yard was bustling with activity. Nobles had come from all over the area to participate. There were art pieces to buy, foods to eat, and games to play. Cards, lawn balls, and even grappling for the men—and all of it supported the charity.

Lady Paltrow had informed Clare that even though the event was always well-attended, the princess's unexpected presence was yielding a larger number of participants—and donations.

Clare was glad there was at least one positive side to the delay; King Newlan certainly hadn't appreciated it.

After Clare had been injured, Bennick had written to Newlan, Desfan, and Serene, informing all of them about the anticipated delay so they could make any needed adjustments. Serene, Cardon, and Dirk would take their time traveling slowly between inns to avoid staying in one place too long, or reaching their next stop too soon. Even more letters were sent to host families they would no longer have the time to stay with, and several social events had to be canceled. The dedication of the king's new road had been postponed, and even the prisoner exchange in Stills had to be pushed back.

Even though they had cut out as many unnecessary stops as possible, the tour would be nearly three weeks behind by the time Clare was allowed to travel. The physician was impressed with her healing, and the scar on her side was small, and pain only sparked if she moved too quickly. But the mark served as a painful physical reminder of her brother's betrayal.

She had heard nothing from Eliot, not that she had expected to.

His silence still hurt.

She felt guilty, though she knew she shouldn't; Eliot's actions were not her fault. But it still felt like she was somehow to blame for being manipulated by him.

Getting out of her room, being outside and surrounded by merriment . . . it was a distraction she needed. Normally she tired easily while pretending to be the princess, but she was actually enjoying the reprieve of so many conversations. But then, no one stayed overlong.

Wilf towered behind her, his arms crossed over his wide chest. A single stare from him kept most people from lingering too long—and some from even approaching her entirely—which helped her avoid feeling the usual strain.

Clare kept hold of Bennick's arm as they wandered the fair, their progress slow, but perfectly enjoyable on her part. When they reached the grappling area, they paused to watch. It was a challenging twist on a simple grappling match. The opposing men each held onto the same long staff, their grips close together on the center of the staff. The goal was to put the other man on his back—without either man letting go of the staff. Men shoved, twisted, and jerked the staff, trying to force their opponent to the ground, or at least surrender their grip.

Venn, who stood on Clare's other side, whistled lowly. "Here's the plan, Wilf. You take on four of those noblemen at once, and I'll place the bets. We'll split the winnings—after taking out the entrance fee, of course."

Wilf growled a little.

Clare grinned. "I don't think anyone is foolish enough to bet against Wilf."

"Come now, I'm giving them four against one!" Venn elbowed Wilf. "Try to look smaller."

Wilf shoved Venn.

Clare laughed, though the flash of pain in her side ended that quickly. She tried to cover it up by clearing her throat, but Bennick's sudden tenseness made it clear she hadn't fooled him.

His brow furrowed. "Perhaps we should go back inside for a while."

"No, I'm fine." Clare gently rubbed her side. "I've had enough of inside. And I would think you have, too." He had rarely left her side during the last two weeks.

He sidled closer, his voice dipping so others wouldn't hear. "I don't want you to overexert yourself."

Wilf and Venn had drifted back slightly, but Clare still kept her tone quiet. "I know you're worried, but I'm perfectly fine. I'll tell you if I need to rest."

His lips pressed together, but he didn't argue.

"Excuse me, Princess, but I'm pleased to see you looking so well."

Clare turned, her smile genuine as she recognized the man before her. "Lord Finch. It's wonderful to see you again." She extended a hand, which he took at once.

"You're too kind." He dipped his head, pressing a barely-there kiss on the back of her hand, brown hair falling over his forehead. He had a simple grace and a charming smile, something that made him memorable even though they had only shared one dance at the Paltrow's ball. A feat not all noblemen could claim.

When he straightened, his eyes carried a gentle hint of concern. "I was horrified to hear what happened. Are you feeling all right?"

"Much improved, thank you."

"Thank the fates." He glanced at Bennick, and Clare recalled their conversation on the dance floor.

"Lord Finch, may I introduce you to my guards? Venn Grannard, Wilford Lines, and Bennick Markam." She shot Bennick a small smile. "Lord Finch mentioned he has followed your career."

"The princess is too kind," Finch said, shuffling his feet. "I'm afraid I'm quite the enthusiast, much to my father's chagrin." He extended a hand, and after a slight pause, Bennick shook it.

"I'm not sure why," he said.

"Don't be so modest," Venn cut in.

Finch flashed a smile. "Indeed. Though, you're all quite legendary, aren't you?"

"Indeed we are," Venn agreed with a grin.

"Princess!"

Finch twisted aside, revealing Lady Paltrow and Imara. The Zennorian princess had been an immense help during the last two weeks. Not only had she distracted the noblewoman from constantly visiting Clare, but Imara had spent hours in Clare's room, sharing stories of Zennor, her family, and the many and varied adventures she and Serene had taken part in over the years. She also asked Clare to share stories of her own, and it had been healing to talk of home. Imara had become a true friend.

Imara spared Lord Finch a quick smile before her eyes shifted to Clare. "Sorry to interrupt, we merely wanted to check in."

"Do you need anything?" Lady Paltrow added. "Anything at all?"

Clare sent the woman a smile. "No thank you, I'm quite all right."

"Perhaps a chair," Bennick said.

Clare shot him a look, but the gray-haired lady was already nodding. "Of course." She signaled to a servant. "We can all have a chair and watch the grappling for a while."

Imara moved closer, her eyes wandering the men gathered around them. "Are any of you planning to grapple?"

"No," Bennick said.

"Oh, but it would be lovely to have your participation! I'm sure there are many here who would love to pit themselves against a royal guardsman." Lady Paltrow glanced at Wilf, her head tilting back so she could see all of him. When she looked back at Clare, her eyes were round. "It would be the match of a lifetime. Especially with you watching. It would help raise more coin for the children."

"I think that's a splendid idea." Imara glanced to her guards, who stood like silent shadows. "You're both up to it, aren't you?" They glanced at each other, then silently bowed their heads.

Lady Paltrow beamed. "Wonderful! What about your guards, Princess?"

Clare eyed the three men beside her. "What do you think?"

Wilf's stare was telling, but Venn nodded enough for them both. "I think it sounds fun," Venn said.

Lord Finch eyed Bennick, a smile climbing his cheeks. "I must admit, Captain, the idea of trying myself against you is most exciting. Are you up for the challenge?"

Bennick's stare was almost as impressive as Wilf's, but Imara spoke before he could. "Of course he is." She grinned at him. "Aren't you? I'll cover the entry cost for you both."

Finch grinned. "Thank you, Princess. But as it is a benefit for children, I don't think they'll mind if we both pay the fee." He tipped his head to Bennick. "I'll add our names to the next available match."

Lady Paltrow's smile widened. "I shall spread the word so others have a chance as well." She hurried off, and Imara turned to face Bennick.

"Oh, don't look so unhappy," she said. "Consider this a gift, Markam. You've needed a moment to relax."

He lifted an eyebrow. "Grappling with a pompous lord is relaxing?"

Imara raised an eyebrow. "He didn't seem pompous."

"He isn't." Clare frowned at Bennick. "But if you don't want to—"

"He wants to," Imara cut in. She turned to her guards. "Let's find you some partners as well."

As she walked away, Clare peeked up at Bennick, noting that his jaw was rather firm. She winced. "Sorry."

"It's fine." He stepped closer and lowered his voice, keeping his words between them. "As much as I'm not in the mood, I think I'll enjoy knocking that charming grin off his face."

The corner of her mouth lifted. "You do realize you have no reason to be jealous?"

His only answer was a grunt.

Lady Paltrow returned at the same time the chairs arrived. Clare allowed Bennick to help settle her into one, as that seemed the least she could do for him. Lady Paltrow sat beside her, and Imara returned to sit on Clare's other side. Lady Paltrow must have done a good job spreading the word about the royal body-guards being available to grapple, because not only did many men step forward with an interest in grappling, but the crowd itself swelled with spectators.

Clare sent Venn to pay the entry fees, and she was quite certain some of his own coins would join the betting pool before he returned.

As they waited for the next match, Bennick flipped open the top button on his uniform collar and stretched his arms and neck. Clare tried—and failed—to ignore the way his uniform strained as his muscled body flexed. But when his shoulders rolled and the dark blue jacket pulled over his chest . . . she couldn't look away.

Of course, he glanced over and caught her staring.

Her cheeks warmed, but his quick half-grin made up for the

swell of embarrassment.

A cheer rose from the grapplers and Clare looked over to see the victor offer a hand to the loser. As they cleared the grassy square, Bennick and Finch were called forward.

They stood across from each other, only a pace between them as they took hold of the long staff. Their hands flexed beside each other, testing and tightening their grips, while the crowd finalized their bets.

The game master stepped beside them, raising one hand as he called for them to prepare.

Bennick shifted his stance, his eyes on Finch. The nobleman flashed him a smile.

The game master threw down his hand and cheers erupted as the competing men pushed against the staff. Clare felt a spark of surprise that Finch did not crumple at once, but he was well-built for a nobleman, and he seemed to be matching Bennick's strength. Their heels dug into the ground, leg muscles straining as they pushed against each other.

Bennick suddenly shoved forward and Finch stumbled back, his grip on the staff sliding a little. Bennick jerked the staff, twisting it in on Finch, but the man only grunted and struggled to find his footing. He was twisting his body, absorbing each push that Bennick delivered and even turning some of them back on him. Their faces grew red as they continued to grapple, heels digging into the grass that had been well-trampled even before their tense dance.

Clare's fingers curled in her skirt, her heart beating faster as they continued to twist around each other, dipping, shoving, and spinning each other. She wasn't worried about Bennick. This was only a game. But for every moment it continued, the knot grew in her gut. The building tension made her shoulders rise.

While the crowd continued to call out, a muscle ticked in

Bennick's jaw, and the tendons in Finch's neck bulged as the staff wavered between them. Almost too fast to track, Bennick yanked on the staff with a brutal twisting movement. Unprepared for the sudden lack of resistance, Finch stumbled forward—and then was promptly shoved back.

The crowd shouted as Finch's back hit the ground, his hands slamming into the grass.

Bennick stood over him, the staff still gripped in both hands, his chest rising and falling with each heavy breath.

Applause broke out, and Clare watched as Bennick held out a hand to Finch. The nobleman took it at once, allowing Bennick to haul him to his feet.

The game master took the staff, thanked them for their participation, and called up the next match.

Bennick and Finch walked together off the field, and Clare pushed up from her chair, Lady Paltrow and Imara only a moment behind her.

Sweat dotted Finch's forehead, and his hands were braced on his hips as he breathed raggedly. "That was more exhilarating than expected. Thank you, Captain."

"You're stronger than I expected," Bennick admitted, smiling a little.

Finch huffed out a laugh, still breathing hard. "Yes, well, I'm afraid my boyhood dream to become a soldier never quite went away. I spend more hours training than I should."

"What a thrilling match!" Lady Paltrow enthused, her hands clasped in front of her. "I think you lasted longer than any other today. Perhaps you'll choose to participate in another round?"

"I don't believe I'm up to it." Finch pushed the hair off his flushed forehead. "In fact, I think I'll excuse myself to recover." He bowed to the ladies. "Until our paths cross again." He offered a final nod to Bennick and then strode away, heading back toward the manor.

Lady Paltrow smiled after him. "Such a charming boy. It's nice to have him back in Lindon. He rarely stays long. He's always off traveling. It's a shame when he leaves the house locked up."

"What of his sisters?"

"Oh, he—"

"Lady Paltrow!" A servant darted up, pale and breathing hard. The shock and fear in his eyes made Clare's stomach drop.

"Fates, what's wrong?" the woman asked.

The young man's throat bobbed as he swallowed, his eyes darting to Clare. "It's the prince. He's just arrived, along with twenty Mortisian prisoners."

Lady Paltrow blinked quickly. "The prince? Prince Grandeur?"

"Yes. He's inside."

Clare shot a look at Bennick, shock freezing her blood. What was Grandeur doing here?

The servant wasn't done. "There's also a city guard commander in the courtyard with the Mortisian prisoners—you know, for the exchange—and he wants to know where he can put them during their stay."

"Their stay?" Lady Paltrow fairly squeaked.

Bennick stiffened beside Clare, his gaze focused on the boy. "Commander Markam?"

The servant shrugged. "I don't know. I didn't ask."

"Oh, dear." The lady's fingers twisted together, her shoulders stiffening. "I haven't the faintest clue where to put prisoners. Go find Lord Paltrow at once."

The boy nodded. "I will, but . . ." He glanced at Clare, bending into a slightly awkward bow. "Forgive me, Princess, but the prince is demanding to see you. Now."

Nerves twisted inside her as Clare stepped into the drawing room, Bennick, Venn, and Wilf behind her, and Imara beside her. Confusion and anxiety threaded through every rapid beat of her heart as her eyes cut right to Prince Grandeur.

The Devendran prince sat on a chair near an open window, sipping from a glass of red wine. His dark skin and even darker hair showed his half-Zennorian heritage, but his usual smile was absent, making his handsome features oddly cold. He was seventeen years old, but he looked far older in this moment. Two bodyguards stood behind him, their shoulders back as they stood at attention.

Grandeur slowly pushed to his feet, still clutching his wineglass as he eyed their approach. "Quite the entourage, when all I asked was to see my *sister*." The emphasis on the word made it sound derisive, as well as the fact that it was unnecessary; everyone in the room knew who Clare really was. The hostility in his voice tightened every muscle in Clare's body. She had a horrible sinking feeling that something bad had happened, and that, somehow, she was to blame.

The prince's focus turned to Imara. "My father and I were quite surprised when news of your presence here reached Iden."

"You know me," she said with a tight smile. "I love surprises."

The tension between the cousins was clear, and Clare's concern about the prince's strange mood only grew. She cleared her throat. "Your Highness, we didn't expect you."

"The king deemed it necessary for me to come," Grandeur

said, fingering the stem of the wineglass as he eyed her. "Considering recent events, he thought it best to show our lack of fear of the rebel mob, as well as demonstrate our strength. We can't have them think we can be hurt."

Clearly, Grandeur and Newlan blamed Clare for her injury. Fates knew they would truly blame her, if they knew about Eliot's involvement.

She swallowed, her mouth suddenly dry.

Grandeur wasn't finished. "I will attend the road dedication with you in Halbrook, then make my way to Lythe."

"Why Lythe?" Imara asked.

Grandeur set the wineglass aside and straightened, lifting his chin. "I'll be taking over the hunt for the rebels as well as review our forces. A large part of our army is stationed there, and we don't want them to become lax just because the alliance is all but secured."

"A prince visiting a military fort positioned near the border during these tenuous times sends a strange message, don't you think?" Imara asked.

Grandeur forced a thin smile. "Aren't you supposed to be getting married to some primitive tribal lord?"

Imara's answering smile was sharp. "Don't worry, Cousin. I wouldn't dream of letting you miss the occasion. After all, you haven't been rejected by *every* woman in Zennor. Yet."

The prince's eyes narrowed.

Bennick took a step forward, breaking the glare between Imara and Grandeur. "Forgive me, Your Highness, but the king's latest letter said nothing of this. I don't know if having you, Serene, and Imara at the same place is advisable."

Grandeur's gaze cut into Bennick. "Your concern has been noted, but I suggest you keep your focus on your job, where it is clearly needed."

A muscle in Bennick's jaw ticked. "Of course. But I do have concerns about the Mortisian prisoners."

Grandeur expelled a breath. "It was my father's wish that I travel with them to this point, for added security. Now that I've joined you, Commander Markam will continue with the prisoners to Stills. After tonight, you won't see them again until the border. Does that satisfy you?"

Bennick inclined his head, though the motion was a bit stiff. "Thank you, Your Highness."

The door opened behind them and Clare turned to see Commander Markam stride in. Her body reacted by stiffening, and she wondered if that would always be the case. This was the man who had interrogated her, and then decided she could be the decoy. He had brought the king to her cell, and convinced him, too. In many ways, this man had stolen her life. He had certainly changed the course of it. And while she had gained much, it was hard not to look at him and only see what she had lost.

The commander's expression was grim, his jaw set. The hair at his temples seemed grayer than before, as if he had aged in the weeks they had been away. His stern gaze was just as fierce, however, as he scanned them all, his focus falling on her. She was startled at the reminder of how similar his eyes were to Bennick's—and yet so fundamentally different. Because while Bennick's eyes were always warm, his father's were cold, even as he turned to view his son.

"Captain," he said in greeting.

Bennick's shoulders tightened. "Commander."

Commander Markam's focus shifted to the prince. "The prisoners are secure in the stable. They're being fed and watered."

"Good."

Clare chafed at the way the prisoners were being discussed. And clearly she wasn't alone, because Imara's eyes narrowed.

"They're not animals. They should be given better accommo-dations."

"They're no doubt being treated better than the Devendran prisoners," Grandeur said, his throat working on a swallow of wine.

"Mortise follows the Garvins Treaty," Imara said. "As we all do."

Grandeur snorted. "Do they? We got the names of the prisoners Desfan's releasing, and do you know what was different about their list? Ours held the names of men. Theirs belong to men *and* women, and barely a soldier among them. They were simple farmers, captured by the enemy during the border skirmishes."

Imara stiffened. "Devendra is not without blame in this. My father has been asking Newlan to release all Mortisian prisoners for years, and your father wouldn't listen."

"No. He refused to give them up without Saernon Cassian's promise that the Devendran prisoners would also be released."

"And the serjan refused to give up his prisoners without a promise that all Mortisians would be returned," Imara retorted. "So you were both locked in a years-long debate because neither one of you dared to offer any trust, and innocent people lost years of their lives trapped in prison cells. I believe my father even volunteered to be an intermediary, and Newlan flatly refused." One eyebrow arched. "An insult no one in Zennor's court has forgotten, I might add."

Grandeur's knuckles whitened as he tightened his grip on the wineglass. "It was not meant as an insult."

"Of course not," Imara said, her smile thin. "A refusal to trust one's ally is never an insult."

"Zennor insulted Devendra when your father refused to cease trade with Mortise during the border wars."

"Your skirmishes with Mortise were your affair. And if you'll recall, my father begged your father to consider the consequences of such a useless battle."

"Useless?" Grandeur leaned in, his jaw hard. "Mortisians were stealing Devendran lands. We had to act."

"Saernon Cassian insists it was Devendran farmers who were taking Mortisian land."

"A lie," he snapped. "One that should never have been believed by our family in Zennor."

Clare eyed the two cousins, shocked by how rapidly the argument had escalated. Their distaste for each other had been clear from the beginning, but this had moved far beyond that. Both royals were clearly incensed, and it was difficult to say which one seemed the most out of character—the always cheerful Imara, or the mild-tempered Grandeur who had been Clare's first friend at the castle.

But then, hadn't Clare learned by now that everyone wore a mask?

Commander Markam cleared his throat, the low sound cutting through the tension. "Perhaps this discussion should take place at another time."

"I'm not sure this is a discussion that will ever lead us anywhere." Imara turned to Clare and took her arm. "We should return to the fair."

"I require a word with Clare," Grandeur said. "A private word."

A chill skated down her spine, and she wished she could refuse. The Grandeur before her was so different from the man he had been at the castle. This version of the prince was cool. Detached. And his eyes, which used to spark with kindness and humor, were sharp as he stared at her.

Her fingers curled in her skirt but she nodded. "Of course."

Imara crossed her arms over her chest, and Clare knew instinctively the princess would not leave—even if Grandeur dared to order it. So she turned to face her. "Please rejoin Lady Paltrow. I would hate to disrupt the fair any more than we have."

Imara's shoulders dropped as she expelled a breath. "Very well." She shot a last look at Grandeur, and Clare's heart warmed at the protective gesture.

Beside her, Bennick also seemed intent to remain. But before he could voice any protest, his father spoke. "Captain, I'd like a word with you."

Bennick's mouth pressed into a line and he eyed Clare. "Wilf and Venn will be just outside."

She gave him what she hoped was a reassuring smile, then watched as the guards filed out. Even Grandeur's bodyguards left, leaving her alone with the prince as the door clicked shut.

Grandeur dropped back onto his seat and lifted his wineglass, taking a generous swallow. His throat worked on the wine, and then his gaze raised to meet hers. "Sit."

Clare moved to the nearby settee and perched on the extreme edge, her hands shaking a little in her lap. She needed to latch onto Serene's confidence so she could make it through whatever this was.

The dipping in her stomach told her it wasn't going to be good. It felt like an interrogation, and it hadn't even started yet.

The prince's face was smooth, revealing nothing of his thoughts. But the corners of his mouth were drawn. "Why didn't you send me a message about Imara's arrival on the tour?"

Clare's tongue darted over her suddenly dry lips. "I . . . didn't think it mattered. And she had a letter from Newlan, so I assumed you—"

"Which was it? You didn't think it mattered, or you thought I already knew?"

Her heart pounded, the fine hairs on her arms rising. "Both, I suppose. I assumed you knew, since Imara had that letter. And I truly didn't think her presence meant anything to you."

The wineglass clinked as Grandeur set it on a side table, the small sound amplified in short silence. "My cousin is a talented forger." His voice was carefully measured. Quiet.

Dangerous.

"I didn't know," Clare said, her voice nearly a whisper.

"Perhaps you didn't. But that's not what troubles me, Clare. What troubles me is that you didn't tell me that my sister's greatest friend and confidante was unexpectedly now traveling with her."

"She hasn't even seen Serene yet—"

"That isn't my point." Grandeur leaned forward, his eyes narrowing. "You promised to watch Serene for any signs of treason, any sort of plotting. And yet you failed to inform me about Imara's arrival. They could be exchanging letters. They could have laid plans even before this. And they will most certainly be planning something the moment they see each other. The fact that you didn't see the danger raises some concerns for me, as I'm sure you can understand."

"I do. And I'm sorry, I didn't think of Imara in that way."

His head listed to the side. "In what way?"

Clare blinked. "As . . . dangerous. To Devendra."

His lips twitched, and Clare honestly couldn't tell if he was amused or upset as he shook his head. "You'll need to do better, or you won't even know the moment Serene strikes. She can be devious, and with Imara's help?" He waved a hand toward the closed door. "You saw how incendiary she is. She thinks little of Devendra, and even less of my father. She would help Serene in any scheme. She is exactly the sort of person I need you to watch."

"Of course."

Grandeur leaned back, his elbows propped on the arms of the chair, his fingers laced as he studied her. "It seems Imara likes you. That will work in your favor. Get closer to her. And when she and Serene are together, you need to tell me what they discuss. I need to know what they're planning."

"I don't think they're planning anything."

"You're not *thinking* at all."

Clare's mouth snapped shut.

His shoulders tightened. "Fates, Clare, I'm sorry. I didn't mean that." One hand stretched over his eyes, rubbing gently. "I don't mean to be upset with you at all. I'm not. Not really. I'm upset with . . ." His voice trailed off and his hand dropped. This time when he looked at her, she could see the prince she'd first befriended, though a graver version of him. Regret twisted his features as he shook his head. "I'm grateful for your friendship, for all you're doing for me. For Devendra. I shouldn't have let my frustration get the best of me. I just fear that Serene is already laying her plans, and Imara being here only confirms that."

A voice in her head cautioned her to tread carefully; to simply nod and leave it at that. But something had happened to Grandeur. Something had changed in him, and she needed to learn what it was. Serene would want to know. "Grandeur," she said carefully. "Is something wrong?"

His eyebrows drew together, his eyes shifting to the half-empty wineglass beside him. "A friend of mine delivered some . . . difficult advice. I don't want to accept it, but I may have no choice."

Clare's lungs tightened and she was suddenly back in the castle garden, overhearing Grandeur and a stranger discuss things like killing Serene and threatening Clare's brothers. She wasn't sure if that was who Grandeur referenced—or if she was simply being paranoid in hearing the danger of his words—but terror flashed through her, making her mouth dry. "This friend . . . do you trust him?"

"Completely. At times, I feel he is the only one I can trust." Grandeur glanced up at her, a slight smile tugging the corner of his mouth. "It makes me all the more grateful that I have you on my side." He nodded to her. "Now. Tell me everything that has been going on."

CHAPTER 28

BENNICK

BENNICK CLOSED THE DOOR OF HIS BEDROOM and turned to face his father. The commander had asked for privacy, and this was the only place that would give them that during the Palrow's charity fair.

As much as Bennick didn't want to talk to his father, at the moment, his biggest reason for dreading this was because he wanted to be with Clare. Leaving her with the prince when Grandeur was clearly in a bad mood didn't sit well with him. His skin itched and his movements were stiff. Knowing Wilf and Venn were watching her helped only marginally.

The commander was scanning the room, his hands clasped behind his back. Though the window was closed, the excited shouts from the fair below still drifted in, filling the otherwise quiet space.

They hadn't spoken a word since leaving the drawing room.

Their relationship was beyond complicated. Showing his father any deference or respect always filled him with the urge to break the commander's nose, but he had no choice but to keep his hostility in check. Commander Markam was one of the king's most trusted military leaders. He commanded the city guard and oversaw the king's prison. And while he wasn't Bennick's direct superior, he could not blatantly ignore him—or attack him.

The commander finally turned to face him. "It's good to see you, Ben."

Bennick bit back the first retort that sprang to mind. "How is Mother?" Normally he avoided speaking about her to the commander, but Gweneth Markam was a woman of delicate health, and her deterioration had been quickening of late.

"She is actually doing well," the commander said. "Better than she has been in months. She tires easily, but the physicians have given her some new powders, and they help immensely. She even managed to ride a horse."

Bennick's jaw loosened. "Really?"

"Yes. She's also been taking walks in the garden. The summer weather seems to be agreeing with her. She even asked if we might spend the winter in Zennor."

"Will you?"

The commander's shoulders tightened. "This year will be a difficult one, politically speaking. The king will need me in Iden."

"Of course," Bennick snorted. His mouth twisted wryly, bitterness coating his words. "You never have put her before your career. I don't know why I thought you might this time."

"She understands my dedication to Devendra." His eyebrows pulled together. "I don't know why you don't. You're a soldier.

You should—"

"Do not tell me what I should or should not understand. Not when it comes to you."

His mouth snapped shut, and he lifted his chin, his gaze sharp. "Very well. We have other things we need to discuss."

"Like why you're the one escorting the Mortisian prisoners?" Bennick asked. "I would have thought it beneath you."

"The exchange must go smoothly. I volunteered to oversee it, and the king agreed it would be best. I also wanted to see you."

Bennick snorted. "Sentimentality? From you?"

His father's eyes darkened. "You're in danger, Ben, and it was clear from your letters that you refuse to realize it."

"Danger is part of my job."

"This is different. You've been targeted by the Rose."

"I'm not his target."

"I think that's debatable. He sent you poison."

"I don't see that as a threat."

"Then you're blind." The commander straightened. "The last message I received from you was the note purely addressed to you. Have there been any new notes?"

"No." Frankly, it bothered him. The Rose had been completely silent during their stay with the Paltrows. He wasn't sure what that meant, but it had him on edge.

The commander's eyebrows pulled together. "You mentioned in your letter that the last note was found in your room." He shot a look at the space around them. "You also said there was not an accompanying message for the princess."

"Correct." He was still grateful for that, because it meant Clare had been easily left out of the latest terror. He had found the note the evening before the Paltrow's ball, and he had decided against sharing it with Clare. There was no advantage to frightening her with it—especially after she had been injured, and needed to focus on healing.

Besides, the message had been for him.

He'd found it on his bed, which had been covered in thorns and blood.

Captain Markam,

Did you receive my gift? I don't normally give poison to anyone, let alone a bodyguard. But I couldn't resist. Do you like playing this game with me? I must say, I'm enjoying myself.

Could you do something for me? Could you please keep the princess alive? I've heard rumors that others want to kill her, but if you could keep her breathing long enough so I can be the one to end her, I would greatly appreciate it.

Oh, and your horse was a very beautiful creature.

The Rose

Bennick ground his teeth just thinking about the letter. He remembered the moment he read that final line—realized where the blood had come from. His horse had been a loyal companion for years, and the Rose had slaughtered him in his stall in the middle of the night. No one had heard anything.

As much as he hated to see his father's point, he had to admit the Rose seemed fixated on him. He just didn't know why.

"He's taunting me," Bennick allowed. "But I'm merely a part of his larger game. His target is Serene."

"The princess may be his ultimate target," the commander said. "But the threat against you is real. The Rose is known to escalate things, and that is the pattern I see with you. He started by sending you a vial of poison—now he's killed your horse." His jaw stiffened. "You may refuse to see this as a threat, but that is the only objective way to see any of it."

He pulled in a breath, trying to keep his pulse from snapping. He needed to keep his temper in check, keep things as professional as possible between them. "It doesn't make sense for him to target me. It isn't his normal process."

"Exactly what has me worried."

Bennick shook his head. "I've had this conversation with Wilf and Venn, and I still think I have no personal connection with the Rose."

"But you do."

His stomach dropped at the unexpected response. "What do you mean?"

The commander lifted an eyebrow. "Two years ago, the Rose killed one of the captains under my command, and I hunted him. While I didn't catch him, my search would not have gone unnoticed by him. It would not be hard for him to make the connection between us."

"So you think he's targeting me because of a grudge he holds against you?"

"It makes sense. Well, as much sense as anything where that

deranged killer is concerned." He shook his head. "Regardless of why he's targeting you, I think you need to consider the fact that your presence here is making the situation with the Rose worse."

Bennick frowned. "What?"

"Your presence has antagonized him, and I think it's clear his fixation with you has only grown."

"Which could work in our favor," Bennick said. "For whatever reason, he's obsessed with me. Wilf thinks he might believe we're competing somehow, and that in his effort to win, he will be more likely to make a mistake. He's already done things he has never been known to do on a hunt before."

"True. Which is why I think it would be best if you returned to Iden."

Bennick jerked, his body straightening away from the wall. "You can't be serious."

"I'm completely serious. We can say you fell ill, or were injured. You can leave in the morning with a group of my men. I've already discussed this with Grandeur, and he has graciously offered Captain Dervish to take your place. Your men can stay under his command."

"No." The shock was wearing off, and heat flashed through Bennick's body, curling his fists at his sides. "I'm not leaving."

"Why?"

"Because this is my job."

"Ben—"

"I'm not returning to Iden," he cut in firmly.

A growl percolated up the commander's throat. "You're being a fool. Your presence here could very well be making things worse. If you're suddenly gone, the Rose will be divided. Torn. He will want to complete his mission in killing Serene, but he has also made this personal with you. My gut tells me he will choose to go after you first, before you're out of reach. He'll be angry that you left his game. He'll want to punish you —taunt you with what he has planned for Clare and Serene."

"You're making a lot of predictions about his thoughts."

"He killed one of my men. I've studied him, and I know he's a sick-minded killer, and the fates will rot me before I let him hurt you."

The impassioned, protective words took Bennick by surprise, not that his hard expression revealed that. He was still too angry to show anything else. "I'm not leaving."

A muscle in the commander's jaw ticked. "If it will set your mind at ease, I'll stay with the decoy."

"No. I disagree with your assessment of the Rose. I think the best thing I can do is stay so the Rose can remain fixated on me —he'll be less likely to hurt anyone else, and more likely to make a mistake."

"You're being hunted, Ben."

"Then I hope he finds me so I can stop him." He turned for the door, done with this entire conversation.

His father snagged his wrist, jerking him close. Every muscle in Bennick's body tensed at the sudden contact, but he didn't jerk away as his father leaned in, his voice low and sharp. "I refuse to stand by and do nothing while you blatantly ignore the danger. The Rose is stalking you. If you're not willing to see that, then you are blind, stupid, or both."

Bennick ground his teeth. It took every bit of control he possessed not to break his father's hold and only meet his glare. "Let go of me. Now."

The commander's fingers tightened around his wrist, then suddenly released. His father took a step back and his nostrils flared, frustration pouring off him in waves. But his tone was surprisingly even as he spoke. "Please, Ben. I know our history is not good, but I'm begging you to listen to me. Just this once."

"I listened to what you had to say, but I refuse to return to Iden. The Rose will make a mistake, and I'll catch him. He will stand trial for every crime he's ever committed."

There was no softening in the commander's stance, but the edge in his voice made it clear that Bennick had won the argument, at least for now. "If you manage to catch him," he said darkly. "Do all of Eyrinthia a favor and kill him. He doesn't deserve a trial."

CHAPTER 29

MIA

MIA WAS STILL EATING BREAKFAST WHEN the cell door swung open and Tyrell walked in.

Seeing him was a shock, because it had been ten days since she'd seen him. She'd started to wonder if he no longer intended to follow King Henri's orders to visit her.

It was also a shock because last time he'd been in this room, she had hit him with a chair, and he had triggered one of her panics.

He didn't quite look at her as he closed the door. "Good morning."

She watched silently as he moved for the table and lowered himself into the chair opposite her. "I was beginning to think you weren't coming back."

His lips pressed into a line. "My father sent me away from

307

Lenzen on an errand. I wasn't avoiding you."

"I didn't say you were."

He ignored that. "Are you well?"

Surprise flashed through her. Though his eyes were still not quite meeting hers, she could see the concern in them. "I'm fine."

He dipped his chin. "Good. I . . ." He swallowed, his throat bobbing. He shook his head a little. "Good," he repeated.

There was an awkward silence and Mia picked at her slice of bread. "You've never come so early in the day."

A muscle in his jaw ticked. "I was anxious to see if you were well."

"Oh."

This was a new version of Tyrell, one she hadn't seen before. She didn't know what to expect from him.

His hand slipped into his pocket and he withdrew a deck of cards. "I thought we could play a game today." He nodded to her plate. "You can finish your breakfast first."

"I'm finished." She pushed the plate aside, truly not interested in the remains of her breakfast. Not with him acting so strangely.

He began shuffling the deck. "Do you know how to play Assassins? It's a Mortisian game."

Mia eyed the worn cards in his hands. "Grayson taught me."

He snorted, sounding more like himself as he dealt. "He's terrible at it."

Mia gathered her cards and viewed them. She rearranged them in her hand, then took another from the pile.

In two turns, Mia laid down a winning hand.

Tyrell stared at the cards, his eyebrows lifting.

Mia smiled, a slight edge to the action. "*I'm* not terrible at it."

"No," Tyrell said quietly, dropping his cards. "No, you are not."

He gathered the cards and shuffled them between his long fingers. "How long have you been a prisoner here?"

She frowned. "Why do you ask?"

"I'm curious." He watched the cards as he dealt. "My father gave the impression that it's been a while."

"I've been in here since I was seven."

Tyrell froze, the deck hovering over the table. "How old are you now?"

"Sixteen."

He stared at her. "Nine years."

"Yes."

He muttered under his breath, finished dealing the cards, and then they each looked at their hand. "What did you do to catch the king's attention? I can't imagine you as a criminal. At least not at seven years old."

Mia shuffled the cards in her hand. "You don't know me."

"You're right. I don't." They went three rounds before Tyrell won. He didn't crow his victory, just gathered the cards and shuffled again. "I haven't traveled much beyond Ryden, but I've been to Mortise. If I had to guess, I'd say you're Mortisian."

She surprised herself by nodding.

"Is your family still in Mortise?"

In her mind, she heard her mother screaming. The horrible sound ripped through the already terror-soaked night. She saw the fear in her sister's eyes—

She shook her head, cutting off the memories before they could swallow her. "I don't want to talk about this."

Tyrell said nothing, just passed out her cards.

She fanned them out, forcing herself to concentrate.

She won this time.

She grabbed the cards before Tyrell could and shuffled briskly. The stiff fluttering of the cards was the only sound in the room.

"You can ask about me, you know," Tyrell said.

"There's nothing about you I care to know."

The corner of his mouth twitched. "You wound me."

"If only."

He snorted a laugh as he gathered his pile of cards. "Liam taught Grayson and me how to play this game. I was probably only six years old. He found a deck somewhere. It was the first card game I ever learned. I loved it."

Mia glanced up from her cards, catching the almost wistful look that crossed his face.

His eyes remained on his cards as he spoke. "I stole Liam's deck and convinced Grayson to play with me at night, when no one would know." He smiled a little. "I'd forgotten about that. But we would sneak into a sitting room no one ever used, and we'd play for hours. In the beginning, we both brought our knives, worried that it was a trick and the other might turn on us. But at night, in that room, we could just . . . play." Lost in his thoughts, his smile faded.

Mia's gut tightened. "What happened?"

"Peter caught me sneaking back to my room one night. He beat me for keeping secrets, and then he held a knife to my face and told me to lure Grayson into another game. I did. Peter and Carter were lying in wait, and the moment Grayson entered the room, they tackled him. They beat him, and then Peter made me burn the cards." Tyrell set down his cards—a winning hand —and lifted his gaze to meet her stare. "I suppose you hate me for that. Betraying him like I did."

In truth, she just felt horribly sad for both of them.

He swept up the cards, not waiting for a response. "I think I'm done with this game for now."

"You're leaving?"

He shook his head. "The hour's not up. What were you planning to do this morning?"

"I was going to paint," she answered honestly.

"Excellent. I can watch you."

"No." The word came out reflexively.

"I really think I can. I'll try not to blink too much." He shrugged. "If you want me to participate, I suppose you can paint me."

Her eyes narrowed. "No."

He flashed a smile. "I truly don't mind posing for you."

"I'm not painting you." But her fingers did itch to paint, and after Tyrell had shared that story from his childhood, she didn't feel like arguing with him. She also knew he wouldn't relent until she painted something.

She wouldn't paint him, though.

She rose from the table and moved for the chest in the corner that held her supplies. She carried the bottles of paint to the table, then crossed the room to find a canvas. She had run out of blank ones, so it was time to paint over something. She found one of a mountainside, and decided that would do. It wasn't her best work.

She took it to the table, where Tyrell was fingering a bottle of yellow paint. He watched as she wordlessly put her wooden easel into place and stood up the canvas. Then she tied her curly hair back into a knot so it would be out of her face while she worked. She didn't like the thought of Tyrell watching her paint, but it wouldn't be the most offensive thing he'd done to her. Not by any account.

She returned to the table, pried off the cap to the white paint, and dipped a brush.

Tyrell watched her wordlessly until the moment she lifted the paint-covered brush to the canvas. "Stop!" He leaped up from the chair and lunged for her, snagging her wrist.

Mia flinched back, her spine stiff as adrenaline shot through her. "Let go of me!"

His fingers flexed around her wrist, his expression twisted in anger. "What are you doing? Why are you trying to paint over that?"

She frowned, her heart hammering against her ribs. "*That's* what bothered you?"

A muscle in his jaw feathered angrily. "Why would you destroy that?"

Mia tugged at her wrist, but he didn't let go. "I paint over my canvases all the time. I only have so many."

Tyrell's eyes narrowed. "And Grayson never bought you more?"

"He couldn't always get them." King Henri had spies everywhere, and they were always watching Grayson. He had to be careful with what he brought her. Too much, and the king noticed. Mia shook her head at Tyrell. "Besides, your mother hates art, so supplies are hard to find in Lenzen."

"They're not lost relics," he snapped. "He could have found them with a little searching."

"Let go of me."

He did, though he was still fuming and he remained far too close to her. "I'll buy you canvases."

"I don't need anything from you."

His teeth clenched, but he didn't stop her when she stepped around him and dragged the brush over the canvas, slowly obliterating the mountainside in white.

Tyrell twisted away, moving to sit back at the table. His back was a rigid line and he shuffled the cards in his hands. She was half-surprised he didn't stalk from the room. But he'd left early only once, and she wondered if Henri had found out. A threat from the king would explain why he was still there, when he clearly wanted to be anywhere else.

While the white on the canvas dried, Mia sorted through her paints and arranged a scene in her mind. She wanted to paint a peaceful scene, something that would calm her. Her thoughts turned to Grayson. To where he was now—or would be soon.

Where she wished she could be.

She grabbed her blue paint and began to mix it with white on the stained palette.

She worked in silence, the ache in her chest slowly loosening as she brushed paint over the white canvas, slowly coaxing life back onto it. Movement. Color.

She was so attuned to her art, she didn't notice Tyrell move to stand behind her. Not until he spoke. "That is . . . beautiful."

Mia eased back, studying the image. It was a beach at midday. Sunny, bright, and warm. Golden sands against clear blue water, tipped with white foam. Green fronds encroached the side of the beach, along with smooth boulders that children would rush to climb.

But the beach was empty. Beautiful, but deserted.

Mia stretched out her fingers, only now registering the cramps. "The sea isn't right," she said. "I can't get the right shade." She shook her head. "The blue is old and doesn't mix well."

Tyrell said nothing, just continued studying the painting. His scrutiny was a little unnerving. Then his gaze turned to her, and she was even more unnerved.

He hesitated, then lifted a finger toward her cheek.

Mia stepped back before he could touch her, her heart hammering.

His hand rolled to a fist as it dropped and his jaw tightened. "You have some paint on your face."

Without another word, or even a backward glance, he strode from the room.

CHAPTER 30

GRAYSON

DUVAN WAS AN IMPRESSIVE CITY. SPRAWLING up from the wide bay were hundreds of sandstone buildings, all painted in vivid blues, reds, yellows, and greens. The streets twisted among the towering structures, filled with people who looked like little more than skittering bugs. Even from this distance, Grayson could see the ropes crisscrossing the streets overhead, hung with brightly colored clothes left to dry under the bright sun. Everything about the city seemed colorful, crowded, and chaotic.

It was nothing like Lenzen, with its dirt streets, poorly thatched roofs, and the depressive gray fortress that loomed over the city. His skin itched at the thought of entering the madness, being surrounded by it, but he was anxious to leave the rocking ship.

He stood at the side rail near the gangplank, Liam beside him, both of them waiting for Prince Desfan—or *Serjah* Desfan, as Grayson should call him. Liam had told him it would be best to use the Mortisian term for *prince*. It showed effort. Respect.

It would help hide the real reason Henri had sent them here: to assassinate Desfan's bride-to-be and launch a war that would probably see the Mortisian prince dead and his kingdom conquered.

The continual sway of the ship made Grayson long to step onto the docks, but they'd been told they could not leave the ship until Desfan came to greet them.

They'd already been waiting almost two hours.

Grayson had known other kingdoms operated on grand ceremonies and traditions, but he had never imagined they could be so ridiculous and stifling. He'd never appreciated the cold efficiency of his father's court until now.

The men on the ship were not happy either. They'd just learned they would only be allowed to leave in rotations of ten men at a time, which meant emotions would run high in this wooden prison. The restricted shore-leave could end dangerously, but luckily it was a problem Grayson would not have to deal with.

Just as well. He already had more problems than he could handle.

His eyes were pulled to the royal palace, seated on the southeastern side of the bay. It was raised above the city, a rocky cliff-face keeping it well above the sea. It was beautiful. A light tan stone had been used to craft it, and even from here he could see that sections had been painted in bright colors and designs, the pillars and arches carved elegantly. There were even statues set on—and in—the walls.

"I often fantasize about Mother visiting Duvan," Liam said suddenly. "The criticisms she would deliver would be amusing. The smaller coastal villages are even more colorful, as are the islands." He clapped his brother's shoulder. "You'll grow used to it."

Grayson was not so confident. His black clothes were stifling in the heat and he imagined he looked as out of place as he felt. This was the sort of place someone like Mia belonged. It was vibrant. Alive. She had never confirmed where she came from, but he had guessed Mortise. Looking at the brown skin of the people milling on the docks, hearing the rolling accent on the air, he assumed he was right. Perhaps she had even been to Duvan—seen this very view.

For some reason, the thought calmed some of his anxiety.

A trumpet sounded, alerting all to the royal presence now entering the docks. Grayson watched as an enclosed carriage came into view and then rolled to a stop. He followed Liam's lead to the plank of wood that had been laid against the dock. The harbor was deep enough that all the large ships were able to anchor near the docks.

They stood at the top of the plank and waited some more. The sun beat down and Grayson barely held back his growl of annoyance.

Finally, Serjah Desfan strode onto the dock.

The man was tall, his build rather narrow, though there was obvious muscle in his forearms. He wore no swords, but Grayson guessed those were his weapon of choice. It was something in the way he carried himself, the way his trim body was shaped. Dark hair curled over his brow and at the nape of his bronzed neck. He wore a gold crown and was dressed as colorfully as the buildings of Duvan, wearing shades of turquoise, red, and ivory.

"Serjah Desfan," Liam called out. "Thank you for coming to greet us personally. It is a great honor." He started down the gangplank and Grayson snapped to follow, his movements less graceful than his brother's; the wood swayed beneath his feet and he had to concentrate on each step to avoid pitching into the harbor.

Desfan smiled cordially at them, though perhaps with a hint of caution.

Wise of him.

"Prince Liam, Prince Grayson; welcome to Mortise!"

Liam stepped onto the dock and tipped his head. "It is a privilege to be here."

Grayson stepped beside Liam, also inclining his head. But he didn't stay focused on Desfan, because the heir of Mortise was not alone.

Several noble men and women dressed in green robes offered courteous bows, their mouths a little too tight. Some of the council members, Grayson assumed. Then there were the guards. Several stood with hands loose by their sides, their curved swords within easy reach. The serjah's personal bodyguard was easy to spot. The young man looked to be just slightly older than Desfan—maybe Liam's age—and he stood so close to the serjah they were nearly touching. His eyes had scanned Liam, assessed the Ryden guards trickling into place behind them, and now were narrowed on Grayson.

He was clearly seen as the biggest threat.

He tried to keep his face as neutral as possible, even though he felt totally off-balance. The ground was still swaying beneath him, even though they'd left the ship, and he didn't know what to do, how to act. Everything Liam had imparted had deserted him. He had not been trained for the useless niceties Liam and Desfan were so easily exchanging. He was out of his element, far from home, and missing Mia so intensely he could hardly breathe.

"I trust your travels were uneventful?" Desfan asked.

"They were. Just a slight storm several days ago, but we rode through the edge of it."

"We're not to the stormy season yet, thank the fates."

Liam nodded. "I hope the weather in Devendra has also been good. Your future bride began her travels, did she not?"

"She left Iden about five weeks ago, and is enjoying her tour."

"Wonderful! As my father wrote to you, we look forward to the official betrothal."

"Mortise is also excited for the alliance," Desfan said. He glanced at Grayson, his brow furrowing. "Are you unwell, Prince Grayson?"

Liam's hand clapped his shoulder. "I'm afraid my brother is not suited to a life at sea."

"Ah." Understanding crossed Desfan's face and he winced in sympathy. "The last couple of weeks must have been most unpleasant for you. We'll do our best to make you forget all that. We've planned a celebratory dinner for tonight."

"That sounds delightful." Liam glanced at Grayson. "Doesn't it?"

Not at all.

"Yes," he said instead.

Desfan smiled. "Good." He gestured toward the shore. "Shall we?"

"Please." Liam fell into step with Desfan and Grayson trailed behind, Desfan's personal bodyguard at his side. The other guards and nobles also made their way off of the dock, and they had nearly reached the carriage waiting at the end when Liam spoke. "Grayson and I would very much enjoy a chance to walk around your city. It is our first time in Duvan, of course, and we're anxious to see it."

"Of course. The carriage can follow us. If you tire, or the heat becomes too much, we can ride back to the palace."

The last thing Grayson wanted to do was trudge through the too bright, too crowded city, where curious eyes were already scanning every inch of him—pointedly lingering on the scars on his face. He gritted his teeth and forced himself to ignore them.

They passed the carriage, and a couple of the older robed nobles climbed inside. Desfan's guards led the way to a narrow street which took them past some warehouses and into the actual city.

With the wider street, Grayson no longer had an excuse to walk behind his brother. And Desfan's bodyguard clearly did not like Grayson anywhere behind Desfan, so he moved to walk on his brother's other side.

The cobbled streets were uneven, and the strange swaying and pitching feeling that he'd experienced on the gangplank continued here. It was like he was still on the ship, and he supposed it would take a little time for his body to adjust to life back on solid land. But it was annoying, and heightened his feelings of agitation. The blasted sun glaring down on them didn't help, either. He was sweltering in the heat.

The ground dipped unnaturally again and he nearly stumbled. He struggled to keep his strides even.

"I admire your bravery, Prince Grayson."

He glanced at Desfan. "What?"

The serjah gestured with his chin. "To wear such a dark color during a Mortisian summer."

Liam chuckled. "My brother is fond of serious colors."

"Well, perhaps I can at least direct you to a place where you could purchase something of a lighter material. It can still be black, but it will breathe easier."

Grayson bowed his head, though his spine had stiffened. "That is most generous of you, Serjah Desfan."

"Please, I insist you call me Desfan. I don't like to stand on ceremony."

He nearly snorted, thinking of all the guards and nobles

around them. This was *not* standing on ceremony?

Liam, ever the diplomat, smiled. "We thank you for the honor, Desfan."

The deeper they moved into the city, the more people stopped to stare. The Mortisian language—which Grayson had barely begun to learn—was spoken so rapidly, he had no hope of understanding anything. The smells were foreign, as well. Foods were being cooked and sold that he didn't even recognize. Bright orange and yellow fruits that would fit in his fist, a spiky fruit as big as his face and topped with a green frond. Brown spheres that looked hard as wood, but people were drinking something white from them, like milk. There were fried pastries covered in sugar, carts with spices so strong his nose itched and his eyes watered. Seeds, nuts, and berries. Fish of all colors and sizes. There were other creatures from the sea as well; some had claws, and others had tentacles. There were also snakes, goats, chickens, and . . . were those insects?

He stopped looking too closely at the carts after that.

Desfan pointed out different things of interest—old architecture, statues, and fountains, facts about the many different markets Duvan boasted—and Liam was a rapt listener, inserting comments, asking questions, always smiling.

The market they walked seemed to have a little of everything, and the area proved that the streets of Duvan were more chaotic than they had appeared from afar.

Sheets, rugs, and clothing snapped in the breeze overhead, hung out to dry. Vendors sang out their wares and prices, merchandise spilling out of the tents, carts, and stalls that clogged the street. Children shrieked with laughter, darting around the crowds. Mothers yelled and bartered. Shirtless men carried heavy burdens while others walked leisurely in their finery. Others knelt on the ground, heads down, empty hands cupped in supplication, wordlessly begging for food or coin. Mercies that would never come in Ryden. Not because there was nothing left to give—though there wasn't—but because begging was a criminal offense, punishable by imprisonment or a rotation at one of the many work camps.

Grayson hung back, watching one old man in particular. The thin white hairs on his head barely covered his age-spotted scalp and his flabby arms trembled, hands empty, but still he raised them. As if he knew something good would be placed in them, even if it took some time.

"Prince Grayson?" Desfan asked.

He jolted. He had stopped walking at some point, and the whole procession had paused to eye him. Liam frowned slightly at Desfan's side, his fingers twitching with the subtle signing language he had been teaching Grayson. *Are you all right?*

Warmth infused his cheeks and he opened his mouth to apologize for the delay, but before he could speak, someone crashed into him from behind.

His reaction was ingrained. Unstoppable.

Even as he stumbled from the surprising blow, he jerked the dagger from his belt. His free hand snatched for a grip on his attacker as he wheeled around, raising the knife to strike.

Horrified wide brown eyes stared up at him and his heart stopped.

Mia.

No. Not Mia. A Mortisian child. A young girl, no more than ten years old, terror stricken into every angle of her face. Tears pooled in her eyes and she gaped up at him, trembling, clutching his wrist with thin fingers.

"P-please," she gasped in Mortisian. "I'm sorry."

Grayson was frozen. Everyone stared at him—spectators on the street, the nobles, the soldiers, Desfan, Liam—but he couldn't move. His heart thundered against his ribs, fingers still wrapped in the collar of the girl's orange dress.

He heard the anxious whispers stabbing the air all around him. *Ryden demon. Bloodthirsty killer. Kaelin monster.*

In that moment, he felt the slicing truth of every hissed word.

"Please." The girl's lips quivered as she begged again, tears rolling down her rounded cheeks. "Don't kill me."

Grayson released her as if he'd been burned. He stepped back, pulse roaring in his ears, his grip on the knife so crushing he thought his knuckles would snap within his gloves. The girl darted away, back into the arms of her playmates who had stood back, watching Grayson with mute horror.

It was not the first time he'd been viewed this way, even by children. As his father's enforcer, he had been feared and reviled for years. So why did this time feel different? Why did this time stop his breath and cause his hands to shake?

That little girl with the deep brown eyes still stared at him, her thin shoulders shuddering, viewing him like a living nightmare. Like he really would have killed her just for knocking accidently into him.

He knew he would haunt her, and that haunted him.

"I'm sorry," he said, struggling to speak the Mortisian words.

There was a brief pause where no one moved. Then Liam cleared his throat. "Perhaps we should take the carriage the rest of the way."

"Perhaps we should," Desfan said, his voice quiet.

Grayson realized only now that Desfan's bodyguard had his sword half out of its scabbard and he watched Grayson as if he were about to attack them all.

He couldn't escape the street quickly enough.

CHAPTER 31

GRAYSON

WELL, THAT WAS QUITE THE FIRST IMPRESSION you made."
Liam reclined against the pillar beside the tall, narrow window
in Grayson's room. The décor was done in many shades: navy,
gold, red, emerald—too many colors, too much opulence.

Grayson's head pounded as he yanked the clothing from his
bag and shoved it into the open drawer beside him.

"You know," Liam drawled, "servants could do that."

"I don't like anyone touching my things."

He chuckled, an edge to the sound. "Our mother taught us
well, didn't she?"

He threw a look at his brother, irritated at being watched.
"Why are you here?"

One of Liam's shoulders lifted. "I wanted to check on you.
Make sure you were all right. It's been a big day for you."

The back of his neck warmed. "I'm fine."

There was a pause, and when his brother spoke, his voice was pitched low. "You were startled. It wasn't your fault. You've been taught to react to a threat."

"She wasn't a threat," he said stiffly.

"No. But you reacted as you've been forcibly taught to react. And once you assessed the situation, you let go. Everyone could see the horror on your face when you released her. No one thinks you attacked her."

Heat blasted his face. He didn't appreciate the reminder that there had been so many witnesses.

"You didn't hurt her," Liam said quietly. "Focus on that."

Maybe he hadn't physically hurt her, but he had frightened her. Badly. She had shaken in his grip, and her eyes had been wide with terror. The fact that her face had reminded him so much of Mia only gutted him more.

He jerked another black shirt from his bag and threw it in the open drawer. "I don't want to talk about this."

His brother was silent for a long moment before inclining his head. "If you insist. But I'm available if you ever want to talk."

Thank you, he wanted to say. But his throat was tight and his fingers had just brushed the vial of Ieannax concealed inside his bag.

Killing Liam after they finished their mission was becoming more difficult to contemplate. If it wasn't the only way to ensure Mia's freedom and save three innocent lives, he would never consider his mother's request.

But he didn't have to think about it. At least not yet.

Keeping the poison in the bag, he dropped the whole thing into the bottom drawer before kicking it closed and finally facing his brother. "You didn't come just to check on me."

Liam's mouth twitched wryly. "Kaelins until the end, aren't

we? Always an ulterior motive." He crossed his arms over his chest, his eyes growing serious. "While I did want to check on you, I also came because there is a conversation I've been wanting to have with you, but it hasn't been safe yet to do so. Now that we have relative privacy in Mortise, we can. As long as we stay away from the door and speak no higher than this, we won't be overheard. Still, I need you to know that this conversation is dangerous. You cannot un-hear what I'm about to say. Do you understand?"

Grayson eyed his older brother. Queen Iris was convinced Liam was a traitor, and that is why she wanted him killed—secretly, of course, because she doubted Henri agreed with her assessment. Grayson had been so focused on the actual threats, and the daunting task of killing his brother, that he hadn't stopped to truly consider if the queen's fears were real.

What if Liam was a traitor?

Grayson's chest tightened, curiosity burning through him. "I understand."

Liam studied him, his eyes intent, his jaw set. "I'm choosing to trust you. I don't do that lightly. I'm sure you can appreciate that."

Fates knew he did. They'd both been raised to distrust everything around them—especially their family.

"I've been watching you for a long time, Grayson. You're different from our brothers. You don't like what you've become. The things Father makes you do. And I think you can guess by now that I don't, either."

His heart thudded in his chest. He was strangely nervous for Liam to confirm his guilt, but he also *needed* to hear it. To know he wasn't alone in despising their parents and the monsters they'd twisted their sons to be.

"I'm working on a plan," Liam continued. "You'll forgive me

if I don't share all the details now. But I do not intend to be father's slave any longer. He's tortured me all my life, turned me into a monster—he did that to all of us." His jaw clenched, and the raw emotion in his eyes—the grief and the rage—pierced something deep inside Grayson. "I will destroy him for that alone. With or without you. I need you to understand that now."

His meaning was clear: If Grayson got in Liam's way, Liam would kill him. Or at least die trying.

Grayson dipped his chin. "I understand."

"Good." He folded his arms over his chest. "I think it's best for us to be honest with each other. I am not on a path of pure revenge. If that had been my goal, I would have already slit Father's throat. My plans are much larger. I mean to annihilate him, and our entire family. They will not hurt anyone ever again. That is my goal. If you cannot accept that, then I will walk out of here, and if you ever repeat any of this, I will deny it—and retaliate. Do you understand?"

"Yes."

Liam took a breath. "I know about Mia."

Silence cut through the room.

Grayson didn't move. Or breathe. He didn't blink as he met his brother's stare, tension crawling up his spine, though he tried to keep the panic from his face. "I don't know who you're talking about."

Liam's expression didn't change. "You met her as a child, in the dungeon. She's been imprisoned there since she was seven years old. It's quite obvious you love her, and if I had to guess, she probably loves you, too. Father has used her to control you. To keep her safe, you do everything he tells you to do, no matter how much you hate it. Hate *him*."

Grayson's throat clenched as he tried to swallow. Liam knew about Mia. Of all the things he'd expected from his brother, it had not been this.

But then, Liam was Henri's spymaster. If anyone in his family would have discovered her, it would be him.

His fingers twitched at his sides, near one of his belted knives.

Liam's falcon eyes caught the movement and he slowly lifted his hands. "Easy. I'm not threatening her."

"You're not?" he asked, an edge to his question.

"No. I'm offering to help her. To help you both."

Once again, Liam had shocked the air out of Grayson's lungs. The words didn't make sense, because the concept was so foreign. So unexpected.

Kaelins didn't help each other.

Suspicion arrowed through him, and his eyes narrowed. "Why?"

Liam's arms dropped along with his shoulders and he suddenly looked much older than his twenty years. "Because Mia is an innocent; she shouldn't be punished for being caught in the mess of our lives. Because you're my brother, and I actually like you. Because as long as Mia is under Father's control, he controls you; and whether you want to admit it or not, you are one of Father's greatest weapons, and losing your support will be a crippling blow to him. Because the man who sired us is a tyrant, and if he is not stopped, he will destroy every last good thing in Eyrinthia. Because I want to destroy *him*." He lifted a brow. "Is that sufficient, or do you need more reasons? I have them."

Grayson eyed his brother. "How exactly would you help her?"

"I have contacts at the castle. People who owe me favors or loyalty—or both. I can ensure Mia's safe removal from the castle. Father will send men after her, so we can't act until we're in a position where we can help her, but I can make arrangements so she'll be brought to us."

"To Duvan?"

"No. Zennor. We'll meet in the port city Zoroya once our work in Duvan is done. Then we can disappear forever."

Grayson's mind was spinning, his lungs tight with possibility—and fear. "Father will come after us."

Liam's eyes narrowed. "No. Once we're through with him, he won't be able to do a fates-blasted thing to anyone ever again. I simply need your trust and your help here in Duvan, and then you can be free of him forever."

The future Liam's words painted was everything Grayson had ever wanted. Freedom from his father. The ability to shed the Kaelin name. The chance to free Mia and live with her in safety—to not have to lose her.

It was his every dream. And that fact alone made him hesitate, because nothing in his life had ever come without a price. "What do you want from me?"

Liam's gaze was serious. "I have a plan, and it *will* work. All I need is your support, and, when the time is right, we can end this."

"That's not very specific."

"Forgive my caution. I'll share the details later, once I have your support."

"How can I trust you?"

"How does one make any decision? Instinct? Reason? All I can promise is that I will destroy our father, with or without your help. But it will be much easier if you stand with me." Liam crossed the room and braced a hand beside a tall closed window, his eyes on the sea, his jaw tight. "Father has done unspeakable things to all of us, but we're not the only ones he's ruined." His throat bobbed, and when he spoke, his voice was low and raw. "He took away the one person who meant everything to me. She's dead, and I . . ." His mouth clamped shut, and

Grayson looked away, allowing his brother a measure of privacy.

His stomach knotted, but it wasn't only in sympathy for his brother and the woman he had clearly loved. No, it was because he knew that he wouldn't be this strong.

If his father killed Mia, Grayson's only thought would be to annihilate Henri. There would be no place he could hide; Grayson would find him and kill him. He wouldn't survive the army that would be sent after him, but then, he wouldn't want to.

The fact that Liam could think beyond simple revenge, that he could develop a plan to stop Henri's evil, and that of their entire family . . . Well, that just showed Liam was a better man than Grayson.

His brother turned, his face carefully smoothed of his inner turmoil. He crossed his arms over his chest as he looked to Grayson. "What do you know about Mia? Who is she?"

He didn't think he would answer, he was so protective of Mia. But something—hope? –loosened his tongue. "Mia is a girl Father found. She was close to my age, so he took her, thinking he could manipulate a friendship between us so I would do anything to keep her safe."

"And that's all he said?"

"Yes." He eyed Liam. "Why?"

Liam's brow furrowed. "What has she told you?"

Nothing.

His silence seemed to convey that. Liam's face softened, and Grayson didn't like that; it felt too much like pity. "Mia doesn't like to talk about her past. And where she came from, who she was . . . it doesn't matter to me."

"But aren't you curious about her origins?"

Yes. No.

The skin around Liam's eyes tightened. "Do you really think Father picked a random child for you to bond with? That his choice was not deliberate?"

Grayson forced his stiff jaw to move. "What do you know?"

"Nothing concrete. I have some contacts in Duvan I hope to confer with, and they may be able to confirm some things." He shook his head. "Whether you decide to help me or not, I'll share anything I learn about her."

Curiosity and guilt twisted inside him. He wanted to know everything about Mia—of course he did. But it seemed wrong. Almost like he was betraying her, because her past was something she had never shared with him.

Liam spoke again, pulling him from his thoughts. "You don't have to make any decisions yet. I know I've given you a lot to consider. All I ask is that you think about what I've said."

As he watched his brother leave, Grayson knew he'd be able to think of little else.

Liam's parting words still rang in Grayson's ears hours later as he sat at the head table in the vaulted dining room. Liam sat beside him, and Desfan was on Liam's other side. They were in a position of honor, but Grayson would have given anything to eat in one of the shadowed corner tables. Or to still be in his room.

The large dining room roared with laughter and boomed with conversation—all of it in rapid Mortisian, of course, which Grayson struggled to follow. Flutes and stringed instruments were being played in the corner, raising the level of sound even further. It was overwhelming, and he felt oddly vulnerable.

Every eye seemed to be on him. One man—bald and middle-aged—watched him so intensely, it was more of a glare. Grayson's face burned while he tried to eat the unfamiliar foods without choking. The flavors were strong, some of the foods spiced with peppers that made his eyes burn. Even the bread tasted different, dusted with seeds he couldn't name. He quickly learned he did not like fish, and when he bit into a cube of yellow fruit, the tartness pinched his mouth and made him cough.

Liam leaned in, his voice low. "Stick to the clam chowder or the seasoned rice. They're more mild."

Desfan glanced at the brothers. "Is there anything I can send for?" He spoke slowly, though not to the point of insult; Liam spoke Mortisian flawlessly, but he'd explained that Grayson was new to the language.

"Perhaps some unseasoned chicken, if you have it," Liam said. "Rydenic palettes are rather simple in comparison to Mortisian ones, I'm afraid."

Desfan signaled for a servant, who hurried to the kitchen. "Is the food to your liking, Prince Liam?"

"Yes, but my tastes have always been more exotic than my brother's."

Desfan gave Grayson a sympathetic smile. "If there is anything you crave, you have only to ask. I want you to be comfortable."

Grayson couldn't imagine ever being comfortable here, but he tipped his head. "Thank you."

"You've been so accommodating already," Liam added smoothly. "The rooms are wonderful, and this feast is a generous welcome for us."

"We're grateful for your presence," Desfan said. "It means a great deal to have you here, supporting the alliance between Mortise and Devendra."

"I hope we can enter discussions for peace between all our kingdoms, once Princess Serene arrives. When do you expect her?"

"Within the month. She would have arrived sooner, but she was delayed."

"Oh? All is well, I hope?"

"She was injured during a protest by some rebels, but I was assured her recovery will be full."

"That is a relief." Liam lifted his wineglass and took a careful sip. "I heard a rumor that the Rose has been hired to kill her."

Desfan's jaw tightened. "Unfortunately, it's not a rumor."

Liam winced. "How awful. I assume you've sent men to her aid?"

"Unfortunately, King Newlan declined my offer. From the beginning, he insisted that our kingdoms be seen as equals, which is why he wants the princess to come to Mortise with only Devendran guards." Desfan used a fork to prod the fish on his plate, his brow furrowing. "Regardless, when I heard she'd been injured, I considered going personally."

"What stopped you?" Liam asked, curiosity threading his tone.

The serjah offered a wry smile. "Responsibility, of all things. With my father ill, it falls to me to run the country. I can't just leave."

Liam accepted this with a nod and set his wineglass back on the table. "Is it true Princess Imara travels with Princess Serene?"

"Yes, I received a letter from King Zaire informing me that his daughter wished to see her cousin safely settled here. She will stay until the betrothal is officially signed."

"A historic occasion," Liam observed. "Royals from all four kingdoms, all in one place."

"I pray to the fates it's a sign of good things to come," Desfan said.

"I pray for the same," Liam said, raising his glass.

As Liam and Desfan continued their conversation, Grayson watched his brother. He wondered once again what his plan was. He couldn't imagine what they could do from here to steal King Henri's power, but Liam was the Shadow, the spymaster of Ryden. Whatever the plan, it would be well-thought out.

He supposed the whole thing could be a ploy—a test orchestrated by Henri to gauge Grayson's allegiance. But the emotion in Liam's voice today as he'd spoken of the woman he'd lost . . . No, he didn't think Liam had pretended that. And his heart ached for his brother, because without Mia, the world would be a void. *He* would be a void.

He would also have nothing to lose. That was something he would do well to remember, since it could make a man ruthless or foolhardy—or both.

Grayson had also considered the fact that Iris wanted Liam dead because she suspected him of treason. That meant his careful brother had let something slip, which meant his plans were not as secure as Liam might think. His entire revolution might be doomed to fail—yet another reason to turn away from it.

He had briefly thought about telling Liam that the queen wanted him dead, but he'd almost instantly rejected the idea. Not only would it put Liam on guard—a problem, if Grayson did have to follow-through and kill him—but it could ruin the tenuous trust they were starting to build. *Liam, Mother asked me to kill you, but I promise I won't . . .* Fates, it sounded horrible enough in his head, and the truth was, it wasn't a promise he could even make. Because Mia's fate mattered more to him than anyone else's.

And he wasn't sure he could risk her life. Not even for the future Liam had painted; a future where Grayson and Mia could both be free—together.

In the end, he wanted to believe in Liam. He just wasn't ready to plunge into treason with him. At least not yet.

Grayson's milder food arrived, and he tried it cautiously. He didn't care for the clam chowder, but the rice was flavored lightly, as was the chicken. Maybe he wouldn't starve here, after all.

Liam and Desfan chatted as the meal continued. Grayson followed most of it; he'd quickly learned that he could understand Mortisian far better than he could speak it.

He heard when Liam's voice grew a little more serious. "I have heard talk of olcain coming into Duvan."

"Yes," Desfan said, fingering the stem of his wineglass. "But the drug was seized, and an investigation is ongoing."

Liam shook his head. "Terrible stuff. Who brought it into the city?"

"It was smuggled on a merchant ship."

"Oh?" Liam's eyes widened a little, and Grayson could not decide if the spark of surprise was genuine or an act. Because clearly, his brother was fishing for information. "I would think most merchants would stay far away from such things."

"Yes, well, the Nassars have a history of taking risks."

"Hmm," Liam frowned. "Nassar . . . the name is familiar."

"Their family has a long history in the shipping business. I'm sure they have come to Ryden as well as Zennor." Desfan lifted his wine for a quick sip. "They also have a history of avoiding any accusations we throw at them. The head of the business —Rahim Nassar—is apparently in Zennor, and his second in command claims the Nassar ship was stolen." He shook his head. "At the moment, the Nassars are a dead end."

"Have you any leads on the buyer or seller?" Liam asked.

"None that I am at liberty to discuss at this time." Desfan smiled a little, to soften his words. "But answers will be forthcoming."

Liam nodded, but Grayson was getting to know his brother enough to see his thoughts were racing. He was piecing together some puzzle only he could see—or filing away this information to use later.

After a slight pause, Liam cleared his throat. "I heard that you and Newlan worked out a prisoner exchange."

"Yes, it will be taking place at the border."

"A merciful gesture on both sides."

"Thank you. We hope it sends a clear message of peace. Ser Ashear, a great man on our council, was sent to oversee things."

"Oh. I did not realize you could have an empty seat on the council." His tone was the perfect balance of surprise and interest, but Grayson knew his brother understood everything about Mortisian politics. Why would he be pretending otherwise?

"He appointed a second to sit in his stead," Desfan explained. "We do this so a full council is always available to cast votes and serve the people of Mortise."

Liam nodded once. "Ah. Very wise. And who is his second?"

This, Grayson assumed, was what his brother actually wanted to know.

"Ser Sifa," Desfan said, taking a quick sip of wine. "Actually, we have two seconds at the moment, as another councilman—Ser Zephan—needed to take some time to tend to his estate, so Ser Anoush was appointed to his seat."

"And are they here tonight?" Liam asked.

"Yes, they—"

"Serjah, may I have a word?"

Grayson stiffened at the harsh tone and turned to see the young man who stood behind Desfan.

He was wearing clothes as bright as all the rest, but his were slightly wrinkled, and his beard was not as well trimmed. He appeared to be in his early twenties, and frustration bracketed his mouth with tension.

Desfan lowered his fork, his voice low. "Amil, this is not the place—"

"You refused my audience this morning."

"I was otherwise engaged." Desfan gestured to Liam and Grayson. "I was greeting our guests, the Kaelin princes."

The man—Amil—cut them a quick look, his eyes sharp with disgust. "So, you dine with the enemy while my father's death goes unpunished?"

Desfan stiffened, but before he could form a reply, his bodyguard—the tall, extremely silent one—gripped Amil's arm. "Don't cause a scene," he said quietly. "The serjah will see you tomorrow morning, as scheduled. Join the feast, or retire to your room."

Amil's nostrils flared and he jerked away from the bodyguard's hold. He focused back on Desfan. "Until tomorrow, then." He bowed stiffly and marched from the dining hall.

Liam whistled lowly. "I knew some would be against our presence, but that seemed especially hostile."

"It's not because of you," Desfan said, his jaw tight. "I'm afraid Amil recently lost his father. They were serving as emissaries in Devendra, and his father was caught in an unfortunate attack targeting the royal family."

"How horrible." Liam winced. "That must complicate things between your kingdoms."

"It is a tragedy, but I refuse to let it complicate the peace. The emissary was killed by a Devendran, but not on royal order."

"Some may see it differently." Liam lifted his glass of wine and took a sip. "And how is your father's health? We pray to the fates for his quick recovery . . ."

The conversation continued, and Grayson tried not to show his unrest as the feast dragged on. Finally, after desserts so rich they made Grayson's stomach turn with only one bite, he excused himself from the table. His temples pounded and the noise, colors, smells . . . they were all too much.

He strode from the room, hurried down the hall, and when he reached the first Mortisian guard he asked for the quickest route out of the castle. The somewhat wary man spoke quickly, stumbling a little over his words, and Grayson struggled to understand. But he gathered enough information and hurried down the hall. Towering columns, ornate art pieces, and stone carvings—everywhere he looked, he was overwhelmed by the foreignness of it all.

Pulse racing, lungs aching for freedom, he finally reached an outer door and clipped his way past the guard. He burst out into the Mortisian night, the air still warm, but at least it was fresh. The smell of the sea was thick in the air, and waves crashed against the cliffs the castle was built on. A path trailed away from the castle, and Grayson followed it, winding his way down the cliffs to a stretch of beach that was clearly private to the castle.

He was on the south side of the castle, further from the docks and the busy city center. And for the first time in weeks, no one was around him.

Grayson walked over the sand, moving toward the water, grunting a little as the grains shifted underfoot. So far, he was not impressed with Mia's sand. But even though he didn't like it, walking through it made him think of her.

When he neared the water's edge he kicked off his boots and reluctantly stepped onto the sand with his bare feet, as Mia had asked him to do.

As expected, he did not find the sand comfortable. It was a contradiction—soft, but grainy. It got between his toes, and when he stepped closer to the water he touched wet sand, which clung to him in filthy clumps.

He realized he was smiling a little. Disgusting or not—ridiculous, certainly—this was something Mia had done before. Why else would she have asked him to do such a thing? And even though they were so incredibly far away from each other, doing this brought him closer to her.

He stood inside the water's lapping edge and let the frothy waves roll over his feet, rising above his ankles. He looked out across the water, then tilted his head up so he could gaze at the stars. There were so many. An endless stretch. The rushing sound of the waves—rising and falling, coming then going—was oddly soothing, and the tension eased from his shoulders.

Perhaps he didn't hate everything to do with water.

He rolled the black legs of his pants higher and took another step forward, deeper into the sea.

He whispered her name—barely breathed it. "Mia."

The distance separating them had never been so vast. He missed her so much the sharp longing filled every part of him, lodged in his gut.

He stood there for a long time, the glow of torches so distant in the towering palace that they seemed barely there. It was the silver moonlight that illuminated the sea, the beach. And it was moonlight that revealed Serjah Desfan, as he slowly approached.

Grayson stiffened, turning slightly to keep Desfan and his bodyguard in his sights.

The crown prince of Mortise looked tired, but he smiled at Grayson. "Sorry to disturb you, I didn't know you were here. I usually have the beach to myself at night."

"Sorry. I'll go."

Desfan waved a hand. "No, please stay."

Grayson remained where he was, the water splitting around his calves as the newest wave rolled in.

Desfan tugged off his own boots and came to stand in the waves, a few paces from Grayson. "You left so quickly, you missed the drunken singing."

Grayson couldn't stop his cringe.

Desfan laughed softly. "Your brother told me Ryden's court is very different. Let me know if there is anything I can do to help ease you into Mortisian customs."

"Thank you." It was all he could think to say.

The serjah nodded, his hands braced on his hips as he looked out at the sea. "Karim, when was the last time you stood in the ocean?"

"I'm fine here," the bodyguard said, his tone edged.

It was clear he would not relax around Grayson.

Desfan squinted at the moon hanging above them. "Sometimes I forget the simple pleasures."

With a ridiculously lavish court, Grayson could see how simple things would be forgotten.

Desfan eyed him. "You don't talk much, Prince Grayson."

"No."

"Would you prefer me to speak the trade language? Or Rydenic?"

"No." Liam insisted that Grayson speak Mortisian as often as possible, so he could learn it more quickly.

There was a short silence, and it was entirely uncomfortable. But then, Desfan did not seem particularly bothered. Perhaps Grayson was the only one feeling the uneasy prickle?

"I have little experience with court life," he said at last. As if that would explain his inability to have a conversation with this foreign prince.

The corner of Desfan's mouth lifted. "Neither do I. I was never very involved, until several months ago."

He referred to his father's illness, clearly. "I'm sorry about your father." It was the right thing to say, but Grayson didn't know how to convey sympathy. Mostly because he wished a similar ailment would seize his father.

"Thank you," Desfan said, his voice quiet. "You are lucky, Grayson, to have your family around you."

It wasn't luck, it was a curse. But he knew what Desfan meant—what he mourned.

Liam had reminded him that Desfan had lost his mother and sisters when he was just a child. To have his father ill now . . . He supposed that was difficult, if one had a loving family.

The Mortisian prince eyed him. "May I ask a question?"

"Yes."

"Does your family truly seek peace?"

He glanced away, unsure of how to answer. Perhaps it was the moment, but he felt compelled to say, "Not all of them."

Desfan exhaled slowly. "What about you? Do you want peace?"

His fingers twitched at his sides, aching still to hold Mia. "Yes," he said quietly. "All I've ever wanted was peace."

There was a moment of silence, then Desfan said over the crashing of the waves, "Thank you for your honesty."

They did not speak again. Desfan didn't mention the incident with the little girl, and Grayson didn't say anything about his father's plan to throw Eyrinthia into chaos.

They just stood together on the beach, under the silver eyes of a thousand stars.

CHAPTER 32
CLARE

CLARE EXPELLED A HEAVY BREATH AND lowered herself onto a wooden chair. It creaked under her weight, but it was the pinch of pain in her side that made her wince. She gingerly fingered the area, feeling the slight bump of the scar through her simple maid's dress. It was a relief to be wearing it. After pretending to be Serene for weeks, she had been overjoyed to hand the mantle back to the princess. The dedication of the king's new road was one of the few stops Newlan had insisted Serene handle personally on this tour. The threat to her had been deemed minimal due to several factors, including the nearness of the inn and the brevity of the actual event. Newlan had wanted a royal presence, and he was certainly getting that, with Imara and Grandeur in attendance as well.

The prince had been with them for a week now, and truthfully, a break from him was making this private moment in the room she would share with Ivonne and Vera all the more of a relief. She had yet to feel at ease around him. His paranoia had grown sharply since she'd left Iden, and she knew she needed to find a moment to talk to Serene about her concerns. It seemed safest to wait until after the road dedication, which would be underway in an hour or so. After the royal appearances were done, Grandeur had made it clear he planned to set out for Lythe. He wasn't even planning to spend the night, and he had barely spoken to Serene before excusing himself to a private room at the inn.

The reunion between Imara and Serene, however, had been very warm. They'd embraced in Serene's private room, squeezing tightly until Serene had finally reared back so she could eye her cousin seriously. "You really shouldn't have come. It's far too dangerous."

Imara had shrugged. "I couldn't let you go to Duvan alone. How would you get into decent trouble without me?"

Serene had cracked a smile, though there was a slight sheen over her blue eyes. "Thank you." She had then turned to Clare, and in typical Serene fashion, had begun demanding what Clare needed. A physician, a chair, a bed, food, medicine. When Clare had declined all of that, the princess had stepped forward and gripped Clare's hand, leveling her with a firm gaze. "I'm sorry about what you've been through. I don't know what to say. How to apologize, or thank you."

The words were unexpected, but warming. She cracked a thin smile. "Thank you."

Bridget had entered the room then, declaring they had no time to waste.

Clare's skin had been scrubbed clean of all makeup, her expensive gown traded for a maid's gray and white dress, and she had left Serene standing in the center of the room in all her royal finery. Clare had slipped out while the maids worked in a flurry to get Serene prepared for the dedication ceremony, and she'd retreated to this empty room.

It was a nice, quiet place to read her letters from home, which had arrived just this morning. She settled back in the creaky chair and rifled through the letters, an ache in her chest easing as she saw Mark's familiar handwriting, read Thomas's words. Hearing from her younger brothers, knowing they were well—it helped with her homesickness. Mistress Keller confirmed that additional guards from the castle had been provided, which Clare knew Commander Markam had arranged after the rebel attack in Lindon. Clare had yet to tell her brothers what Eliot had done. She wasn't sure if she would ever find the words. She had penned a letter to Mistress Keller while recovering with the Paltrows, but she hadn't given any details. She'd merely asked that Eliot—if he returned home—not be allowed to be alone with the boys, and that if he attempted to take them, he must be stopped. She didn't think he would hurt them, but after his betrayal, she was feeling extremely protective of Thomas and Mark, and these extra precautions felt entirely warranted.

She had just finished reading the letters when there was a knock on the door. "Come in."

The door pushed open and Bennick stepped into the room. He spied the letters and smiled a little. "Are Thomas and Mark well?"

"Yes." She folded the letters away, swallowing back a wave of melancholy. When she focused back on him, she noted the tension in his shoulders. "Are you all right?"

"Yes, I just wanted to check in with you before we leave. Wilf and a handful of guards will remain here. You'll be safe."

"I'm not worried about me." She pushed up from the chair,

ignoring the tug of discomfort in her side as she stepped closer to him. "How was your meeting with the captain of the city guard?"

"Good." His eyes tracked her every movement, watching for any sign of strain. "They'll be in place around the square during the dedication. He said the crowd is already large, but he doesn't seem worried."

"Are you?"

"Just cautious. As always." His brow furrowed. "Cardon just told me that Newlan sent a letter to Serene, informing her that Desfan invited two Rydenic princes to Duvan."

Her eyes widened. "What?"

He nodded grimly. "Exactly. It's not something I expected, and I don't really like the idea."

"Why did Desfan invite them?"

"Apparently, they're ambassadors for potential peace. King Henri hasn't confirmed that Ryden will enter peace talks, but he said he thinks the marriage alliance between Devendra and Mortise could be the first step to a promising future for all Eyrinthia."

"Why don't I believe him?"

Bennick snorted. "Probably because he's a snake."

She bit her lower lip, her thoughts racing. "And if the alliance with Mortise goes through, then Ryden is the only kingdom not linked through marriage. Their trade negotiations with Mortise and Zennor are tentative at best, which really makes Ryden the outcast. I doubt King Henri likes that idea."

"Agreed. I think it's far more likely that King Henri wants to stop the peace between Mortise and Devendra, if only to keep us from uniting against Ryden."

A frown tugged at her lips. "Do you know which princes he sent?"

"Liam and Grayson."

Her breath quickened, dread trickling inside her. "Prince Grayson is the Black Hand."

"Yes. And if rumors are to be believed, Liam is a spymaster. They make a dangerous pair. And they'll be arriving in Duvan soon, if they haven't already, so they'll be quite settled by the time we arrive."

"Which changes the dynamic of the betrothal."

"It isn't ideal." Bennick scrubbed a hand over his bristled chin. "It's entirely possible King Henri wants to forge an alliance with Mortise. Which means the Rydenic princes could be trying to sabotage the marriage alliance with Devendra so they can steal Mortise as an ally. Their first step may be to shift Desfan's attention from Serene, create their own alliance, and then both kingdoms might turn against us."

Clare frowned. "Fates, with Imara there, we'll have royals from all the kingdoms in one place at one time. When was the last time that happened?"

"I don't know. The Garvins Treaty, probably."

Which was two hundred years ago.

That certainly put the magnitude of this into perspective.

"I imagine the dinner conversations will be interesting," Clare muttered.

"I'm sure you're right." Bennick chuckled, though his jaw remained hard.

She stepped closer, and Bennick watched her approach with a question in his eyes. When she reached him, she set a hand on his tense arm, feeling his muscles bunch. "Are you all right? You haven't seemed like yourself since you saw your father."

The commander hadn't stayed long in Lindon. He had insisted on keeping the prisoners moving at a slow but steady pace toward Stills, where the exchange would happen in eight days.

Clare had noticed a shift in Bennick's mood since he'd had a private conversation with his father, but she hadn't had an opportunity to ask him about it until now.

"Is it about your mother?" she asked. "Has her illness worsened?"

"No. Actually, she's doing much better." Bennick let out a slow breath. "My father and I . . . we had a disagreement."

She pursed her lips at his cool tone, her hand dropping from his arm. "I don't want to pry, but if you want to talk about it, I'm here."

"It's not . . ." He pushed a hand through his tawny hair, a muscle in his jaw ticking. He took a step back, his gaze dropping even as tension raised his shoulders. "He said something, and I can't get it out of my head."

She kept her voice low. "What did he say?"

Bennick leaned his back against the closed door, his body a hard line. "He believes the Rose has become fixated on me."

Confusion twisted through her; she hadn't expected that. "Why? Because of the poison he left you?"

"That . . . and he killed my horse and left a message on my bed."

Her jaw loosened, her mouth falling open. "What? When?"

"Just before the Paltrow's ball."

"Why didn't you tell me?"

Bennick glanced away, a lock of hair falling over his lined brow. "I didn't want to alarm you."

Her breathing thinned. "What did the message say?"

"It doesn't matter."

"Doesn't matter? He threatened you!"

"And that doesn't matter." He pushed off the door and gripped her shoulders in a firm but gentle grasp. His blue eyes burned into hers. "He was trying to scare me, but I'm not his target. This is some game of his, and I refuse to play. I will not become distracted."

"But the commander thinks you've become a target."

"He thinks the Rose has taken a strange interest in me, yes. But I don't know if I agree." His hands smoothed down her arms, his gaze tracking the motion. "My father thinks if I return to Iden, the Rose will follow me. That he'll be compelled to punish me for leaving, and you'll be safe."

"No."

His eyes cut to her. "What if he's right?"

"He's not."

"How can you be so sure? I keep debating it, and I still don't know if I disagreed with my father because I think he's wrong, or if I disagreed because it's *him*."

She took his hand, twining her fingers with his. "I know he's wrong, because we can't protect each other if we're apart. Whatever we face, we're stronger together."

"I want to believe that, Clare . . ."

"Then believe it."

He studied her for a long moment, then dipped his head. "You're right. We're stronger together."

She squeezed his hand. "You should have told me about what the Rose did. There shouldn't be secrets between us."

The moment the words left her mouth, her stomach knotted. How many secrets was she keeping from Bennick? Serene's plot against her brother and father, the letters she'd carried for James . . .

That's different, she told herself. *They're not my secrets to tell.*

And yet a hint of uneasiness remained.

"I should have told you," Bennick said. "I'm sorry."

She eyed him, the corner of her mouth lifting. "It's hard to argue with you when you agree with me."

"Do you want to argue?"

"No." She eased forward, sliding her arms around his hard middle. Embracing him, she laid her cheek against his chest and whispered, "What I really want is for us to have a moment of peace."

He pressed a kiss to the top of her head, making her insides flip pleasantly. His low words rumbled through his chest. "Maybe tonight we can slip away. See some of the city. Just the two of us."

She leaned back, a smile playing on her lips. "Really?"

His chin dropped as he leaned in, this time kissing her lightly on her mouth. When he drew back, his voice was rougher than before. "Maybe you could bring your garrote, so we can train. You need more practice."

She flashed him a scowl and he chuckled. "Oh, I'll bring it now," she muttered.

A smile bloomed on his face as he stepped back, reaching for the door handle. "I look forward to it."

She shook her head, but she was smiling as he left. The only thing that managed to dim it was the thought of the Rose threatening Bennick. Threatening them both.

She knew the hours would pass slowly as she awaited Bennick's return, so she distracted herself by writing replies to Thomas, Mark, and Mistress Keller, and she was just finishing the last one when Ivonne pushed into the room without warning, her face pinched. "Sorry to interrupt, but someone is asking for you."

Clare blinked. "Someone is asking for *me*?"

Ivonne jerked a nod, still gripping the door's handle. "Vera and Wilf are with him now. He's wounded, but he won't tell us what happened—he just keeps asking for you."

Visions of Eliot jumped to mind, and despite her feelings

about what he'd done, she still leapt to her feet and hurried from the room, Ivonne at her heels.

Clare rushed down the stairs, ignoring the painful stitch in her side. Her palm slid down the smooth banister and she reached the common room, heart in her throat. She drew up short when she saw James slumped in a wooden chair. She hadn't seen him since Tarvin, when she'd given him Serene's last message. His drawn face was pale and glistening with sweat, the heel of one hand braced against his bleeding shoulder.

Wilf frowned down at him, no sign of distress at the blood. Vera was wringing her hands and biting her lip, clearly desperate to help him.

It was also clear Wilf had ordered her to stay back.

Clare's slippered feet were soft against the wooden floor as she hurried forward. "James?"

Wilf shot her a look, his mouth bracketed in hard lines. "You know him?"

"Yes. He's an old friend," she lied.

James made to stand, but grimaced deeply and remained where he was, his face etched with strain. "Clare. I must speak with you."

Wilf snagged Clare's elbow, stopping her from getting too close to the bleeding man. She shot a look up at him. "I told you, he's a friend."

"What I see is a man bleeding from a hole in his shoulder, who won't tell me why. He wants you, not a physician. And the fact that he knew to ask for you here, even if you are old friends? Well, I find that suspicious, too, especially after what happened in Lindon." She winced at the reminder of Eliot's betrayal, but Wilf wasn't done. "Before you get close to him—or before I summon a physician—he will tell me exactly what happened to him, and why he's here." He eyed James, his expression truly menacing. "I anticipate you have several minutes before you succumb to the blood loss, and unless you can convince me you're not a rebel—or a threat in any way—I won't bother waking you up."

"Wilf!" Clare yanked her arm, but he didn't let go. She wasn't quite sure how he managed such a strong grip without it being the least bit painful.

James's throat visibly bobbed as he swallowed. "Please, there's no time. It—It's about Serene. Her safety."

Wilf's broad shoulders stiffened. "What about the princess?"

"She's in danger."

This time when Clare tugged her arm, Wilf released her. She knelt in front of James, one hand braced on the arm of the chair. The wood dug into her palm with a grounding pressure. "Tell me what you know."

James cringed, his dark brown hair falling into his eyes. The clawed fingers of his hand dug into his shoulder, increasing the pressure on the wound. "What I have to say is private. Please. I can only talk to you."

Clare shot a look to Wilf. "Can you give us a moment?"

He growled, the sound so deep it seemed to vibrate through the whole room.

"Please, Wilf."

He was not happy about it, but he eventually retreated to the other side of the room, his sharp eyes still on them, his pox-scarred face twisted into a scowl. Ivonne left to find bandages and Vera left with a soldier to find a physician—which Wilf didn't protest, as he was so focused on watching Clare and James.

She gripped the chair arm and leaned closer to him, her voice a bare whisper. "What happened to you?"

"Doesn't matter." He tried to straighten and hissed through his teeth. "I wouldn't have come at all, but I didn't think I could make it to her. But you can."

"Someone plans to attack her at the dedication?"

He jerked out a nod and glanced at Wilf, who was far enough away that he couldn't pick up everything of their exchange. "I knew he wouldn't believe me. He'd just ask questions. It has to be you. If you don't alert her, she's going to die."

"Who is attacking? How many?"

"Mercenaries. I don't know how many. Twenty? Thirty? Tell Serene that one of the Mortisians on the council hired them —I'm quite certain it was Zephan, but I don't have proof." He stiffened his jaw, pain flashing over his face. "I arranged to have men in the crowd weeks ago, but they don't know what's coming, so they can't warn her. But they'll be ready to help, if the fight is triggered before you can get to Serene."

She stared at him. "Who *are* you?"

He let loose a stiff laugh. "If I told you, you wouldn't believe me."

"Do you love her?" The question rolled out of her mouth before she could consider the wisdom of it.

His eyes darted over her face, his breathing tense. "She is everything to me." He grit his teeth and ducked his head, panting out a hard, pained breath. "Please. Go. Save her."

Clare shoved to her feet and spun to Wilf. "There's going to be an attack at the ceremony. We need to warn them."

His eyes narrowed. "You believe him, then?"

"Yes."

He turned without another word and called a handful of soldiers toward him. They started for the door and Wilf only stopped when he noticed Clare following. He lifted a stern finger. "No."

She met his gaze firmly. "You're all uniformed men. What if we need a bit more subtlety once we reach the square?"

"It's too dangerous."

"This isn't just about Serene. Grandeur and Imara are in danger as well." And so was Bennick. The thought made her heart beat faster. "Please, Wilf. I need to help if I can."

Wilf opened his mouth, then snapped it shut, looking irritated.

Behind them, Ivonne returned with bandages and she crouched in front of James, who was shaking with the pain.

Clare folded her arms, her shoulders braced as she faced Wilf. "We're wasting time. Are you taking me with you, or am I sneaking out after you?"

His eyes narrowed. "Fine," he snapped. "Just stay close."

CHAPTER 33

CLARE

"WHAT DO YOU KNOW ABOUT THE ATTACKERS?" Wilf asked
as they hurried down the street.

"They're mercenaries," Clare said, running at his side. "Maybe twenty or thirty."

Wilf cursed.

They reached the edge of the crowd in minutes, but only because so many had gathered to hear Serene speak. The streets of Halbrook were clogged with people, stretching far away from the actual square Serene was in.

Wilf swore again, then glanced back at the four soldiers with them. "Move as quickly as possible, but don't cause a scene. We don't want to trigger the attack. As we move in, one of the princess's guards will spot us and know something is wrong, and they will get the princess to safety. Keep your eyes peeled for the mercenaries, but stay in a group so we'll be more noticeable to the princess's bodyguards."

The men nodded, their faces set grimly.

He shot a look at Clare. "Stay right behind me. I'll send you ahead only if we have to."

She nodded, and stepped quickly to follow Wilf as he shouldered into the crowd. She kept as close to Wilf's back as possible, the four soldiers trailing behind her.

Even though her footing remained sure over the cobbled street, Clare vibrated with the need to reach the square before it was too late. Serene was the target, but anyone could be hurt. Grandeur, Imara, the guards—even innocent bystanders.

Panic twisted her insides as they pushed their way into the square, but they were on the far side.

A dais had been constructed for the event, so the royals could be seen. Serene stood at the front, surrounded by her guards, with Grandeur and Imara slightly behind her. All of them were far too exposed, considering there was a small army of mercenaries hiding in the square.

At least the guards were alert. Bennick, Venn, Cardon, and Dirk were all eyeing the gathered crowd, searching for any sign of danger. She prayed they would spot Wilf quickly—he was huge and pushing through the crowd, so he had to catch their attention once they got closer.

Serene's speech was underway, her voice carrying through the square, punctuated by scattered cheers. "The road will provide easier access to Zennor's Midlands, opening new trade partnerships with our longtime ally, as well as paving the way for trade to more easily reach the southern cities of Devendra . . ."

Clare bumped into a man and he tossed her an annoyed look. She kept moving.

"It is a great time for our kingdom," Serene continued smoothly. "Alliances—both new and old—will bring us greater prosperity, and a brighter future for our posterity."

The soldier behind Clare knocked into her and she stumbled against Wilf's wide back. She steadied herself by gripping his thick arm, and the recent wound in her side twinged uncomfortably as she twisted a look over her shoulder.

The soldier crumpled to the ground, a crossbow bolt buried between his shoulder blades. The other guards were also falling, all of them shot.

Shouts burst out of the nearby men and women in the crowd as they scrambled back from the fallen bodies, pushing each other in their haste to get away.

Wilf shoved Clare in front of him, sheltering her with his body against the sudden surge of the crowd. With panic breaking out, he abandoned the subtler plan and bellowed, "Mercenaries!"

A man from the crowd threw himself at Wilf's side, actually managing to tackle the giant warrior, but Wilf's shouted warning tore through the crowd. Everyone was suddenly moving. Elbows jabbed, screams pierced the air, and hands shoved.

Clare drew her dagger and ducked around the seething mass of arms and legs so she could assist Wilf, but he hardly needed help.

He rolled, nearly crushing his attacker beneath him, and then a knife flashed as he cut the man's throat.

Clare looked hastily away, her stomach churning. She strained to find Bennick, but the stage Serene had stood on just seconds before was now empty. She prayed that meant they'd all made it down safely, and that the mercenaries hadn't surrounded them.

Wilf grasped her arm with a firm grip and started dragging

her back the way they'd come, away from the stage.

Clare dug in her heels. "Wait! We have to help them."

He flashed her a hard look. "We won't make it to them in this mess, and the risk isn't worth it. We gave them warning—they'll be fine. I have to get you to safety."

She knew he was right, but it still took a moment to wrestle with the need to find Bennick and make sure he was all right. But when Wilf pulled her forward, she didn't resist.

They cut through the crowd, dodging around every knot of people in their way. Pain burst in Clare's side when a man fleeing the chaos of the square unintentionally knocked into her, hurting her still-tender side.

Wilf latched onto her elbow, jerking her in front of him. He protected her with his arms even as he continued to herd her forward. "Are you all right?" he demanded.

"Yes," she gasped, her body shaking from the pain. Or maybe it was the adrenaline.

Probably both.

They were nearly to the edge of the crowd when Wilf grunted, suddenly pushing against her back. "Move for the alley," he snapped.

Clare altered her course without hesitation. They entered the narrow street and Wilf hissed, his body tensing behind her. "Stay against the wall," he ordered, even as he drew his sword. Brandishing a long sword in the crowd would have been nearly impossible, but in the alley he finally could.

She glanced up at his face. It was rigid. Controlled. As he twisted to face the opening of the alley, she got a view of his back.

She clapped a hand over her mouth. Two crossbow bolts were stuck in him. One was embedded in his thick upper arm, the other in his lower back.

"Wilf, you're hurt!"

"Shut up and back up," he huffed at her.

She peered around him and spotted three men who stood shoulder to shoulder, just out of Wilf's sword range. They set aside their empty crossbows and drew their own swords.

The one in the middle was glaring openly. "This is for Galvin."

Wilf cranked his neck to the side, popping it. There was something chilling about his calm. "I assume he's a dead friend of yours?"

The man seethed. "You're dead. And so is your girl."

Wilf lunged, moving his bulky body with surprising fluidity as he spun the sword in his hands. If Clare had not seen the bolts buried inside him, she would not have thought him injured.

She stumbled back. There was no room to fight beside Wilf, even if she dared to join in.

He fought fiercely, but with a horribly efficient ease. He was both terrifying and awe-inspiring. The mercenary on the right was dead in seconds. The man on the left managed to lay a cut to Wilf's arm, but then he was dead, too.

The man who had spoken remained alone, his face flushed as he snarled. "You will suffer for their deaths."

Wilf swung his sword and the man leapt back, avoiding the swipe only barely.

Clare heard a noise behind her and turned. A fourth mercenary stepped out of a side door only a few paces away. He turned toward them, his crossbow clutched in both hands.

He lifted the loaded weapon and Clare flinched, but he wasn't aiming for her. Clearly dismissing her as a threat, he aimed for Wilf's unguarded back.

She wouldn't be able to reach the mercenary in time to even try to stop him. "Wilf!"

He turned at her shout and his eyes narrowed.

The bolt released with a twang and Clare pressed against the wall. Wilf also threw his body to the side, his shoulder crashing into the alley wall. The bolt sped past him and lodged into the other mercenary's chest with a solid thunk.

Wilf dove for the newest attacker, who panicked at the sight of the giant man charging toward him. There was no time to reload his crossbow, so he hurled the empty thing at Wilf's face.

Wilf jerked his head to the side and the thrown weapon only bumped against his shoulder. The man drew his sword, gulping as he backtracked.

Their swords clanged together, and then the mercenary screamed.

Clare whirled away from the violence, bile stinging her throat, her heart thundering in her chest.

Facing the mouth of the alley, she gasped as she saw the man who had been accidentally shot by the other mercenary. He had a crossbow bolt in his chest, blood running down his shirt, but he was still standing. He struggled for every breath, but he was alive. His eyes latched onto Wilf's back and he took a step forward, a dagger in his hand, prepared to throw it. He didn't even glance at her, he was so focused on Wilf.

Clare lunged for him, slamming her arm down on his extended wrist, flinching at the pain that ricocheted up her arm. But the move Bennick had taught her worked. The dagger fell and the man bared his teeth at her in a terrible snarl.

She kicked him between the legs, and he crumpled.

She stared at his fallen body, her own trembling with adrenaline.

The man was no longer moving.

"That was ruthless," Wilf grunted.

Clare spun, catching something like approval on his face.

"Did I—?" She couldn't continue. Had her kick somehow killed him?

Wilf stepped forward, flexing his grip on his sword. "You sent him to the fates with quite a story, but no. Your kick didn't end him. His friend did that." He nudged the man's shoulder with his boot, then his gaze flashed to her face. "You defended my back."

She folded her arms over her chest. "Of course I did."

He arched an eyebrow. "Well, my little defender—how are you at tugging out crossbow bolts?" Her face must have blanched, because he waved a hand. "Never mind. But I may need to lean on you a little as we make our way back to the inn."

He swayed on his feet and she rushed under his uninjured arm, spreading her feet as she braced to take his weight.

"Perhaps this is not the best idea," he muttered. "I'll crush you."

"I can steady you. Just don't lose consciousness."

He huffed and took a step back, slouching one shoulder against the wall. "Will you clean my sword and sheath it for me? I believe we are out of immediate danger."

Clare took his sword, grunting as she hefted it.

"Don't let it fall to the ground," he said.

She managed to keep the longsword from falling, but her arms strained as the tip dipped. "Fates only know how you manage to fight with this," she grunted.

Wilf rubbed a hand over his eyes, his low voice rough and worn. "Use the back of the man's shirt to clean the blade."

Stomach rioting, she did as instructed. When the blade was clean, she helped return it to the sheath at his side. The weight, oddly enough, seemed to balance him. He stood a bit straighter. "We'll stick to the alleys. If I begin to fall, don't attempt to catch me."

She agreed with a nod, wrapping his arm around her shoulders. He staggered a little, but once they started moving, he was able to fall into regular steps beside her. Their progress was slow, and they hesitated at every street opening, scanning carefully for more enemies. But where once the streets had been nearly impassable due to the crowds, now there were only a few scattered people darting for safety.

They didn't see anyone with a weapon, but Clare didn't relax.

A good quarter hour later, they finally meandered their way back to the inn. Clare first recognized the hulking building purely because Bennick stood with Venn just outside the door, speaking rapidly to each other.

Venn spotted them first and pointed. Bennick spun to face them, his shoulders visibly lowering even though his blue eyes flashed with intensity. They rushed across the street and Bennick grabbed Clare's arm, quickly taking her place beneath Wilf's sagging body.

"What happened?" he asked, voice clipped.

Venn was on Wilf's other side and he peeked at the man's back. He whistled lowly. "Aren't you supposed to dodge those? I thought you told me that."

Wilf glowered.

Clare looked to Bennick. "Is Serene safe? Imara and Grandeur?"

"Everyone is fine." His jaw tightened, his gaze digging into hers. "Are you?"

"Wilf protected me."

The large warrior snorted. "You trained her well, Bennick. She saved my life."

Venn's mouth actually dangled open. "She *what*?"

"It's true," Wilf said. "And she kicked the dying man's vitals for good measure."

Venn winced, but Bennick's mouth curved up.

Clare blushed. "I was only trying to stop him."

"Oh, you stopped him," Wilf said with a grunt. "If he hadn't died, he'd have been unable to walk for a week."

"Fates," Venn said, eyeing her with something like caution.

They had started back toward the inn, crossing the now empty street. "How long have you been back?" she asked Bennick.

"Not long."

From Wilf's other side, Venn spoke. "Bennick was already preparing to tear the city apart looking for you, though."

She fingered her throbbing side and sent Bennick a small smile. "Thank you. Did Vera find a physician?"

Bennick frowned. "Why did she go for a physician?"

"A man showed up at the inn," Wilf said, beads of sweat gathering on his brow. "He would only talk to Clare. He's the one who told us about the mercenaries."

Bennick shot Clare a look. "Who was it?"

"An old friend. His name is James." An uneasy prickle rippled at the back of her neck. "He isn't inside? We left him in the common room with Ivonne."

"No, the common room was empty."

Concern tightened her lungs. "Vera should have been back by now."

"Did she take a soldier with her?" Venn demanded.

"Yes. Which left two here with Ivonne and James."

"The room was empty," Bennick repeated.

They entered the inn. Serene, Imara, and Grandeur were in the common room, along with Dirk, Cardon, and a handful of soldiers. But James, Ivonne, and Vera were nowhere to be seen.

"Thank the fates you're all right!" Imara rushed to Clare and took her arm. Her eyes scanned Wilf, who Bennick and Venn assisted into a wooden chair. The Zennorian princess's eyes widened. "*Are* you all right?"

"Fine," Wilf grunted.

Serene stepped around Wilf to see for herself, and her eyes narrowed on the bolts. "We need a physician."

"I'll go," Venn said at once. "And I'll find Vera."

Serene stilled. "Vera's missing?"

He grit his teeth. "Apparently several people are."

"There's no need to panic yet," Bennick said. "They may have moved James upstairs."

Serene jerked, her eyes flashing to Clare.

Grandeur's dark brows drew together. "Who is James?"

"A friend of mine," Clare said quickly. "He learned about the attack and came to warn us. He was wounded."

Serene darted a look at Clare. "Was he badly wounded?"

"A shoulder wound. I think he'll be fine."

Some of the tension bracketing Serene's mouth released. "Good. That's good. I should like to thank your friend for taking such a risk to alert us."

"I'd like to thank James, too," Bennick said. His eyes were on Clare, and it was clear there would be questions involved—like how James knew about the mercenaries, and how he knew to find Clare and alert her.

It was also obvious in the look Serene gave Clare that they would talk more later, in private.

Venn turned for the door, but it burst open before he could take a step, and Vera darted into the common room, breathing hard, her face flushed.

Though Venn had been one of the farthest away, he managed to reach her first. His dark fingers curled around her upper arms, his eyes dragging over her. "Are you all right?"

She blinked up at him, her chest still rising and falling quickly.

"Yes. Fine. Why? What's wrong?"

Venn's shoulders remained tense. "Fates blast it, you were missing!"

She eyed the others in the room, who had gathered around them. "Oh. Sorry. It took longer than expected to find a physician, and then the streets were pure chaos."

Clare looked past Vera and saw a young man clutching a small bag. His throat was bobbing as he swallowed convulsively, clearly winded from their run. Behind him, two soldiers lurked.

"You're a physician?" Bennick asked the young man.

He bobbed his head. "Yes. Well, apprentice actually. Nearly finished with that."

Wilf grunted. "Can't even get me a proper physician?"

The apprentice glanced at Wilf and paled when he realized he was looking at his patient. A very large, very irritated patient.

Vera flushed at Wilf's roughly spoken reprimand and Venn scowled at Wilf. "Don't be such a child, Wilf."

"Me, a child? You fainted with only one bolt in you."

Venn glanced at the apprentice. "Good luck."

Serene stepped forward. "Tend my bodyguard while we find your other patient. Come upstairs as soon as you're able."

The young man gave a jerky bow, then moved toward the glaring giant with only slight hesitation. Clare thought he should get credit for that.

Serene looked to Clare. "Let's check on your friend." Her need to see James for herself was clear, so Clare nodded and led the way to the stairs. She knew Serene, Bennick, Imara, Cardon, Venn, and Vera followed, leaving Dirk and a handful of soldiers with Wilf.

As Clare reached the top of the stairs, unease prickled the back of her neck. The narrow hall of the inn was quiet, as were the rooms behind the closed doors. She thought Ivonne might have had the soldiers carry James into the room she shared with Vera and Clare, as it was the first in the hall.

Clare halted in front of the door. "James?" she called out.

Silence.

A chill skated down her spine. She reached for the handle, but Bennick's hand moved past hers, grasping the knob before she could.

"Let me go first," he whispered, sliding his body in front of hers. A quick glance showed that Venn and Cardon had both drawn their daggers.

Clare's heartbeat spiked as she eased back a step.

Bennick pushed the door open, and Clare couldn't help but watch as the portal swung, slowly revealing the room.

Ivonne lay on Clare's bed, nearest to the door. Her blond hair was combed out around her, drifting over the pillow in gentle waves. The hilt of a dagger stood out above her heart, blood staining her maid's dress.

Her chest did not rise and fall with breath, and a red rose sat in her open mouth. The red petals made it look as if her mouth was gaped in a terrible, silent scream.

Behind Clare, Vera shrieked, the sound raw and terrible.

CHAPTER 34

CLARE

CLARE QUIETLY DRAPED A BLANKET OVER Vera, where she lay curled on the bed. The girl had finally succumbed to sleep after hours of tears and unanswerable questions. Her older sister was dead. The last of her family—gone. Murdered.

Clare could not imagine the agony Vera must be clawing through right now. Her own eyes were swollen, her throat aching from swallowing back her rioting emotions.

Ivonne had been killed by the Rose, her body left as a taunt. The two soldiers who had been left to guard her were also dead, their bodies dumped behind the inn. Both had been stabbed through the heart and left with a crimson rose petal on their tongues.

There had been no sign of James.

Clare's shoulders were heavy as she glanced at the empty bed in the cramped room, but she knew she couldn't sleep. Even though Venn and Bennick had given up their room so Vera wouldn't have to sleep in the room where Ivonne had died, the shadows seemed ominous. Clare was exhausted, emotionally and physically spent, but her skin itched with echoes of terror.

She cast a last look at Vera before she slipped from the room.

Venn straightened from his position beside the door, his eyes darting past Clare, seeking a glimpse of Vera. "Does she need anything?" he asked, his voice a hoarse whisper.

Clare shook her head, tugging the door until there was a soft click. "No, she's sleeping."

She clutched the ends of her shawl, cinching it tighter around her shoulders. "Is everyone else settled for the night?"

Venn's throat bobbed. "Mostly, though I doubt many are sleeping. Bennick is downstairs. He's been there for hours." For once, Venn's long black hair was unbound, the dark locks falling past his shoulders. He shoved a hand through the mass now, his fingers tangling against his scalp. His eyes were lost. "What can I do?"

She set a hand on his arm, which flexed under her touch. "Just be there for her. And allow her time to mourn." After losing her parents, Clare had learned that the pain of losing the ones you loved never really went away. But as time passed, the moments where you felt the agony of their loss came further and further apart, allowing life and happiness back into the moments between the bouts of grief.

But right now, in the shock of such a violent, horrific death, the thought of feeling anything but pain was almost impossible to comprehend.

Venn drew in a shuddering breath, his eyes trained on the closed door that blocked his view of Vera. "I love her," he whispered. "I haven't said it to her, but I love her. I hate that she's in so much pain."

"I know." Clare's lungs tightened as she scanned his haggard face. "You need sleep, Venn."

"Dirk will relieve me in a couple of hours." His tone was dismissive, but his eyes finally focused on her. "You need sleep, too."

"I want to check on Bennick first." She squeezed Venn's hand, then slipped away, drifting toward the stairs. A shiver wracked her body as she passed the room Ivonne had been murdered in, but she didn't let her steps drag. She also didn't let herself run, even though a horrible prickling started between her shoulder blades as she descended the stairs.

The common room was deserted except for Bennick, though Clare knew guards were stationed outside every door. Bennick sat at one of the many tables, the glow of a lantern burning through the darkness of the wide room. The golden flame traced the angles of his face, highlighting the hard cut of his jaw, the sharpness of his bristled chin. His brow was furrowed as he bent over the table, one hand gripping the back of his neck, the other fisted on the table. He was staring at the square of paper that in turn stared up at him.

Clare knew what it said. The message had been burned into her mind after one glimpse of it, lying on the bed beside Ivonne's body.

You have not fooled me, Markam. I know of the decoy. I came for her today, but caught another. The message is the same: I can kill a pretender as easily as I can kill a princess.

You will find my next rose with Clare, then I will kill Serene.

The floor creaked beneath Clare's step and Bennick's head jerked up, both hands landing on the table.

She winced. "Sorry."

His stiff shoulders loosened as he exhaled. "No, I'm sorry. I . . ." His voice trailed off, his eyes skirting back to the Rose's message. He flipped the paper over, hiding the inked words as she took a seat beside him.

His hand remained flattened on the overturned page. "How is Vera?"

"Asleep." Clare laid her hand over his on the table, gently squeezing his fingers. "You look exhausted."

He looked to her, his gaze intent as their eyes met. Held. "Nothing will happen to you, Clare. He will never touch you."

There was a warm shiver in her stomach, a reaction to his fervent vow. She tightened her hold on his hand. "I know," she whispered, knowing it was what he needed to hear. And maybe she needed to hear it, too—speak the words and assure herself that she would survive this. That she would see her brothers again.

Bennick's hand shifted, and suddenly he was holding her hand, their fingers interlocked against the table. Silence stretched between them, but it wasn't uncomfortable. They were together, and there was peace in that, even though Ivonne's death and the uncertainty of the future crept in the shadows around them.

Clare was the one to break the quiet, her words soft. "He

learned about the decoy. How?"

"I don't know. It's possible he's somehow affiliated with the rebels, or has a contact."

She grimaced, because that meant her brother had betrayed her fully.

Bennick glanced at her. "It's also possible the Rose managed to get close to us and overheard something. But I don't think he knew from the beginning. There is a change in tone between this note and the others he's left. We fooled him in the beginning, and he didn't like that."

"How did he know I would be here, and Serene would be at the dedication? Maybe he lied in his note and he really did come here for Serene, but then he overheard something and figured out the truth." That thought terrified her. That the Rose might have been near while she was in her room, writing to her brothers.

Bennick's brow furrowed. "It's possible. If he came here for Serene, he might have questioned Ivonne, and she told him about you."

She shuddered, even though she knew Ivonne's body had not borne signs of abuse, other than the wound that had killed her. But the emotional torture of her final moments . . . that was something Clare knew would haunt her forever.

"I think he came here with knowledge of the decoy," Bennick finally said. "My instincts are screaming that he knew, and he hoped to find Serene here, thinking you would be at the dedication."

Ice filled her veins at the thought. If Newlan hadn't insisted that Serene be present at the dedication so a true royal could consecrate the new road, Serene would have been here. The Rose would have found her.

"When the Rose didn't find her, he settled for sending a

message using Ivonne." His gaze met hers, his jaw tight. "Could James be the Rose?"

Shock jolted through her. "No." The thought had not occurred to her, but was easy to dismiss. Serene trusted him, and his devotion to the princess was clear.

"Are you certain? He showed up here, knowing about an attack, and he was last seen with Ivonne. When we return, he's gone, and everyone else was killed."

"It wasn't James. Trust me."

Bennick let out a slow breath. "I trust you." He spread a hand over his eyes, rubbing gently. "I hate all of this. What happened to Ivonne. The Rose knowing your name—targeting you specifically. The fact that your brother knows you're the decoy, and he's probably already told his leaders. And then there's the prisoner exchange, and Rydenic princes in Mortise." He shook his head, his hand dropping. "It just feels like we're rushing toward something bad. I want to ignore all of it and just get you and Serene somewhere safe. I wish I could rush you to Duvan."

"Newlan wouldn't want that. It would look weak. Like we're afraid." Appearances were more important to the king than avoiding the increased dangers of traveling slowly, with plenty of publicized stops.

There was a moment of silence between them, their hands still joined on the table. Clare smoothed her free hand over his tense arm. "You need sleep," she whispered.

His fingers tightened around hers, his voice low and raw. "I don't know if I can close my eyes. If you had stayed here today . . ."

She brushed her thumb over his, cresting the knuckle in a gentle stroke. "I know." She'd considered the same. She, Ivonne, and Vera may all have been killed. Or perhaps they would have stood a better chance. Wilf would have been here, and she couldn't imagine anyone—not even the Rose—getting past someone so fierce.

Bennick dragged in a shaking breath, his free hand moving to rub his ducked brow. "Clare, if I'd opened that door and seen you on that bed—"

"Don't." She squeezed his hand. "It didn't happen. And what happened to Ivonne . . . Fates, I can hardly believe any of this is real."

He dropped his hand back to the table, his fingers curling into a fist. "We'll catch him. I promise you, he'll pay for what he did."

There was a momentary pause, a silence that pulled them closer together. Bennick's voice was pitched low when he finally spoke. "Does James know you're the decoy?"

Her throat was tight as she lied. "No. He just knew I was the princess's maid."

"How did he know about the mercenaries?"

"I don't know."

"Did he mention anything else to you? Anything else he might know?"

"No." She eyed him. "I promise you, James is not an enemy to Serene."

"Who is he to you?"

Finally, she understood the intensity in his low voice. Her face softened. "He's only a friend." And he clearly had feelings for Serene, which—judging from the widow's braid hidden in her hair—the princess seemed to return.

Bennick dipped his head, acknowledging the words. But she had a feeling he still didn't entirely believe her. Or perhaps he still thought James made a good candidate for the Rose.

He shoved the assassin's note into his pocket and stood, pulling her gently to her feet. "We both need sleep if we're going to face tomorrow."

They walked closely together to the stairs, their shoulders brushing as they went. When they reached the base of the stairs, Clare tugged him to a stop, her fingers tight around his. His eyes dropped to her, a question in his gaze.

She leaned forward, rising on her toes so she could press a soft kiss against his lips. It was a simple kiss, a reassurance for them both in this dark moment, but when she eased back, Bennick's gaze was warm, his breath heated. "Thank you," he whispered, his expression full of awe, appreciation, and . . . love.

Left unable to speak, she wrapped her arms around his neck and pulled him close. He buried his face in the curve between her neck and shoulder, his arms banded around her.

And even though shadows pressed in around them, all she felt was warmth and peace.

Ivonne was buried in a cemetery near the outskirts of Halbrook. Clare stood beside Vera, who clutched a bouquet of white daisies they had picked while the gravediggers prepared the spot.

The burial service was short and the grave marker simple. Serene had commissioned a more elaborate stone marker, which would be laid later. The princess had also offered Vera a chance to return to Iden, but Vera declined. She had no family to return to, and Clare understood her need to be kept busy.

While Vera knelt to arrange the wildflowers on her sister's grave, Serene drifted to Clare's side. "Would you walk with me a moment?"

She fell into step beside the princess, conscious of Bennick and Cardon shadowing them at a distance that afforded them privacy to talk. They tread over the soft grass, their black skirts too warm in the summer sun as they made their way to the back edge of the quiet cemetery.

"Thank you," the princess said quietly. "For protecting James as you did. Claiming he was a friend of yours was smart. My brother, especially, would have been suspicious if you hadn't spoken up so quickly."

"He might already be suspicious." Clare hurried to tell Serene about her private meeting with Grandeur a week ago, in Lindon.

If Serene were surprised by his increased paranoia, she didn't show it. "Pushing him to his breaking point will take less effort than I thought. I'll have to consider the best way to use his frustration and suspicions to the best advantage."

For her part, Clare was just grateful he had already left. Ivonne's death had delayed him, but he had still departed the inn last night. He was anxious to reach Lythe.

A part of her wondered if he was just anxious to be away from the tour. It was certainly a dangerous place to be.

Clare glanced over at Serene. "I know I probably don't have a right to ask, but who is James really? How did he know about the mercenaries?"

Serene exhaled slowly. "I'm afraid my answer will only require more discretion on your part."

"Do you love him?"

She drew up short. From the corner of her eye, Clare saw Cardon and Bennick also stop, keeping their watchful distance. Serene stared at her, shock in her gaze. "James is a friend. Only a friend."

"Serene, you aren't known for trusting people, but James seems to know everything about you. You told him about me, and he told me that you mean everything to him."

She blinked. "He did?"

"Yes." Now that she was talking, she couldn't seem to stop. "You gave him a detailed outline of your alternate route, and when you learned he'd been wounded, I could see how worried you were. And then there is your widow's braid. Is it for him? Is that why you're hesitant to marry Desfan?"

The princess opened her mouth and promptly closed it. It took a long moment before she finally cleared her throat. "I may be slightly apprehensive about marrying Desfan, but that's because he is a stranger. He could be an ally or an enemy. Frankly, he hasn't been in court long enough for me to know anything about his political ideals or his aspirations, but I hope to determine what sort of man he is once I arrive in Mortise. Regardless, I will marry him, because that is what is best for Devendra. And though I can see how you would construe my connection to James as something romantic, I assure you, I do not love him, nor does he love me." She started walking again, forcing Clare to move to keep pace with her.

The princess's voice remained low. "That is all I can say, unless I have your promise that you will never speak of this to anyone else."

Curiosity rose within her. "You already have my promise. I've been keeping your secrets since Iden."

"This is different."

"I won't betray you, Serene. I promise, this will stay between us."

Serene folded her arms over her chest, her head lowering. "I do trust you, Clare. And I'm grateful for your discretion thus far." She swallowed. "What else did James say to you?"

"He warned me about the mercenaries. He said someone on the Mortisian council hired them. He wasn't sure, but he thought it was someone called Zephan. He also said he had men in the crowd, and that they would try to help you if something happened, but that they didn't know about the threat." Clare eyed the woman beside her. "James is not a simple farmer."

"No, he's not. He is one of the key captains of a rebellion against my father."

Clare stopped walking. "He's a rebel? A rebel *captain?*"

Serene twisted to face her. "Yes."

"But . . . the rebels are trying to kill you."

"There is a faction of rebels who want me dead, yes. But James is part of another faction." She arched a brow. "And if you think that's surprising, I can't wait to tell you who the rebel leader is."

Somehow, she already knew, but that didn't keep the shock from her voice. "*You're* the leader of the rebels?"

"You didn't think I was crafting plans of retribution against my father and brother without actual help to see them through?"

Honestly, Clare didn't know what to think. She shook her head. "You're the leader of a rebellion."

"Yes. James is one of the most senior leaders in my rebel force." They began walking again, and Serene kept her voice measured so her words would remain too quiet for Bennick and Cardon to catch. "Both factions are remnants of the civil war that happened ten years ago. Both groups want to see my father dethroned. The big difference is, the rebels who are trying to kill me—the group your brother joined—don't care who they hurt, how much damage they cause. They don't have a plan for who will sit on the throne. They want revenge, anarchy, and chaos. The event that sparked their increase in violence was my betrothal to Desfan. They see an alliance with Mortise as the ultimate betrayal. Their primary target shifted in that moment from my father, to me. If I'm dead, there is no alliance. Then they can tear down my father, or start a war with Mortise. While I want my father off the throne, I do not want my kingdom ravaged by needless bloodshed and war. And I'd prefer to still be breathing in the end. That is what my rebels are fighting for. We will kill, but only if it is strictly necessary. We don't want war with Mortise, we want peace. And we don't want to destroy Devendra—we merely want to take my father's crown, so we can heal the damage he has caused."

Clare's head was reeling with Serene's revelations—the sheer scope of the princess's plan. Back in Iden, when Serene had taken her into her confidence, she had no idea how far-reaching her plans were. How many people were involved already. She had a whole network of rebels, all of them dedicated to over-throwing Newlan and placing Serene on the throne. Devendra's first ruling queen.

Serene glanced back, a small smile flickering into place. "I think Cardon and Bennick are getting curious—they're inching closer."

Clare glanced over her shoulder, a prickle of guilt rising as she saw Bennick.

We're stronger together. No secrets.

She shook her head, focusing back on Serene. "Why didn't you tell me about the rebellion?"

"It was one thing for you to learn the truth about my mother and decide to spy on my brother. Quite another matter to join a rebellion. I didn't want to force you." She lowered her voice even further. "Besides, not many in the rebellion even know I'm the leader. It's safer that way—for them and for me."

"When did you form this rebellion? In Zennor?"

"That's where I got the idea, yes. After learning the truth

about my mother's murder, I wanted to go to my uncle and tell him everything. But if I would have gone to him, he would have declared war on Devendra. He loved his sister that much. I couldn't risk it. The bloodshed would have been too much, and my mother would not have wanted that done in her name. So I began plotting a better way to ensure my father and Grandeur paid for their sins, without killing innocents in the process. I needed help—especially when another rebellion rose and began hurting people."

"How did James learn about the mercenaries? Is he a spy?"

"Among other things. Before I left Iden, I asked him to look into threats that may come from Mortise. Clearly, he found one. Someone on the Mortisian council wants me dead badly enough that they would hire mercenaries—which don't come cheaply—and they want me killed before I can even reach Mortise. Probably because they don't want my death traced back to them. I will need to learn more about Zephan. I trust James will be looking for further proof of the councilman's guilt as well."

Serene looked once more to Clare, her expression almost wistful. "In Zennor, I saw what it was to lead a people with kindness, humility, and respect. My uncle is the kind of king who truly serves his people. My father governs as if he's afraid his people will turn against him again. He imposes taxes people struggle to pay, he punishes even a hint of disobedience as if it were full-on treason, and he focuses on making friendships with his nobles. As if by making the rich richer, and the poor poorer, he thinks to keep balance somehow. All he's done is give blood-thirsty rebels more reason to want revenge.

"I do not want Devendra ruled by his iron hand. I want a kingdom that flourishes, and I want that even more than I want revenge for my mother's murder. Which is why I've taken these last three years to build a network of allies who will help me remove my father and brother from the castle. I will have justice for my mother, but I will also make sure Devendra is protected. I will not have things devolve into war—not if I can help it."

She looked at Clare. "I know you will keep this confidential. You've proven yourself. I'm sorry you were put into a position where you had to handle messages for James, because the contents were treasonous. That was unfair of me. But I'm asking you now: would you consider joining me?"

"You mean, become a rebel?"

"Yes. I would value your help and opinions, and you're in a unique position. As you pretend to be me, there are things you might hear and see that I would never know unless you told me. As my spy, you would be invaluable to the cause."

Clare hesitated. So many of the things Serene had said sounded right. The future she painted for Devendra looked beautiful, and she agreed with what Serene was trying to accomplish. But this would be a line she could not uncross. Rebellion against Newlan, if discovered, would lead to her death—just like rebellion had led to her father's death. Where would that leave Thomas and Mark? And what about Bennick?

While she had already agreed to spy on Grandeur, Serene was right—this decision was bigger. Her current spying only pertained to the prince, and aligning with Serene helped protect her family. Choosing to spy for the rebel cause was another matter entirely.

This was a choice that would alter her life forever. She couldn't make this decision on a whim. And choosing to become a rebel without telling Bennick . . . That seemed wrong.

"You don't have to say yes," Serene said. "And you can take time to think it over before giving me your answer. It's not a small thing I'm asking. I do feel that I can say that many of those in my network are servants, commoners—the people powerful men like my father tend to overlook. The people who work hard every day to provide for their families and want peace for their kingdom. Those are exactly the type of people who will actually manage to change the world. I feel you fit in with them perfectly."

"I will continue to guard your secrets," Clare said. "But I don't know if I can become one of your rebels. If I was discovered, my brothers would be in terrible danger. I don't know if I can risk them."

"I understand. And if you change your mind, you have only to tell me. But if we succeed, you won't have to worry about the safety of your brothers again. They will be safe from my father and my brother, and they will live in a Devendra that knows peace."

"Thank you," Clare whispered. "Not just for that, but . . . for what you're daring to do."

Serene looked toward the blue sky above them. "That means a great deal to me. As does your friendship. Thank you."

Her heart tugged, because somehow—as impossible as it had seemed in the beginning—the princess *had* become her friend. And in times such as these, friends meant everything.

CHAPTER 35

MIA

MIA JERKED FROM SLEEP, HER HEART POUNDING. She wasn't
sure what had awoken her. The room was dark and the door to
Mama and Papa's room was closed. Everything was silent. It was
the middle of the night.

There was a muffled thump against the outer cell door and
Mia clutched the neck of her thick nightgown to her throat.

There was a rough, barking order, and then the key rattled
into place.

Her stomach dropped and she lunged for the dark lamp at
her bedside, gripping it in both hands. It could be a weapon.
She kicked her blankets aside and slipped off the bed, her feet
hitting the cold stone floor with a jarring thump.

She thought about crying out, but Papa and Mama had drunk
heavily before going to bed. They wouldn't hear her. And obvi-

ously the night guard would be no help, because he was unlocking the door for whoever was coming.

The door swung open and a tall, dark form staggered inside, one hand flashing out to brace against the wall.

Mia clutched her lamp and blinked against the torchlight coming from the hall, but too soon the door closed, plunging the cell into darkness.

Heavy breathing came from the shadow near the wall. "Mia?"

Shock blasted through her. "Tyrell?"

There was a low snort, and then a thump. Had Tyrell slumped against the wall?

"What are you doing here?" Mia hissed. "It's the middle of the night!"

He ignored her question. "You know what you are? Moss." He huffed out his breath, a weak laugh. "Not funny. Not funny at all . . ."

Was he . . . drunk?

Her grip flexed on the lamp. "You need to go to your room."

"You're there, too," he argued, his voice heavy. "Not fair. This . . . You . . . Grayson . . . Not fair." He snorted. "Maybe that's why he did it. Had me come here. All this . . . Fates, I hate him for making me come here. Especially that first time."

Mia's heart was still beating faster than normal at his unexpected presence, and she hesitated for a moment, frozen as she wondered what to do. Finally, she set the lamp back on her bedside table and fumbled a little with the match, but soon the lamp was lit. She glanced away from the bright glow and slowly focused on Tyrell.

The prince was indeed slumped against the wall. His shoulders were low, his hands hanging loosely at his sides. His dark hair was a mess and he smelled strongly of ale. He grimaced at the sudden light, blood leaking from a crack in his upper lip.

More blood had dried in a streak under his nose. His unfocused eyes sought her out blearily, and she could see the redness and swelling by one eye and along his jaw.

Mia frowned, her eyes shooting to his hands.

The knuckles were bloody.

"You've been in a fight? While drunk?"

He shrugged one shoulder, but it moved his whole sagging body. "Wanted to lose." He grunted and tipped his head back against the wall until it thunked dully. "But I didn't. I'm too good. Or cursed." His glazed eyes managed to find her, and she was reminded that she only wore a nightgown.

Thank the fates it was thick and long.

Still, she folded her arms over her chest. "You need to leave."

"*You* need to leave *me* alone." He shoved a finger in her direction. "You're one of the fabled witches. I thought they were just part of useless stories for children, but you . . . you're a *witch*."

"If I were a witch, I would have turned you into a toad long ago."

He chuckled, then choked. After a short coughing fit, he shoved a hand into his messy hair. "You really love Grayson. Don't you?"

She eyed him, wondering how he was even standing. "Yes."

His eyes pinched closed and his fingers fisted in his hair. "How do you love someone like him?"

"He's not who you think he is. He's a good person."

Tyrell's hand dropped and he met her gaze, his eyes bloodshot. His voice was quiet. "He's not like me, you mean?"

She gripped her folded elbows. "Yes. He's nothing like you."

His throat bobbed. "None of us are good, Mia. We're Kaelins. Evil is in our blood."

"Evil is a choice."

He glanced away and when he spoke, his voice was raw. "I

made a choice a long time ago and I haven't doubted it once. Until now."

Her forehead wrinkled. "What choice did you make?"

His eyes slid back to hers, and there was a sorrow there she had not expected to see. "You asked me if I'd always been cruel, and I said yes." His chest rose with a deep breath. "I lied. I wasn't always cruel. But . . . I chose to be. I had to. I didn't really have a choice. Can you understand that?"

Mia looked at him, and she thought maybe she did understand, at least a little. And it broke her heart, because she wondered how often Grayson had been tempted to make the same choice. To be cruel and enjoy it, rather than be tortured by what he was forced to do. To excel at being a Kaelin prince, rather than take the punishments their parents devised.

Her voice was thin in the shadowy room. "You chose to be cruel because—if you enjoyed doing what your parents ordered —then you didn't feel as much pain. Right?"

Tyrell's head dropped, and both hands sank into his hair as he clutched his head. "I am cruel. I'm sadistic. I'm evil. I . . ." His shoulders curved inward. "I'm a Kaelin."

Something in Mia ached for him. Because in this moment, she saw the child he had once been. A child like Grayson. Tortured by his parents, preyed upon by his brothers, groomed to be a weapon—a puppet. But Tyrell wasn't Grayson. Grayson had refused to be cruel. He had refused to lose his morality. He cared for others, even when he had to pretend that he didn't.

"I'm sorry," she finally said, because it was the only thing she could think to say. And she *was* sorry for him. She was sorry for all of them.

Tyrell's legs gave out and he crumpled to the floor, his back still to the wall. With his legs sprawled out and his head in his hands, he looked more vulnerable than Mia would have ever imagined.

"You make me remember things," he said. "I don't like to remember." He looked up at her, hands falling to his lap. "Did you know I had a dog?"

She shook her head. "No, I didn't know that."

"I did. I never named him, though." He huffed a short, hard laugh. "Stupid. Should have just picked a fates-blasted name. But I couldn't. And so now I just think of him as *the dog*. My dog."

Mia lowered herself to the floor so they would be eye level, but she was still a pace away from him. She wrapped her arms around her knees, her eyes intent on him as he continued his story, his voice quiet, his face lit with glowing light on one side, leaving shadows to play on the other.

"I found him when I was nine or ten. My father sent us all hunting. He had us separate, told us each to take down a deer on our own, and he made it clear there would be a punishment if we failed to kill it. I . . . I was so scared I would fail." He squeezed his eyes shut. "I was tracking a deer when I heard a horrible, pitiful whining." He shook his head, his eyes still closed. "It was a dog. Just a pup. He had a broken leg. He was in pain, screaming for help. Who knows how long he'd been screaming."

"You saved him," Mia whispered.

Tyrell's whole body shuddered as he released a breath. "He was an ugly, muddy mess, but he looked at me, and . . . I had to save him. He needed me. And sometimes I think that I . . ." His eyes peeled open.

They were rimmed in red.

"I smuggled him back to the castle, kept him in my room. I healed his leg. Stole food for him. Kept him hidden. He was mine. My one rebellion." His breaths grew thin. "I had him maybe two months before my father walked in and caught me playing with the mangy cur. He'd always known I had it, of course.

I hadn't managed to keep any secret."

He looked right at Mia. "He put it there. On the mountain. Broke his leg and left him for me to find. He left a dog for each of us and had trackers watching us, to see how we'd react. Peter found his injured dog, and he . . . *played* with it until it died. Carter found his dog, but he just left it lying there. Liam lingered for a moment before slitting the creature's throat; putting him out of his misery, I suppose. Grayson found his dog, and like me he picked it up and took it down the mountain. But in Lenzen, he gave the dog to a couple of boys playing outside their house. I was the only one foolish enough to think I could keep it."

Mia stared at his face, etched in shadow. Sympathy she didn't want to feel blossomed in her chest. He just looked so . . . broken.

Tyrell sniffed, his head tipping back against the wall. "He let me keep the dog for months, let me bond with it. And then he decided it was time to teach me a lesson. So he made me kill it."

Tears stung her eyes and her stomach clenched. "I'm sorry, Tyrell. That's horrible."

He rubbed the back of his neck, his head ducked. "I learned the lesson, though. Caring about something—someone—is the absolute worst mistake you can make. It causes you nothing but pain."

"You can't believe that. You obviously still care about that dog, even after all these years."

"Yes, but that didn't stop me from snapping its neck when my father gave the order." He glanced aside. "He would have given the dog to Peter to torture. I made the choice I had to make." He lifted his hands, held them up to the glow of the light. They were shaking. "I think I held that broken neck for hours. I couldn't make myself let go. And I cried. I never cry anymore, but I couldn't stop then. I buried him in the garden. There's no marker, but I know. I always know . . ."

Tears spilled over her cheeks, but she didn't brush them away. She couldn't move.

Tyrell met her eyes. "My father said I was like Grayson. We both took the dog because we were weak. But when I killed my dog, he said I became strong." His jaw stiffened. "I won't be weak again. I promised myself I would always be strong the first time, so I wouldn't be put in that situation again. Better to ignore the dog, or put it out of its misery, rather than come to love it. Because eventually someone will learn it is your weakness, and the inevitable death will hurt more."

Mia stared at him, so many emotions swirling inside her.

Tyrell was not Grayson. He was not someone she cared about. But looking at him in this moment, telling her things he would never admit while sober, all she could see was a little boy who had loved his dog, and a father who had destroyed them both.

"I'm sorry," she whispered.

He just looked at her, his eyes carrying a thousand pains.

"The things your parents did to you . . . to all of you . . . it's disgusting and wrong," she told him. "A loving father would have been proud of you for helping that dog. Showing mercy, love, and kindness . . . those are strengths, Tyrell. Not weaknesses."

He stared at her for a long time, and when he spoke, his voice cracked. "I hate you."

She recoiled, but there was no venom in his words. Just desolation.

"I hate you so much it hurts," he continued. "Sometimes when I'm with you, or think about you, I can't even breathe. I hate what you've done to me." He shook his head, his words growing more mumbling. "You drew him. A waste. Me . . . I'm a waste too, but you would never draw me. Would you?" He tipped his head back until it again bumped into the wall and then he closed his eyes tightly. "Kaelins are a waste . . . A waste of everything. And you . . . you are . . ."

He didn't finish his thought. He was already snoring lightly, and Mia studied him in the soft glow of the lamp. Silently, she rose to her feet, lifted a quilt off the end of the bed, and laid it over him.

She kept the lamp on as she climbed into bed and closed her eyes, not at all sure what she was feeling in this moment.

She woke hours later when she heard Papa open his door, and her heart jumped. What would he think when he saw the prince sleeping on her floor?

Her eyes darted to the wall, but the spot on the floor was empty. Tyrell was gone, and the blanket she'd given him . . .

It was stretched over her.

CHAPTER 36

GRAYSON

THEY HAD BEEN IN DUVAN FOUR DAYS, and Grayson was losing his mind.

The first full day had been filled with extensive tours of the gardens and the castle. Art was everywhere, and they seemed to stop at nearly every painting, sculpture, or tapestry. Liam had used the spy sign language to say it was all about showing off Mortise's wealth.

But then the tours were over and Grayson had nothing to do. With the exception of over-crowded dinners nearly every night, he had been left on his own. Desfan was occupied, and Liam said tentative peace talks would not begin until after Serene was in Duvan—possibly not until the betrothal was legalized.

Liam had asked Grayson to practice his Mortisian, memorize the palace layout and shortcuts, and consider his offer of alliance against their father.

It seemed all he was doing these days was thinking. And until he had more information, he couldn't come to any real conclusions.

The inaction made his skin itch.

In the beginning, he had mostly kept to his room. He sharpened his blades. He studied the drawing Mia had given him, though he had already committed it to memory weeks ago. After a while, he asked for some charcoal and paper, and he had begun to draw—something he hadn't done in years. He tried to draw Mia, and failed. Not because he couldn't remember every detail of her face, but because he couldn't do her justice. So he drew landscapes. The pine-covered mountains of home, and the endlessly stretching beaches of Duvan.

Finally, when his blackened fingers cramped, he left his room. He dismissed his guards and wandered the palace, checking his memorization of the layout. He knew he made the Mortisians nervous, but no one told him to go back to his room. They didn't speak to him at all, actually. Just watched him.

And so here he was this morning, venturing into one of the palace wings that housed what had to be a thousand paintings. In their initial tour, their Mortisian guide had explained that it was a museum, because the Cassian family had long adored art. The gallery was placed near a side entrance into the castle, and sometimes outsiders were allowed in.

Today, the halls were deserted.

Grayson wandered the empty space, the portraits of a hundred men and women staring down at him, and a hundred landscapes taunting him with their views.

He didn't know if he'd ever felt this trapped. He was surrounded on all sides, by his mother's order to kill Liam, the bargain he had made with his father to secure Mia's freedom, and the temptation to join Liam's rebellion. The reward would be everything—a chance to have Mia in his life forever, the two of them free. But Liam could fail. The fact that Iris knew about his treasonous leanings was proof enough of that.

It didn't help matters that he was missing Mia. The ache of being without her had grown until it was a multi-layered knot in his gut, a constant pounding in his head. He wished he could talk with her about Liam. About all of this.

There was a scuff on the carpet ahead of him and Grayson's head snapped up.

A middle-aged man froze when he saw Grayson. He'd just come around the corner, and he clearly hadn't expected anyone else to be here. The man wore a red kurta and white pants. His scalp was bare, and it wasn't until the man's eyes narrowed on Grayson that he remembered. Their first night in Mortise, this man had been at the feast. He had watched Grayson and Liam so intently, it had almost been a glare.

The man was certainly glaring now. "What are you doing here?" he demanded.

Grayson refused to cower in front of this man. He straightened, his chin lifting. "Admiring the art."

The man's nostrils flared. "I did not realize you were allowed to wander unsupervised."

"I am a guest of Desfan's."

"You are the enemy," the man said, his tone sharp.

Grayson forced a thin smile that lacked all amusement. "If you know who I am, then you know that being my enemy is not advisable."

His eyes narrowed. "I know you, Grayson Kaelin. You're the Black Hand. Your own people despise you."

"No. They fear me."

The man's jaw tightened. "Our serjah might trust you, but

I assure you, the rest of us do not." He turned on his heel and marched away, his spine rigidly straight as he moved deeper into the gallery.

The hairs on the back of Grayson's neck lifted, a warning that someone was behind him. He twisted to see Liam striding toward him, his eyes on the retreating man. His voice was low as he reached Grayson. "That seemed like a charming conversation with Ser Sifa. I don't know much about him yet, but from what I've gathered, he doesn't much like Ryden."

Grayson's eyebrows slammed down, his irritation with everything now focused solely on his brother. "Where have you been?"

Liam arched a brow. "I didn't realize you missed me so much."

He noticed his hands were balled into fists at his sides. He forced them to loosen, but his voice remained tight. "Sorry, I've been having a . . . bad day."

"I can see that." Liam put his hands on his hips. "I've actually been quite busy these past few days. I needed to get a feel for the palace, gauge the sentiments and mood, from the nobles to the servants. Seeing Sifa reminded me that I need to make time to research him and Anoush, since they're effectively members of the council right now. But right now I need to go into the city, and sneaking in and out of the palace gets tricky. I thought you and I could publicly attend a play, as an excuse to leave."

While Grayson was still undecided about his future with Liam, he did need to get out of these stone walls. So he agreed, and within the hour they were on the streets of Duvan. They had several Rydenic and Mortisian guards, but Liam's fingers moved quickly and discreetly in the spy language, informing him that they wouldn't have the guards for long.

As they walked in the open air, some of Grayson's tension

seeped away, and with it came a flash of shame. He had slipped into the role of the Black Hand when Ser Sifa had faced him, and he did not like how easily that had happened. He didn't want to be that person. One who inspired fear. But it was his shield. A mask he had been forced to hone.

"You'll love this play," Liam said suddenly, his voice carrying on the slight breeze coming up from the sea. "It's about a pirate who falls in love with a kiv's daughter . . ." He spoke excitedly about the play, saying that he hoped Mortisian actors compared to the ones he had seen perform in Zennor. Grayson had a hard time paying attention, and he assumed the guards were losing interest as well.

Perhaps that was his point. His fingers moved even as they walked the crowded streets. *We'll go to the private box entrance, and then our guards will make sure no one knows we aren't inside. The room will be shadowed—no one will notice we are not there. We'll have three hours.*

Where are we going? Grayson asked.

Liam signed back quickly, still chattering on about the details of the play and the theater. *To see some friends of mine, hopefully.*

Grayson frowned. *You hope to see them, or you hope they're friends?*

Liam flashed a grin, a dimple winking into view against his stubbled cheek. *Both.*

They reached the theater, and Grayson was surprised to see how many people flocked to a midday performance. It seemed a waste of time and coin. He followed Liam, shouldering past the crowds as they made their way through the vaulted anteroom and to the actual performance hall. They had been given leave to use the private box that sat beside the royal Cassian box. It was empty, of course, as Desfan was not in attendance.

Liam instructed the Rydenic guards to remain in the hall,

and then Grayson followed his brother through the dark curtain and into the box. There were several cushioned chairs, their arms and legs heavily carved with intricate designs. Yet another bit of excess that would irritate the Poison Queen.

Liam sprawled into a chair, his eyes on the empty stage.

Grayson frowned as he lowered himself into a chair as well, his gaze sweeping the other boxes, the floor below them. The chatter of the crowd as they meandered toward their seats was increasing steadily, and it seemed everyone was taking a moment to steal looks up at them.

"Relax," Liam drawled.

Grayson shot him a look. "Everyone is staring."

"Let them. It will only help confirm that we were here—even after we sneak out. I've ordered the guards to let no one in, and two of them will take our chairs, just so their shadows will be seen. We'll be back before intermission. Hopefully."

"And if we're not?"

He shrugged. "The guards will improvise."

Grayson's mouth tightened. "These people we're going to see . . . are they your contacts who might know about Mia's past?"

"No. But I've already been asking some discreet questions among my contacts." He glanced at Grayson. "Gathering information can be time consuming, but I will find the truth."

Below them, a cluster of young women had spotted them. They huddled together, giggling and blushing as they pointed and stared.

Grayson's own cheeks heated and he forced his gaze away, watching as the rest of the audience filed in and found their seats. He bristled under the many stares that found him, unable to relax as Liam clearly had. His brother reclined in his chair, legs stretched out, shoulders settled back against the cushion. His eyes hovered somewhere above the empty stage, his fingers lazily twisting his leather wristband. It was an unconscious gesture, something he did frequently; not a nervous tic, since he never seemed agitated when he played with it. If anything, it seemed to soothe him. Center him. Grayson had first noticed the bracelet about two years ago, and he had never seen Liam without it. Curiosity rose, but Grayson didn't ask for the story; he doubted it was something his private brother would want to discuss.

Finally, the lights dimmed and music swept over the room, the majestic strain announcing the beginning of the play. When Liam stood, Grayson followed, and two Rydenic guards wordlessly took their places.

No one followed them as the brothers slid down the empty hall and out a side door that led into an alley.

"Someday I'll actually take you to a play," Liam said, leading the way back into the crowded streets. "You might like it."

"Sitting in the dark with a room full of strangers doesn't sound like something I'd enjoy."

"Well, when you put it like that . . ." Liam chuckled. He guided them through the street with ease, matching the fast pace of the city and dodging the carts and animals like he'd walked these streets a hundred times.

Perhaps he had.

Grayson felt clumsy in comparison, but he was grateful he'd at least listened to Liam when he'd insisted Grayson wear a white shirt. He fit in much better, as no one else seemed to wear black here.

"Have you thought about my offer?" Liam asked. Grayson glanced around them, but his brother chuckled. "Trust me, no one is paying attention. They couldn't hear us anyway."

That was probably true. They were in the market district now, and people were shouting their wares and haggling loudly on all sides.

He still lowered his voice. "Can you really get Mia out?"

"Yes." Liam's confidence was clear.

He swallowed. "I'm . . . interested in learning more."

"Interested, hmm? Not actually committed yet?" Liam lifted a hand. "No need to answer that. I understand your hesitation. I could be trying to trick you, or my plan could be impossible." He shrugged. "You'll just have to trust me, as I am trusting you."

Grayson didn't like it. At all. But he would do anything for Mia, and Liam . . . well, he actually liked his brother. He didn't want to kill him. He also didn't want to be his father's assassin for the rest of his life. Trusting Liam seemed to be the best way forward—even if he had a hard time taking that risk.

They exited the market and entered the warehouse district. They were getting closer to the docks.

Grayson eyed the thinning crowds. "Who are these friends of yours?"

"To be honest, I'm not sure who we'll find." With that cryptic response, Liam strode for a whitewashed building and pushed through the vibrant blue door without knocking. Grayson followed, trailing his brother through a small room to a desk where a man sat, tallying numbers in a ledger.

The Mortisian looked up after a slight hesitation, still scrawling something on the page as he focused on them. "Do you have an appointment?"

Liam flashed one of his charming smiles. "No, but is Rahim Nassar in?"

"No, I'm afraid not. You can try back tomorrow."

Liam laid a palm on the desk. "I'd really like to speak to someone in charge today, if at all possible. Perhaps his second?"

The man glanced back at his number sheet, clearly annoyed with the interruption. "I'm afraid his second isn't available, either."

"What is his name, might I ask?"

"Neev Sal."

The corner of Liam's mouth tightened. "I see. Is he here today?"

"As I said, he is busy."

"Tell him Azul is here. He'll ask to see me."

The man's eyes narrowed. "He can get quite irritated with interruptions. Are you sure you want me to ask?"

"Quite sure, yes."

The man grumbled but stood and made his way to a door on the left side of the room. He disappeared, but the door had barely closed before it was swinging open again. The man blinked as he faced them. "Please do come in."

"Thank you." Liam brushed past him and Grayson followed, entering an office crammed with shelves laden with books, ledgers, and fine items that clearly came from all around the world. Grayson's eyes moved quickly past the corners of the room to settle on the man seated behind the desk.

He was large, impressively so, with brown skin and slight wrinkles around his eyes. There were throwing daggers on his belt, the handles worn from repeated use. As he came to his feet, the fighter in Grayson reacted, his spine stiffening and his hands drifting to his own belt.

But while Grayson tensed, the man seemed to dismiss Grayson almost entirely, his focus completely on Liam. There was recognition on his face, but also shock.

Liam's face was blank, revealing nothing.

"Shall I bring tea?" the man still standing at the door asked.

"No," Neev said, his voice deep and chilling, his Mortisian accent thick. "Find Zeph and tell him to come here immediately. And no other interruptions are to be allowed."

"Yes, sir." Curiosity etched the man's face as he closed the door.

There was a beat of silence, then Liam spoke lowly, his tone dangerous. "What by all the blasted fates are you doing here?"

Neev's jaw worked, his fists pressing into the desk he still stood behind. "You should know the answer to that."

Every muscle in Grayson's body was ready to attack once the large man made his move, and he cursed his brother for not warning him of exactly what they might face.

Then everything in the room shifted when Liam leaped for the man and embraced him. Hard.

Neev's arms crushed Liam, but not in violence. It actually looked like there were tears in the man's eyes.

Confusion swamped Grayson as Liam finally pulled back, still gripping the man's thick forearms. "Fates rot you, you fool. And if Akiva is Zeph, I'm going to murder you both."

Neev grinned. "You might try."

Liam shook his head, emotion shining in his eyes as he glanced at Grayson. "You won't need to draw a blade here. This idiot is a friend. He's going by the name Neev, but his real name is Kazim."

"And you're using the name Azul, I see." Neev—or Kazim—grunted. "That name got us into trouble."

"So did Neev."

Kazim flashed a grin. "So it did."

The corner of Liam's mouth twitched. "Use Azul if you must speak to your associates about me, but I am in Duvan officially as Liam."

Kazim turned to Grayson. "And you're his bodyguard?"

"Yes," Liam answered for him. He didn't add that Grayson was also his brother.

The man extended a hand to Grayson, which he slowly took.

"You have my sympathies," Kazim said. "I was once Liam's bodyguard, and it is no easy thing. Fool takes more risks with his life than any sane man would dare."

Liam rolled his eyes.

Kazim cocked his head as he studied Grayson. "You seem young."

"He's not untried," Liam said, a small smile twisting his lips. "You would lose against him, Kazim."

The large man lifted a thick eyebrow. "Really?"

Liam nodded.

The man grunted. "I'll take your word for it." He nodded to Grayson. "What is your name?"

"Saimon," Liam said.

Kazim frowned. "Do you ever let him talk?"

"Saimon prefers to keep his silence." Liam crossed his arms over his chest, his dark brows lowering as he studied Kazim. "I left you in Zennor with clear instructions."

"You did," the older man allowed. "But someone used one of Rahim's ships to transport olcain into Duvan, and we decided to investigate."

"Do you know who it was?"

Kazim's mouth thinned. "Sahvi."

Every part of Liam froze. "Impossible. He died two years ago."

"That's what we thought. But he's alive."

Liam's eyes darkened, his jaw hardening. "I *watched* him die."

"Well, you must have blinked and missed his final breath. He's been keeping to the shadows, not that I blame him. You caused him a lot of trouble, and he made some powerful ene-mies. But he's inserted himself back into the drug trade. Akiva and I figured you would want to know everything he's doing, considering who his business partners are. When we heard Liam

Kaelin and the Black Hand were coming to Duvan, we knew we'd see you. I just didn't think you'd pay us a visit so soon."

"I didn't know you were here. If I had, I would have come sooner."

The door banged open and Grayson spun.

A young man who looked to be Grayson's age kicked the door closed behind him, took one look at Liam, and then threw himself at Grayson's brother.

Liam caught him in a tight embrace, and Grayson could see the young man's scarred hands clutching at the folds of Liam's shirt. Neither of them said anything for a long moment, simply gripped each other in a fierce embrace. When Liam did speak, his voice was thick. "You shouldn't have left Zennor."

"And you shouldn't have left us there," the young man retorted.

Liam pulled back to make introductions. "Akiva, this is my bodyguard, Saimon."

Akiva barely spared Grayson a glance; his focus was on Liam. "Did Kazim tell you about Sahvi? We think he must be working to hurt Mortise with the olcain. What's your plan—?"

"Slow down, boy." Kazim clapped a hand on Akiva's shoulder and looked to Liam. "But what is your plan?"

"There isn't time to go into that now," Liam said. "Have you found evidence to link the olcain to Sahvi?"

"Not yet. But we will." Akiva nodded to Kazim. "We're getting closer, and we're not the only ones. Rumors say the pirate Syed Zadir is also looking into the olcain, and Kazim swears he saw the serjah himself at The Red Cobra, confronting the drug master Fang for answers."

"Interesting," Liam murmured. "I suppose I shouldn't be surprised, given Desfan's past. He would feel more suited to hunting criminals than ruling from his throne. Still. It's a wonder his council lets him do it."

"Maybe they don't know," Akiva said.

"It's hard to keep secrets when you're living in a palace with hundreds of people." Liam frowned. "If this is Sahvi, we need to incriminate him. There's too much at stake if we don't."

"We'll find the evidence," Kazim promised.

"Do you have any other news from Zennor?" Liam asked.

"Unrest between the monarchy and the clans is building," Kazim said. "Skyer's betrothal to Princess Imara is being touted as the way to peace, but we all know he can't be trusted. And the princess isn't even there right now."

"Yes, I heard," Liam mused. "Her father sent her to travel with Princess Serene."

"If the rumors are true, he didn't actually send her," Akiva chimed in.

Liam snorted. "I'd heard the princess had a talent for forgery. I assume she sent the letter to Desfan in Zaire's name, confident her father won't publicly denounce her. It would create a scandal." His jaw firmed. "Is Skyer still in Zennor?"

"Yes," Kazim said, and there was a hard edge in his voice. "He's in Kedaah, speaking for the clans in Buhari's court."

"Good. Keep an ear out, in case he moves. I need to know where he is. Always." The thread of steel in his voice was unmistakable: hatred.

Grayson had felt like a spectator through this whole exchange, an observer who had come in halfway through a game and didn't understand the plays that had already been made— or even the end goal.

Akiva pushed a scarred hand into his dark hair. "Don't worry. We have someone watching Skyer at all times. He won't go anywhere without being tracked."

"Good." Liam blew out his breath. "You really should have

listened to me. Things will get messy."

Akiva shook his head. "No. Your fight is ours. We're going to destroy Henri Kaelin for what he did. We'll destroy them all."

Kazim nodded, his eyes burning with fierce agreement.

Liam glanced at Grayson, as if finally remembering his presence. "We should go." He turned back to the others. "I'll return when I can. Where are you staying?"

"Just here, in the warehouse," Kazim said. "But what would you like us to do?"

"Find out everything you can about Sahvi and the olcain," Liam said. "I'll be in touch."

As they left the warehouse and re-entered the sunny street, Grayson glanced over at his uncharacteristically quiet brother. "They weren't just informants," he said slowly. "They're your friends."

"No," Liam said, squinting up at the bright blue sky. "They're family."

Grayson wasn't sure why that answer made him feel a little hollow. He cleared his throat. "Why didn't you tell them who I am? They know who you are."

"True. But they don't need to know who you are. At least not yet." He glanced over at him. "There are few people I truly care about. Pose a threat to them in any way, and I will be forced to defend them."

Grayson met the edge of threat in Liam's eyes. "They have nothing to fear from me, as long as they don't threaten Mia." Unlike his brother, Grayson had only one person he truly cared about.

Because clearly, Grayson had not made Liam's list of *family*. The distinction shouldn't bother him, because he understood it. They may be developing a tenuous trust, but they each had other priorities. People who were more valued. More important.

And Grayson wasn't wounded by that.

Not at all.

He glanced at his brother. "Who is Skyer?" *And why do you hate him?*

He couldn't quite voice the last part. It seemed too personal a question, after the line that had just been drawn between them.

Liam's eyes remained focused on the street ahead of them, his jaw clenched. "He's a walking corpse."

His brother said nothing more, and Grayson didn't, either. But as they walked back to the theater, he realized he'd forgotten something vital in these past weeks with Liam.

His brother was a Kaelin, too. Ruthless. Secretive. Dangerous.

He would do well not to forget again.

CHAPTER 37
CLARE

THE MOMENT CLARE STEPPED OUT OF THE carriage she was greeted by Lord Francin, who was hosting them for their one-night stay on the outskirts of Wexon.

The old lord stood in the courtyard with his mansion towering behind him. Trees from the surrounding forests bled onto the grounds, creating a natural, wild beauty. The afternoon sun turned the leafy treetops a vivid green while casting deep shadows underneath. The encroaching forest was oddly comforting —as was the sight of Lord Francin. He was thin and bald, a little bent with age, and he relied heavily on his cane. Unlike most of the lords and ladies they had stayed with on the tour, this man seemed purely genuine as his watery green eyes found hers. "Princess, it is an honor." He straightened from a short bow, and quirked a bushy eyebrow. "Now, I'm not much on fuss and fanciful things, so that's about all you'll get from me."

Though exhaustion pulled at every aching muscle in Clare's body, his words made her smile. "Quite frankly, I appreciate that."

"Good. We'll get along splendidly." He tightened his grip on his cane, his eyes darting to Imara, who had just descended from the carriage. "I'm pleased to have you here as well, Princess Imara. If half the rumors are true, I think we'll get along as well." He winked.

Imara grinned. "I think you're right, Lord Francin."

"Thank you for being so accommodating," Clare said. "I'm sorry we're so delayed, and that our stay had to be shortened."

He waved an age-spotted hand. "No apologies necessary. I'm just pleased to have you here at all. Cursed rebels, trying to kill you. What a disgrace." He turned toward the mansion. "Come, let me give you a tour, and then you can rest up. You'll need your strength for tonight, as the king still asked that I put on a dinner. I had to invite several people I don't like, so I decided I might as well make them all jealous. We've refinished parts of the house, and I've got my best riches on display." He shot her a grin. "And of course I took great pains with the seating arrangements for dinner, so they can sit by people they despise."

Imara chuckled. "How wonderfully devious of you."

He winked. "My late wife always said I would make a wonderfully mean old man . . ."

Clare followed them as they moved toward the house, but she stole a peek back at the carriage and saw Venn helping Vera down. The instant the maid's feet touched the ground, she tugged her hand away and turned her back on Venn, hurrying to direct Lord Francin's servants who had arrived to help unload the carriage. Venn's empty hand rolled into a fist, his gaze focused on Vera.

It had been two days since Ivonne's burial in Halbrook, and Clare had not seen Vera so much as speak to Venn. She knew her friend was hurting for the loss of her sister. It was obvious in the tears she cried at night, and the stoic face she wore throughout the day. She didn't want to talk about anything. She wanted to lose herself in work. It was something Clare had experienced when she lost her parents, so she knew not to press Vera.

But Venn's pain was obvious as well, and Clare's heart hurt for them both.

As Clare walked toward the house, she sensed Bennick move into position behind her, leaving Wilf and Venn to secure her room.

Lord Francin's tour proved long and thorough. Clare thought he must have been a bit starved for company, as he talked almost the entire time. He had a comment for every painting and a story for every room. Imara's eyes glazed after a while, but Clare found him amusing. And his loneliness was obvious, so she was happy to let him talk. Several times during the long tour she caught Bennick staring at her, and her cheeks warmed as she shot him a secret smile.

After an hour, Lord Francin led them to the corridor with the guest suites. Imara excused herself rather quickly and slipped into her room, but Clare turned to Lord Francin with a smile. "Thank you for the tour, it was lovely."

He scoffed. "I'm an old man who doesn't know when to stop talking, and you're a gentle soul who lets me."

She smiled. "I enjoyed your stories."

"Now I know you're too kind." Lord Francin waved toward her door. "Please, take some time to rest. I have final preparations to make for tonight. A storm is coming in, which means most of the guests will want a room for the night." He shook his bald head as he turned, leaning on his cane as he headed for the stairs. "Simpering fools," he muttered under his breath.

Clare grinned after him, aware of Bennick turning to face her. "I don't think I've met another nobleman like him."

"I like him." She glanced up at Bennick, perfectly aware that they were the only ones left in the corridor. The warmth in Bennick's intent gaze warmed every part of her. "I don't think you were paying much attention to his tour, though."

Bennick's eyes remained fixed on her. "You're right. I barely heard a word he said."

Something low in her gut tightened. Her smile widened and her voice turned lightly teasing. "That's a shame."

Bennick eased closer. "Oh?"

"You didn't hear him mention the private sitting room in this very wing that no one ever uses?" She shook her head. "A pity."

His chin dipped along with his voice. "Well, I may have heard him mention it, and I admit I was intrigued."

Heat spread through her chest. "Did you manage to hear where it is located?"

"I admit that I did not."

"Hmm. That's too bad."

"Ah, but I trust you were paying attention."

The flirtation felt good. Normal. And Clare wanted to embrace it fully. She grasped his hand, squeezing his fingers. "Luckily for you, I *was* listening, and we have a few moments." She tugged him down the hall and he followed without hesitation, the two of them glancing around to make sure they remained unobserved.

They slipped into the room at the end of the hall, and Bennick nudged the door closed with the heel of his boot. The room was dimly lit, since the drapes were drawn, leaving the sunlight barely peeking around the edges, but Clare didn't need to see much to know that they were actually, truly alone for the first time in weeks, and that Bennick wanted this moment just as much as she did.

Her fingers curled in his uniform and she dragged him closer, their mouths coming together easily in the semi-dark. His hands were also moving, one curling around her side while the other dragged up her back until he cradled the back of her head.

Her fingers lifted to his face, then got lost in his hair and her heart pounded as her back was somehow pressed against the wall. Had they moved? Crossed the room? Or was it the door beside her? It didn't really matter, especially as Bennick eased closer, until there was no space between them.

Her skin hummed and warmth exploded in her chest when he tilted his head, changing the angle of the kiss. He captured her mouth, taking over what she had started. His body curved around hers, as if he could not resist some invisible pull.

They were both breathing raggedly when he finally dragged his mouth away from hers. His stubbled jaw rasped against her cheek as he ducked his head, his lips at her ear, his voice rough with emotion. "That wasn't exactly what I thought would happen when I closed the door."

Her short laugh was breathless. "What did you think was going to happen?"

"I don't know. I thought maybe we would talk. Sit together. Maybe kiss a little."

"Sorry."

He leaned back, his eyes serious even though his mouth twitched. "*Never* apologize for that."

Her hand drifted across his cheek. "Did you want to talk now?"

"Talking isn't as enjoyable as what we were just doing." His chin ducked as he lowered his lips to hers, but she kept a hand on his jaw, holding him back.

He groaned, and she smiled a little. "I love kissing you, but we can talk."

"What do you want to talk about?"

"How are you feeling about your father?"

He drew back. "Do you really want to discuss my father right now?"

"I just want to make sure you're all right." Her brow furrowed. "The more I've been thinking about the latest note from the Rose, the more I think his obsession with you is dangerous."

He frowned slightly. "I agree. But I still think leaving you isn't the answer."

"Neither do I. But I think it's clear your father only wants to protect you. He cares about you, Bennick."

He sighed, his shoulders dropping. "I know. And it bothers me."

"Why?"

His hands shifted to her waist as he let out a slow breath. "He didn't care about me or my mother in the past. Why should he get to now? He certainly shouldn't dictate to me, or expect me to do everything he wants."

"I don't think you're wrong. Everything you're saying . . . it makes sense." She balanced her hands against his chest, prompting him to meet her gaze. "But for all your father's flaws, he does love you. He doesn't want to risk losing you."

"But I can't lose you. That's why I can't leave." His fingers tightened against her waist. "And yet I'm fates-blasted terrified of making a mistake and having you pay the consequences. If my father is right and the Rose would follow me if I left . . ."

"We're stronger together, remember?" She tipped her head back, meeting his hooded gaze. "You have good instincts, Captain Markam. You have my unwavering trust. Trust yourself in this and don't let anyone—especially your father—make you question yourself."

His thumbs drew small circles against her flat stomach, and it was entirely distracting. "How are you so perfect?"

She snorted. "I'm not."

"You're perfect for me." He searched her face, and when he spoke again, his words were soft but sure—simple, and beautiful. "Clare Ellington, I'm in love with you."

Her heart pounded and her eyes flew wide.

His grip on her waist tightened, his gaze steady as he met her startled eyes. "I have been for a long time, and I've been wanting to tell you, but I didn't want you to think I was just saying the words. That it was too soon. Because I mean it, Clare. I love you with everything I have. Everything I am." His throat bobbed and he lifted one hand to brush back a strand of hair that had escaped her braided crown. She shivered as he tucked it behind her ear, his fingertips trailing down her skin.

She could not look away from his intense gaze.

"I love how you defended Serene in that hallway, before I even knew you. I loved watching you with your brothers, seeing how much you love them—how much they love you. I love that you didn't forgive me right away for lying about who I was. I loved our conversations—your wit. You challenged me. Surprised me. And I loved every second I spent with you on the training ground, loved watching you discover the strength and courage you've always had. I loved every excuse I had to touch you, and every time you would touch me. I love how you showed kindness to my mother, and how you stood up to my father for her. And even though it terrified me, I admired how you stood up to Newlan at the banquet. I love your compassion—that you still love Eliot, even after all he's done. I love your smile. Your spirit. Your loyalty." A furrow pulled between his eyebrows. "The only moment I ever hated is when you walked away from me, and I thought I'd lost your friendship forever. Because I knew then that what I felt for you went beyond friendship—beyond anything I'd ever felt before, for anyone."

Tears stung Clare's eyes and she blinked rapidly, her throat swollen with emotion.

Bennick lifted one hand to cup her cheek, his thumb brushing across her quivering lower lip. His eyes never left hers. "I never want to give you any reason to walk away from me again. I want you in my life forever. I don't care what obstacles are in our path—I will do anything to keep you with me."

A tear slipped from her eye and Bennick's thumb was quick to swipe it away. "You don't have to say anything," he whispered. "I don't expect anything at all, I just needed to—"

Clare grabbed the back of his neck and pulled his mouth to hers, kissing him deeply. When she pulled back, she couldn't stop her grin, or her happy tears. "I love you, Bennick. Of course I do." She wanted to say more, tell him all the reasons and the moments, make her declaration as wonderful as his had been, but her voice failed her.

His grin was slow, the light filling his eyes a steadily increasing glow.

If she had not already been completely in love with him, she would have fallen for him in that moment. With that look. The absolute joy and adoration on his face was something she would never, ever forget. Nor would she forget how beautiful, strong, and courageous he made her feel when he looked at her like that.

He planted his free hand on the wall beside her, his other still cupping her cheek, no doubt feeling her grin. "Well," he whispered. "I think we should find private sitting rooms more often."

"I agree." To emphasize her response, she lifted up on her toes and kissed him again.

The storm Lord Francin had predicted was already lashing the mansion when the first guests arrived. Heavy rain beat at the roof, with gusts of wind buffeting the walls. The torches and lamps that glowed in the entry hall guttered as drenched nobles dove inside, sloughing off their heavy cloaks and hurrying to adjust their hair and clothes before they joined the line.

Clare and Imara stood beside Lord Francin at the dining room entrance, personally greeting each guest. She was a little surprised how many nobles had braved the rough summer storm, but Lord Francin merely rolled his eyes and whispered, "The lot of them wouldn't normally venture out in a drizzle, but for a chance to see you, they'd probably swim the length of the Lambern. Ridiculous."

Clare leaned in, keeping her voice low. "Can you imagine them swimming in the lake with their finery?"

The old man chortled, gripping his cane planted firmly before him. "Lady Riven's ridiculously voluminous skirt would terrify any ghastly lake monster."

Clare grinned, the tug on her lips reminding her of the moments she and Bennick had shared earlier. Her skin still tingled with the memory of his touch.

He loved her. And she loved him.

Saying it out loud was freeing. Empowering. And it made it extremely hard to focus on anything else, which is why Francin's humorous asides were all that helped keep her somewhat present as they greeted the seemingly endless stream of nobles.

Clare had chosen to wear the blue dinner dress that matched

Bennick's eyes. It was perhaps a little less formal, but it seemed the perfect choice for tonight. The flowing skirt rippled to the floor, the bodice snug at her waist. Silver embroidery twisted in basic but lovely designs at the hem. Vera had helped tame her thick hair into an elegant bun at the nape of her neck, and Clare had disregarded the gloves she normally wore as the decoy, which helped to hide the small scars on her hands from her life as a kitchen maid. The garrote bracelet Bennick had given her was tucked under the edge of the sleeve, and her knife was sheathed at her calf.

She was perfectly aware of Bennick's eyes on her. He and Wilf stood behind her, along with two of Imara's towering body-guards. Venn was stationed at the bedroom and Vera was inside, claiming a headache. Clare's heart was breaking for her friend, but she didn't know how to help her through this grief—except to be near, for whenever Vera was ready to talk.

As they stood in the entryway, Lord Francin made intro-ductions and Clare greeted each noble with a smile and polite greeting before smoothly passing them to Imara. Lord Francin would then lean in and whisper some comment about them or their ancestors, and Clare would have to smother the urge to laugh.

She recognized several faces in the sea of nobles she greeted; all people she had met at previous stops on the tour who were interested in seeing the prisoner exchange. Some even planned to journey all the way to Duvan to show their support for the alliance.

One of the many guests to arrive was Lord Finch, the young man who she'd met at the Paltrow's ball. She hadn't seen him since the fair in Lindon, where he had grappled with Bennick. She smiled genuinely as she offered her hand. "Lord Finch, I'm pleased to see you here."

"Princess." He took her hand and brushed a quick kiss to her knuckles, his grin stretching wide. "I must say I'm glad to hear that. Wouldn't want you to be sick of me."

"Nonsense, familiar faces are always welcome." She peered past him. "Are your sisters with you?"

"No, but they insisted I commit every detail to memory to recite to them later."

"I'd nearly forgotten, you said you were coming to the prisoner exchange."

The corner of his mouth twitched. "If you forgot, I must not have made enough of an impression. I'll have to remedy that." He glanced beyond her, no doubt catching sight of Bennick. Clare could feel him standing behind her, and she had to fight a grin when Finch immediately dropped her hand. His smile was a bit apologetic as he faced her again, lowering his voice conspiratorially. "It seems I still have the unwitting ability to make your bodyguard nervous."

"At least there will be no dancing tonight," Clare said.

Laughter sparked in his eyes. "True, he does seem to particularly dislike that."

Lord Francin leaned over. "You do realize you're holding up the line, Lord Finch."

"Apologies. You're going to regret sending me an invitation."

"I already do," he said blithely, before shaking his head. "Frankly, I'm surprised you accepted." He looked to Clare. "Don't let his charming ways fool you. Lord Finch is a bit of a recluse."

"Nonsense." Finch met Clare's gaze with a slow smile. "I merely require something remarkable to grab my attention."

Clare hoped she was the only one to hear the low growl in Bennick's throat, but it was quickly overridden by a commotion at the front doors. They all turned to see the crowd scrambling back, making way for the last person Clare expected to see.

Commander Markam's cloak was drenched, his hood thrown back to reveal his severe expression. Soaked strands of darkened hair were plastered to his face and he seemed to belatedly realize that he had stepped into the middle of a procession. He drew up short, his motions stiff.

Clare excused herself from the line and hurried toward him, conscious of Bennick and Wilf following her. When she reached Bennick's father, she had to crane her neck to meet his gaze. "Commander Markam. What an unexpected surprise."

"Princess." He bowed his head, though the action was tense. "May we speak in private?"

"Of course." She gestured to an open sitting room just off the entry hall, and he preceded her inside. Once they were all inside, Wilf pushed the door closed.

Bennick faced his father. "What are you doing here?"

The commander's mouth thinned. "It was a last resort."

"What does that mean?" Clare asked. "Where are the prisoners?"

"Outside. I put them in the barn."

"Why?" Bennick asked. "You should have been far past Wexon by now."

"We ran into some . . . complications."

"What kind of complications?"

The commander frowned at his son. "Some of the prisoners fell ill. We've been moving at a crawl ever since."

"Are any of them still sick?" Clare asked.

"Yes." His eyes narrowed. "With this storm, I had little choice but to seek shelter, and this was the nearest place with a stable large enough to house them."

"You made the right choice," Clare said. Everyone shot a look at her, but she ignored their cut of surprise. "The Mortisians must be cared for. It could be disastrous if we arrived at the prisoner exchange without all twenty."

"Indeed," the commander agreed, eyeing her. He shifted his attention back to his son. "I knew you would be here, which is why I wanted to let you know we'd arrived. We'll keep to the barn."

There was a beat of silence, so Clare rushed to fill it. "I'll inform Lord Francin. We can bring food, blankets, clothing, medicine—whatever the Mortisians or your soldiers need."

The commander tipped his head. "Thank you. The aid is much appreciated."

Clare nodded and led the way back into the hall.

Lord Francin and Imara were both curious about the commander's presence, and Clare hurried to explain what had happened. Lord Francin immediately sent servants to find anything the prisoners needed.

In the dining hall, since dinner had yet to be served, the nobles were sipping wine from tall glasses and milling amongst each other. It became obvious in seconds that word had already spread, and the conversation buzzed with speculation about the prisoners in the stable.

"I can't believe those criminals are out there right now . . ."

"We're not safe with them so close! They'd murder us in our sleep if they got the chance."

"Their sickness is probably a fates-blasted curse for their crimes."

"Filthy Mortisians; they'll spread their plague to all of us!"

The ignorant, insensitive comments grated on Clare, and she was all too grateful when Lord Francin declared dinner ready and everyone took their seats at the long tables.

Despite Clare's irritation with the Devendran nobles, and her worry for the ill Mortisians, the meal was delicious. A creamy vegetable soup. Roasted vegetables and liberally seasoned chicken served with a rich brown gravy. Plump rolls that steamed when pulled apart, and a variety of jams, butter, and honey. The long table stretched to somehow hold them all, and servants dashed expertly between courses. Lord Francin assured her there was plenty, and even now, the Mortisians were being served the same fare.

The conversation was punctuated by bursts of laughter, the mood in the room growing more jovial as the wine poured freely and the prisoners were largely forgotten.

The meal was well underway when Clare caught sight of a servant hurrying to Bennick's side. They exchanged a brief word, and Bennick's tension was palpable as he motioned for Wilf to stay even as he strode from the room, the servant at his heels.

Clare's heart thudded as she saw the darkening of Wilf's face. The chatter and laughter of the nobles was suddenly too loud, and the need to escape the room—and follow Bennick—took over. She leaned in to Lord Francin and Imara, who sat beside her. "I must leave for a moment. Excuse me."

The princess frowned. "Is everything all right?"

"I don't know. Just stay here and keep up appearances."

Imara nodded, though her eyes tracked Clare as she slid from the table and moved for the door. The noise from the nobles didn't stall or drop—they hardly seemed aware of her leaving.

Wilf fell into step beside her, his voice low. "Are you all right?"

"I just needed to get away for a moment." She eyed him. "What's happened?"

"I don't know," he said grimly. "Bennick just said to stay with you."

As they entered the shadowed entryway, a flash of lightning tore through the upper windows, illuminating the tense knot of people standing in the corridor.

Once again, the commander was drenched with rain. Water pooled around his boots and he was focused solely on Bennick, whose stiff back was to Clare.

A few of the commander's soldiers were also dripping wet, silently watching the tense exchange between father and son.

"No," Bennick was saying, his voice tight. "I can't do that."

The commander's eyes narrowed. "I'm ordering you to assist me."

"And I refuse. I can send one of my men to the city guard station for reinforcements, but—"

"Fates, Ben, I need you!"

"What's happened?" Clare asked.

The commander's head cranked toward her and Bennick spun, his brow furrowing. "Go back to the feast."

Her arms crossed her chest, staying firmly in place. "What happened?" she repeated.

The commander's jaw worked. "Most of the prisoners have escaped."

Clare's stomach dropped. "What? How?"

"It must have happened after the servants brought food. When I returned to check on them, my men were dead, and any of the prisoners who could walk were gone." The commander sliced a look at his son. "I require the captain's help getting them back."

"I'm not leaving the princess," Bennick said.

"Without those prisoners, the alliance is threatened. At the moment, I've only managed to recover six of them. I need your help."

Clare could feel Bennick's tension as he breathed low and deep.

She exhaled slowly. "He's right, Bennick. We can't lose them."

Bennick ground his jaw, his eyes trained on his father.

The commander shoved a hand through his gray-tinged hair. "I wouldn't ask, but you and Grannard are some of the best trackers we have. The princess is secure, and I'll leave some of my men as an extra precaution, but those prisoners must be found."

Bennick stood there for a long moment, the roar of the buffeting winds and hammering rain the only sound. Then he turned away from his father. "I'll get Venn." He pointed a finger at Wilf. "You don't leave her. I don't think the prisoners will come here, but be on alert."

Wilf dipped his chin.

Bennick strode for the stairs, grinding his teeth as he left to find Venn.

The commander ordered away a few more of his men before he turned back to Clare. "You may rejoin the guests. It would be best not to let them think anything is amiss."

Clare eyed him, certain the man had other things he wished to say. He was clearly upset that Bennick had listened to her, and not him. She did not like the commander—at all—but she wished he could be a better person for Bennick's sake.

The commander's eyes narrowed. "Why are you shaking your head?"

She hadn't realized she was, but now that she had his attention, she found she had plenty to say. "If you wish to earn his respect, you need to treat him like the man he is. Not a child you can attempt to control."

The corner of his mouth curled with a sneer. "What do you know about him?"

"More than you, clearly."

Wilf's grunt sounded a little like a swallowed laugh.

The commander's expression tightened, but before he could speak, Bennick came down the stairs with Venn just behind him.

He glanced at Clare. "We won't be gone long."

She forced a smile. "We'll be fine here. Be careful."

"Always." Bennick turned to his father, his expression hardening. "Ready?"

The commander stalked for the door without a word, leaving Bennick and Venn to trail after him.

CHAPTER 38

CLARE

RETURNING TO THE DINING ROOM AND acting like there weren't Mortisian prisoners missing was not easy, and Clare was relieved when Lord Francin declared the festivities over. Servants arrived to show the guests to their rooms, and the few brave enough to venture out in the storm were escorted out by Lord Francin.

Clare and Imara walked together up the stairs, and Clare was grateful that Lord Francin had put them in a quiet wing, away from everyone else.

Imara was shaking her head. "I can't believe they ran. Didn't they realize how close to freedom they were?"

"I don't know." Clare bit her lip at the deep roll of thunder outside, the lashing waves of rain.

"They've been caged too long," Wilf said from behind them.

"They saw a chance for freedom, and they took it. They aren't thinking logically."

Imara's shoulders dropped. "I feel so terrible for them. I hope they don't come to harm. How did they even manage to escape?"

"Desperate men always find a way," Wilf said.

Clare bit her lip. "If we can't recover them all, do you think the Mortisians at the border will believe us that they escaped?"

"I don't know." Imara frowned. "Regardless, it will make the situation more tense."

Unfortunately, Clare knew she was right.

They arrived at their suites. Imara disappeared into hers across the hall, and Clare left Wilf at the door with the other guard with instructions to tell her the moment any word reached them.

Inside the room, she found Vera repacking one of the trunks, and she told her about the prisoners escaping while Vera helped pluck the pins from her hair. As the tension released across her skull, leaving waves of hair to fall around her shoulders, Clare's nervous energy increased. She knew sleep would evade her until she learned the fate of the search, and she couldn't sit still. She turned to Vera before the girl could move to unfasten her dress. "I'm not ready to sleep. Can I help you with the repacking?"

Vera shrugged. "Of course."

Lightning slashed the sky outside, ripping a flash of light across the room. Rain drummed against the window, dampening all other sounds. Clare hated to think that the Mortisians were out in this, running scared. She didn't like to think of Bennick and Venn out there, either.

She tried to focus on sorting and folding clothing with Vera beside her. The work was minimal, but proved an effective distraction. Between the muffling torrent of the storm and her focus on the task, she did not realize that Wilf must have been tapping at the door until he prodded it open. From her position at the foot of the bed, she caught the motion from the corner of her vision and turned.

Shock stiffened her muscles when she saw it wasn't Wilf at all.

She straightened, confusion rushing through her. "Lord Finch? What are you doing here?"

The nobleman shoved a hand through his brown hair, pushing it back off his brow as he smiled at her.

Though his smile was familiar, the chilling edge was new.

Her heart thudded in her chest, and it was suddenly hard to breathe.

He dipped his pointed chin in a slight bow, his brown eyes almost glowing in the lamp light. "Clare."

Everything about this moment was wrong. His presence. His smile. His mocking gaze.

The fact that he knew her name.

The blood drained from her face and she took a step back, bumping into Vera who stood frozen behind her.

Lord Finch took a step forward, then paused. "Oh. I nearly forgot."

He twisted away, reaching into his pocket as he looked down.

Clare smothered a gasp with her hand.

Wilf lay unmoving in the corridor, and Clare could see the boots of another guard as well.

Lord Finch bent over the fallen giant and slipped a rose petal into Wilf's mouth. When he faced Clare again, the Rose's smile curved wide. "I've been looking forward to this moment."

Vera clutched Clare's arm, her nails digging through the sleeve. "It's him," she gasped.

Clare slid protectively in front of Vera, her stomach writhing with fear. "You—you're not Lord Finch."

It was a stupid thing to say, but her thoughts were sluggish.

"Oh, but I am. I created this persona long ago. With enough gold and tutoring, you can be anyone. Surely you of all people understand that, Clare."

Vera's cry strangled in her throat as the Rose kicked the door closed and strode forward, obviously relishing each step. Clare swore his falcon eyes caught every tremble that shook her body.

He flashed a smile. "I need various identities. They help me get where I need to be. Creating Lord Finch was easy. I bought a derelict estate near Lindon years ago and pretended that I'd simply been living elsewhere for years. No one questioned me. And when I'm not living as Finch, they think I'm staying at another of my many homes. It's quite perfect. Just like your performance." His head tilted to the side as he studied her. "At the Paltrow's ball, I was convinced I was dancing with the princess. I wanted to meet her, and I really thought I had, up until that moment in the garden when your name was called out." He smiled. "Clare. A beautiful name, for all its simplicity. *Clare.*" He shivered a little, his grin stretching wider. "I can't wait for Bennick to scream it. You, of course, won't hear that, but I plan to hide close enough so I won't miss it."

Clare itched to grab the knife strapped to her leg, but she forced herself to slowly back up instead. She had to get Vera out of here. "Please. Let her go."

One eyebrow lifted. "Not begging for yourself, Clare?"

Her teeth clenched. That familiar, charming voice was like a hundred spiders crawling over her skin. "You have no reason to hurt her."

"Untrue, unfortunately. She's seen me. I have no choice but to kill her."

There would be no reasoning with him. She should have

known it the moment she looked into those cold eyes.

Clare made a dive for her knife, but before she'd even hiked up her skirt, the Rose moved in a blur and grabbed her wrists.

She spread her feet and twisted against his grip as Bennick had taught her, managing to jerk him forward. She slammed her foot against his knee, and he grunted as he staggered, his head ducking. She managed to rip her hands free, and she clawed at the silver bracelet on her wrist, her nail catching on the small latch. As she jerked the garrote wire free, she dodged around the Rose, wrapping the wire around his neck.

"Run!" she screamed at Vera.

She pulled the wire tight, but even though she had moved quickly, the Rose had thrown up a hand, catching the wire with his fingers, trapping his hand at his throat and giving him space to breathe.

His elbow drove into her side, hitting the place she had been stabbed.

She gasped in pain and her hold on him loosened.

It was all he needed to shove into her, then drag her over his shoulder.

She was flipped over him and landed hard on her back, the air knocked from her lungs, the garrote wire trailing uselessly on the floor beside her.

"Clare!" Vera cried out.

The Rose stood over Clare, his face red, his eyes excited. He lifted his foot, and then his boot slammed into her unprotected gut.

The impact was brutal. She choked, her eyes stinging as she tried and failed to suck in air, and she watched with blurry vision as the Rose grasped Vera's swinging arm—which held a knife— and threw her as if she weighed nothing. Vera's head cracked against the wall and her body slumped to the floor. She didn't get up.

The scuff of boots came toward Clare and the Rose snagged her wrists, binding them together with the garrote wire, which bit painfully into her flesh. She struggled, but was still dazed from the pain. The Rose's every move seemed terribly practiced and smooth as he finished tying her wrists, and then he drew out a leather cord from his pocket and reached for her ankles.

Clare kicked out at him, her foot catching his jaw. He grunted, falling back.

She turned and wriggled against the floor, trying to scramble away.

The Rose reached her, one knee digging into her back. She managed a breathless scream before his fingers dug into loose hair, curled into a fist, and he slammed her forehead against the floor.

Clare did not black out, but her vision blurred and her hearing grew distorted with a high-pitched ringing. She was only half-aware of him dragging her closer, tying her ankles together. Then he hefted her into his arms only to carry her to the bed, where he dropped her.

He scrubbed a hand over his jaw, where she had struck him. "Bennick taught you well. I'll be sure to mention in my note to him that you fought hard. I'm sure he'll appreciate knowing that."

Tears stabbed her eyes. Her ears still rang from the blow to her head, and bile climbed her throat.

The Rose lifted the edge of her skirt and she squirmed when his fingers brushed against her bare leg. He tugged her knife free of the sheath and balanced it on his palm. "I think I'll use this one to kill you. There's a poetic beauty in that."

Clare glanced past him, to where Vera lay sprawled on the

floor. Her breath hitched at the sight of her friend's still body. She couldn't tell if she was breathing.

"I'm glad Bennick went to help find the missing prisoners," the Rose said conversationally. "So much better than if I'd had to overpower him. I couldn't have killed him—I need him to find your body. I want him to hate me for what I did to you." He grinned. "That night at the Paltrows, when we were dancing, I saw his feelings for you. I just thought he loved Serene, but later, in the garden, I saw him hold your bleeding body, and I knew it was *you* he cared about. And that's when I knew exactly how I wanted to destroy him."

"Why do you want to torture him?" Clare asked, her voice shaky.

"Because I hate him." It was a simple, terrible answer. He leaned over her, setting the edge of the blade against her throat with enough pressure that she didn't dare swallow. "Hold still," he whispered. With his other hand, he began running his fingers through her hair, carefully teasing it out across the pillow.

Clare shivered and closed her eyes, hating the ghosting feel of his fingers stroking through her hair, brushing her scalp. A tangle snagged his fingers and she winced. He worked through the spot with terrible gentleness, and a tear slid from Clare's eye.

In this moment, all she saw was the image of Ivonne stretched out on the bed, hair carefully spread, rose in her mouth, and a dagger in her heart.

That was how Bennick would find her, unless she could fight her way free.

His thumb brushed the high curve of her cheek and Clare barely resisted the urge to jerk away. The sharp press of the blade at her throat was all that kept her from lashing out.

He smiled as he returned to combing through her hair with his fingers. "A decoy. A genius idea. The rebels were as surprised as I was, weren't they? Especially the one who knew you. Was he your brother, or a former lover?"

"Why do you hate Bennick?" Her voice rasped with emotion she did not want to show. But if she could keep him talking, someone might come. If the storm hadn't been so loud, someone would have heard their screams. But all it would take was for someone to find Wilf's body in the hall . . .

Her heart constricted, and new tears stung her eyes. First Ivonne, then Wilf, and possibly Vera—then Clare would be next.

The Rose finished smoothing her hair over the pillow, and then he set the flat part of the blade against her lips. His brown eyes stared into hers. "That's a long story, and I'm afraid we don't have time for it just now." Keeping the knife in place over her mouth, he reached to the side, and when he straightened back in her view, he held a long-stemmed rose, droplets of rain rolling over the petals. "I picked this one for you. Lord Francin grows beautiful roses."

Her eyes watered, and the red rose blurred as he dipped it toward her. The damp, velvety petals brushed her nose and her nostrils flared. The overwhelming perfume flooded her senses, making this horrible nightmare all too vivid.

"I'll leave two notes with you, I think," the Rose mused. "One in your left hand for Serene, assuring her I have not forgotten her, and the one in your right hand will be for Bennick. And I'd like you to help me compose it."

He pulled back the rose, setting it against his own nose. He breathed in deeply, mouth curving. "What would you like to tell him, Clare? What final message would you give him? Wait—I know. Perhaps: *Bennick, I died thinking you would save me, but you failed.*"

"Stop it," Clare whispered, her breath clouding against the blade held to her mouth.

He grinned, continuing in a falsely high voice—a mocking imitation of her own. *"I cried for you, and you didn't come."*

"Stop it!"

The blunt side of the knife pressed against her lips, stopping her protests. He tapped the rose against her sharply rising chest. "You think he won't appreciate your final words? Should we leave him with nothing?" The soft petals dragged against her cheek now, guided by his steady hand. His awful smile was unbroken. "This is a beautiful moment for me. I'll kill the woman he loves, and then the princess he has dedicated his life to serving. He will truly hate me then, almost as much as I hate him."

The Rose smiled, the blade still sealing her lips. "I'll be sure to tell him you loved him—even though he failed to save you. It's sure to hurt him. He'll blame himself for leaving you."

His words were all the more terrible because she knew they were true. Bennick would blame himself. He had blamed himself before, and if he came in here and found her dead . . .

He would have to tell Mark and Thomas.

Fates, she couldn't just lie here and let the Rose kill her. She would fight. She would—

She gasped as the edge of the knife nicked the soft skin above her lip as the blade was shifted, the tip now resting over her pounding heart.

The Rose grinned. "Goodbye, Clare."

CHAPTER 39

CLARE

CLARE WAS TRAPPED ON THE BED BY the press of the Rose's body and the tip of the blade that rested against her chest, ready to plunge into her heart.

There was no point being careful any longer. Her ankles were tied together, and so were her wrists, but she still kicked and punched, bucking against him in her effort to throw him off.

The Rose laughed, his hand clamped around her shoulder, his knife still resting against her heart. She felt the moment his grip on the knife shifted. She knew he was about to kill her, and she could do nothing to stop it.

Without sound or warning, the Rose was knocked off of her.

She jerked up from the bed, struggling to track the blur of movement as Bennick shoved the Rose onto the floor and then slammed a fist into the assassin's surprised, gaping face.

Bennick kept hitting him. Blood splattered and cartilage cracked. The Rose choked. He lifted the knife, but Bennick knocked it out of his hand. The assassin clawed at Bennick, but each blow Bennick delivered jolted the Rose's entire body. Finally, he slumped, his eyes rolling back in his head.

Bennick's fists didn't stop.

Clare's stomach clenched, her vision wavering as her eyes burned.

"Bennick," a rough voice barked.

Clare whirled, her throat tightening when she saw Wilf standing with one shoulder propped against the doorframe, a hand pressed against his bleeding side. He was pale, with sweat beading his forehead, but his voice was firm as he spoke again. *"Bennick."*

Bennick delivered a last punch and then rocked back, his chest heaving as he stared down at the Rose's battered face.

"We need him alive," Wilf said, darkness in his tone.

A shudder wracked Clare's body, and Bennick's eyes snapped to her.

His expression was hard, fury still churning in his eyes. Rain drenched him from the storm outside, curling the ends of his hair and spilling droplets down his face. His curled fists were splashed with blood. Every muscle in his body was tensed and his chest rose and fell with heavy breaths.

She opened her mouth, but nothing came out. The horror of everything that had happened since the Rose stepped into the room smothered her. The terror, the shock, the pain.

The first tear leaked from her eye, and Bennick was in front of her in an instant. His hands skated over her body, checking for injuries.

"I'm fine," she gasped, her gut aching as memories flashed through her mind. The Rose's smile. The weight of his body, pressing down against hers.

The terror that came with knowing she was about to die.

Bennick's eyebrows drew together, his hands still moving, still searching for any sign of harm. His eyes lingered on the blood streaking over her mouth, and his jaw tightened. He drew a knife from his belt and cut the ties binding her ankles, and then he carefully unwound the wire of the garrote, freeing her wrists.

Blood rushed back into her fingers, sending needles of pain through her hands. She flinched, and Bennick froze. Then his thumbs spread over the deep lines left in her skin. The wire had only drawn blood in a few places, but Clare could feel anger vibrating through Bennick's gentle touch.

He remained crouched on the floor in front of Clare, his voice hard as he glanced at Wilf. "Check Vera."

Wilf pushed off the wall, but immediately swayed and slumped back, blinking slowly. His skin was turning gray. "I . . . don't think I can."

Footsteps pounded through the hammering sound of the rain, charging toward them down the corridor.

Clare tensed, and Bennick's fingers curled around her forearms, but it was Venn who swung around the doorframe. His dark hand gripped the jamb, his chest rising and collapsing with each harsh breath. His long ponytail was wet, strands of loose hair plastered to the sides of his face. His sweeping gaze cut to Vera, and panic exploded in his eyes. He choked out her name and darted forward, falling to his knees beside her. His shaking hands cupped her face, brushed back strands of blond hair, slipped to her neck to search for a pulse.

"Venn?" Bennick asked, his voice edged.

Venn didn't look up, and for every second he didn't speak, Clare's heart refused to beat.

The tension in his shoulders suddenly dropped and he bowed

his head. "She's alive." He muttered what sounded like a Zenno-rian prayer to the fates, but all Clare could hear was a rushing in her ears.

Vera was alive.

Clare was still alive.

And somehow, even Wilf was still breathing.

Fear and relief crashed inside her, tightening her lungs and making her body tremble.

Bennick's hold on her tensed.

The commander dodged into the room, taking in the scene with narrowed eyes before he turned to Wilf. "Was it the Rose?" he asked as he checked the wound.

"Yes." Bennick's voice was dark.

The skin around the commander's eyes tightened. "Is he dead?"

"Not yet," Bennick said, lethal promise in his voice.

"Why wait?" Venn snarled, not looking up from Vera.

"We need answers," Bennick said.

Commander Markam raised his head. "He's a professional assassin. He won't tell us anything. We should kill him now."

Bennick looked past the commander, to where two soldiers hovered in the doorway. "Secure the prisoner. Don't take your eyes off him."

The guards moved to obey, and Clare couldn't help but watch as they bound the Rose, who was still unconscious, his face swol-len and bloody.

Beside him lay the long-stemmed rose he would have shoved down her throat.

Her gut twisted and her eyes stung.

Bennick's hands cupped her face, forced her to look at him instead of that horrible rose. "You're safe," he whispered firmly. "He will never touch you again."

If Bennick had come even a moment later, she would be dead.

Her stomach rolled. The shock that had held her while the torrent of emotions swirled inside her chest finally broke. Tears leaked from her eyes and she sucked in a ragged breath. A sob clawed up her throat, her body shaking. Bennick's intense expression cracked, grief flashing in his eyes as he gathered her in his arms and sat on the bed, one hand pressing against the back of her head. She buried her face in the curve of his neck and clutched his shirt with knotted fingers, dragging him impossibly closer as she cried.

She didn't care what Venn, Wilf, or even the commander thought of her clinging to Bennick. Not in this moment. She wanted to be held. She wanted to feel safe. She wanted to forget what it had felt like to almost die.

Voices spoke over and around her, but no meaning penetrated. All she knew was the strength of Bennick's arms banded around her. His hold was unyielding, and the rumble of his voice was comforting, though in her tears she couldn't quite make out the words he spoke. His heart thudded steadily under her cheek, the predictable rhythm grounding.

It took several long moments for the worst of the shaking to pass. Her breathing was still unsteady and tears still fell from her eyes, but the cries that had wracked her entire body slowly subsided. Bennick still held her, one palm smoothing up and down her back. "I have you," he whispered in her hair, his breath warm against her temple. "You're all right." There was an edge to his words, as if he was trying to convince himself as well.

When Clare finally eased back on the bed, Bennick's hands remained on her shoulders—as if he could not fully let her go. Moisture continued to leak from her stinging eyes and her throat ached. Her head pounded, though she wasn't sure if it was from crying or from when the Rose had smashed her head against the floor.

Bennick's eyes narrowed on her forehead, and she wondered if the swelling was more visible now. His jaw clenched and he lifted a hand, thumb brushing just below the tender spot. His eyes drifted, and she could feel the sting from the small nick above her lip.

His eyes burned. "I will kill him." The vow was spoken in a rough exhale.

She didn't doubt him.

A glance around the room showed that they were alone, and her gaze snapped back to Bennick. "Are Vera and Wilf all right?"

His eyes were still scanning her face. "Yes. The physician said Wilf is lucky. Nothing vital was hit. Wilf said he only lost consciousness because he hit his head when the Rose attacked him. And Vera stirred when Venn carried her out. She'll be fine."

"Thank the fates," she breathed, her eyes squeezing shut.

Bennick's fingers stroked against the side of her face, prompting her eyes to open. "Are you hurt anywhere else?"

She shook her head. "No. A little bruised. Nothing serious."

"The physician will check on you once Wilf is settled." His throat bobbed, and he stood. Clare swallowed back her flash of fear, because it was clear he wasn't leaving her. He had only moved to the washstand and was pouring water into the shallow bowl. He lifted a folded cloth and dipped it in the water, then squeezed out the excess water with one hand. The quiet dripping sounded strangely loud in the otherwise quiet room; a mere echo of the rain glancing against the roof and windows.

Bennick returned to the bed, and Clare's eyes were drawn to his wet hand. His knuckles were already swollen from beating the Rose, and though the blood streaking his fingers did not all belong to him, she could see some cuts oozing crimson.

"Your hands," she gasped.

He barely glanced at them as he sat on the edge of the bed, his body angled toward her. "I'm fine."

She snatched hold of the hand clutching the wet cloth, her fingers tracing over his hurts. "This will take days to heal."

"I don't even feel it." She peeked up at him, and the flare of emotion in his eyes stole her breath. His voice deepened—roughened. "I would have killed him with my bare hands if Wilf hadn't stopped me. I can't believe he got so close—that I let him distract me."

"Distract you?"

Bennick slid his hand from hers and cupped her cheek. His focus was on her upper lip, where he gently dabbed the wet cloth. "The Rose cut the prisoners free. Some of them confirmed it. He caused a distraction, knowing there would be fewer guards on you."

Fates, she'd nearly forgotten the prisoners. "Did you find them all?"

"Yes. They didn't get far in this storm." He tilted his head for a better view of her cut and a muscle jumped in his cheek as he resumed his work. His touch was so gentle, it was barely there. "I left Venn to help the commander finish securing them in the stable, and to look more closely at their story about a Devendran cutting them free. The whole thing felt wrong, and then I saw the fallen guards and . . ." His hand against her cheek trembled, and he lowered the cloth. His voice was hoarse, his eyes haunted. "I thought I was going to be too late."

Clare leaned in, her lips gently settling against his. It was the barest kiss, barely there, but it was everything. It centered her. Strengthened her. Warmth slid through her veins, driving out some of the chill that still clung to her. Some of Bennick's tension seemed to drain as well, and when she pulled back, his breathing was even again.

She slowly pried the rag from his hand and, using a clean corner, began to dab at his torn knuckles. His hand flexed, as if he might pull away. But perhaps he knew she needed to do this—needed to take care of him.

Or maybe he needed this, too.

"Thank you," she whispered. The words didn't seem adequate, but her throat closed off, stopping all other words.

Bennick was silent for a long moment. When he did speak, his voice was worn. "Sometimes I wish you had never worked at the castle. That you had never been forced to become the decoy. The fates know my life never would have been complete without you, but . . . I hate that you're here. Constantly hurt or in danger."

"None of this is your fault. You saved my life, Bennick. So many times, you've saved me." She gently squeezed his swollen hand, still held in hers. "You helped me find myself. You love me, and that is worth any risk."

The skin around his eyes tightened, but he said nothing.

Clare lifted his other hand and began to tend the abused flesh. Her heart thumped hard against her ribs, and sweat broke out on her palms. She forced her voice to remain flat as she asked. "Where is the Rose?"

His hand tensed in her soft grip. "He's been secured in one of Lord Francin's cellars."

She swallowed, her pulse skipping. She still could not believe that the Rose had been Lord Finch. Even now, after seeing her own death in his soulless eyes, she could still see his easy smile. How he had danced so smoothly with her at the Paltrow's ball. How he had pointed out two young women watching them. *My sisters*, he'd claimed. Clearly a lie. Something to put her at ease, perhaps, but he hadn't known those girls. They had simply been watching their princess dance.

Her insides churned, thinking of how he had held her hand. Kissed it. Even tonight, he had smiled at her, knowing he would kill her tonight.

She eyed Bennick, remembering everything the Rose had said about him. How much he clearly hated him. She also couldn't forget the image of Bennick losing control as he had. She'd never seen him so furious. So violent. Her lungs were suddenly too tight. "Will you interrogate him?"

"We need to know who hired him," Bennick said.

She bit her lower lip. "I don't think you should be the one to question him."

Bennick frowned. "Why not?"

She hesitated, unsure of how to convey the sheer hatred that had burned in the Rose's eyes. And she wasn't about to mention the way Bennick had attacked the Rose. "He hates you, Bennick. So much. I . . . I'm scared of what he'll do."

The skin around his eyes tightened and he ducked his head so their eyes were level. "I don't know why he hates me. But I'm not afraid of him. And you don't need to be afraid, either." His free hand lifted, fingers ghosting against her cheek, then slipping into her hair.

Tingles exploded along her scalp, and ice bolted down her spine.

All she felt was the memory of the Rose's hand in her hair.

She jerked back, a shiver wracking her body.

Bennick froze. "Did I hurt you?"

"No." Tears sparked in her eyes, tightened her voice. Fates, she hated this. Hated feeling so fragile. Hated that her skin crawled at what should have been a soothing touch.

Bennick stared at her, his eyes burning. She knew there were a thousand things he wanted to say, a hundred assurances he wanted to give. But his mouth compressed and his eyes shuttered. The tension dropped from his shoulders and his expression seemed to close out every emotion.

Clare almost felt sorry for the Rose.

Chapter 40

Bennick

Pain blasted across his knuckles as Bennick hit the Rose again. The thud of flesh hitting flesh, the assassin's grunt—the sounds were as familiar as a heartbeat now.

He'd been interrogating the Rose for an hour, and the man hadn't broken.

The Rose was not unaffected. He flinched and hissed. He strained against the ropes that bound him to the wooden chair. Sweat slicked his skin, glistening alongside the blood that streaked his face.

But the Rose remained silent when Bennick repeated his question, his voice cold, his emotions carefully leashed. "Who hired you?"

The Rose sagged in his bonds, his face a swollen mass of purpling flesh. Several cuts oozed blood, though it was hard to tell if they were new, or simply reopened from Bennick's first assault, when he had tackled the Rose off of Clare.

Bennick tensed at the thought of her. Of the memory of the Rose on top of her.

He kept seeing that moment Clare had flinched away from his touch. The fear that had flashed in her eyes, the unspoken pain. He saw the blood on her lips. Felt her tears against his skin like they were blades. He had not been able to hold her tightly enough to stop her shaking.

He had to shove the memories away. Kick back the terror, fury, and helplessness before they could rip through the shield of ice he'd erected.

He needed to feel nothing right now. It was the only way he could stop himself from outright killing the Rose.

His fist slammed into the assassin's jaw and the man's head snapped to the side. "Who hired you?" he asked again.

He could feel Venn bristling by the door. They were in one of the cold storerooms in Lord Francin's cellar. The air was musty, the earthy scent of the pale dirt floor mixing with that of the cool stone walls. Two guards stood outside the door, but everyone else in the manor was probably asleep.

Bennick had left Clare only after sleep had claimed her; she hadn't asked him to stay, but she hadn't needed to. He had stayed close, murmuring soft words and soothing her with gentle touches. Once her red eyes had closed and her breaths had gone deep and even, he'd slipped away. He left several guards at her door and checked briefly on Wilf, who was sleeping. He learned that the commander had gone to bed an hour ago, and that was just as well—his father might be the commander of Iden's prison, but Bennick was the captain of the princess's guard. The Rose belonged to him.

He had brought Venn so he wouldn't be alone. So he wouldn't

go too far.

But Venn hadn't stopped him yet, and a part of him doubted Venn ever would.

He glanced down at his hands, saw the blood smeared over his throbbing knuckles. He thought of Clare's gentle touch as she had cleaned his hands mere hours ago, and he felt a needle of guilt.

He stomped it out and hit the Rose again, gritting his teeth against the agony in his hand. "Who hired you?"

The assassin opened his mouth and spat a glob of blood onto the dirt floor. It splattered near Bennick's boot, but he didn't know if the Rose had been aiming for him, or if it was a coincidence due to Bennick standing so close. Saliva and blood dribbled from the corner of the man's mouth and his head rolled a little as he craned his neck to look up at Bennick. One eye was swollen shut, the other already turning black. His jaw worked for a moment before he finally spoke, his words hoarse. "Does it feel good?"

Bennick's eyes narrowed. "What?"

The Rose's split lip tipped up at one corner, blood glistening on his teeth. "Hitting me. Does it feel good?"

Bennick's hand flexed at his side, his fingers stiff and sparking with pain. Pain he definitely deserved to feel. "Who hired you?"

The Rose wheezed out a short laugh. "You may have noticed, Captain. I don't register pain. Not the way other people do. You can hit me until you break your hand, but I won't say anything I don't want to."

Bennick grasped a handful of the Rose's brown hair and yanked his head back, forcing their gazes together. He leaned in, his hand fisting in the Rose's hair until the man winced. His voice was darkly level. "Who hired you?"

The man's nostrils flared. "You should ask me the question I *want* to answer."

Bennick released him, only to hit him. While he shook out his hand, the assassin spat more blood on the ground—along with a tooth. "You're not in control here."

"Neither are you, Captain." The Rose stretched his neck. "Why don't you stop pretending you are?"

Bennick had never wanted to kill a man so badly. But he needed answers to ensure Clare's safety, as well as Serene's, and he would get them.

And then he would kill him.

To prove he was in control, he didn't even hit the Rose again before repeating his question. "Who hired you?"

The assassin rolled his shoulders as best he could with his arms wrenched back, his wrists secured to the back of the chair. "I'm quite certain that little secret is the only reason I'm still breathing. Forgive me for wanting to keep it." One eyebrow lifted, straining against a barely clotted cut. "However, there are other secrets I could share. For a price."

A growl vibrated up his throat. "I'm not here to bargain with you."

"But you will. Because if you don't, Clare will be dead ten times over before you reach Duvan."

Bennick heard the sound of his fist hitting the Rose before he registered the pain of the impact.

When the Rose lifted his head, strands of limp hair stuck to a bloody cut on his cheek.

"You have no power to threaten her," Bennick said, his voice edging toward a snarl.

The Rose sniffed, his nose dripping blood. "So protective of the decoy. But then, we both know she's more than that to you. Dear, beautiful Clare—"

Bennick had a knife pressed against his throat in the space of a blink, and he could feel his eyes burning as he glared at the man. "Speak her name again, and the next thing to pass your lips will be your last breath."

The Rose's eyes flared with an emotion Bennick couldn't read. It wasn't fear, anger, or pain. It was closer to resentment. Then he blinked, and there was nothing in his eyes as he calmly said. "Someday I will kill you."

His mouth twisted in a cold, dark smile. "If you do, I swear to the fates I'll drag you with me."

The Rose's eyes narrowed. And then his expression smoothed. "Lovely threats, Captain. But aren't you curious how I can save both your decoy and your princess?"

Bennick's grip on the knife tightened, and the edge pressed deeper into the assassin's skin. He could feel Venn watching him. Could feel the blistering fury that pounded through his friend's veins, because it was starting to course through his own body.

He needed to stay calm. Cold. Detached.

He pulled back the knife, spinning the blade in his hands. "What do you know?"

"Many things," the Rose said. "I know which of your stops in Mortise will be hosted by men and women who plan to kill the princess. I know the names of all the notable people who want the alliance to fail—and the ones who will take action to make sure it does."

"Give me their names."

"It's not that simple." The Rose's legs flexed; with his ankles tightly bound to the chair legs, the movement was impeded. He still somehow managed to look like he was reclining, perfectly at ease. "You want to keep the decoy and the princess alive. I want to keep breathing. So. You will take me with you to Mortise, and I will identify threats as they become relevant."

"No." Venn peeled away from the door, his voice hard as he moved to stand beside Bennick. "As soon as we've bled everything useful out of you, you're dead."

The Rose blinked, his focus shifting to Venn. "You're Venn Grannard. Youngest man to ever be promoted to the royal guard. I can't imagine why you hate me."

Fury swirled in Venn's eyes. "You're a sick, sadistic killer. I hate everything about you."

The Rose's head listed to the side. "Hmm, it seems more personal than that. Did you perhaps have feelings for the maid I killed in Halbrook? What was her name . . . Fates, she told me while she was crying for her life . . . Ivonne?"

Venn lunged, his fist cracking against the Rose's jaw. Then he shot a look to Bennick, one that clearly said, *I'm not apologizing for that.*

Bennick didn't blame him. He faced the Rose. "Why do you think we would trust your information?"

The Rose spat out more blood. "Perhaps because you have no other choice? Face reality, Captain. Even if you avoid every pre-arranged stop in Mortise—which would offend every Mortisian, as you well know—and take every precaution to ensure a safe arrival in Duvan . . . Eventually, someone will get through your defenses. And you will always blame yourself. Always wonder if something I knew might have made the difference between life and death."

Bennick's hold on the dagger flexed. He hated every word the Rose said. Hated the corner he was being backed into.

Because the Rose was right. If Clare or Serene died in Mortise, Bennick would always blame himself. And he would always wonder.

"Take me to Mortise as your prisoner," the Rose said. "Keep me alive, and I will give you the identity of each enemy as they become relevant. It's a near-perfect solution; you won't be able to kill me, because I won't divulge everything all at once, and I will steer you safely to Duvan one stop at a time."

Venn ground his teeth. "You would try to escape at the first opportunity."

The Rose smiled thinly. "Then you'd better guard me well."

Bennick's eyes narrowed, his thoughts racing. He could feel Venn's eyes on him, but he didn't look away from the Rose.

He wanted to say no. But the same force that had kept him from killing the assassin also screamed for him to carefully consider his options. This was not a time for rash decisions. He knew that enemies lay in Mortise. If the Rose could identify them . . .

Fates, the last thing he wanted to do was bring the Rose with them to Duvan. He hated the thought of the assassin so close to Clare.

But if it saved her life . . .

His hold on the dagger tightened when he realized there was only one answer he could give right now. Because in the end, this choice wasn't his to make.

"The princess will decide your fate." He turned to Venn. "We'll take him to Stills."

Venn's nostrils flared. "He deserves to die."

Bennick didn't disagree, but he sheathed his knife. He had to swallow back the words that wanted to come out. "If he attempts to escape, we'll kill him."

The Rose smiled slowly. "You won't regret this."

Bennick ignored him and turned on his heel, knowing Venn would follow his lead—much as he might not want to.

He'd only managed one step before the Rose spoke again. "You still haven't asked me the question I really want to answer."

Bennick paused, throwing a look over his shoulder. "Unless you're going to tell me who hired you, we're done."

The lantern's glow cast a yellow light across the Rose's battered face. His voice was low. "I saw you that night, at the Paltrow's ball. I was in the garden, and I saw the rebels strike. That's when I learned she was a decoy. I heard Clare's name. I heard you scream it as she bled out in your arms."

Bennick's lungs compressed as that horrible memory crashed into him.

A grin stole across his bloody face, and the effect was chilling. "That night was one of the greatest gifts the fates ever gave me. Because I knew then that my success would mean more than just your failure. When I took Serene's life, I would ruin your career; but when I ended Clare's life? Well, I knew that would rip out your heart."

His jaw ached as he clenched his teeth, his breath coming out on a hiss. "What did I ever do to you?"

"You exist."

Bennick stared at him, bewilderment slicing through him. "Who *are* you?"

"Finally, the right question." The Rose's shoulders eased back against the chair, his expression going so smooth, it made Bennick's spine stiffen. "You were twelve years old the first time I saw you."

"Was this at the academy?" The Rose was a few years older than him, so it was possible they'd spent some mutual years there. But while Bennick had had rivals, he could not think of any actual enemies. Certainly no one with this level of loathing.

"No." The Rose shook his head. "It was at the royal prison in Iden."

Confusion drifted through him, tensing his body. "I don't remember you."

"I'm sure you don't. Our meeting was brief, and I meant nothing to you. But when I saw you . . . That was the first time

I felt the urge to kill."

Bennick stared at him, left without words. Beside him, Venn was also silent.

The assassin rolled his neck. "I was in the commander's office. We were arguing when you walked in. I could see instantly that you favored him." A cold smile, devoid of all humor, stretched his bloody lips. "I favor my mother."

The words meant nothing to Bennick. Not for an eternal moment.

And then there was no air in his lungs. No thoughts in his head, except an endless echo of denials he didn't have the breath to utter.

The Rose's attention was fixed on Bennick. "You knew the commander sired other children. Is it really so surprising that one of them learned about you?"

Bennick shook his head as he fell back a step. His throat constricted, stopping any words that tried to claw their way out. It felt like the ground was spinning. Like his entire *world* was spinning.

"I envied you that day," the Rose said quietly. "Seeing you standing there in his office. Well dressed, bright-eyed, and eager to please our father. I wanted to be you. I *should* have been you." His eyes narrowed. "Your life should have been mine. *Would* have been mine, if he had only claimed me as his firstborn."

Bennick's heart pounded. There was no way this killer—the Rose—shared his blood. It was impossible.

It would explain so much.

Why the Rose had singled him out; why he hated him.

Why his father had been so desperate to send Bennick back to Iden, to keep him away from the Rose.

Why he had wanted to kill him before he could regain consciousness.

"You're lying," Venn snapped.

"If I were interested in telling lies, I would tell you that there was no link between me and Commander Markam. But there is." The Rose focused back on Bennick. "The truth can be a curse. Half of the curse is that we're so persistent in seeking it out, even when instinct screams that we'd be better off not knowing." He cocked his head to the side. "Your instincts are screaming at you now, aren't they?"

Bennick's jaw nearly cracked as he ground his teeth.

"My mother was a young widow," the Rose said. "Her late husband had been one of Markam's soldiers, and she was still living at one of the northern outposts. She caught the commander's eye." He shook his head. "I never met him. He left her before I was born. But she always told me that my father, the great Commander Markam, had to leave us for our own safety. That he had many enemies, and we would be targets. That's why we lived on the northern edge of Devendra in a drafty cabin. He sent coin sporadically to support our simple lifestyle, and my mother was desperate for the day he would return.

"I was beaten, spat upon, mocked as a fatherless whelp. But I took every thrown fist without ever telling anyone I *did* have a father. That he was protecting me by keeping his distance— just as I was protecting him by keeping my silence." Tension bracketed his mouth. "My mother died when I was sixteen. I made the trip to Iden alone, prepared to grieve with my father. When I arrived and gained an audience with the commander, well . . ." The corner of his mouth ticked up. "At first he tried to tell me there was some misunderstanding. That I wasn't his. When that failed, he offered me gold if I would leave him alone. That's when you came walking in. I saw the man's eyes light up, and I knew he would never look at me like that. He didn't want me. He wanted you." His jaw stiffened. "I could see his fear. He worried I would say something to you, so he was quick to usher you out. He threatened to imprison me if I didn't leave. So I did. But I swore that he would respect me someday. That I would give him true reason to fear me." The Rose's thin, empty smile was back. "I leave the roses for him. So he knows it's me. They were my mother's favorite flower."

Bennick's stomach churned.

"Fates," Venn breathed into the heavy silence.

"I love that he lost your adoration," the Rose said to Bennick. "That something happened to dim your view of him. You were the son he chose, but you turned your back on him." A grin slashed across his face. "I love the poetry of that."

The door creaked open and Bennick knew without turning that it was his father. The room grew colder. Darker.

The Rose's smile widened. "Ah, Commander. I've been expecting you. When the captain came in earlier, I was sure it was going to be you, sneaking in to murder me."

His father's voice was gruff. "Ben. I told you I would handle his interrogation in the morning."

The Rose chuckled. "You're a little late, Commander. Or should I say, Father?"

Silence.

Bennick's spine was so rigid, he barely managed to turn and face his father.

If he had been clinging to any hope that the Rose had been lying, he would have had to abandon that now. The commander's face was splashed with anger, guilt, and horror. He took a step toward Bennick, one hand lifting. "Ben . . ."

Bennick strode around him, his chest tight and his throat locked.

"Ben!"

Fingers grasped his arm, but he jerked away and kept walking. He didn't look back. Not when Venn fell into step behind him, or when his father ordered him to come back. Not even when the Rose's laughter echoed off the cold stone walls.

CHAPTER 41

MIA

MIA WAS SKETCHING AT THE TABLE WHEN Tyrell entered the room. She looked up from the pinecone she'd been studying; the one Grayson had given her.

Tyrell's movements were slower than usual. Almost cautious. It had been five days since he'd come to her cell in the middle of the night, completely drunk. She hadn't seen him since, though having a few days between visits wasn't uncommon. What felt different today was his hesitancy. She wondered if his mind, like hers, was flashing to the emotional confessions he'd made in this room the other night. His cut lip was still in evidence, though visibly healing, and the bruising from his drunken fighting had mostly faded as well.

He lowered himself into the chair across from her, eyeing the partially completed sketch. "It looks good."

"Thank you." She fingered the pencil in her hand, the uneasiness that she'd been feeling ever since his late night visit growing and twisting in her belly.

"I have a surprise for you," he said.

"Oh?"

He plucked up the pinecone, spinning it slowly between his fingers. "I've made arrangements for you to spend the afternoon outside."

She froze, her breath caught in her lungs. "What?"

He glanced up. "I thought I'd take you outside today."

She slowly shook her head. "But—you can't. I can't leave."

The corner of his mouth quirked. "You remember I'm a prince, right? I can make things happen."

No. Impossible. The king would never allow it, or Grayson would have taken her before.

Tyrell seemed to read her thoughts. "If Grayson had ever tried to exceed Father's expectations, he would have been able to ask the same favor and have it granted. It's not my fault he never tried."

Mia barely heard him over the pounding of her heart. Outside.

For the first time ever, she could walk out that door. For the first time in nine—almost ten—years, she could see the sun.

She squeezed her pencil so hard, it was a miracle it didn't snap. "No," she breathed.

The word was quiet, but it silenced them both for a long moment.

Tyrell still held the pinecone, though it was motionless now. "What do you mean, no?" he finally asked.

She straightened her spine, her heart thudding loudly as she met his stare. "I meant exactly what I said. *No.*"

His eyes narrowed. "Don't you want to leave your cell?"

"No."

He set the pinecone down, his eyebrows drawing together. "I can take you to the garden. Father said we can stay there all day. I've arranged a picnic, and I bought—"

"I'm not going anywhere with you."

Tyrell pulled back, his shoulders stiffening along with his jaw. "If this is about what happened the other night . . . I wasn't myself. If I said anything to offend you, I'm sorry."

Mia stood, too agitated to remain sitting. Her quick movement pushed back the chair, made it scrape loudly over the stone.

Tyrell rose to his feet as well, though far more smoothly than she had. His frown deepened. "What's wrong?"

"I don't want to go outside."

"All right, fine, we won't go." He shoved a hand through his dark hair. "Fates, I'm only trying to give you something."

"I don't want anything from you."

His tone was forcefully level. "I'm sorry. I thought you would want to go outside."

"Well, I don't!" She threw the pencil onto the table. It bounced and rolled to the floor.

Neither of them moved to pick it up.

"I can't stop you from invading my room," Mia said firmly, "but I'm not going anywhere with you." She barely knew her own thoughts, they were flying so quickly, one panicked fear after another.

What if she went outside and panicked? What if this was a trick? What if Henri had planned some new horror for her? What if Tyrell was trying to hurt her? What if one taste of freedom wasn't enough? What if glimpsing what she couldn't have —what she hadn't had for so many years—drove her mad? What if she left this cell and couldn't get back, and Grayson couldn't find her?

What if that look in Tyrell's eye was actually what she feared it was?

She wanted Grayson. She wanted him to be with her if she ever left this cell. She wanted her first breath of fresh air to be with *him*. She wanted his hand wrapped around hers as she was blinded by the sun again.

She didn't want Tyrell.

Her breathing had turned ragged. Tyrell cursed and took a step forward. "Are you—?"

She threw out a hand. "Stay back!"

He stopped, his eyes flashing with something like hurt. "Fates, I'm not going to hurt you. What's wrong?"

"I love Grayson," she snapped.

Tyrell reared back, his shoulders tensing. "I know that."

Her hands fisted at her sides. "No, I don't think you do. I don't love you, Tyrell. At all. I never will."

He stared at her, his chest rising and falling with deep breaths. He shook his head, snorting once. "You're so arrogant. You think everyone might lose their minds over you, just because Grayson fell at your feet. Well, I can assure you, that will never happen for me." He stalked to the door, jerked it open, and didn't look back as he slammed it.

Her throat was strangled with unshed tears and she moved stiffly to pick up the pencil she'd thrown.

The tip was broken, and for some stupid reason, that was what caused her first sob to escape.

She cried for a long time. The ache of missing Grayson had never been stronger, and it was as if every bad decision she had ever made, every horrible thing she had ever done, was trying to strangle her.

Eventually, her tears dried. She set about tidying her room, for a lack of anything better to do. That was when Fletcher eased the door open.

He carried in a small crate of bottled paints—far more colors than she had ever had—and then he brought in five new canvases of varying sizes.

"Prince Tyrell just brought them," Fletcher said. "There's a note with the paints and brushes."

Mia was grateful that the guard didn't ask questions about her red-rimmed eyes. He simply deposited the gifts and left.

Mia knelt in front of the crate of paints, saw the cluster of new brushes and the folded piece of paper peeking out between the rows of bottles.

She lifted the note and opened it, her stomach clenching as she read the words.

I know you don't want anything from me,
but please don't paint over your beach.

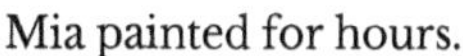

Mia painted for hours.

She felt terrible for snapping at Tyrell. She had never thought of herself as cruel, but she had been horrible to him. Regret was a bitter taste in her mouth. She never should have lashed out at him like that. She'd been shocked by the chance to go outside. She'd been afraid. Angry, even.

But she should have never said those things.

Tyrell, like Grayson, had endured punishments for showing anything like kindness. It had always made her so sick and angry that Henri could do that to his children. But what had she done?

Tyrell had bought her paints, brushes, and canvases. She knew he had set them up in the garden for her, tried to give her something. He had dared to be kind, after kindness had all but been beaten out of him.

And she had attacked him.

She had not forgotten how Tyrell had treated her, or the things he had done to Grayson. But whether she had wanted to or not, she'd glimpsed Tyrell's humanity, and she couldn't see him as wholly monstrous. Not anymore.

When her back and arms ached, Mia finally stopped painting. She ate her dinner, which had grown cold, and then she sat on her bed and pulled out her sketchbook.

The open pages were soon filled with two drawings, one on each page. One of Grayson's face, one of Tyrell's. Both had a vertical line drawn down the center of the page, bisecting their faces. The line drawn down the middle made the divide clear: one face, two different fates.

Grayson's left side bore no scars and he was smiling, his expression open and at ease. The right side was scarred and cautious.

She had done the same to Tyrell on the opposite page. One half of his face was the sadistic, cruel Tyrell who had beaten her. The other half belonged to a young man with a slow grin and a kind gleam in his eye.

She had always hated Grayson's parents. They had destroyed so many lives and brought so much pain to so many people. But their greatest sin was perhaps how they had twisted and tortured their children. None of them had been given love. They had been raised on pain, fear, and hatred. Was it any wonder they were the way they were? It was a miracle Grayson had held onto his goodness.

Mia studied Grayson's face, her grip on her pencil too tight. Her gut twisted, and she blinked against the tears building in her eyes.

She wanted Grayson here with her. She needed him.

She also wanted Tyrell to come back so she could apologize. She had treated him badly, and she didn't want to be the kind of person who lashed out at those around her, just because she was scared.

She wasn't sure he would return, though. Not after the way she had hurt him.

The cell door banged open without warning and Mia jumped, clutching her pencil and sketchbook. She'd been so lost in her thoughts, she lost track of the hour.

Papa staggered in. He wasn't walking straight and the soft glow of the lamp revealed the ruddiness of his bearded face. He'd clearly been drinking.

Mia tensed. Even though Papa hadn't taken a hand to her in years, every instinct still screamed that he would hurt her whenever he entered the room. She had learned to remain quiet and still, and she prayed to the fates he would cross quickly to his room.

He slammed the door and ambled for the back bedroom door, not even glancing at her. Some of the tension bled from her shoulders.

But then he veered sharply to the left and stumbled toward the crate of paints she had left on the floor.

"Look out!"

The warning came too late.

Papa tripped on the crate and crashed to the floor. He roared, fists slamming against the stone. "Fates-blasted fool!" he snarled.

"What have you done?"

Mia shrank back on instinct, every hair on her body rising.

Papa snagged the crate, the bottles of paint rattling. "What is all this?" he demanded.

"Nothing. Just paint."

Papa looked around, saw the paintings propped up against the bookcase to dry. He snatched one, muttering a curse as he threw it at her.

His aim was off, but she still ducked as it rushed past her to smack into the wall. Her heart pounded riotously against her ribs.

It had been years since she'd seen him so upset.

She shoved the sketchbook aside, but still gripped the pencil. For some reason, it felt like a weapon, and that was comforting when Papa turned his furious eyes on her.

"You," he whispered, and that lowering of his voice sent a horrible chill racing down Mia's spine. "You're the one that's been taking my coins. Spending all my savings on useless things like paint."

"No. I haven't touched your—"

He hurled a bottle of paint at her and Mia cried out as she dived to the side to avoid it. Glass shattered on the wall near her head and green paint splashed over her face, neck, and shoulder.

Mia leaped off the bed and ran for the back bedroom. If she could get inside, Mama might be able to—

A bottle of paint hit the back of her head and shattered. Mia gasped at the sharp pain and stumbled.

Papa grabbed a handful of her hair, his boots crunching the glass on the floor as he threw her to the ground.

She hit hard on her chest and the air was knocked from her lungs. Panic exploded inside her and she clawed the floor, the pencil still clutched in one hand. She choked on fear as she tried to crawl away from him.

His knee dug into her lower back, crushing her. Her breaths were uneven and harsh, and there wasn't enough air inside her to scream.

His hand fisted in her hair again and he jerked her head back.

"Please," she gasped. "Can't—breathe."

He had another bottle of paint in his fist, this one red. "I thought it was her," he sneered, his words slurring. "I thought my own wife was stealing from me, for her drinking and gambling. But it was you. You've always been the ruin of us, when you were supposed to be our way to an easier life. The king was supposed to reward me, but nothing changed. A little more gold, but where did it go? Into your stupid pocket!"

Mia's lungs were empty, yet bursting at the same time. She was on fire, but she was shivering. Panic had sunk claws into her body, and she could not get free.

Papa smashed the bottle of red paint into her temple, and agony exploded along with the glass. The impact alone was bruising, but the broken shards cut into her skin, paint and blood mingling.

Mia screamed and her hands flew to the wound. Paint got in her eyes, and when the pressure of Papa's knee left her, Mia rolled onto her back, crying as she clutched her head.

Fight. Grayson's voice was a growl in her mind. *Fight back. Don't stop until your attacker does.*

Through the pain and the panic, Mia pried her eyes open. Papa was fumbling to draw a knife at his belt.

She still held the pencil, though it was splattered with paint and blood now.

Do what you have to do. Don't hesitate.

Papa tugged the knife free from its sheath at the same moment Mia dove for him.

Her pencil slid into his eye—his blade sank into her stomach.

Papa howled and clawed at his face, trying to find the pencil so he could rip it out.

Mia stumbled back with a gasp, shaking hands grasping the handle of the knife that was stuck inside her body.

The door shoved open and she blinked up at Tyrell, whose chest was rising and falling too quickly. He'd been running.

Behind him, the night guard was pale.

Tyrell's eyes darted over the scene, dismissing Mia almost at once to focus on Papa, who roared as he jerked the pencil from his eye.

"I'll kill you!" Papa snarled, cursing her. "I'll—" He spotted Tyrell and gaped, his drunken brain, overwhelmed with pain, struggling to process the prince's sudden appearance.

Tyrell's voice was dark. "You raised a hand against her."

Papa blinked, his skin paling, blood dripping from his ruined eye. He lifted his hands. "Your Highness, I—"

Tyrell's sword flashed and Papa's right hand dropped to the floor. The man howled, clutching the stump of his arm to his chest.

But Tyrell wasn't done. His sword sliced again, and Papa's head rolled off his shoulders, his shout silenced forever as his body crumpled.

Mia gagged, pinching her eyes shut against the scene. But she would never forget Papa's face, or the sound of his screams.

The pain in her stomach flared, and that combined with the violence of the last few moments brought her to her knees.

She heard Tyrell curse, heard his sword clang against the ground. Then his hands were wrapped around her shoulders and he was kneeling with her. "Mia?"

She peeled her eyes open, and though her vision was hazy, she saw his eyes drag over her—saw him freeze when he saw her clutching the knife embedded in her gut.

All color left his face. "No." His fingers curled painfully into her arms. "No," he repeated, his voice raw.

Mia's hands were covered in blood and the warm substance was spreading out from the knife wound, staining her blue dress. She struggled to breathe, and when she shuddered, the blade cut deeper, shredding her insides. "Tell Grayson I'm sorry," she gasped. "I tried to fight."

Tyrell's jaw hardened. "You're going to be fine."

She wasn't going to be fine. She knew it. The color was already seeping from her vision, and her heartbeat was lagging, then thumping too hard.

"I'm sorry," she repeated. "Tyrell, I'm sorry . . ."

"Mia!" He grabbed her in his arms, pulling her across his lap. With her head against his chest, she could hear his heart racing. "Fates, Mia—No!"

Her eyes fluttered closed, and she thought she saw Grayson's face.

It was her last thought.

CHAPTER 42

DESFAN

DESFAN SLIPPED FROM THE COUNCIL CHAMBER before anyone could try to stop him, Karim right behind him. The meeting
had gone long—as it often seemed to do—and he had spent
most of it trying to assuage any concerns the council had.

There had been many.

Serai Essa was worried about Princess Serene's health and
wanted to know if the delays in the tour would stop the prisoner
exchange.

Desfan assured her that the exchange would still happen, and
that he had no new word on Serene's health, but he assumed she
was recovering well.

Ser Sifa—who was temporarily filling a council seat, since
Ashear was overseeing the prisoner exchange—wanted to discuss the Rydenic princes. He was particularly concerned that

they were allowed to roam the palace and the city without close supervision.

Desfan did not want to smother the princes, or risk offending them; they were not prisoners, after all.

Serai Yahri was concerned about the drain on the royal treasury, which was currently funding Desfan's orphanage reform.

He was working on letters to wealthy nobles, who he would ask to become patrons of their local orphanages, which would help meet costs.

The meeting had dragged, and Desfan's head ached. He pulled off his crown the moment he entered the corridor, though it didn't stop the throbbing at his temples. He had a mountain of reports that needed to be read before dinner, and he had a dozen letters to write.

He forgot all about them when he spotted Kiv Arcas standing outside the serjan's office.

The soldier bowed. "Pardon me, Serjah, but do you have a few moments?"

"Of course." Desfan waved him into the office, trying not to get his hopes up. After so long with no new findings from Arcas, Zadir, or Desfan's own investigations into the nobles, he was beginning to think he would never find answers about the olcain, or what had happened to his father.

"You asked me to look into who was guarding the serjan the night he collapsed," Arcas said.

"Yes, do you have the names?" Desfan asked, tossing his crown on the desk.

"No." Arcas's eyes darkened. "The kiv in charge of the ledger that outlines royal rotations said he would get me the report, but he kept avoiding me. Last night, he finally confessed that the volume holding the record of that night was lost a week or so after the serjan's collapse. He seemed terrified that he would be blamed, but I don't think he lost it. I believe it was stolen."

Desfan loosed a curse. "Does the kiv not remember who was on duty that night?"

"No. For what it's worth, I believe him. But for the last week or so I've been asking around to see if anyone knew who was on the serjan's guard that night. A couple of names were mentioned, but, Serjah . . . none of them are employed by the palace guard anymore."

Desfan's eyes narrowed. "They were discharged?"

"No one seems to know for sure. One man swore he heard the guards involved were offered retirement, and they all left Duvan, but I'm concerned something more sinister may have befallen them. Perhaps they saw something they shouldn't have, and someone took action against them."

"What about their written reports?" Karim demanded. "Surely they were all ordered to write a report about that night. The serjan collapsed on their watch!"

"Their reports are also missing."

Desfan shoved a hand through his dark curls, a curse shooting out with his vented breath. He began to pace, too frustrated to remain still. "Why wasn't this discovered sooner?"

"I don't know. Bribes, perhaps? Or whoever made evidence —and men—disappear, has more influence than I'd care to fathom."

"A kiv?" Desfan asked. "Someone with access to records?"

"Or a council member," Karim muttered.

"That brings me to my second bit of news," Arcas said. "I have had the royal physician tailed, as you asked. Nothing suspicious has been reported—until now. Early this morning he met with Serai Yahri in the back gardens. The guard could not get close enough to hear everything that was exchanged, but he did hear Yahri say that the physician needed to keep silent. That there were things you, Serjah, could never know."

Desfan's heart beat a little faster. "Anything else?"

"No, unfortunately." Arcas's chin dropped. "Would you like me to bring either of them in for questioning?"

He hesitated. "No. Not yet. Thank you, Arcas. And please, keep this to yourself."

The man bowed and left the room.

Karim eyed Desfan. "Between that conversation and the one Jamal overheard between Yahri and Zephan—not to mention the way she spoke to you of abdication—I think Yahri should be brought in for questioning."

"She will be."

Karim's brow furrowed. "You have that look again. The one I hate."

Desfan smiled grimly. "I don't think you'll like what I do next, either."

That was confirmed by Karim about ten minutes later as they stood outside Yahri's palace apartment. "You're right," he muttered. "I absolutely hate this idea."

Desfan ignored his friend as he stooped in front of Yahri's door, silver lockpicks catching the light from the nearby torch as he fitted them into place. "If there's any evidence, I need it before I confront her."

"Why not have Arcas do this?"

"Because I need to see it for myself. I need to find it, hold it in my hands. I need to know it is indisputably real."

If all this was true . . . Serai Yahri, the senior member of the council, was a traitor. Potentially a murderer.

This would rock the very foundation of Mortise. He needed to tread carefully.

But he would learn the truth.

The lock clicked open and Desfan removed the picks and pushed in the door. He knew Yahri was in the royal library, because she always spent an hour or two there after every council session. When he was young, he and his sisters would be with their tutor and they'd see Yahri come in. They always got excited when they saw her, because they knew their father was done with meetings and he would be coming for them soon.

He jerked back from those memories, because they didn't belong here. Sometimes, they didn't feel like they belonged in his head at all. They were from a different life. A life that had been torn away from him.

If that woman had plotted to kill Desfan's father, she would hang.

Desfan stepped into her suite and Karim followed, easing the door closed behind them. Afternoon sun poured in through open windows, illuminating the suite. It was minimally decorated, with plenty of books on the shelves and vibrant flower arrangements on the tables.

He moved for her desk in the corner and Karim silently moved for her bedroom.

Desfan rifled over every inch of the desk, glanced at every paper stored in the drawers, but he found nothing incriminating. He moved to the towering bookcase, stuffed with volumes and scrolls. He started taking the books down, one by one, and flipped through the pages. It was time consuming, but he forced himself to be meticulous. Book after book, page after page . . .

A letter slipped free of the old pages and Desfan caught it before it hit the carpeted floor.

His heart thudded as he thrust the book back on the shelf and eyed the folded letter.

It was a single page, heavy paper, folded into thirds. The sealing wax bore no insignia, and the simple crimson dot had been split.

Desfan flipped the letter open, his eyes scanning the words.

> *Yahri,*
>
> *Difficult decisions lie in our path, but hiring the Rose to dispose of Princess Serene was easy. Thank you. The time will come when all of us can be known to each other, but until then, I appreciate your support in our efforts. You took powerful steps to ensure no one learned the truth about what happened to the serjan, and I continue to admire you for that.*
>
> *I know you will continue to take all necessary steps to protect the crown.*

The message was signed with a symbol—an X created by the crossing of two curved swords.

But the writer of the letter didn't concern Desfan at the moment. No, the anger vibrating through his body was for someone else. The woman who his father had most trusted, and who had betrayed him.

She had betrayed them all.

"Des?"

Desfan lifted his head, his jaw rigid as he turned to Karim. "We're getting Arcas and arresting Yahri. Now."

CHAPTER 43

GRAYSON

GRAYSON KNEW THERE WAS A TRAINING ground somewhere outside the palace, and whether he was allowed or not, he intended to use it. He needed the activity, something to focus on. He sheathed some weapons and asked his guards to actually follow him this time. He didn't think the Mortisian soldiers would want to fight with him, so he would train with his guards.

He was nearly to the side door when Liam called out from behind.

He turned, along with his guards, and his brother smiled. "I'm sure you've got fun plans, but I have something I want to show you."

Grayson's eyes dipped to Liam's fingers, which flicked out a quick message.

I have news of Mia.

The training grounds were forgotten in a single, thudding heartbeat. "Of course." He followed Liam, the guards trailing behind them. He eased closer to his brother's side, so Liam could see his fingers as he asked, *Is it news from Ryden? Is she all right?*

Nothing from Ryden. His angular jaw tightened. *I've learned who she is.*

Grayson's stomach dropped, his boot scuffing the stone floor of the corridor as he nearly stumbled.

Liam shot him a look, concern sparking in his brown eyes.

Grayson glanced away, his throat bobbing. He had dreaded this moment almost as much as he had been desperate for it. He had wanted to know the truth about Mia's origins for so long . . . but learning about her past meant he had to share her with it. And he knew there were reasons Mia never spoke of her life before that cell. Not only because Papa had cruelly silenced her, but because whatever circumstances had brought her to Ryden must have been horrific.

He didn't know if he was brave enough to hear it.

But he knew he had to. For her.

Liam spoke—clearly more aware of their surroundings than Grayson was, since he'd forgotten about the guards who observed them. "Sorry to take you from wherever you were going, but I found an interesting volume in the library and I couldn't wait to show you."

"That's all right." He didn't have the concentration to think of any other reply. His fingers flicked less gracefully than Liam's as he asked, *Where are we really going?*

Liam's fingers flew. *The library. There is a private room we can use. No one will hear us. Dismiss the guards.*

Grayson glanced back at the men following them. "This may take a while. You can return to my room."

The men shuffled away at the next turn, leaving Liam and

Grayson alone to enter the library. It was late afternoon, and the lofty space seemed deserted but for a few scattered people silently searching the towering bookshelves, or sitting at small tables, bent over large tomes. Liam led them without hesitation toward the back of the library and into a small room. He closed the door behind Grayson, then grasped Grayson's arm and tugged him to the far end, near a closed, dirty window. The sole light in the room came through the grimy glass, but the dimness wasn't enough to obscure Liam's fingers as they twisted, flicked, and dipped. *No one should be able to hear our whispers, but some things I will speak, and others I will sign. All right?*

Grayson jerked out a nod, his heart hammering in his chest.

Liam's voice was barely there. "Her name is Mia Sifa."

Shock at hearing a surname paired with her name hit him hard. But not as hard as the surname itself, once he actually heard it.

Sifa.

A pit opened in his gut.

Liam's lips pursed, clearly reading Grayson's thoughts. "Yes, she is a relation to Ser Sifa, whom you've had the displeasure of conversing with. The temporary second on the council is her uncle." He pointed to an open book on a small table beside them, which Grayson hadn't noticed. He followed Liam's finger as it brushed over an ancestry chart.

Grayson's eyes leapt to the familiar lines and curves of Mia's name, reaching it before Liam's finger did. The entry was short, just like all the others on the page. Her name. A date of birth.

And another date, only seven years after the first.

Grayson had not met Mia until she was eight, but she had already been a prisoner for a year.

Liam's finger tapped the names of Mia's parents.

Vil and Mari Sifa

And then he touched two other names.

Vari and Kema

Mia's older sisters.

All of their death dates were the same.

Liam's hand lifted from the book, and he signed. *I pulled this registry to research Abeil Sifa, since he is currently on the council. I wanted to know about his family. When I saw Mia's name . . .* His fingers faltered, then he continued. *I didn't want to assume anything. Mia is a common enough name in Mortise. But I asked some of my contacts to trace everything about what happened to Vil Sifa's family, and it fits, Grayson.*

His whisper came out a little rough. "Tell me."

Liam's lips pressed together. "She was born here, in Duvan, but the family moved to Shebar when Mia was six. Serjan Saernon charged Vil Sifa with keeping peace with Ryden. There were many skirmishes in and around Shebar, but more than that, the serjan suspected the last ser to have governance of the city was taking bribes from Ryden."

Grayson folded his arms over his chest, bracing himself. "What happened?"

"The previous ser had been taking bribes, and it wasn't long before Vil Sifa was approached by men from Ryden who asked if he could also be corrupted." His fingers took over. *His answer was no, which of course angered Father. Sifa was left threatening notes. His favorite dog was killed, left on the front steps as a message. He began to fear for his family. Sifa hired more guards for them, but he still woke one morning to find Mia gone—stolen from her bed.*

Liam's fingers were moving too rapidly now—or perhaps Grayson's vision was hazing. His heart was racing. He grabbed Liam's hands. "Please slow down or speak," he said through his teeth.

Liam paused, then nodded. "There was no note. No call for gold. Nothing. Not for three days. From what I could learn, Sifa went mad with grief and rage. He publicly blamed Ryden for her abduction and he rallied a small army of the city guard. They searched every part of Shebar and the surrounding areas, and he was ready to march his small force across the river into Ryden—an act of war that his serjan had forbidden. Sifa would have forfeited his life for the mere chance to save his daughter, though." He swallowed, his throat bobbing. "If he had hoped to make Father afraid, he was mistaken. Father wanted a public example made of Sifa. The more he blamed Ryden, the happier Father was. It would only make his ultimate message stronger: that the next lord sent to Shebar should fear him. Bow to him."

Liam's fingers moved carefully, his eyes intent on Grayson. *During the fourth night after Mia's abduction, Sifa's home was attacked. His small army fought, but when Mia was revealed to be with the attackers, Sifa ordered his men to stop fighting. They swore fealty to Ryden, or were slaughtered. Sifa and his family were forced to watch it all.* He hesitated, then added, *Including Mia.*

Grayson could barely breathe. He had so many questions—questions that Liam likely couldn't answer. Fates, what horrors had Mia faced in those terrifying days of captivity?

His hands fisted at his sides. His voice was low but throbbed with fury. "Did she see them die?" He didn't have to clarify who he meant.

"Yes. She watched as Rydenic soldiers killed her parents and sisters, then set fire to the bodies. Everyone must have assumed Mia was killed as well."

Grayson twisted away from Liam and paced across the floor. Cold rage gripped him. If his father had been in the room, Grayson would have killed him without hesitation.

I'm a killer. Mia had once said those words. She'd been so vehement, and now he understood why.

She blamed herself for their deaths. For the horrible slaughter of her family. She was the one who had been taken. She was the one who had been held hostage, threatened. It was only too easy to imagine how the soldiers would have ridden up to her family's house, a knife to her throat. They would have made them stand down in order to spare her life.

She had done nothing wrong, but she still thought blood covered her hands. Her *family's* blood.

Grayson's pulse roared in his ears.

Liam wasn't done. "Abeil Sifa—Vil's brother—demanded that the serjan retaliate against Ryden, but there wasn't enough proof. It appeared to be the work of thieves, nothing orchestrated by our father. Ryden was never officially blamed."

It explained Sifa's anger. All Mortisians looked at Grayson and Liam with distrust, but Abeil Sifa . . . he had faced Grayson with hatred.

"Father must have already decided to use a girl to manipulate you," Liam continued quietly. "He must have seen Mia as a golden opportunity—a way to bring Sifa down and send a terrifying message to the next ser sent to govern Shebar, as well as control you. That's the only reason she would have been left alive that night. It's the only reason she was brought to Lenzen." Liam hesitated. "Grayson, in a way, you saved her life."

He coughed out a harsh laugh and shoved a hand into his dark hair. "That's supposed to make me feel better?"

"She's alive," he said quietly. "Focus on that. She can still be saved." He moved to Grayson's side and gripped his shoulder.

The bite of his fingers actually helped to ground him. "I can get her out of there. And whether you agree to help me or not, I promise you, Father will suffer for all he's done."

The vow in Liam's eyes was blatant, and in that moment, Grayson knew Liam was not lying. His plan was no trick designed by Henri to test Grayson. He intended to lay waste to the Kaelin family. And he wanted Grayson at his side.

Grayson had to choose a path. He could no longer live stuck between choices, torn between those who wished to use him.

This was his choice, and he realized he had already made it.

Grayson eyed his brother. The room around them was silent except for their breathing. It felt like they were the only ones in the palace. Maybe the only ones in Eyrinthia.

"I'll help you."

Liam's stare was intent. "Are you sure? There will be no going back."

"I'm sure."

Finally, his brother's smooth expression cracked and the corner of his mouth lifted. "Father will never see us coming."

CHAPTER 44

DESFAN

DESFAN, KARIM, ARCAS, AND TWO OTHER guards entered the royal library. No weapons were drawn, but they still snared the attention of the head librarian as they entered the vast room.

It was late afternoon and Desfan couldn't see any patrons as he paused in front of the librarian, who gave a belated bow. "Is Serai Yahri still here?" he asked, his voice clipped.

"I—well, yes."

"Where?"

The woman's hands twisted together as she straightened from her bow. "She usually does her reading in the south corner. Shall I show you?"

"That won't be necessary. Please wait outside."

She dropped into another bow before she eased past them and slipped from the room. Her alarm had been clear, but Desfan couldn't linger to assuage any fears. He strode forward, Karim at his side. They saw a couple patrons as they moved through the shelves, and Karim or Arcas quietly asked them to leave. Everyone obeyed at once, though they cast questioning looks over their shoulders.

As they drew nearer to the south corner, Karim gripped the hilt of the sword belted at his side.

Desfan had forgone his double swords for the sake of time, but he had a knife sheathed at his waist. He doubted Yahri would make him draw it—especially once he showed her the letter he'd found.

She had hired the Rose to kill Serene.

She had lied about the night of the serjan's collapse, and had bribed or destroyed all evidence.

She would be in a cell tonight, never to step foot in this library again.

Karim touched Desfan's arm, a silent order to stop.

Desfan did, and he was aware of Arcas and the other two guards pausing behind him.

Karim's voice was barely audible as he whispered, "She's not alone."

Desfan strained his ears and caught the low male voice. It was too quiet for him to decipher the words, or who the speaker might be, but this unexpected development was enough for the guards to quietly draw knives—the bookcases were too close together for a sword to be effective here.

Arcas leaned in. "We'll approach from the other side. They'll be boxed into the corner."

Desfan nodded, and the guards followed the kiv back down the narrow aisle.

Karim took the lead and Desfan didn't bother arguing. They eased forward until they were at the end of the aisle, the bookshelf hiding them from view.

"... don't know why you chose to make your move now," Yahri's voice was low and shaky. More so than usual. But she spoke measuredly, as if trying to hide her nerves. "I didn't know it was you. Your secret was safe."

"I could not take that chance."

Desfan jerked at the familiar voice, confusion ripping through him.

Jamal?

The youngest member of the council continued smoothly, "I knew my mistake might cost me everything, if you put it together."

"Ahh," Yahri exhaled in dawning surprise. "You've been framing Zephan to be the mysterious writer, but you didn't know he'd already left Duvan when you sent your latest message. If I had thought about it, I would have realized that. But it was a close thing, so I assumed he'd merely left it for me before he left the city. But it's you. You're the one who has been manipulating all of us."

"I've been so careful," Jamal said. "I have to fix my mistake."

"I assume you mean to kill me."

"Yes."

Desfan shifted silently, but Karim caught his elbow, holding him back. His bodyguard's glare spoke volumes, but Desfan set his jaw and pulled free. He moved around Karim and peered around the edge of the bookcase.

Yahri sat in a cushioned chair, her cane planted between her legs and gripped by both hands. Her fear was obvious in her white-knuckled grip, but her drooping shoulders were pushed back and her chin lifted as she stared across the few paces that separated her from Jamal.

Jamal's stance was relaxed. He wasn't the least bit nervous

about admitting treason, or the fact that he was about to commit murder.

And he was not alone. Eight men stood with him, five of them dressed as palace guards—perhaps they *were* guards. The other three men wore the clothes of servants, but their stances made it clear they were trained fighters.

Desfan lifted his fingers, signing to Karim that there were nine enemies, not counting Yahri.

Not the best odds, but if Arcas and the other two guards could get into position, they could surround them and have the element of surprise. They just had to give Arcas a little more time.

"Honestly," Jamal drawled, "I feel I should thank you. Your habits are so predictable. You chose the most silent part of the library, as you always do, during the quietest part of the day. You've made this very easy for me."

Yahri was staring down nine men, and yet she still managed to look regal as she lifted a silver eyebrow. "Don't you think my death will be suspicious?"

Jamal laughed. "Woman, you're ancient! No one will question your heart giving out." He lifted a small vial, the afternoon sunlight highlighting the crimson liquid. "I assure you, it will look completely natural."

She grunted. "It does seem as if you've thought this through."

"I have. And I must say, my plans are looking a lot less complicated without you. You've been talking to the other council members, trying to learn who else has been receiving my letters."

"I thought I was being discreet in my investigations."

"Oh, you have been. But not all of my allies require blackmailing, Yahri."

The councilwoman didn't seem surprised by this. "No, I

imagine some were simply blinded by greed, and they were only too eager to betray me to you because you gave them so many pretty promises. Some would love the fact you hired the Rose to kill Princess Serene, thus ending the alliance. Others would be interested in your protection. That's why you've been trying so hard to befriend Desfan, I assume? You thought to make yourself invaluable to him, let your voice be the one in his ear, guiding his choices on who will replace the council members you decide to dispose of." Her head tilted to the side as she studied him. "Of course, some would be content with a promise of wealth, which you have in great supply because you're a drug master. You're the one who bought the olcain."

Desfan's jaw loosened in shock.

Jamal also seemed surprised. "Very good," he murmured. "However did you figure it out?"

"It wasn't too difficult. All your new, nice clothing. The new mansion on Dorma. The renovations to your estate in Yamir. It didn't make sense, until I took into account the increase of drugs in Duvan. That was something Desfan failed to recognize because he wasn't looking far enough back to relate the overall increase in drugs to the most recent olcain, which was merely your newest market."

"Why didn't you tell him?"

"I didn't support him in his investigation because I didn't think he should be dedicating all his time and efforts into something so trivial. Not when there are so many other things happening. But I did have a conversation with Kiv Arcas about it."

"You told him about me?" There was a hint of anxiety in Jamal's raised voice.

"No, unfortunately. I didn't actually realize everything until this conversation. But I told him the investigation into the olcain might make more headway if he looked into all the drug activity over the last year." She sighed, a long-suffering kind of sound that Desfan had heard from his tutors all his life. "Say what you will about Desfan, but that boy is tenacious. He will figure everything out, I have no doubt."

"Perhaps I'll arrange an accident for Kiv Arcas," Jamal said. He shook his head, fingering the bottle of poison. "Not that any of that matters to you."

"Because you're about to kill me?"

"Yes."

"Well, I had to ask, because you keep putting it off."

Desfan was torn between the desire to curse the woman, and to smile at her boldness.

Jamal huffed a short laugh. "You have been a unique challenge, Yahri. When I initially wrote to you, I knew I was taking a risk. You're unflinchingly loyal to Mortise, which is annoying. But when I learned about all the lengths you took to make sure you were erased from the night of the serjan's collapse, I knew I could use that to manipulate you into helping me."

"How *did* you know?" Yahri asked.

"I have employees in the guard. You were seen that night, when you stole the ledger." Jamal's head listed to the side. "Tell me, what is it you were so desperate to hide? When writing the letters, I had to pretend I knew more than I did. But now I can admit I'm curious. Did you poison the serjan? Did you want the throne?"

Yahri's eyes narrowed. "If you think that, then you're more of an idiot than I thought possible."

Jamal's shoulders tensed and Desfan silently cursed. Yahri had pushed him too far.

Karim read the situation even without seeing it, and he crept forward, not as shielded by the bookcase anymore.

At least Jamal and his men had their backs turned. He hoped

Arcas was nearly in position; he and Karim might not be able to take on Jamal and all his men—especially since Desfan had left his swords behind.

Jamal's anger bit through his rigid tone. "I'm smarter than you, Yahri. I've outsmarted all of you. I should be the senior seat on the council. After you're dead, I think I'll convince Desfan to give me your seat."

The woman snorted. "He won't be fooled forever. He's not an idiot."

"Sometimes I wonder why I even wanted you in my employ."

She stiffened her slightly curved spine. "I was never in your employ, Jamal. You blackmailed me, and I nearly reported you at once. But I knew if you were coming after me, you were going after others. I knew I needed to get to the bottom of everything. I needed to know who was working with you, what your plans were—and I needed to discover your identity."

"Too bad you figured it out too late. Now you won't be able to tell anyone. And when they search your rooms, they'll find evidence that shows you hired the Rose to kill Serene. And who knows? There might even be some olcain in your room."

Serai Yahri snorted. "I highly doubt Desfan will believe me to be a drug master, Jamal. But do go on with your silly plans, because the more you try to get away with, the sooner you will be caught."

Jamal took a threatening step forward, and Desfan and Karim both tensed.

Jamal's voice was a deep growl. "I wish I could strangle you, or shove a knife in your heart. But this will be a natural death." He lifted the bottle of poison. "Although I assure you, it won't be painless."

Anger flashed in Yahri's eyes. "Then you'd better get on with it. I won't tell you anything, and I will not scream and bring an innocent to their death."

Jamal took another step forward and Desfan nodded to Karim, prepared to attack. Because whether Arcas was in position or not—whether Yahri was still considered a traitor or not—they needed to act before she was killed.

Jamal's men turned as one to look down one of the aisles, their backs still turned to Desfan and Karim.

A guard stepped into the open space, a bloody knife in his hand. Desfan recognized him as one of the men who had left with Arcas only moments ago, and he immediately tensed.

Jamal straightened as he faced the guard. "What are you doing here?"

The man's face was grim as he spoke quickly. "They came to arrest Yahri. I just killed Arcas, but the serjah is here. He probably heard everything."

CHAPTER 45
CLARE

THE MORNING OF THE PRISONER EXCHANGE dawned brightly, the summer sun gilding every rooftop in Stills with golden light.

Clare hoped it was a sign from the fates that all would go smoothly.

Bennick walked her through the plan as they stood in the inn's common room. The exchange would happen on an open field just outside the city of Stills. Devendra would stand on the east side of the field and watch the Mortisians approach from the west. The prisoners would be in front of them, a perimeter of soldiers guarding them. Each side had been allowed twelve soldiers for the exchange, which included royal bodyguards.

The Mortisians would stop at a careful distance with the Devendran prisoners, men and women who had been imprisoned in Duvan for years. Ser Ashear, the nobleman Desfan had appointed, would then come forward, and Clare would meet him at the edge of the Devendran line and they would exchange the requisite speeches. After that was concluded, Clare would retreat to a safe distance and the prisoners would be released. Ser Ashear would remain behind with a small retinue and they would dine at the inn.

"I'll be with you at every step," Bennick assured her. "Venn and Dirk will be assigned to you as well, which will leave Serene here with Cardon and Wilf."

Clare nodded, carefully watching Bennick. He had been quiet since leaving Lord Francin's four days ago. Distant, and distracted. They hadn't had an opportunity to be alone while traveling, but Clare could see the tightness in his shoulders, the deep frown on his face when he thought no one was looking. And she wasn't the only one who had noticed his heavy mood.

She had caught Venn standing close to Bennick several times, their heads tipped together, concern etched in Venn's serious expression. Even the commander kept sending looks to his son, though Bennick had stalked around him any time he'd tried to approach.

Somehow, Clare knew the change in Bennick had to do with the Rose.

Just the thought of the assassin sent chills through her body, lifting the hairs on her arms. Every nerve still felt raw after his attack, and the fact that he remained nearby terrified her more than she would ever admit. Even now he was locked in a room above them. It didn't matter that he was under heavy guard. The tang of fear remained on her tongue.

"There will be a large crowd," Bennick said, drawing Clare's attention back to the present moment. "We'll keep them back as much as possible, and we'll be watching them for any sign of trouble."

The innkeeper had told them the city was overflowing with nobles and commoners alike who had gathered to see the exchange. The small border city was completely overrun. Every room in every inn had been rented, and even then the people kept coming, choosing to camp in the nearby fields rather than miss this historic moment.

Perhaps the most surprising spectator had arrived at the inn this morning, seeking an audience with the princess before the exchange.

The middle-aged woman's posture was regal, her dark hair piled into an elaborate bun atop her head that made her willowy frame seem even taller. The bright pink of her dress contrasted beautifully with her warm brown skin. When she greeted Clare, she curtsied gracefully, her Mortisian accent thick as she said, "Princess Serene, it is an honor. I am Serai Tamar Nadir."

The name sparked recognition, though it took Clare a moment to recall why—she was to be their first Mortisian host. "Serai Nadir, you honor us with your presence. I didn't realize you would be attending the exchange."

The woman straightened, her hands clasped neatly before her. "I live too close to miss such an important moment in our history. And it would be my privilege to help escort you to my home afterwards, so we can celebrate the day." Moisture entered the woman's eyes, though she pushed out a tenuous smile. "Forgive me, I did not intend to become emotional. My husband was killed in a border dispute nearly twenty years ago. We had been married only a year. I've been praying to the fates for peace ever since." She swiped at tears that leaked from her eyes, and Dirk stepped forward, a handkerchief in his hand.

Serai Nadir took it, murmuring words of thanks as she dabbed her eyes. After a deep breath, she squared her shoulders and met Clare's gaze. "Standing here with you, Princess . . . This is a dream come true."

Clare's lips pressed into a smile, her throat surprisingly tight. "It would be an honor to have you stand with me." She glanced at Bennick, hoping she had not overstepped. He gave a subtle nod.

Serai Nadir grinned. "Thank you, Princess."

Clare was grateful to have Tamar Nadir with her when it came time to stand on the grassy field. The woman's assured presence was calming, and Clare admired the way she did not seem affected by the stares—or the few glares—of the Devendran crowd. And her genuine joy brought back Clare's own desire for peace. She had seen so many shadows of late, so much evil. She needed the reminder that there were good people in Eyrinthia—that peace was possible.

Banners bearing the Devendran standard snapped in the warm breeze and the prisoners bound in front of them stared toward the trees bordering the far side of the field. Their yearning for home was palpable, and it made Clare all the more grateful that this exchange had been brokered. It was a beautiful prelude to the alliance between their kingdoms.

A warm breeze tugged at the tendrils of hair that had escaped Clare's bun. The soft strands brushed against the column of her neck, which was growing stiff under the weight of Serene's silver crown. She was focused on mentally rehearsing her speech, so she hadn't realized how long they had been standing there until Venn twisted slightly toward Bennick.

"They're late," he whispered. "How long do we stand here?"

Clare looked to Bennick, who stood beside her. His jaw was set, his eyes trained on the distant treeline. "I don't know," he murmured.

Behind them, the large crowd of Devendrans was growing restless as well. Speculating whispers cut through the air and unease rippled from them.

On Clare's other side, Serai Nadir shifted her weight. "I don't know what could be keeping them," she said quietly. "The roads were clear."

A furrow grew between Imara's dark eyebrows. "Perhaps something happened to delay their journey."

"There," Dirk said suddenly.

Clare darted a look to the trees, her pulse thrummed faster when she spotted the column of men threading their way through the edge of the woods. Sweat broke out on her palms and she wiped her hands discreetly on her skirt, her insides tightening when the first Mortisian soldiers stepped onto the sun-drenched field.

Their swords were sheathed but their eyes were alert. Behind them, a ragged line of prisoners stumbled into view, hands tied to the man in front of them, looking ready to fall over from exhaustion. As they drew closer, Clare could see many tears in their dirty clothes. Her heart constricted when she saw that not one of them seemed to have the strength to look up. Every head was bowed. They were completely submissive. Defeated.

A quick count of the Mortisian soldiers—and the prisoners they led—proved they had kept their word. Twelve soldiers. Twenty prisoners. Some of the tension in Clare's shoulders eased as she released a slow breath.

Ser Ashear was easy to pick out. The nobleman's clothes were clearly expensive, colorful and flecked with gold designs that matched the gold necklace hanging from his neck. His eyes were riveted on Clare, and she could read nothing in his expression.

The spectators had all gone quiet, bringing an eerie quietness to the field.

The Mortisian line halted several paces away, maintaining

a careful space between them.

Commander Markam and his men coaxed their prisoners to stand, leaving a path so Clare would be able to walk through them, once the signal came.

Tamar Nadir frowned. "That is not Ashear," she whispered.

Clare tensed, aware that Bennick, Venn, and Dirk also stiffened around her.

"Princess Serene Aren Demoi of Devendra," the nobleman called out. "I bring the greetings of his highness, Serjah Desfan Cassian, current regent of Mortise." His eyes flicked to Tamar, and a slight frown broke his smooth expression. "Serai Nadir, I did not realize you would be present."

Her chin lifted. "I would not miss it, Ser Zephan."

Zephan.

The name shot through Clare, making her jolt. She was suddenly back in Halbrook, looking at James as he bled in the inn's common room. He'd suspected a man on the Mortisian council had hired mercenaries to kill Serene. A man named Zephan.

Clare darted a look to Bennick, though he wouldn't recognize the name. His gaze was firmly on the Mortisian nobleman in front of them as Serai Nadir continued, "I did not think Ser Ashear would miss this. He was such a staunch supporter."

Ser Zephan lifted his chin. "Unfortunately, Ashear became ill on the journey. The serjah asked me to complete the exchange." His eyes pinned Clare. "Shall we proceed?"

Every muscle in her body screamed in protest, and she was momentarily frozen. Zephan's presence was unexpected, and potentially more dangerous than anyone else realized. If James was correct, this man had already tried to kill Serene once.

But that had been with mercenaries, while he had remained safe in the shadows. Surely he wouldn't attempt something here, in front of so many witnesses?

She wanted to warn Bennick, but she didn't know how. There was no way to be discreet with so many eyes on her, and the tension on the field was an oppressive force; the smallest spark could destroy this pivotal moment—and the peace.

Hundreds of eyes watched, waiting for Clare to move.

It was the prisoners that finally centered her. Seeing the Mortisians, their eyes drawn toward home, and the Devendrans, their downcast eyes and hunched shoulders speaking of a pain she could not fathom . . . She could not let them down. She needed to trust that Zephan would not risk a strike against Devendra while on official business.

She stepped forward, Bennick, Venn, and Dirk moving with her as she walked past the Mortisian prisoners. She halted at the invisible edge, just beyond where the last soldier stood guard.

Ser Zephan had done the same, and now he was only three paces away from her. He had two guards, one on either side of him. None of the bodyguards had drawn their weapons, but Clare could feel the tension in all of them as she met Zephan's gaze.

One wrong move, and she knew that all the tightly coiled soldiers would snap, ending this moment in disaster. If a fight broke out, it would be a bloodbath, and the weaponless prisoners would be the first to be slaughtered.

She lifted her chin, channeling Serene in every careful breath as she began the practiced speech. "I welcome you to Devendra in the name of my father, King Newlan Demoi. Once, this field was a battleground. Now, it lays the groundwork of peace between our great kingdoms. This exchange of prisoners creates a bond of trust between our monarchs, our courts, and our peoples. Our kingdoms take this vital step together toward peaceful unity in full confidence, knowing that both our peoples will benefit from the future alliance, just as these forty men and women, and their loved ones, feel the benefit of freedom to-day."

Ser Zephan dipped his dark head. "Your words express completely the thoughts of Serjah Desfan. He apologizes that he could not come himself, but with his father's health it is quite impossible for him to travel. He did ask that I pass along his hope for the future, with our kingdoms joined forever in peace . . ."

From the corner of her eye, Clare caught movement. One of the Devendran prisoners kneeling near Zephan had lifted his head just enough to peek up at her. His face was streaked with dried mud and dirt covered his hair. But when his familiar blue eyes met hers, her breath rattled out of her.

Eliot.

It was impossible, but it was him. Her brother. Staring up at her with dawning horror in his eyes.

Breath locked in Clare's lungs. She no longer heard Ser Zephan's words. She was no longer aware of Bennick beside her, or anyone else around her. She couldn't see anything except Eliot. Her hands twitched at her sides, longing to grab him, shake him. A thousand questions burned in her mind but her tongue was stiff, useless.

This moment seemed eternal, and yet it could have only lasted seconds.

Eliot's chest lifted on a sharp breath, his throat bobbing hard. His eyes moved deliberately to the prisoners beside him, then shifted back to her.

Confusion twisted through her.

There was a weighted pause, and then Eliot looked back at the prisoners.

The skin around Clare's eyes tightened as she followed her brother's pointed gaze. She saw the ragged clothing, the bowed heads, the grime on their bodies . . .

That was when she saw it, and a pit opened up in her stomach. It was so obvious, and yet she had missed it. They had *all* missed it.

Every last prisoner was a man.

The prisoner list Desfan had sent included women.

Her scalp prickled, and Clare shot a look back to Eliot, her heart pounding loudly in her ears.

His jaw tightened.

I'm sorry.

She could practically hear his voice in her head.

Her eyes stung, the pain of betrayal ripping through her chest. Her fingers curled, nails biting into her palms.

She knew Zephan was still speaking. She could hear the roar of his empty words in her head, but they meant nothing.

Her body trembled, her mouth dry even as her vision blurred. She was frozen. Unable to do anything but stare at her brother.

"Princess?"

Her eyes snapped to Ser Zephan, who stared at her. His mouth was a thin line, irritation clear in his gaze and the set of his shoulders. One eyebrow lifted as he watched her, waited for her to speak.

Clare's pulse thrummed inside her, a quickening beat that made it hard to breathe. She could feel Bennick's eyes on her face, a wordless question weighting the space between them.

Impatience tightened Zephan's dark features. "Princess?" he repeated, more firmly than before.

"Yes?" Clare barely knew her own voice.

Zephan's eyes narrowed.

Bennick turned slightly toward her, concern flashing in his gaze.

She needed to speak. There was something she was *supposed* to say, after the initial speeches were done.

Bennick's light touch to her arm helped ground her.

She swallowed hard, the practiced lines rushing back. "Thank you for your words of peace and hope. They warm my heart, and brighten our shared future. I look forward to entering Mortise on such beautiful terms. Thank you."

Zephan dipped his head, accepting her words.

Clare watched him for any sign of danger. She didn't know what the plan was, but it couldn't be good. Not if Devendran rebels had united with a dangerous Mortisian like Zephan. Something bad was going to happen, and she needed to get herself, Bennick, and the others as far away from Zephan as possible—without alerting Zephan and making things worse.

It was time to retreat and release the prisoners. Tension gripped Clare's shoulders and her fingers curled in her long skirt, prepared to lift it so she could step back. She darted a look to Eliot, her gaze colliding with his.

Her brother was still kneeling on the ground. He hadn't moved, but he seemed closer. She could see the hard angle of his chin, the hair that curled over his dirty brow. His hair was too long. She had always cut it, when they were younger.

Before he had left.

A familiar pain pierced her heart, sharpening the sting in her eyes.

"Princess Serene," Zephan said, calling her attention. "Serjah Desfan sent a gift for you. He asked me to personally put it in your hands." He slipped a box out of his pocket and balanced it on one palm, the velvet case perfectly suited to holding a small piece of jewelry. "May I approach?"

Clare's hands clenched in her skirt and she shot a look at Bennick. A gift exchange had never been part of the plan. Warning blazed through her. Her lips parted, but no sound came out. Anything she wanted to say was strangled in her tight throat.

Bennick shifted to stand partially in front of Clare, his hand extended. "I will accept the gift for the princess." His firm tone brooked no argument. It was clear he didn't appreciate the surprise gift, but he knew they could not refuse it.

Clare's heart beat against her ribs as Zephan stepped forward, and she darted a look to Eliot.

Her brother watched her, a muscle in his cheek flexing as his jaw tightened. Too many emotions flashed across his face. Frustration. Guilt. Pain. Regret.

His eyes closed, and his shoulders rose with a measured breath. When his eyes opened, a new emotion had settled on his dirty face. One Clare had never seen before.

It terrified her.

"It's a trap!" Eliot shouted, the warning ripping through the air. He jerked his hands apart, breaking the ropes that had been only loosely wrapped around his wrists as he shoved to his feet and dove for Zephan.

Everything happened at once.

Bennick drew his sword.

Zephan reared back, his guards jerking out their weapons.

Venn grasped Clare's arm, but she barely felt his touch.

A Mortisian soldier grabbed Eliot and plunged a knife in his back.

"*NO!*" Clare's shriek tore through her.

Eliot's body jerked, face carved with pain. His mouth opened, then slackened. His eyes glazed as he crumpled to the grass, the blade buried in his back, one arm reaching for her.

Instinct, training, and adrenaline converged. Clare twisted her wrist and tore free of Venn's hand.

Shock burst across his face and he cursed, reaching for her

again.

But she was already running, her heart fracturing as she darted toward her brother. She needed to reach him—needed to stop the bleeding.

The sounds of battle waged around her. Screaming had erupted from the spectators, and she heard the pounding of feet, the ring and clang of metal striking metal. From the corner of her eye, she saw Imara being pulled away by her guards. She also saw Serai Nadir had drawn a throwing dagger from somewhere within the folds of her dress, and she hurled it at one of the Mortisians running after the Zennorian princess. It struck him in the back, and he fell.

Beside Clare, Dirk cut off one of the Mortisian soldiers from reaching her.

The world was nightmarish. Nothing seemed real, even though Clare could feel the sweat rolling down her spine and the tightness of every ragged breath.

Bennick's voice cut through the chaos. "Get her out of here, *now*! Venn!"

It was her only warning before Venn's arms were thrown around her shoulders, yanking her to a stop.

Keeping her from Eliot.

Deep inside her, something snapped.

Clare clawed Venn's arms, drove her heel into his foot, hammered her elbows into his ribs. She rocked them both with the fierceness of her attack and Venn hissed in pain. His hands grew bruising, but then he lightened his hold—as if afraid of hurting her.

She used that reticence against him, continuing her attack until he stumbled, unbalanced. She threw her weight down and broke his hold, but she could already feel him grasping for her again.

She rounded on him, her nails raking his cheek. Crimson lines split his dark skin and he gasped, rearing back.

A prickle of guilt rose, but she slammed it down and spun, kicking his knee.

His leg buckled and he crashed to the ground.

Clare bolted, heart throbbing in her chest, tears clogging her throat as she drew closer to Eliot.

It was Dirk who tackled her.

The hard ground knocked the air from her lungs, and his weight kept her pinned. She barely noticed the knife that hit the grass nearby—the knife that had been thrown, and would have killed her.

"Let me go," she rasped, grass and dirt scratching her palms as she pushed against Dirk. "I can save him!"

Dirk's breath was hot at her ear, his voice horribly thin as he whispered, "I'm sorry, Clare. He's dead."

Agony ripped through her, even as denial surged. But when her eyes lifted and she saw Eliot, lying motionless not far from her, his face turned away from her . . . she knew Dirk was right.

Her chest caved in, compressing her heart and lungs.

The truth had never hurt this much.

Dirk's hands squeezed her arms. "I'm sorry," he repeated, urgency leaking into his voice. "We have to go."

Clare's darting eyes took in the space around them. Saw Bennick, fighting two men at once several paces away. She saw Venn—his face bleeding from her scratches—swing his sword at a Mortisian who darted for Dirk's unguarded back.

Her gaze went back to Eliot, her heart burning, her vision hazed with tears.

Her brother was gone. He had died for her.

But no one else had to.

Dirk felt the fight ease from her body, and he pulled her to her feet.

Venn grasped her hand and Clare met his gaze, her stomach twisting as she saw the blood she'd drawn.

There was no censure in Venn's gaze as his fingers flexed around hers. Grim determination set his features, compassion sparking his eyes as he noted her tears. "Stay close," he said.

Clare jerked out a nod and moved with Venn, Dirk protecting them from behind as they ran together toward the city.

CHAPTER 46

DESFAN

DESFAN'S SHOULDER PRESSED INTO THE bookshelf, a curse on his tongue. Beside him, Karim tensed.

"What?" Jamal hissed.

The guard who had betrayed them pointed at the bookcase Desfan and Karim crouched behind. "The serjah is there. Him and his guard. They'll have heard everything."

Jamal and his men spun.

Desfan tightened his grip on his knife as he stepped out next to Karim.

Jamal's face went pale, then flushed red. So many thoughts could be seen streaking through his mind, but he clearly settled on the easiest solution. His voice dropped low. "Kill them."

Karim hurled a throwing knife, which embedded in the nearest man's chest, and then his open palm slammed into

Desfan's chest, shoving him back. "Run!" he shouted, plucking another knife from his belt.

He wasn't going to run. Was Karim insane?

Jamal turned toward Yahri, who still sat in that chair, clutching her cane, her eyes wide.

Fates blast it. The woman couldn't die. Not when Desfan had so many questions. But getting past the wall of enemies would be too time-consuming. "Hold their attention," he snapped at his friend.

Karim didn't respond, just threw his second knife. Desfan darted back down the aisle they'd hidden in.

"Don't let him get away!" Jamal screamed.

Desfan's boots pounded over the stone floor, running so quickly the spines of the shelved books blurred. The row seemed to go on forever, but finally he reached the end. He grasped the wooden edge and hurled himself around it, charging down another row. He counted the shelves that flashed by, then—after he guessed it had been enough—he darted up one of the aisles, running back toward the south corner.

Somewhere behind him, he heard the sounds of pursuit. He'd have to tease Karim later for letting them slip past him.

He could hear blades clashing as he drew closer to the fight. Karim was no longer throwing knives, then.

With a burst of speed, he reached the end of the aisle and burst into the south corner of the library, this time entering closer to Yahri.

Jamal was just reaching for her when her white cane swung in a blindingly fast arc, cracking against his hand.

Jamal cried out and doubled over, cradling his hand to his chest.

He didn't see Desfan coming.

Desfan slammed into Jamal's side, knocking them both to

the unforgiving floor. The vial of poison bounced away with a soft clinking sound, quickly drowned out by the sounds of fighting.

Jamal kicked at Desfan, trying to throw him off, or at least roll them so he could be on top. One of his knees caught Desfan's ribs and he grunted, his grip shifting on Jamal's wrists so he could pin them down. "You can't win," he said through his teeth. "Give up."

A vein bulged in Jamal's forehead. "No!"

"Look out!" Yahri cried.

Desfan looked over his shoulder just in time to get a boot in the jaw. His head snapped to the side and he flew back, losing his hold on Jamal as he landed hard. Blood spurted in his mouth and his hands flinched up to his throbbing face. The pain was intense, but he didn't think anything was broken.

"Desfan!" Karim shouted.

He blinked through the involuntary tears and rolled, barely missing a knife as it plunged for him. He rolled until his shoulder hit a bookcase.

Jamal pushed to his feet, but the more immediate threat was the man who had kicked Desfan. It was the soldier who had betrayed them. He was advancing, a knife in each hand, the blades covered in blood.

The sight of that helped Desfan push through his pain-filled daze.

That blood was probably Arcas's, and that of the other innocent guard. They had trusted this man, and he had killed them.

Desfan grit his teeth, head spinning, jaw throbbing. He fumbled to draw his knife, but it was stuck, pinned between his hip and the bookshelf.

The soldier crouched, his knife striking for Desfan's heart.

Desfan snatched a book off the shelf and the dagger thunked into the thick volume. The man blinked at the book on the end of his blade, but before he could strike with the other, Desfan grasped another heavy tome and slammed the spine into the man's temple.

The man crumpled.

Desfan rolled away from the shelf, his breathing deep and ragged. His head felt ready to explode, and he still tasted blood on his tongue. He groaned when he saw two more men running toward him.

Meanwhile, Jamal had just grabbed Yahri's cane when she swung it, and he yanked it from her. The woman stumbled and fell, hitting the floor with a horrible thud.

She looked stunned as she blinked up at Jamal, who had a knife in his other hand.

"This ends now," Jamal snarled.

A dagger sliced end over end through the air and slammed blade-first through Jamal's wrist.

He screamed and dropped his blade, clutching his wounded arm to his stomach, the blade still buried in his flesh.

Desfan's eyes widened as Prince Grayson leaped from between the row of shelves. He already had knives back in both hands, even though he'd clearly just thrown the one that had stopped Jamal's killing blow.

He threw both daggers at the same time and they struck the two men who had been advancing on Desfan.

Desfan watched the men crumple. "Impressive."

Grayson's gaze snapped over Desfan's shoulder, and his hands dove for more blades. "Behind you!" he shouted.

Desfan whirled, managing to spin away from the man who had been sneaking up on him. Before he could even raise his knife, Grayson had already thrown another blade and it found the man's neck.

"This may be a touch late," Liam Kaelin's voice rang out as the body fell. "But can we kill them?"

From the corner of his eye, Desfan saw that Karim was no longer fighting alone. Liam fought beside him.

Karim ducked a swinging blade and shouted, "Yes!"

Liam grinned and drew a second knife, spinning it in his hand. "Well, that makes things easier."

Desfan had no idea why the Kaelin princes were in the library or why they'd chosen to join the fight, but he thanked the fates they were here.

Grayson jumped over Serai Yahri, who was still on the floor, and—on his way back down to the floor—punched Jamal in the face. The councilman slammed into the ground, blood spurting from his nose. Then Grayson whirled and engaged two more attackers, spinning around them with an ease that should have been unnerving.

Would have been, if he hadn't been on Desfan's side.

Grayson moved like he was possessed by a demon, fluid grace and deadly accuracy in every powerful movement.

Desfan ducked an enemy blade and jerked his attention back to his own fight, since the man he'd struck with a book had recovered.

And he looked livid.

"I'm sorry," Desfan said. "Do you not like books?"

The man charged.

Desfan darted to the side, kicking out and buckling the man's knee. The man fell, and Desfan couldn't resist when he saw the book sitting on the small reading table. He lifted it and smacked it down on the man's head.

Karim snarled from across the room. "Stop playing around with books!"

Desfan smiled. "It's called improvising."

"No." Karim ducked a swinging sword and shot a look over Desfan's shoulder. "*That's* improvising."

Desfan twisted in time to see Grayson jump, his hand grasping the lip of an upper shelf so he could kick a towering candelabra onto one of his attackers. The heavy iron piece—taller than a man and three times as heavy—knocked the man down, pinning his chest to the floor.

Grayson dropped from the shelf, spinning a knife in his free hand.

Liam snorted. "Show off."

Grayson flashed a thin smile.

"Stop!"

They all turned at Jamal's shout. The man had hauled Yahri up and held her like a shield. A knife was against her throat. "I'll kill her," he said, blood smeared over his face. "You let me walk out of here, or I kill her."

Desfan's stomach dropped. He really didn't know how he felt about Yahri, but he needed her alive if he was going to learn the truth about what had happened to his father.

But Jamal could not walk out of here.

"Do you need him alive?" Grayson asked, his voice a deadly murmur, that knife still in his hand. It would be a risky throw with Yahri there, but Desfan somehow knew Grayson could make it.

"Preferably alive," Desfan grunted. "But she's more important." Yahri knew the truth about his father's collapse; that mattered far more than gathering the details of Jamal's treason.

Jamal was backing up, his eyes darting between them all.

Liam and Karim had finished their attackers as well and were slowly approaching.

"Stop!" Jamal said again, his voice edging higher. "Don't

come closer!"

Desfan lifted a placating hand. "Jamal. You can't make it out of the palace. You know that. Let Yahri go, and you won't die here."

The man's tongue darted frantically over his lips, his eyes still bouncing between them all. He was nearly to a row of bookshelves, and if he made it there, he would disappear from view. "I never meant to harm you, Desfan. Everything I did, it wasn't meant to harm you."

Desfan grit his teeth. "You brought olcain to Duvan. You were the buyer and the one promising protection, weren't you? Was it to make a profit, or destabilize Mortise?"

Jamal's eyes flashed and he growled. "Mortise is already destabilized. And you would make it worse by marrying a Devendran. I'm not alone in thinking so; I wasn't the only one who paid for the Rose to kill her!"

Desfan's hands fisted. "You blackmailed Yahri, and others."

"I'm not the only one who has committed crimes." His hold on Yahri tightened until the woman gasped. "She knows what happened to your father. She has fought to cover up her involvement, but she was there with the serjan that night. Why don't you ask her why?"

Desfan couldn't let himself even look at Yahri. His focus needed to remain on making sure Jamal—and Yahri—lived through the next moments.

Jamal eased back another step, moving into the shadow of the towering bookshelf. "You're stalling, but you have a decision to make. Let me go, or Yahri dies—along with the truth about what happened to the serjan."

That wasn't how this would play out. Beside Desfan, Grayson was holding the knife, ready to make the throw.

Jamal would die.

"It's your choice," Jamal said with a slow grin. "You must choose how this ends."

"No," a new voice said, low and pained yet still somehow strong. Arcas stepped out of the shadows and stopped behind Jamal, one hand pressed to a bleeding wound in his side while the other laid the edge of a blade against the side of the councilman's neck. "You decide, Jamal. Release her, or die."

Jamal's face twisted with rage, but he dropped his knife from Yahri's neck. She stumbled without her cane and Desfan leaped to steady her. He quirked a smile at Arcas, ignoring the pain in his jaw. "I'm glad you're alive."

The man huffed a short, heavy breath. "So am I."

Liam eyed the bodies on the floor. "You Mortisians certainly know how to throw a party."

Desfan almost laughed, but that tugged painfully on his face and he grasped his jaw with a groan.

Karim cursed. "Fates rot you, did you break your *jaw*?"

CHAPTER 47

BENNICK

BENNICK SLICED HIS BLADE ACROSS THE GUT of a Mortisian soldier. The man had tried to edge around him so he could pursue Clare—Serene, as they all thought she was.

He guarded her retreat with Venn and Dirk, the brunt of the battle going on in front of them.

The prisoners the Mortisians had brought were now all armed and fighting. Twelve enemy soldiers had turned into thirty-two in one horrible moment. The Devendrans were woefully outnumbered.

Bennick cursed himself as he fought a new enemy. Everything had devolved too quickly. He'd been suspicious of Ser Zephan purely because he wasn't Ashear, but there had been other clues. He'd just been too focused on watching Zephan to notice the fact that none of the Devendran prisoners were looking up. Not one. As if they were hiding their faces. And there hadn't been a single woman among them, even though Desfan's letter had said there would be.

And why had that enemy prisoner called out, warning them it was a trap? It was something else about this whole disaster that didn't make sense. But even though Bennick didn't understand, he was grateful. The warning had cost him his life, but it had given them a better chance to fight. To get Clare to safety.

He wanted to be with her, but he needed to guard her. He would not allow anyone to slip past him to follow her. But as he fought the Mortisians, he could feel the distance between him and Clare stretching, growing. It killed him.

He spotted his father in the fray, parrying the blows of a younger Mortisian soldier with his double-edged blade. Commander Markam was a powerful warrior, but he had spent years behind the desk of the king's prison, or advising the king on security matters. He was not in shape for this battle of overwhelming odds. A spark of concern he didn't want to feel lit inside his chest.

Two of the false prisoners, dressed in their ragged clothing, reached Bennick, attacking him with long knives. Even under all that dirt, he could see they were Devendran.

Bennick cursed as one of the blades got past his guard and nicked his arm between the leather armor plating. The cut wasn't deep, but it stung.

Pounding footsteps announced the arrival of Devendran soldiers from Stills coming to their aid. The reinforcements charged into the core of the battle with swords drawn and teeth bared.

Commander Markam did not seem surprised by their appearance, and Bennick wondered if the king had ordered the commander to have reinforcements on hand, or if the thought had been his own. Either way, Bennick felt grudging gratitude. At least now they stood a chance.

He killed the last of his attackers and twisted to observe the fight, sweat streaking his face, his chest rising and falling with heavy breaths. The arrival of the reinforcements had changed the dynamics of the fight, leaving Bennick free to go after Clare.

He didn't hesitate. He tightened the hold on his sword and jogged after Clare, Dirk, and Venn. He could see them through the blur of fighting men, and his stomach dropped as he watched two Mortisians charge them.

Venn's long ponytail swung as he ducked, spun, and attacked the men. Dirk twisted to help, yelling for Clare to keep going. She darted forward, but had only made it a couple of steps before a shout rent the air.

"Clare!"

Bennick jerked at the unexpected sound of her name, his eyes darting to one of the dirt-covered prisoners. He was running toward Clare from across the field and Bennick's heart stopped when he saw Clare stumble, then bolt toward him.

Dirk stabbed his attacker and tore after Clare, leaving Venn to finish off the last attacker. The older bodyguard called for Clare to stop, but she was running quickly, moving deeper onto the field.

Bennick altered course, forcing himself to move faster, desperate to intercept her. He didn't know who the Mortisian was, or why he knew Clare, but his instincts were screaming that this was an enemy.

"Michael?" she shouted, her voice cracking.

Bennick wanted to curse. Eliot's friend. A rebel. And, apparently, the traitor was working with the Mortisians.

It made a horrible kind of sense. The Mortisian prisoner who had called out a warning was not a Mortisian at all. It must have been Eliot.

And from the rage twisting Michael's face, it was clear he blamed Clare for his friend's death.

Bennick drove himself harder, ignoring the burn in his lungs.

"It's your fault!" Michael snarled

Clare jerked to a stop, as if slapped. "Michael, I—"

"You killed him!" He threw a knife and Dirk leaped for Clare, but he would be too late.

Bennick's heart stopped.

Clare slammed to her knees, ducking as the blade sailed over her head. Her hands braced on the ground, her chest rising and falling too quickly. Shock splashed her features, as well as pain.

Michael ground to a halt when he saw Dirk reach Clare, and then his eyes jumped to Bennick, who was nearly to her as well.

His hands fisted, and then he dashed for the cover of the trees.

He wasn't the only one retreating. Bennick could see Mortisians darting for the treeline as well, fleeing from the reinforcements.

Bennick nearly charged after Michael, but Clare was sobbing on the ground with Dirk's hand on her back, and leaving her when she was in pain was impossible.

As soon as he reached her, he fell to his knees, gripping her hunched shoulders. "Clare. Are you hurt?"

Her fingers latched onto his uniform as she pressed against his chest, her body shaking. "He's dead," she sobbed. "Eliot is dead."

Bennick's insides knotted, his heart aching for her. His feelings toward Eliot would always be complicated, but that didn't stop him from tightening his hold on Clare, holding her tightly as she cried.

CHAPTER 48

MIA

AWARENESS CAME AND WENT WHILE Mia died.

At first, it was a bolt of agony that ripped her to the surface. Sharp, stabbing pain in her gut as she was lowered onto a bed.

"Gently," a deep voice cautioned. Devon?

"Will she live?" That was Tyrell, though he sounded strange. Tense. Worried.

"I don't know. I need more light. Water. Bandages." Devon clipped out orders, and someone scurried out of the room.

"Hold on, Mia," Tyrell ordered, his voice rough.

Mia's eyes fluttered closed.

The next time she woke, the room was brightly lit with a roaring fire, and there were lamps and candles all around the bed. Devon crouched over her, his hands on her stomach.

There was so much pain.

Mia cried out and lost consciousness again.

The next time she surfaced, it was more gently.

She could feel the mattress against her back, feel the warmth of the fireplace against her face.

"How long?" Tyrell asked, his voice low and tight.

"I don't know. Her body is fighting hard. Infection is the true danger now . . ."

A soft rag brushed her skin, her hair. Cleaning her, perhaps?

Long fingers wrapped around hers. A soft, desperate whisper. "Please, just open your fates-blasted eyes."

A cool, deep voice that resonated through the room. "What is she doing here?"

Mia shivered, shying away from that terrifying voice.

"She was badly hurt," Tyrell said. "I had no other option."

"She needs to be back in her cell."

"She cannot be moved, Sire."

"And her caretaker. He had to lose his head?"

Tyrell's voice was flat. "Yes."

There was a short silence. "Will she live?"

"Yes," Tyrell said again but this time the word was edged with doubt.

Mia drifted again.

Consciousness once again seeped in, but this time Mia knew she was not dying.

She blinked her heavy eyes and peered around the unfamiliar room. It was much larger than her cell and there was a fire crackling in a large hearth across the room. The shadows were heavy in the corners, obscuring the edges of the room. But she was lying on a large four-post bed with heavy drapes pulled back.

Beside her, Tyrell sat in an armchair, his eyes on the flickering flames in the fireplace. His profile was washed with the orange light, his jaw hard. Dark hair hung over his brow and blood and paint smeared his white shirt. The sleeves were rolled up and muscles tensed in his forearms as he fisted his hands, which were braced on his knees.

Mia shifted, and Tyrell's eyes snapped to her. The sudden twist cast his face with light on one side while the other was now shadowed.

He straightened in the chair, angling toward her. "You're awake."

She glanced around them, her throat dry and her entire body aching. "Where . . .?"

"My room. It was the only place I could think to bring you." He reached for a glass and pitcher sitting on the bedside table. He poured water into the cup, the soft rippling sound filling the room.

Confusion tugged at her. "Was Devon here?"

"Yes. The night guard summoned him. He said he's tended you for years." Tyrell's hand slipped under her head and tilted her up.

Pain rippled over her stomach as muscles flexed, and she had to force her body to remain as still as possible while she drank. The cool liquid slid comfortingly over the dryness in her mouth and throat, until Tyrell suddenly pulled the glass away. "Devon said you needed to drink slowly."

She winced as he lowered her back to the pillow. "My head

hurts."

"He gave you something for the pain. Said it might keep you sleeping, and give you headaches when you woke. I'm sorry."

She glanced down at herself, noting the blankets that had been carefully tucked around her. She was also wearing a clean nightgown, and she could feel no blood or paint on her face.

It was as if he read her thoughts. "After Devon stitched the wound, we had a woman change and clean you."

"But you're still wearing your clothes."

He glanced down at his shirt, which was stained with blood and paint. "I honestly forgot."

Mia's fingers curled in the blankets. "Is . . . is Papa really dead?"

Tyrell's brows slammed down. "I won't apologize for killing him. That man was lower than vermin."

She shuddered at the assault of memories. Jamming that pencil into Papa's eye. Feeling that knife slide into her middle. Watching as Tyrell's sword cut off Papa's hand—and then his head.

Fates, was it wrong that all she felt was relief? She would never again have to see him. Hear him.

Fear him.

The man had hurt and terrorized her since she was a child. Perhaps guilt for feeling peace over a violent loss of life would come later, but for now, she was almost dizzy with relief.

She reached for her necklace, her heart lurching when the familiar pebble wasn't there.

"Here."

She darted a look at Tyrell, saw the necklace dangling from his fingers.

His gaze was hooded. "I was keeping it safe while the woman cleaned you. It was in the way."

She reached out a hand.

His fingers clenched around the necklace before lowering it onto her palm.

She fisted the pebble, tension leaving her once she felt it against her skin. "Thank you," she breathed.

Tyrell swallowed and straightened in the chair. "There's still some paint in your hair. The woman who cleaned you said her ministrations seemed to be bothering you, so she stopped. Now that you're awake, I can fetch her. Or I can do it."

The answer on her tongue was *No*. But if she refused him, a stranger would come and touch her. In her vulnerable, exhausted state, she didn't like that thought. Besides, rejecting Tyrell's kindness went against her resolution to treat him better, so she nodded.

Tyrell rose and rounded the bed, grabbing a basin that was already filled with water. He also snatched up a cloth before moving to sit on the bed beside her. When the mattress shifted and she hissed out a breath, he froze. "Sorry."

She shook her head and closed her eyes, trying to focus on keeping her breathing shallow and even.

His fingers were tentative as they brushed her hairline. She could feel the cuts on her brow and temple—places where the paint jar had sliced her skin. And her curls were stiff with dried paint and blood. That is where Tyrell focused his efforts, taking a length of her hair in hand, and then gently dabbing it with the wet cloth.

"You saved my life," she whispered into the quiet. "Thank you."

"I'm sorry I wasn't there sooner," Tyrell said, his voice dark.

She peeked up at him, but his gaze remained wholly focused on his task. "How did you know to come?"

Tyrell eased back, dipped the rag in the basin, then returned to another lock of hair. His touch was far more careful than she would have ever imagined him capable of. "I paid the night guard weeks ago to fetch me if anything out of the ordinary happened. The moment he saw how drunk that fetid cretin was, he thought I should know. I—" He cut himself off, tendons standing out in his neck. He dipped the rag back in the water, turning it pink. "I didn't realize he'd stabbed you at first. I didn't know until you fell . . ." He leaned over her, the wet rag touching her hair again. "I thought you died in my arms. I swear you stopped breathing."

Mia forced herself to meet his eyes. Her pulse raced. She was tired and in pain, but she needed to say this. "I'm sorry, Tyrell."

His brow furrowed. "You have nothing to apologize for."

"But I do. You bought me those paints. The canvases and brushes. You tried to do something nice for me, and I . . . I'm sorry for the way I reacted. I . . . I was afraid. I didn't want to go outside."

His jaw flexed. "You don't have to explain yourself."

"But I want to. Because I appreciate what you did." She wet her dry lips. "Being afraid doesn't excuse me for how I treated you. I never should have attacked you like I did, or said the things I did." Her cheeks reddened. "I shouldn't have suggested that you loved me. It was insane of me to think that. Please forgive me."

Tyrell lowered the rag, his pale fingers clenched tight. "Yesterday . . . I didn't react well, either. When you said you didn't love me . . . That hit me hard, because I . . . I have feelings for you, Mia."

She stared at him, shock and denial and so many other emotions stabbing her. She didn't know how to respond. What to say. "I love Grayson," she finally whispered.

Tyrell huffed a short, coarse laugh. "Trust me, I know." He glanced away, the tendons in his neck stretching. "What if you had met me first?" he asked quietly. "What if Grayson had been the one ordered to hurt you that night?"

She shook her head slowly. "I love him. Speculating about the past won't change that."

His eyes narrowed on the flames dancing in the fireplace. His profile could have been cut from stone. "And if he doesn't return from Mortise?"

"He will come back."

He turned to her. "But if he doesn't?"

She stared back at him. "I would still love him. That will never change. What you want from me . . . It will never happen."

Tyrell looked down at the rag in his hand, his shoulders tensed. "He's been ordered to assassinate the princess of Devendra."

She stopped breathing.

Grayson had killed before. She'd seen his difficulty with it over the years, but the night that he'd saved her from Tyrell, he had broken in her arms because he'd been forced to kill a defenseless man. It had been murder.

It had been a test.

If Grayson was forced to kill a young woman . . . it could break him completely.

Mia swallowed, her heart drumming against her ribs. "He can't."

Tyrell eyed her, his expression hard. "If he doesn't kill her, you will die."

She closed her eyes, her heart aching.

He wasn't done. "The princess will be in Duvan to finalize her engagement to the prince of Mortise. Her death will trigger a war between their kingdoms, and then Ryden will strike. My father will control three of the four kingdoms, and one day he will have Zennor, too. Thousands will die." He paused. "Can you still love Grayson after that?"

She met his gaze, even though her eyes stung. "You know my answer."

He didn't respond. He finished cleaning her hair the best he could with the basin and rag, and then he dropped them on the bedside table and stood. "I'll send for Devon. He should look you over, make sure you're all right." He moved for the door, and when his fingers grasped the handle, he glanced back at her over his shoulder, his eyes shadowed due to the fire behind him. "You need to know something, Mia. I've been raised to fight, and I don't give up. Not if it's a fight for something I want."

CHAPTER 49

DESFAN

JAMAL WASN'T TALKING, BUT WITH EVERYTHING the man had already revealed in the library, the pieces were falling into place. Kiv Arcas—despite his injury—was leading the search of Jamal's apartment, and he had already dispatched a contingent of guards to seize and search all of Jamal's properties.

Karim had finally managed to get Desfan to see a physician about his jaw. Not the royal physician, of course—he was still in a cell, and by the last report, he had confessed all he knew about Yahri's involvement in Serjan Saernon's collapse. Which really wasn't much—just that she had been with the serjan when he'd collapsed. She had asked the physician not to say anything, and since they were friends—and the physician saw no sign of poisoning—he had agreed to keep silent.

Desfan didn't know what to think. He didn't know if Yahri

had poisoned his father, but she was clearly hiding something. And he would get answers.

Yahri was currently locked in a cell, also being tended by a physician. Before they'd left the library, she'd told Desfan where he could find a box hidden in her room, filled with letters from Jamal—all signed with the now-familiar crossed swords—and also letters from others on the council who she knew Jamal had either corrupted, blackmailed, or recruited.

Five names in all. Seven, including Yahri and Jamal.

In one night, Desfan had arrested seven members of the council. He didn't think such a thing had ever happened in Mortisian history.

Half the night was gone by the time he and Karim left the physician's tower. They both had bruising and some minor cuts, but Desfan's jaw was *not* broken. It could have been much worse.

Would have been, if not for the Kaelins. Thank the fates they'd been in the library and heard the fight.

"Do you want to question Yahri tonight?" Karim asked as they descended the spiral staircase.

Yes.

No.

He was mentally and physically done. It was only a few hours until dawn. Karim looked as exhausted as he felt.

Desfan paused on the stairs, one hand braced against the stone wall. "I trusted Jamal."

Karim had stopped a step below him, the muted glow of a torch around the curve barely highlighting his face as he peered up at Desfan. "He fooled everyone."

"I know. But I feel like I should have guessed."

Karim didn't answer, just watched him. After a moment, he said, "While you were busy arresting half the council, Ori came by."

"He did?"

Karim nodded. "He had an urgent message from Zadir. The pirate thought you would want to know that a Zennorian drug master named Sahvi sold the olcain to Omar Jamal."

Desfan stared at him. "You're kidding."

He shook his head. "Ori said Zadir wanted you to know as soon as possible so he didn't expect payment first. Although the boy made it clear Zadir still expects it." The corner of Karim's mouth twitched. "Apparently, the pirate considers you a friend."

The ridiculousness of the fact that—even if they hadn't overheard Jamal's confession—the truth would have come out tonight, made Desfan huff out a laugh. When he considered that a pirate had been a better friend than a councilman, a deeper laugh followed.

Karim cracked a grin, chuckling as well.

After the laughter spluttered out, Desfan shook his head. "The fates have a sense of humor."

Karim clapped a hand on Desfan's shoulder. "Come on. Yahri can wait until morning."

"I shouldn't put this off."

"You need sleep. The fates know you're hard enough to deal with when you've had a good night's rest."

Desfan snorted. "I am not."

"You're a monster without sleep," Karim argued.

The debate continued as they walked through the sleeping palace, and Desfan was struck with how lucky he was. The fates had stolen so much from him, but they had given him his best friend. And, apparently, he also had a pirate captain, and possibly two Kaelin princes on his side.

The fates did indeed have a sense of humor.

CHAPTER 50

GRAYSON

"I THOUGHT YOU MIGHT STILL BE AWAKE."

Grayson turned from the window to track Liam as his brother closed the bedroom door and moved toward him. "Counting the stars?" he asked.

Grayson's brow furrowed. "Why would I be doing that?"

Liam stopped beside him at the window, looking out at the full moon that hung above the dark, reflective sea. "It's a Zennorian legend. Count all the stars in the midnight sky, and whatever you wish for will come true."

"That's ridiculous."

The corner of Liam's mouth twitched. "Yes, but that doesn't stop people from counting until their eyes burn." He eyed the sky, his profile shadowed—hidden but for the silver moonlight brushing his upturned face.

"Have you counted the stars?" Grayson asked.

Liam took a slow breath, his eyes fastened on the sky, his voice edged with sadness as he said, "Yes. Many times."

There was a lot Grayson didn't know about his older brother, but he knew Liam had experienced a great loss at their father's hand. He sensed the loss had broken something inside him, even though it had given him resolve—the final push to seek revenge and tear down the Kaelins once and for all.

If his loss was akin to losing Mia, then Grayson thought his brother was the strongest man in Eyrinthia.

And it was time he told Liam the truth.

He took a breath. "Mother ordered me to kill you."

Liam's eyes remained on the stars, his expression revealing nothing. "Why didn't you?"

Not the response he'd expected.

Grayson frowned. "I didn't want to."

Liam tipped his head. "I appreciate your honesty. Did she say why she wants me dead?"

"She suspects you're no longer loyal to Ryden. She wants you eliminated."

"I suppose I shouldn't have expected anything less from her. She's been harder to convince." He eyed Grayson. "I assume she brandished some lovely threat in order to secure your obedience."

"Yes."

"Mia?"

Grayson's jaw tensed. "No. She doesn't know about Mia."

"Well, that's a rare blessing. How did she threaten you, then?"

"There's a family I helped a few months ago. She found them, and she'll kill them if you return home."

"Oh, I won't be returning to Ryden," Liam said. "And soon,

she won't have the ability to hurt anyone ever again."

It sounded too good to be true, but Grayson prayed that day would come.

"You fought well in the library," Liam said suddenly. "It was quite something to watch."

"Your technique could use some work."

Liam chuckled. "Perhaps I should ask you for some lessons." He propped his shoulder against the window frame, his eyes on Grayson. "How are you doing? After learning everything about Mia?"

His fists tightened at his sides. "I don't know. I'm angry at Father, and I wish Mia had shared the truth with me. I know she must have been scared, and I know she was conditioned not to even think about it, but . . ."

"Some things are too painful to talk about," Liam said. "Too horrible to share. And sometimes we might blame ourselves, or feel shame about what happened. Her not telling you has no bearing on how much she trusts you."

"I know. I just . . ." He wanted to be there for her, for everything. Always.

"You haven't failed her," Liam said quietly.

Grayson's jaw firmed. His heart ached with missing her. Being apart from her like this was agony.

Liam seemed to hear his thoughts. "This won't last forever. You'll be reunited soon enough."

The words Grayson had been thinking since learning the truth about Mia came out low but strong. "I want to kill Father for what he did to her. To her family."

"We will kill him," his brother promised. "After we destroy his ability to be a threat to anyone ever again."

He looked to Liam, finally asking the question that made his rebellion real. "What's your plan?"

His brother glanced out the window. "It's simple, really. Father sent us here to spark a war, and that's exactly what we'll do." Liam met Grayson's gaze, his eyes gleaming with a focused light. "But it will not be the war he asked for."

524

CHAPTER 51

CLARE

"We will not return to Iden." Serene looked every bit the ruler standing in the common room of the inn as she addressed them. Darkness had fallen outside, and the lamps that glowed on the nearby table highlighted the determined tilt of her chin. Her shoulders were back, eyes uncompromising as she stared down Commander Markam.

The older man's mouth tightened. "With all due respect, there is no point continuing. Mortise has betrayed us."

"No." Serene shook her head. "Some Mortisians betrayed us, along with a group of Devendran rebels."

"Yes. The rebels." Commander Markam's eyes shot to Clare, who stood in the shadowed corner of the room, Vera's arm wrapped around her.

Venn was on her other side, his arms crossed over his chest.

The scratches on his cheek were vivid, but he had barely left Clare's side in the aftermath of the attack. Even now, his body stiffened, and he glared at the commander. "What are you trying to say?"

Commander Markam's eyebrows pulled together, his gaze still focused on Clare. "Somehow, Miss Ellington, it was never reported that your brother was a rebel. And from what I've gathered today, you've known since the Paltrow's ball."

Clare flinched under his condemning words, and Vera's arm tightened around her.

Venn took a step forward, but it was Bennick who grabbed the commander's arm. His voice was low, his eyes dark. "How dare you accuse her of anything?"

The commander ground his teeth. "I'm merely stating fact. Her brother's involvement with the rebels should have been reported to the king immediately. Keeping that secret was treasonous."

"You dare lecture me about secrets?" Bennick growled. "You're a fates-blasted coward."

"And you're blind when it comes to the decoy," his father snapped. "After what happened today, how can you—?"

"Enough," Serene cut in, giving the commander a hard look. A look she then turned on Bennick.

Slowly, finger by finger, Bennick released his father's arm. But his fury was still evident as he shifted back a step.

Serene straightened. "We have interrogated Ser Zephan, and all the other survivors, and I think it is clear that what happened this morning was not sanctioned by Desfan." She turned to Serai Nadir, who had been a silent observer thus far. "I would like to know your thoughts on what happened today, and how it reflects on Mortise as a whole."

The Mortisian noblewoman still looked a little disheveled

after the attack; she had thrown four knives, killing two enemy Mortisians in defense of Imara. But her expression was fierce as she said, "I *know* the serjah would never have sent Zephan to do this."

Serene nodded and glanced at Bennick. "What do you think?"

His shoulders were hard with tension, but Clare thought that had more to do with his proximity to the commander than Serene's question. "I don't see this as an act of war on Desfan's part. I believe if we blame him and Mortise at large for the actions of a few evil men, that could be the act that destroys the peace."

Serene tipped her head. "I agree. Zephan's design was to ruin the peace, and I will not let him succeed."

"I still don't think it's advisable to continue to Duvan," Commander Markam said.

"Your opinion has been noted." Serene turned to Tamar Nadir. "Will you still house us?"

"Yes, of course." She frowned. "What of Zephan?"

Clare had wondered if Serene would tell everyone that Zephan had orchestrated the attack in Halbrook as well, but she hadn't. She was clearly protecting James and her rebel network.

Serene's mouth tightened. "We will take him to Duvan to stand trial."

"I can accompany you and bear witness to the council of his treason," Tamar said.

"Thank you." Serene turned to the commander. "I would like you to leave several of your men with us, but I want you to return to Iden."

The commander's eyes narrowed. "Very well. And what of the Rose?"

"I have decided to accept his offer. He will come with us as our prisoner. Serai Nadir should be able to help us gauge his honesty, since she knows most of the people he will be informing us about."

The commander glanced at Bennick, who refused to look at him. "Fine," Commander Markam said. "I will return to Iden with the Mortisian prisoners we were able to recover."

"No." Serene once again looked to Tamar. "I would like to set them free, with you as a witness. Do you have the means of making sure they are helped to their homes?"

The woman looked a little surprised, but there was relief and joy in her eyes as well. "Of course, Princess. It would be my pleasure. Thank you."

The commander blinked. "Forgive me, but we have nothing to gain by doing that."

"We have everything to gain," Serene argued. "By freeing those men, we will show our compassion to all of Eyrinthia." She then turned to her cousin. "Imara, I strongly suggest you return to Zennor."

"No," the petite princess answered calmly. "I fully intend to look Serjah Desfan Cassian in the eye and know for myself if he deserves you."

Serene's mouth twitched, but her eyes were serious. "That is your final word?"

The Zennorian princess grinned. "You're quite stuck with me."

Serene's chest lifted on a breath, and she nodded. "Then our course is decided."

Clare stood alone on the quiet balcony that overlooked the grounds of Tamar Nadir's manor, watching the sun rise. It looked like it always had, a subtle glow that spread over the sky, slowly dispelling the heavy darkness of night. Only this time, she was watching it happen from Mortise.

The sun warmed her skin, but the dented tin soldier was cool in her hand.

It hardly seemed real that she was in Mortise. That she had buried her brother yesterday.

Bennick had pulled Eliot's body aside so he could be buried in his own grave. It was a kindness she didn't have the words to thank him for. Bennick and Venn had dug the grave and Wilf, Dirk, and Cardon had helped her and Vera prepare his body.

She didn't think she would ever forget what it had felt like, standing beside Eliot's grave as his wrapped body was lowered inside.

Bennick had stood beside her, his hand wrapped around hers. His silent strength, the comfort his nearness brought her . . . it was what kept her from feeling like she might float away.

She had loved her brother, despite everything, just as he had loved her. In the end, despite his many betrayals, he had chosen to save her life. He had known what would happen when he shouted that warning—and he had done it anyway.

After Eliot's burial, Bennick had to leave to help prepare for their departure. Wilf had remained with her, just the two of them staring at the freshly covered grave.

It was strange to think that mere months ago, she had thought this hulking bear of a man might be trying to kill her. Somehow, they had become friends.

"Death is not easy to understand," Wilf had said, his low voice softer than she had ever heard it. "Especially when one is taken unexpectedly. But you cannot let the grief overtake you. You can feel it, but don't let it consume you."

"I won't." She pursed her lips. "I don't know what to tell my brothers," she admitted. "I want to send a letter with the commander, but . . . What can I say to them? He was a traitor."

"Tell them he died protecting you. That is the truth, and they don't need to know the rest."

Tears built in her eyes and she slipped her hand in his, feeling the rough calluses on his skin. "Thank you, Wilf," she whispered.

He looked startled by the contact, but he did not pull away. And when he squeezed her hand a second later, a smile pulled at her lips.

Even now, standing on Serai Nadir's balcony, Clare smiled again as she remembered that moment.

Footsteps sounded behind her, and her body tightened as Bennick joined her, a physical reaction to his nearness. She wondered if that innate awareness of him would ever go away.

He came to stand at the stone railing beside her, his eyes sweeping the view. Dawn had washed the trees with shades of yellow, orange, and pink. It made the surrounding forest seem otherworldly. "Were you able to sleep?" he asked.

"A little. You?"

He nodded, but she wasn't sure she believed him. The purple shadows under his eyes were dark and he looked worn. "We'll be ready to leave within the hour," he said. "Serai Nadir will catch up with us in a couple of days. She wants to make sure the Mortisian prisoners are taken care of first."

"I like her."

"So do I." He squinted toward the sprawling forest they would have to pass through. "Traveling together is the right decision," he said, almost to himself. "Sending Serene on an alternate path, splitting our forces . . . It wouldn't be wise. Serai

Nadir has reviewed our stops, and we've made a few adjustments. I don't care if it offends Desfan or upsets Newlan. We'll only be staying with nobles Serai Nadir recommends."

"And we'll be following the Rose's advice as well," Clare added quietly.

Bennick's jaw tightened. "Yes." He glanced at her closed fist. "What do you have there?"

She was sure he was trying to distract her, but she opened her hand anyway, revealing the toy soldier.

A fleeting smile crossed Bennick's face. "Mark would be glad to know you still carry it."

"It's a piece of home." The corner of her mouth lifted slowly. "It also makes me think of you."

He grunted, studying the chipped paint. "We're both battered, I suppose."

She shook her head. "You may not be perfect, Bennick Markam, but you're perfect for me."

He didn't respond, and his gaze dropped.

Clare felt a tug low in her stomach. "Something is bothering you," she said quietly. "You haven't been yourself since Wexon."

Since he'd interrogated the Rose.

Tension bunched his shoulders, and she expected him to deny it.

He didn't.

"I learned something about my father," he said, the dawn outlining his strong profile. His throat worked, as if he had to force the words out. "It's his fault, Clare. All of it. The reason the Rose hates me, why he specifically targeted you . . . It's all his fault."

Her forehead creased. "I don't understand. How is it his fault?"

His jaw locked, his eyes on the horizon.

Clare touched his arm, her voice soft. "You can tell me anything, Bennick."

He twisted toward her, his eyes shadowed, his expression almost sick. "The Rose is his son."

Clare could only stare, her breath frozen in her lungs. The words were impossible. Horrible.

Bennick shoved a hand through his hair, his short laugh brittle. "Fates, it sounds insane, doesn't it? The Rose and I share blood. He's my half-brother. And my father knew the truth the entire time and didn't tell me."

Her fingers tightened on his arm. "Bennick, I . . . I'm sorry."

He shook his head. "You don't need to be sorry. I shouldn't have brought it up. You have enough on your mind."

She increased the pressure on his arm, forcing him to face her. She met his gaze, her jaw set. "I love you, Bennick Markam. That means I'm always with you. No matter what comes, we face it together."

He swallowed, his fingers catching hers. "I spoke with Serene this morning."

The unexpected words threw her. "What did you talk about?"

The skin around his eyes tightened. "You returning to Iden."

She blinked. "I don't understand. Why would I go back? I'm needed here. I'm the decoy."

"I know. But if you wanted to go back and mourn Eliot's death with your family . . ." Bennick's hand flexed around hers. "I can send Wilf and Dirk with you. My father isn't far ahead— you can catch up to him easily. We'll make it look like Serene is returning to Iden by using you as a decoy."

Her chest felt too tight. "Would that protect Serene? My go- ing back?"

"It might, for a while." His brow furrowed. "But I don't want you to think about her. I want you to make this decision for *you*. The king won't release you from your oath, but you would be safe."

"Safer than here, with you?"

A muscle throbbed in his cheek. "Yes."

Her heart pounded. "It seems you've thought this through."

"I have. Do you wish to go?"

"Do you *want* me to go?"

He stared at her, his face nearly expressionless, it was so carefully blank. "What I want is irrelevant."

Her eyes did not leave his as she eased closer, their chests brushing. His breath caught, and her heart tripped. "I disagree," she said quietly.

His blue eyes were serious. "I don't want you to feel trapped. Fates know you haven't had enough choices, but I can give you this one."

"I rather love you for that," she whispered.

Tension bracketed his mouth. "Will you go, then?"

Clare studied his face before shaking her head. "No. I want to help protect Serene. I want this alliance with Mortise to succeed. I need there to be peace, so Thomas and Mark don't have to grow up afraid. I will see this through. With you." She squeezed his hand. "I'm always with you, remember?"

He searched her face, his expression unreadable. He wasn't even breathing. "Are you sure?"

"Yes."

He reached out with his free hand, his fingers sweeping back a lock of brown hair from her temple. He looped it behind her ear and then his palm cupped her cheek. Her heart thrilled when he dropped his chin and pressed his mouth to hers.

His kiss helped to calm every storm in her heart, and she knew she would always love him.

In the chaos of her ever-changing world, he was one thing that remained absolute.

Clare's head rested against the rocking carriage. She wasn't asleep, but her eyes were closed and she let the conversation drift around her. Serene and Imara sat side by side across from her, and Clare knew without looking that Serene wore a maid's dress. Clare had foregone the crown, but even her traveling gown was fine enough to mark her as the princess. Even though they traveled together, she still needed to be the decoy. The target.

Vera sat next to her, and she had also been quiet for the past several minutes.

Outside the carriage, horses snorted and soldiers spoke to each other, some even joking.

Clare didn't enjoy riding horses, but she wished she could be out there with Bennick. Even if it meant she might be within sight of the Rose.

Fates, she still couldn't believe they shared blood. In the end, it didn't mean anything. Bennick was the best man Clare had ever known, and his character was unmarred by his relation to the Rose. But she knew it troubled him.

The carriage rolled to a halt, and Clare opened her eyes. A peek through the curtains proved that they were still deep in the Mortisian forest.

"What's going on?" Imara asked, ending her earlier conversation with Serene. "Why are we stopping?"

"I don't know. It's too soon to set up camp." Serene frowned, then reached to push open the carriage door.

She didn't get far. Cardon was there, his hand out to stop her descent. "Stay inside, please."

Serene frowned. "What's going on?"

"A tree fell over the road. We can't go around, and the road is too narrow to turn around. It will take us a little time to move it." He looked back toward the front of their procession, and his eyes suddenly narrowed. His shoulders tensed. "Get back inside."

Unease wavered in Clare's gut.

Serene's eyebrows lowered. "Why? What—"

"In the trees!" Bennick's shout boomed a second before the first volley of arrows hit the carriage, the soldiers, the horses.

The animals shrieked in pain and men screamed. Clare heard Bennick yell orders, heard swords being drawn.

Cardon shoved Serene inside, slamming the door closed and sealing them in. Serene grabbed the handle with a curse, but it wouldn't budge.

Clare jerked and Vera cried out when the next round of arrows slammed into the carriage. One shot through the curtained window, shattering glass.

Serene growled. "We'll all be killed if we stay here." She turned back to the door and thudded her fist against it. "Cardon!"

Clare's heart thundered in her chest, and she could feel the blood drain from her face when she heard the yells of men, the clash of swords—the enemy was on the ground with them now.

Serene muttered a curse and pounded the door again. She nearly fell when it was wrenched open. Cardon's expression was fierce, and he grabbed Serene's arm and hauled her to him. "Dirk brought the horses," he gritted out. "You ride with me."

"But—"

Locked in the shelter of Cardon's arms, Serene was dragged away from the carriage, her words left unspoken.

Wilf took his place at once. He grabbed Clare, lifting her like she weighed nothing. Worry cut through her—he hadn't fully healed since his stabbing—but as he crushed her to him and carried her away from the carriage, she had a bigger concern. "Vera!"

"Dirk will get her," Wilf said, his voice rough.

Clare managed a peek around his shoulder and saw that Imara's bodyguards were already grabbing her, and that Dirk was waiting beside them, ready to grab Vera.

Her heart pounded as she took in the rest of the chaos that she managed to see. Bodies and arrows littered the ground. "Bennick?" she gasped.

"He's fine," Wilf growled, tightening his hold on her. "Stay in my arms."

He wasn't really giving her a choice. His hold was crushing, and he was hunched over her. She didn't notice any more arrows flying. Was it because they were fighting on the ground now, or because they'd already managed to kill most of their attackers?

Her stomach heaved when she saw a soldier on the ground, riddled with several arrows. His eyes were vacant.

Beside him, Zephan also lay dead, the Mortisian traitor's hands still bound.

Panic gripped her. Fates, where was the Rose?

They reached the horses. Cardon shoved Serene onto the nearest one and then he swung up behind her and gathered the reins. With little urging, the horse bolted down the road, hooves pounding up clouds of dust as they headed back toward Serai Nadir's manor.

Wilf threw Clare into the saddle and she scrambled in her long skirts to find her seat as he jumped on behind her. The poor horse let out a protest at the combined weight, but Wilf ignored that as he shoved the reins into Clare's hands. "Steer us up the road," he ordered, the rasp of steel announcing the draw of his sword.

Clare kicked the horse forward, her grip on the reins too tight as the horse shot forward. She gripped hard with her knees, desperate to keep her seat as she bounced along with the animal's fast gait. Throwing a glance over her shoulder and past Wilf's hulking mass, she saw Vera alone on a horse, quickly gaining on Clare.

Imara was on her horse, one of her guards riding behind her to protect her back. The other Zennorian guard remained with Dirk, the two of them turning to face the attackers who rushed toward them, screaming at each other in Mortisian.

Stop her! Get the princess!

They wore no uniforms, but it was clearly a well-organized trap.

Heart in her throat, Clare searched through the fighting, past the abandoned carriage. Her heart nearly stopped when she finally caught sight of Bennick and Venn on the road, fighting together to keep the attackers at bay.

They were outnumbered, fighting three men each. And there weren't enough Devendran soldiers left standing.

Wilf's chest was hard behind her, and his sword caught the light as he swung the blade, striking out at an attacker who lunged for them.

The horse threw its head and stumbled, trying to jerk away from the enemy.

Then suddenly Wilf was gone, dragged off the horse by one of the attackers.

Clare cried out his name and fought to keep her seat on the stomping horse, but Wilf was already rolling to his feet, his sword swinging in a wide arc that kept his attacker back.

The horse continued to sidestep, and Clare could not pull him into submission. His eyes were rolling, his head tossing as he nearly hit into one of the trees.

The branches swayed, then snapped, and Clare screamed as one of the archers dropped from the leafy canopy and landed behind her on the horse.

Fear exploded in her chest and Clare tried to shove him off, but one steely arm clamped around her chest, pinning her arms and pulling her close against him.

His horrible voice rasped in her ear, "Got you, Princess." He jerked the reins from her and wheeled the horse around.

Clare struggled, desperate to get away, not caring if she fell off the panicked horse.

Wilf roared like an enraged bear, fighting the men that blocked his way to her. And beyond him, Clare spotted Bennick in the same moment he spun and caught sight of her.

Even from this distance, she could see the fury flare in his eyes.

The man behind her whistled sharply, a trilling sound that pierced through the sounds of battle.

It needed no interpretation. It was a call to finish. A call to retreat. They had gotten what they came for.

At least, they thought they had.

They thought she was Serene. This was an abduction.

"*No!*" Venn's gutted shout jerked Clare's attention, and fear blasted through her when she saw one of the Mortisian attackers had also gotten onto Vera's horse. Though the girl screamed and struggled, the man held her fast as he galloped for the trees.

Venn bolted after her, but there was no way he would reach her. Not before she disappeared into the forest.

An attacker lunged at Venn.

Clare cried out, but the warning came too late; he was too

focused on chasing after Vera.

The Mortisian tackled Venn to the ground, and Clare saw the flash of a knife.

Panic gripped her, but she lost sight of their struggle and her eyes locked on Bennick.

He stood on the road, several long yards away from her, but his blazing eyes were trained on her. His sword was drawn and bloody, his face set as he darted forward. He was coming for her.

It happened in an instant.

A man sprung up behind Bennick and his sword punched through his unprotected back, tearing through his body and coming out his front.

Bennick's entire body jerked, his eyes wide with shock and pain.

Clare's heart stopped.

"BENNICK!"

She hardly recognized that the horrible shriek came from her.

Bennick fell to his knees as the attacker wrenched the sword from his body and Bennick shuddered as he fell, his body going still when he hit the ground.

Clare was still screaming, she realized distantly. She didn't stop, even as she thrashed against the man who held her. She shouted Bennick's name over and over, an endless cry that consumed every part of her. Every muscle strained and burned. Every nerve screamed to be at his side, to somehow save him.

But the arms that held her were unbreakable.

The horse wheeled around and Clare lost sight of Bennick as they plunged into the trees, the air still ringing with her screams.

THE STORY CONTINUES IN

ROYAL CAPTIVE

BOOK 3 OF THE FATE OF EYRINTHIA SERIES

FIRST THE FLAMES . . .

When Desfan Cassian, the future ruler of Mortise, skips his fifteenth birthday celebration so he can gamble in the slums, he knows his father won't be pleased. Then again, the serjan hasn't been happy with him in years. And while Desfan anticipates a reprimand for his latest transgression, he doesn't expect to be thrown out of the palace and exiled onto a patrol ship for the next year.

THEN FROM THE ASHES . . .

Furious to be trapped on the same sea that stole his family four years ago, Desfan is fully prepared to hate his new life. After all, the *Phoenix* is run by a strict captain, and Desfan's annoying new bodyguard, Karim, is his constant shadow. But when Desfan learns that a group of dangerous pirates may have been behind the deaths of his mother and sisters, he's suddenly committed to hunting down the truth—no matter the risk.

HE WILL RISE.

Fire & Ash* is a novella set in the world of the *Royal Decoy* series. While it is a prequel story, it is best enjoyed after reading *Royal Spy*.

THE DECOY

AND THE

BODYGUARD

A FATE OF EYRINTHIA SHORT STORY

HEATHER FROST

THE DECOY

AND THE

BODYGUARD

A FATE OF EYRINTHIA SHORT STORY

HEATHER FROST

BENNICK

BENNICK SWUNG DOWN FROM HIS horse, taking in the narrow street with a practiced sweep of his gaze. Lower Iden could be a dangerous place, even in daylight. People walking the street had edged back from the mounted palace guards, but they'd frozen mid-step when they recognized the royal crest on the carriage. Men, women, and children had stopped to gawk, and even more spectators leaned out of their windows, craning their necks for a better look.

Bennick's shoulders tightened under their stares. He didn't appreciate the attention the carriage had drawn, but he hadn't planned this excursion. The king had spoken, and the commander had made arrangements—one of them slightly treasonous.

Bennick wasn't supposed to be here. Despite the king's

wishes for total secrecy, the commander had sent Bennick as an extra precaution.

He glanced at the house they'd stopped in front of, noting the door that sagged a bit on old hinges. Despite that sign of disrepair, the windows were clean, especially compared to the others along the street. The building row was a mix of shops and homes, all smashed together. Scents from a nearby bakery helped cover some of the uglier smells of the city, but the signs of poverty were obvious in the wear of the buildings—and the people—who called Lower Iden home.

Bennick handed the reins of his mount to a palace guardsman and strode to the carriage door, cutting off the guard who had just reached for the handle. The look the middle-aged man gave Bennick was filled with several questions, but Bennick only flashed a wordless smile.

He wasn't here to assuage the man's curiosity. His job was to make sure nothing happened to the young woman inside the carriage, because she was not the princess's newest maid. No, she was much more than that.

Bennick pulled open the carriage door and extended a hand.

Long fingers emerged and slid over his. The contact was simple, but it tightened something in Bennick's chest. Her dark hair was braided into a crown around her head, curling tendrils of loose hair brushing her rounded cheeks. The faded blue of her dress complimented her darker skin and her deep blue eyes were focused beyond him, her jaw set as he helped her down to the cobbled street. Though her face was carefully smooth, he could feel the tension through their joined hands.

He squeezed her fingers, an instinctive offer of comfort, and her eyes snapped to his.

The full force of Clare Ellington's attention stalled his thoughts, but he managed a small smile.

It was only meant to be reassuring, but when her eyes flared with recognition, he wanted to curse.

He hadn't expected to be recognized; he'd even assured the commander that Clare would *not* recognize him. They had only met once, briefly, last night—when she had saved the princess's life and forever changed all their fates.

Clearly, he'd underestimated her. Something he swore he'd never be foolish enough to do again.

Her spine straightened and her soft face hardened with an expression he couldn't quite read. Suspicion? Anxiety? Perhaps both?

His mouth opened, though he wasn't sure what he would say. His father would want him to remain anonymous, so a denial would be best: *You must be confused. We've never met.*

What he wanted to say was: *Yes, it's me, but please don't say anything in front of the guards. I'll explain later.*

He never got the chance to decide on a reply. The crooked door banged open and two small boys shot into the street, calling Clare's name.

She dropped Bennick's hand immediately and ran forward, catching her brothers and pulling them into a fierce embrace.

"What happened?" the taller boy demanded. "You didn't come home!"

"I'm sorry," she said, her low voice sincere even though she didn't offer an explanation.

Her brothers didn't seem to even notice her lack of answer. Their focus had shifted to the carriage and soldiers. The older boy eyed Bennick, his eyes widening. "Fates," he muttered in disbelief.

Bennick tried for another reassuring smile, but he wasn't sure this one succeeded either, because when Clare glanced over her shoulder and saw him watching, she stiffened. "Let's go inside," she said to her brothers. "I'll explain everything."

The smaller boy—maybe ten years old—grabbed onto her hand, and the way Clare held fast and led him toward the open door of the house . . . It was a clear act of comfort, protection, and love.

When the commander had informed Bennick that Clare Ellington had accepted the decoy position, Bennick had assumed her reasons were simple—coin. Knowing her status as a kitchen maid, learning the location of her home in Lower Iden, it had made sense. The position was dangerous, but Clare had demonstrated her bravery last night in the castle hallway when the rebels had ambushed them, and the promise of gold was a powerful motivator.

But standing here now, Bennick realized the real reason she had agreed to become the decoy. It was for her brothers. Because whether she lived or died in service to the crown, her brothers would be provided for, and that was clearly a sacrifice Clare was willing to make.

That level of love was staggering, and as Bennick watched them disappear into their home, he made them a silent promise.

Whatever it took, he would protect Clare Ellington so she could always come home to those boys.

———————

Rain slashed down in a furious deluge, drenching Bennick and the other soldiers as they made their way back to the castle. Though it was late afternoon, early darkness covered the city due to the storm clouds that crowded the sky.

Bennick blinked rapidly to clear his vision. He couldn't afford to duck his head or pull his hood too far forward. He needed to remain alert. The horses tossed their wet heads, their hooves spraying water from the puddles on the cobblestones, and the carriage rattled in front of Bennick. He preferred to keep it in view, so he let other soldiers ride ahead of it. Rain pelted off the canvas roof and streamed over the rotating wheels, and thunder rolled. He knew the spring storm fit the mood of the young woman inside.

He had given the Ellingtons all the time he could. Mistress Keller—the caretaker hired for the boys—had lingered in the carriage at first, giving Clare time alone with her brothers. But once she'd joined them, she had pushed open the curtains in the kitchen window, giving Bennick glimpses of Clare and her brothers as they'd talked and played throughout the day.

He hated that he'd had to end things for them. He could still hear the cries of the younger boy as he'd begged for Clare to stay. Mistress Keller had been forced to hold him back as Clare exited the house and moved for the carriage. Her eyes had been covered with a wet sheen and her hands fisted at her sides. Her pain was impossible to miss, and she flinched when her youngest brother screamed her name.

Bennick should probably be worried about what he'd say to Clare once they returned to the castle, because he would need to pull her aside and explain the delicate situation he was in. Being an anonymous guard wasn't an option at this point, and he couldn't risk the king finding out he had been with her today. Newlan did not take any betrayal lightly, no matter how slight or well-intentioned.

That was what he *should* be worried about but, truthfully, he was just worried about Clare. Saying goodbye to her brothers— even if it was only temporary—had clearly been torturous.

Lightning split the sky, and in that breath before the glow of light faded and the crack of thunder boomed, Bennick saw masked men rush into the street ahead of them.

Bennick yelled a warning, though the thunder's roar nearly drowned him out. Thankfully, the other guards were paying attention. They drew their swords and half of them yelled an attack while the others rallied around the stalled carriage, taking defensive positions.

Bennick kneed his horse forward, his grip on his sword tight despite the rain. He put himself between an attacker and the carriage. The man glared up at him, a kerchief tied around the lower half of his face. A rebel, no doubt.

The blade spun in Bennick's hand and the man leapt back, only to dodge around Bennick's horse and leap for the carriage door.

Bennick jumped off his horse, tackling the man to the ground. The impact jolted him to his bones, but he kept a grip on his sword as he rolled, ignoring the bruising bite of the cobblestones. He slammed a hand onto the road, grounding himself as he shoved to his feet and swung his blade, meeting the sword of his attacker. The man was strong, but not skilled—Bennick felled the rebel and pivoted, rain sluicing off his blade.

Screams filled the street, punctuated by the clash of swords and the pounding of the rain. They were being attacked on all sides, outnumbered and unable to move the carriage forward because crates had been shoved into the narrow street, blocking the way.

The perfect ambush.

And then everything got worse.

Clare Ellington was in the street, her fingers wrapped around the carriage door handle, her posture crouched as she peered through the blur of rain that was quickly soaking her.

"Get back inside!" The shout ripped up his throat and Clare whipped toward him, her blue eyes wide.

She had heard him, but she wasn't moving.

He gritted his teeth. "Get inside!"

Her eyes flashed behind him, horror striking her face. "Look out!"

He pivoted without hesitation, ducking to avoid the blade swinging for his neck. He brought his sword up, feeling the jarring blow throughout his whole body. From the corner of his eye, he saw Clare dart for the nearest alley, and he cursed when he saw one of the rebels tear after her.

They couldn't know who she was, but they had to assume she was important. They would kill her just to show they could—to prove no one associated with the royals was safe.

Bennick kicked out at his opponent, his boot crashing into the side of the man's knee. There was a terrible crack and the man collapsed with a howl. Bennick didn't even take the time to kill him. The man was no longer a threat, not able to stop him from chasing after Clare. That was all that mattered.

Bennick ran, charging away from the ambush and past the hunched figures of the beggars and thieves that lived in the alley.

He burst out of the alley and muttered a curse at the size of the crowd that congested the street. He had to shove through them, but thanks to their shouts and pointing fingers, he knew exactly which alley to dart into next. He had to leap over a pile of broken crates, but near the end of the alley he caught sight of the rebel.

He pushed himself faster, ignoring the burn in his lungs. It came more from panic than strain, and he was desperate for more speed. By the time he emerged on the next street, he was drawing closer to the attacker—and Clare.

She ran with surprising speed, her long skirt fisted in her hands. She threw a look over her shoulder, looking past the people who scrambled to get out of their way and clearly spotting the rebel who was steadily gaining on her. Fear flared in her eyes, and then she was diving into another alley.

Once Bennick had a clear shot, he jerked out a throwing dagger and hurled it at the rebel.

The blade sank into his back and he fell with a grunt, hitting the ground hard.

He didn't get up, and Bennick didn't slow down to check if he was still alive. He needed to stop Clare. She was running *away* from the castle, and for how well-organized the ambush had been, he was fairly certain there would be more rebels nearby. If she didn't stop, she might run right into their arms.

"Stop!" The command burst out of him, but she didn't slow. In fact, she seemed to speed up.

He threw his sword aside, not daring to risk hurting her as he lunged. His fingers brushed her arm but failed to grasp her.

She cried out from the ghosting touch, and he didn't have enough air in his lungs to assure her she was safe. She was too close to the end of the alley, and they couldn't afford to plunge into the street and garner more attention.

He grabbed the only thing he could—her skirt.

He only meant to tug her to a halt but she tripped, falling hard to the ground with her palms flashing out to catch herself. He tried to rear back, but the momentum of her fall dragged him forward and he landed on top of her.

Breath slammed out of his lungs, and for a moment he was stunned. Then he realized he was probably crushing her and he quickly pushed up, knees bracketing her sides as he grabbed her shoulder and twisted her onto her back so he could see her face.

Her palms hit his chest, her own chest rising and falling too quickly, her entire body shuddering as she pushed against him. Strands of hair that had fallen from her braided crown were plastered on her forehead, cheeks, and neck. The rain splashed against her skin and soaked her dress.

Clare's eyes leapt to his face, which hovered mere breaths above hers.

Something about her wide blue eyes staring up at him made his own fears spike.

A simple shift of the fates, and it would have been the rebel who tackled her. She could already be dead.

Tension coiled in his shoulders. "I told you to stop," he ground out. "Why didn't you?"

She stared up at him, a shiver wracking her body. Lightning flashed, a crack of thunder right behind it.

His fingers curled more tightly around her shoulders. "Why didn't you stop?" he demanded.

"I didn't know it was you!" she snapped, anger rolling over her face.

That was the moment he became aware of every place their bodies touched. The way he was crouched over her. The warmth seeping from her body into his. His knees were braced against her sides, and he could feel the knife belted at her waist as it pressed into his leg. They were so close, he could feel her shallow breaths fan his cheek, feel the pounding of her heart.

Fates, he had frightened her. Perhaps even more than she had frightened *him*.

A raindrop fell from his nose and hit her chin, and it was her flinch that broke the tense moment that stretched between them.

He let go of her shoulders and levered back, moving into a crouch beside her. He searched her for any sign of harm, his voice was more temperate as he asked, "Did I hurt you?"

"No." She pushed into a seated position, glancing past him.

"What happened to the man chasing me?"

"He's not a problem anymore."

She blinked, and he realized that may have sounded ominous, rather than reassuring.

Clare crossed her arms over her chest as she shivered, clearing her throat before asking, "What happened to the other soldiers?"

"They were losing," he said grimly. He extended a hand. "We need to get you to the castle."

Clare eyed his offered palm, and for a moment he thought she wouldn't take it. But then her hand was in his, just like it had been hours before. But instead of helping her down from the carriage, he was pulling her to her feet in a cramped alleyway.

Oh, the difference several hours could make.

A wince crossed her face, and he immediately flipped her hand over.

Red scrapes cut across her palm, blood welling from the largest one. He thumbed the edge, feeling his jaw set. "I'm sorry. I didn't mean to hurt you."

She eyed him almost warily, as if surprised by his words. She pulled her hand away. "You didn't hurt me. I'm fine."

He dropped his chin in a half-nod, accepting her words. His empty hand fell and he moved to retrieve his sword. A quick examination revealed some minor scratches, but it could have been worse.

He sheathed the blade at his waist, fingers wrapped around the hilt. When he looked back at Clare, it was to see her scowling at a toy soldier in her hand.

He quirked an eyebrow. "An interesting choice of weapon."

Her head snapped up, and she studied him carefully.

He kept his expression smooth and remained where he was. Having a little distance between them seemed like a wise course, since he'd clearly terrified her with his tackle.

Clare's fist closed around the tin soldier. "It was a gift from my brother," she finally said, her voice a little edged. "He thought it might protect me."

The corner of his mouth lifted. "A kind gift, then."

She said nothing, only stared at him.

Fates, it was impossible to tell what she was thinking.

Why it was so important to know her every thought—especially when it came to him—was a mystery. They had more pressing things at the moment, like getting to safety.

Bennick's fingers clenched around the hilt of his belted sword. "We need to get back to the castle. Stay close to me."

Clare pocketed the toy soldier and walked beside him to the end of the alley. They paused there, standing so close he could feel her arm brush his.

He pushed through that distraction and eyed the street. It was emptying quickly as everyone rushed to find shelter from the storm.

Beside him, Clare cleared her throat. "Those men who attacked us. Who were they?"

The street was empty of visible threats, so he stepped out of the alley. "I think they were rebels," he told her. His voice was low, even though no one was close enough to hear anything through the drumming of the rain.

"Why would they attack the carriage?" Clare asked.

"It came from the royal stable," he said. "That would have been enough for them. Most likely one of their spies saw the carriage leave this morning. They had hours to plan the ambush."

"Are they loyal to Carrigan?" she asked, hesitancy in her tone.

"Doubtful. Rumors say he fled to some mountaintop in Zennor."

Clare became quiet as they walked through the rain, skirting around the larger puddles. There was a worn sort of sadness around her, and it shriveled something inside of him. Maybe that was why he felt compelled to say, "It's good you didn't get back in the carriage. One of them got past me." He gave her a half-smile. "You could have obeyed when I asked you to stop running, though. My sword would've appreciated it."

Her mouth twitched. "Was it damaged?"

"Merely scuffed."

"Then it and my hands have something in common."

He huffed a soft laugh, the wryness of her tone catching him by surprise. "I *am* sorry for hurting you, but I didn't think you'd stop."

She eyed him. "I didn't get your name."

He didn't look at her, even though he could feel her studying his profile. "Venn Grannard." The lie came easily, though after it was out, he wanted to wince.

The truth would come out eventually. After the events of the day, he had certainly made an impression and she would remember him. He would hopefully have a private moment where he could fully explain things, but for now, it was *vital* that the king not learn he had been here.

It wouldn't be ideal for her to say Venn had been with her, but it would be better than the truth. The king would not take kindly to the fact that the commander had spilled his secret to Bennick. But if Venn had been sent, the commander could probably convince the king that he'd merely told Venn that Clare was a new maid. The king might believe that.

He would not believe it if Bennick had been sent. He would guess that the commander had told his son everything.

If Bennick had the time—and the ability to think clearly— he might have considered telling Clare the truth now. But as it was, they needed to focus on getting out of this mess. He would deal with the repercussions later.

"You must be well-trusted," she said.

He looked to her. "What makes you say that?"

"You must be the youngest royal bodyguard to ever serve in Devendra."

The corner of his mouth tipped up. "You wouldn't believe how many people underestimate me because of it." He spotted three masked men as they stepped out of an alley a dozen yards ahead of them. He touched Clare's arm, slowing their steps. He knew the moment she saw them, because she shifted closer to him.

"There's a tavern to the left," he said quietly. "We'll hide there until they pass." He kept his hand on her arm as he guided her across the street, careful to keep his body between her and the rebels searching for them.

The tavern was crowded, but he shouldered his way through the thick knot of people. Clare was right behind him, echoing his steps as they tried to lose themselves in the crowd. The men and women in the common room were eating, drinking, and laughing, and they needed to blend in.

Bennick stopped and drew Clare around so he could block her body from the view of the door. He smiled down at her, ignoring the raindrops rolling down his hair, face, and neck. "Act as though nothing is wrong," he told her. "Smile."

Her mouth lifted into a small grin, though anxiety sparked in her eyes.

"I think they saw us," he said, still smiling, in case anyone around them was looking. Her hands were shaking, and he went on instinct, folding his fingers around hers with a gentle pressure. "Easy," he whispered. "This will be over soon."

Her tension was still obvious, but at least the shaking mostly stopped. She peeked around his arm and stiffened, her hands tightening against his. "I see one," she whispered.

Battle calm had already settled around him from the moment he saw them on the street. "Has he seen us?"

"No, he's still searching the crowd."

Bennick glanced past her, toward the group of men standing right behind them. They were clearly friends, enjoying a drink. "Any sign of the others?" he asked her.

"No." Clare's gaze darted to his. "What do we do?"

His lips pressed together. "Forgive me."

She frowned, but he didn't take the time to explain. He pushed her into the nearest man behind her, who spat out a curse when his drink spilled.

"Oy!" He rounded on Clare with a heated glare, shaking out his ale-drenched arm. "Watch it, fool!"

Clare stumbled back a step, her shoulders knocking into Bennick's chest.

"You yelling at my girl?" Bennick demanded, the boom of his voice making Clare jump.

He didn't wait for the man to answer before swinging his fist, and Clare ducked under his arm as his knuckles connected with the drunk man's jaw.

Bennick only had to throw a few punches before the brawl he had intended to spark broke out with full force. As the room exploded into chaos, he ducked away from the center of things and spotted Clare. He grabbed her wrist and yanked her to his chest. "We'll hold out until the city guard gets here," he called against her ear, the crashing sounds of hurtled chairs, overthrown tables, and shouting nearly swallowing his words. "The rebels won't risk capture."

A man stumbled into them, his elbow jabbing Bennick's side. He threw his arms around Clare, sheltering her as much as possible.

Her fingers dug into his arms, her head ducked against his chest. The trust in that gesture surprised him—and warmed him.

A moment later, a shout cut through the room. "The Guard! City Guard is here!"

The fighting continued, but those who heard the warning disentangled themselves and bolted.

One of the men rushing for the door would have clipped them if Bennick hadn't twisted away, pulling Clare with him.

A gasp burst out of her. "Venn!"

The warning in her cry was clear and Bennick didn't hesitate. His own belt was hard to reach with her standing so close to him, so he snatched the knife at her waist. He spun, shoving Clare aside in the same motion as he buried the knife in the rebel's gut.

The man gasped and Bennick jerked the blade free, watching as the man collapsed. Adrenaline pounded through him as he turned back to Clare.

His heart stalled.

She was sprawled on the floor, unmoving, her eyes closed.

He dropped to his knees, his stomach a yawning pit as he lost hold of the bloody knife. It clattered to the wooden floor. "Clare? Clare, can you hear me?" He laid the pads of his first fingers along the column of her neck, searching for her pulse even as his eyes darted over her. Her chest was rising and falling—she was alive, and there were no apparent signs of injury. The corner of a table was near enough that he could guess what had happened, though.

He'd pushed her and she'd fallen, hitting the table on her way to the floor.

He cringed, feeling the knot already rising on the back of her head. Thankfully, there was no blood.

Footsteps scuffed the floor behind him and the point of a sword touched his back. "Get away from the girl," a soldier barked.

Other members of the city guard moved throughout the room, putting an end to any lingering fights.

Bennick glanced over his shoulder at the guard standing over him. "I'm Captain Bennick Markam. I—"

"I know who you are." The blade was lowered at once and the young guard actually reddened. "Sorry, Captain."

"Do you have a horse?" Bennick asked. He needed to get Clare to the castle. He didn't think the damage to her head was serious, but he wanted a physician to be the judge of that.

"No. But I can get one." The guard sheathed his sword and hurried away.

Bennick twisted back to Clare, seeing the bloody knife he'd dropped. He attempted to clean it, but the quick job wasn't great, so he pocketed the blade; he would clean it and return it to her later.

As he shifted his attention back to Clare, he caught sight of the toy soldier her brother had given her. It was lying just under the table. It must have bounced out of her pocket when she hit the floor. His fingers wrapped around it just as another city guard member strode up to him.

"What can you tell us about the brawl?" he asked.

Bennick slid the tin soldier into his pocket as he faced the guard. "I suspect there's a link to the rebels." He nodded to the body lying nearby. "I killed him, but he had friends. They may come looking for him. If they do, I need you to detain them for questioning."

The guard blinked. "But—you're leaving?"

Bennick gathered Clare into his arms, his heart tightening when her head lolled to rest against his chest. His grip on her firmed as he faced the guard. "I'm taking her to the castle. I'll be back as soon as I can." He told the soldier where the ambush had taken place and asked for the city guard to secure any bodies or prisoners at that scene as well.

Then he strode from the tavern, holding Clare close to his chest as he stepped into the rain.

The guardsman was waiting with a horse. "Borrowed him from the stable," he explained, speaking loud enough to be heard over the storm. "I assume his owner was mixed up in the brawl."

Though Bennick was loath to let go of Clare, he passed her to the guard so he could swing up onto the horse. Once she was settled back in his arms, he gathered up the reins. "Make sure no one disturbs any of the bodies until I return," Bennick told the guard. They may not recover any prisoners, but it was possible the bodies held clues.

The guard nodded, but Bennick was already turning the horse toward the castle, urging the animal into a trot.

He half-expected Clare to regain consciousness, with the rain still pouring down and the jarring clop of the horse, but her body only rocked against his, her cheek against his chest. His worry doubled with every moment she remained unconscious.

Finally, after minutes that stretched like hours, they rode through the castle gate. By some miracle of the fates, Venn was standing at the door.

His best friend's eyes narrowed as he bolted down the steps, his long dark ponytail swinging in the rain.

"What are you doing out here?" Bennick asked.

"I could ask you the same." Venn's gaze tracked over Clare, his brow furrowing.

"Later," Bennick said, cutting off any questions. He carefully lowered Clare into Venn's ready arms, his own feeling empty now. "Take her to the commander's suite. Use a side door."

Thankfully, the rain ensured only a minimal guard was outside to see them; they didn't need any more witnesses.

Venn frowned. "Is she all right?"

"She hit her head on a table. She needs a physician."

One of Venn's dark eyebrows ticked up. "And where are you going?"

"Back into the city."

"Do you need help?"

"No."

Venn's grip on Clare tightened. "Well, I'll be upset with you later for going into the city without me in the first place. I was on my way to find you. The commander said you left the grounds, but he wasn't specific about *why*."

Bennick ignored the unspoken question. "Take care of her, Venn."

"Of course." He glanced down at her rain-streaked face. "Who is she?"

"Clare." It was the first time Bennick had said her name aloud. It felt soft as it passed his lips, and yet every nerve in his body seemed to rise and take note.

He straightened in the saddle and wheeled the horse around before Venn could voice any more questions. And as he rode hard through the gate, he was already counting down the moments until he could see her again.

GLOSSARY

AKIVA *(ah-KEE-vah)* One of Liam's Mortisian contacts. Alias: Zeph.

AMIL HAVIM *(uh-MEEL hah-VEEM)* A Mortisian nobleman who served in Devendra with his father as an emissary of peace. Due to his father's murder in Devendra, he no longer supports the alliance.

ANOUSH *(ah-NOOSH)* A temporary member of the Mortisian council.

ARCAS *(AR-kus)* A kiv in the Mortisian city guard. Full name: Manusch Arcas.

AREN BUHARI DEMOI *(eh-RUHN boo-HAR-ee de-MOY)* The late queen of Devendra, mother to Serene and Grandeur. Was married to Newlan Demoi. Sister to Zaire Buhari, king of Zennor.

ASHEAR *(uh-SHEER)* A member of the Mortisian council. Full name: Duman Ashear.

BENNICK MARKAM *(BEN-ick MARK-ahm)* Captain of Serene's bodyguards. Commander Markam's son.

BRIDGET *(BRI-jeht)* The senior maid for Serene.

CARDON BRINHURST *(CAR-den BRIN-herst)* One of Serene's bodyguards. He has a distinctive scar on his cheek.

CARTER THELIN KAELIN *(CAR-tr THEL-in KAY-lin)* The second prince of Ryden and a close follower of Peter's. Also a dutiful pupil of his mother's.

CLARE ELLINGTON *(CLAIR EL-ing-tun)* The decoy for Serene. Former maid in the castle kitchen. Sister to Eliot, Thomas, and Mark Ellington.

COMMANDER DENNITH MARKAM *(DEN-ith MARK-ahm)* A high-ranking Devendran commander. Father to Bennick and married to Gweneth Markam.

DESFAN SAERNON CASSIAN *(DES-fawn SAIR-non CAS-ee-uhn)* The heir to the Mortisian throne and currently serving as regent due to his father's illness. His official title is *serjah*.

DEVENDRA *(duh-VEN-druh)* One of the kingdoms of Eyrinthia, ruled by the Demoi family.

DEVENDRAN *(duh-VEN-drun)* Relating to the kingdom of Devendra or its people.

DIRK ARKLOWE *(DIRK ARK-low)* One of Serene's bodyguards. He is the oldest of the guards and has protected the princess since birth.

DORMA *(DOHR-muh)* The largest Mortisian island.

DUVAN *(DOO-vahn)* The capital city of Mortise.

ELIOT ELLINGTON *(EL-ee-uht EL-ing-tun)* Clare's older brother. He is a Devendran city guardsman and a rebel who opposes King Newlan. Also known as Eliot Slaton. (Slaton was his mother's surname.)

ESSA *(EH-suh)* A member of the Mortisian council.

EYRINTHIA *(air-INTH-ee-uh)* The name of the known world. The four kingdoms of Eyrinthia are Devendra, Mortise, Ryden, and Zennor.

FARAH CASSIAN *(FAIR-uh CAS-ee-uhn)* Desfan's mother, the late seraijan of Mortise.

FLETCHER *(FLEH-chr)* Mia's day guard. Full name: Alun Fletcher.

GRANDEUR NEWLAN DEMOI *(GRAN-jer NEW-luhn de-MOY)* The crown prince of Devendra and heir to the throne. Serene's younger brother.

GRAYSON WINN KAELIN *(GRAY-suhn WIN KAY-lin)* The youngest prince of Ryden. He is the enforcer of his father's laws. Also known as the Black Hand.

GWENETH MARKAM *(GWEH-neth MARK-ahm)* Bennick's mother. She is married to Commander Dennith Markam.

HENRI KAELIN *(HEN-ree KAY-lin)* The king of Ryden. He is married to Iris Kaelin, and they have five sons.

IDEN *(EYE-den)* The capital city of Devendra.

IEANNAX *(EYE-ahn-ax)* A rare poison that delivers painless death. Originates from Zennor.

IMARA AIMETH BUHARI *(ih-MAR-uh AY-meth boo-HAR-ee)* The third Zennorian princess and daughter of Zaire Buhari. She is Serene's cousin.

IRIS KAELIN *(EYE-ruhs KAY-lin)* The queen of Ryden. She is married to Henri Kaelin, and they have five sons. Also known as the Poison Queen.

IVAR CARRIGAN *(EYE-vaar CARE-i-guhn)* King Newlan's cousin. He led a failed uprising in Devendra ten years ago. Alive; current location unknown.

IVONNE SMALLWOOD *(ee-VOHN SMAHL-wood)* One of Serene's maids and older sister to Vera.

JAHZARA *(jah-ZAR-uh)* A Zennorian noblewoman and Peter's mistress.

JAMAL *(jah-MAHL)* The youngest member of the Mortisian council. Full name: Omar Jamal.

JAMES *(JAIMZ)* A Devendran commoner who is a friend to Serene.

KARIM SAFAR *(kah-REEM sa-FAR)* Desfan's bodyguard, as well as his best friend.

KAZIM *(kah-ZEEM)* One of Liam's Mortisian contacts. Alias: Neev Sal.

KEDAAH *(ke-DAH)* The capital city of Zennor.

KIV *(KIV)* (rhymes with *give*) A Mortisian military title, similar to the rank of captain.

LAMBERN *(LAM-burn)* A lake located in Devendra.

LENZEN *(LEN-zuhn)* The capital city of Ryden.

LIAM KELL KAELIN (*LEE-um KEL KAY-lin*) The third prince of Ryden. He is the spymaster for his father. Also known as the Shadow of Ryden.

MARK ELLINGTON (*MARK EL-ing-tun*) The youngest of Clare's brothers. She has raised him since his birth.

MEERAH JEMA CASSIAN (*MEER-uh JEH-muh CAS-ee-uhn*) Desfan's youngest sister, one of the late seraijahs of Mortise.

MIA (*MEE-ah*) The young woman who loves Grayson. She has been a prisoner in Ryden for several years.

MICHAEL BYERS (*MY-cull BY-urz*) A Devendran city guardsman, rebel, and best friend to Eliot.

MORTISE (*mor-TEES*) (rhymes with *geese*) One of the kingdoms of Eyrinthia, ruled by the Cassian family.

MORTISIAN (*mor-TEE-shun*) Relating to the kingdom of Mortise or its people.

NEWLAN DEMOI (*NEW-luhn de-MOY*) The king of Devendra, father to Serene and Grandeur. Was married to the late queen of Devendra, Aren Buhari Demoi. Cousin to Ivar Carrigan, who led a rebellion against him ten years ago.

OLCAIN (*OHL-cain*) A highly addictive drug that originates from Zennor.

ORI (*OR-ee*) A Mortisian street urchin.

PETER HENRI KAELIN (*PEE-tr HEN-ree KAY-lin*) The heir to the throne of Ryden and the oldest Kaelin brother.

RAHIM NASSAR (*rah-HEEM nah-SAR*) A Mortisian merchant and suspected smuggler.

RYDEN (*RYE-den*) One of the kingdoms of Eyrinthia, ruled by the Kaelin family.

RYDENIC (*rye-DEN-ick*) Relating to the kingdom of Ryden or its people.

SAERNON JARON CASSIAN (*SAIR-non JAIR-uhn CAS-ee-uhn*) The ruler of Mortise and Desfan's father. Currently incapacitated by illness. Official title is *serjan*.

SAHVI (*SAW-vee*) A Zennorian drug master.

SER (*SAIR*) The Mortisian term for *lord*; title used to address noble males.

SERAI (*SAIR-ay*) The Mortisian term for *lady*; title used to address noble females.

SERAIJAH (*sair-AY-zjaw*) The Mortisian term for *princess*.

SERAIJAN (*sair-AY-zjawn*) The Mortisian term for *queen*.

SERENE AREN DEMOI (*ser-EEN EH-ruhn de-MOY*) The princess of Devendra. She is Newlan's firstborn but not in line for the throne, because in Devendra women cannot wear the crown.

SERJAH (*SAIR-zjaw*) The Mortisian term for *prince*.

SERJAN (*SAIR-zjawn*) The Mortisian term for *king*.

SIFA (*SEE-fah*) A temporary member of the Mortisian council.

Full name: Abeil Sifa.

SKYER (*SKY-ur*) A ruler of one of the Zennorian clans. He is betrothed to Imara.

SYALLA (*sy-AL-uh*) A pain-causing potion that is often applied to blades. Generally used in Ryden.

TAHLYAH FARAH CASSIAN (*TAHL-yah FAIR-uh CAS-ee-uhn*) Desfan's younger sister, one of the late seraijahs of Mortise.

TAMAR NADIR (*tah-MAR nah-DEER*) A Mortisian noblewoman who lives near the Devendran border.

THE ROSE The most feared assassin in Eyrinthia. His signature is to taunt his targets before killing them, and he always leaves a rose with his victims.

THOMAS ELLINGTON (*TAH-mus EL-ing-tun*) Clare's younger brother.

TYRELL ZEV KAELIN (*ty-REL ZEHV KAY-lin*) The second youngest prince of Ryden. Grayson's closest rival. He oversees the training of Ryden's soldiers.

VENN GRANNARD (*VEN GRAN-ard*) One of Serene's bodyguards and Bennick's best friend. He is half Zennorian; his father was a Devendran soldier who died when Venn was young.

VERA SMALLWOOD (*VER-ah SMAHL-wood*) One of Serene's maids. Younger sister to Ivonne and friend to Clare.

VYKEN (*VY-ken*) The main port city of Ryden.

WIDOW'S BRAID A Zennorian custom for widows to mark the stages of mourning.

WILFORD LINES (*WIL-ford LINES*) One of Serene's bodyguards. He nearly died from the pox five years ago, an illness that killed his wife, Rachel.

YAHRI (*YAH-ree*) The senior member of the Mortisian council. Full name: Amna Yahri.

ZADIR (*zah-DEER*) A Mortisian pirate captain. Full name: Syed Zadir. Also known as Crush.

ZAIRE BUHARI (*ZAIR boo-HAR-ee*) The king of Zennor. Imara's father and Serene's uncle. Brother to the late Aren Buhari Demoi.

ZENNOR (*ZEN-or*) One of the kingdoms of Eyrinthia, ruled by the Buhari family.

ZENNORIAN (*zen-OR-ee-un*) Relating to the kingdom of Zennor or its people.

ZEPHAN (*ZEF-uhn*) A member of the Mortisian council. Full name: Ganem Zephan.

ZOROYA (*zo-ROY-uh*) The main port city of Zennor.

ACKNOWLEDGEMENTS

Almost ten years ago, I published my first novel. This book in your hands makes number five, and I'm feeling very blessed. This journey—like so many things in life—is filled with ups and downs, triumphs and challenges, elation and discouragement. So many people in my life have helped me live my author dream—family, friends, fellow authors, bloggers, librarians, teachers, and, of course, my incredible readers. There are too many people to list here, but please know I'm so grateful!

Mom, you are the best proofreader, cheerleader, and champion. Dad, you taught me so much and encouraged me to work for my dreams. I love you both so much!

Kimberly, words can't express my gratitude for you. You're my best friend, the best designer, and the best at talking me through my issues—both writing-related and life in general. Thank you!

Kevin, thank you for the map—it is still brilliant!

To all my brothers and sisters and their amazing spouses— thank you for always supporting me, loving me, and laughing with me. Being part of such an amazing family is a gift, and I treasure you all.

My phenomenal beta readers! Thank you for the emails, texts, phone calls, video chats, visits, and for reading multiple versions of this book. It would not be what it is today without your insightful feedback. Thank you for loving these characters as much as I do! Rebecca McKinnon, Anna Brown, Laurie Ford,

Cynthia Ford, Kimberly Frost, Crystal Frost, Rachel Wilson, Jonnie Morgart, Michalla Holt, Amelia White, Elyce Edwards —I love you all!

Thank you to the early readers who helped me fine-tune things, and who gave me the encouragement I desperately needed. And a huge shout-out to the book reviewers and bookstagramers who fell in love with this world and these characters—your passion for this series shows, and means so much to me. Thank you!

Finally, thank YOU. Thank you for reading, writing reviews, and sharing this story with others. I am endlessly grateful for your support!

If you liked this book, please consider leaving a review! It seriously makes a WORLD of difference. Thank you!

Want more books by Heather Frost?

Don't miss the Seers Trilogy

seers are not just **spectators,**

they are also **prey**

When Kate Bennett survived the car accident that claimed her parents' lives, she knew her world would be forever changed. But her life is more dramatically altered than she first realized. Not only is she able to see auras on the people around her, she's even started seeing invisible people with no colors at all. And no matter how attractive the new addition to her American Lit class is, Kate sees what no one else can—the dangerous truths this mysterious boy threatens to pour into her life.

Patrick O'Donnell was killed in the Irish Revolution in 1798. He's here now to try and keep Kate alive, and stop her life from spinning out of control. The one thing he's not going to do is fall in love with her.

But plans change, especially when Demons are involved . . .

Kate is about to enter the world of Seers; where immortals are at war with each other, and unfortunate mortals like Kate are in over their heads.

ABOUT THE AUTHOR

Heather Frost writes mostly YA fiction and has a soft spot for tortured characters, breath-stealing romance, and happy endings. She is the author of the Seers trilogy and the Fate of Eyrinthia series. Two of her books have been Whitney Award Finalists, and Royal Decoy was a Swoony Award Finalist. She has a BS in Creative Writing and a minor in Folklore, which means she got to read fairy tales and ghost stories and call it homework.

When she's not writing, Heather likes to read, travel, and re-watch Lord of the Rings. She lives in a beautiful valley surrounded by towering mountains in northern Utah.

To learn more about Heather and her books, visit her website: www.HeatherFrost.com.